Raves for *Please Say Kaddish For Me*

\*\*\*\*\*\*

From the first sentence, Wisoff-Field's writing seized me, transporting me to Russia just before the turn of the twentieth century. I became the young Jewish girl, Havah, struggling to survive amid extreme prejudice, hatred and conflict. I felt Havah's grief, anguish, strength, determination and grit. I feasted on the words of the Torah, as well as the Holy prayers, which I'd never heard. I wondered who would be the lucky man to stand beside her as her husband. Would that decision be hers to make or would the elders make it for her? Filled with suspense, beauty, love, and true-life horror, **Please Say Kaddish For Me** is a riveting read.

~Diane Yates, author of **Pathways of the Heart** and **All That Matters**

\*\*\*\*\*\*

For those who have never suffered discrimination or persecution, **Please Say Kaddish For Me** will bring empathy toward all who have. Reading this book will ignite the fire of indignation in your soul against all forms of intolerance, as well as the fire of faith in the face of despair. This work presents us with insight into the bond and traditions of what it means to be Jewish. I recommend this work of Rochelle Wisoff-Fields. Whether Christian, Muslim, Hindu or agnostic, reading it will raise your consciousness toward the revelation of our one world, one family of man, one Creator of all . . . .

~JAMES C. WASHBURN author of **Touching Spirit: The Letters of Minominike**

\*\*\*\*\*\*

*Please Say Kaddish for Me* is an adventure, a love story and a tale of survival against all odds that would be too much for most adults, let alone a sixteen-year-old girl. Hope, courage and strength shine through in Rochelle Wisoff-Fields' novel.

~HOLLY MCCLURE, author of *The Vessel of Scion*

\*\*\*\*\*\*

*Please Say Kaddish for Me* is a poignant window into the world of Eastern European Jews of the 19th Century. Ms. Wisoff-Fields's beautiful prose takes readers through history to experience devastating challenges as well as tender moments. A captivating read!

~ JAN MORRILL, author of *The Red Kimono*

# PLEASE SAY KADDISH FOR ME

## By

## Rochelle Wisoff-Fields

W & B Publishers
USA

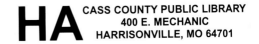

*Please Say Kaddish For Me* © 2015. *All rights reserved by Rochelle Wisoff-Fields*

W & B Publishers

For information:
W & B Publishers
Post Office Box 193
Colfax, NC 27235
www.a-argusbooks.com

ISBN: 9781942981114
ISBN: 1942981112

Book Cover designed by Kent Bonham
(kdbonham@me.com)

Book artwork by Rochelle Wisoff-Fields

Author photograph by Victoria Bernal Forbes

Printed in the United States of America

Dedicated to
Jan Wayne Fields,
*my best friend*

# ACKNOWLEDGEMENTS

Countless people have helped me along the path from rough draft to publication and I want to take the time to thank them.

First, thank you to Annie Withers who believed I had an important story to tell. Without your guidance I wouldn't have known where to begin.

To videographer Kent Bonham who set the wheels in motion when he asked me what I'd like to write about. Thank you for the support and the book trailers.

My undying appreciation goes to the Dinner Writers who critiqued my earliest drafts and encouraged me to keep writing: Polly Swafford, Annette Williamson, Julie Harris, Pat Clothier, Jan Duncan O'Neal, Betty Mordy, Jane Miles-Smith and Roberta Silver.

*Todah rabbah* to my rebbe Shmuel Wolkenfeld who took the time to read one of the first drafts on our flight to Israel in 2006. I appreciate your *brakhas, nakhas* and support.

Lois Spears, you were more than just my junior high art teacher, you made me feel special at an awkward time of life. As with my first book, this novel is part of your legacy.

To Jean L. Hays, my fellow artist, who shared Mrs. Spears, thank you for your keen eye and listening ear.

Fellow writer Douglas M. MacIlroy sacrificed long hours to help me smooth out the rough spots with skill and brutal honesty. *Mahalo nui loa, hoaloha.*

To William Conner of W&B Publishers, thank you for welcoming my Havah and putting her in print.

A very special thank you goes to my agent and advocate, Jeanie Loiacono, whose belief in my book, my artwork and me has never wavered. I know that ours was a divine appointment, Jeanie.

Others who have helped me along the way include Louella Turner, owner of High Hill Press, Delois McGrew, Dusty Richards, Regina O'Hare, Scott Harding, Susan Hawes, Terry Thompson, Lois Hounshell and Marie Gail Stratford.

My biggest thank you goes to my husband Jan Fields. Thank you for your patience, love and support.

# Part I

## *CAST FROM HER FATHER'S HOUSE*

Chapter One

NATALYA, MOLDAVIA,
THE PALE OF SETTLEMENT,
EASTERN EUROPE, NOVEMBER 1899

Gunshots and screaming woke sixteen-year-old Havah Cohen from a sound and dreamless sleep. She ran to her window and saw flames shooting through the roof of the synagogue. Dense clouds of black smoke poured through the windows as men with shovels and rocks smashed the stained glass. By moonlight she could see her older brother lying beside the road in a bloodstained night shirt. Her other brother, a few feet away, lay face down.

"Papa!" She screamed when she saw him run from the inferno clutching the sacred scrolls. Before she could utter another word her bedroom door crashed open. A strange man grabbed her around the waist and a rough hand covered her mouth. She struggled to free herself. He pushed her down on the bed, his body pressing against hers. Paralyzed with fear and repulsed by the odor of liquor, she choked and gasped for breath.

Out of the corner of her eye she saw her mother creep through the doorway and inch toward the bed with a wooden rolling pin high over her head. She slammed it down on the back of the man's head. With a sudden jerk and a grunt he released Havah. He rolled off her and fell to the floor unconscious.

She sat up, clutching a pillow and stared down at him. Blood pooled under his head and seeped into the cracks between the floor boards. This had to be a dream. In the morning Papa would wink at her over breakfast and assure her it had all been a horrendous nightmare.

Her mother yanked her hand, dragged her from the bed and held her for a moment, her tears hot on Havah's neck.

"Hurry, Havah. May the God of Israel go with you." Taking Havah's face between her hands her mother kissed her forehead.

"But Mama—"

Tugging Havah's arm, her mother dragged her to the back door of the house and shoved her out. "No arguing. *Go!"*

Heart thumping, she ran. Thick smoke stung her eyes and burned her throat. She stopped and turned to look one last time. The blazing synagogue crumbled to the ground.

"No, Havah, don't look back!"

The man who had attacked her appeared in the doorway wielding a meat cleaver.

"Mama, behind you!"

"Run, Havah!" The sound of her mother's last scream filled Havah's head and pounded in rhythm to her footsteps.

Beech trees loomed in the forest ahead, their gnarled roots circled above the ground like dancers at a wedding feast. They whispered somber melodies.

Rocks, frozen grass and thorns stabbed the soles of her bare feet. There had been no time for shoes, no time to dress.

Who would pray for their souls? Who would remember David, the artist or Mendel, the poet or Mama or Papa?

She forced her heavy mouth to shape the Hebrew prayer—Kaddish—prayer for the dead and prayer for the bereft. *"'Magnified and sanctified is your great Name…'"* She detested its beauty.

Her hands, held her over her ears, could not blot out the anguished cries of friends and neighbors, fast becoming memories. *"'…in the world which you have created…'"*

Thorns grabbed at her nightgown and she fought to ignore the fire in her lungs. *"'…according to Your will.'"*

Run.

Brambles ripped into her flesh.

Run.

The muscles of her legs burned.

Don't stop. Run.

Havah shivered as the wind whipped around and through her. But stronger than the cold was her determination. When she could no longer run she walked keeping the glow of the flames at her back.

Her tongue stuck to her frozen lips. *"'Let His great name be blessed forever and to all eternity.'"*

Tears streamed down her cheeks and she chided herself. "No, Havah. No time to cry. Pray." *'Though He be high above all blessings and hymns, praises and consolations which are uttered in the world…'"*

She could no longer feel her feet but still she walked. How many times had she repeated the Kaddish? She neither knew nor cared.

In the distance she saw a row of roughhewn buildings, golden in the faint morning light. She stopped. The icy air racked her heaving lungs. Standing on a hill she looked down on a village that reminded her of her own dear town, Natalya, sweet Natalya.

Havah shielded her eyes with her hand and searched. A majestic building, the tallest on the street, caught her eye. The Hebrew words carved above the door told her she had found the synagogue. Relief flooded through her.

Was it not the Sabbath? Where else should a rabbi's daughter go?

Numb with cold, she staggered down the dirt road unable to feel the ground beneath her. She looked down at her cut and bleeding feet. They seemed to belong to someone else.

Twisting her head from side to side, she chewed her lower lip. "Everyone must still be asleep."

*"'He who makes peace in his high places, may he in his mercy make peace for us and for all Israel.'"* As she reached for the door's handle the bitter wind whipped through her thin gown. *"'And all say, Amayn.'"*

****

"More pogroms. And so close." Rabbi Yussel Gitterman's sightless eyes filled with tears.

Eighteen-year-old Arel Gitterman pulled his coat around his ears and shivered, partly from cold and partly with rage. What had they done to make the Christians hate them so much? "We should retaliate. We should gather all of the young men—"

"Shah! Such nonsense!"

"Ouch! Papa, is it unreasonable for men to protect their homes?"

"Remember, my son. A soft answer turns away wrath."

"How can you say that, Papa? Last night innocent people were murdered in their beds all over the countryside. Did they have time to make an answer—*of any kind?*"

Hershel Levine's green eyes flashed. "The lad makes sense, Yussel. There is much cruelty in the world. Sometimes one has to wonder what the Almighty is thinking."

"So, Hershel, my old friend, do you think the three of us, an old cantor, a blind rabbi and a boy who's barely able to squeeze out a whisker are going to seek revenge on those animals with their guns and Czar Nicolas, may his name be blotted out?"

Arel gritted his teeth. "Reb Pinkas said he heard the Christians burned down a synagogue. A rabbi died trying to protect the sacred scrolls. Papa, it could just as easily have been you."

"Reb Pinkas is up early bearing his tales. Yes, it could have been any Jew in this land, my Son." Yussel patted his shoulder. "It's dangerous to be a Jew in this Pale of Settlement. But now let's tend to matters at hand. It's *Shabbes,* the Sabbath, and we have a synagogue to prepare for morning services."

"Yes, Papa." Arel knew from experience arguing with his father would not accomplish anything. Still his anger boiled because they were Jews who lived in poverty under the tyranny of the Russians. Prisoners in their own country, unable own land and denied education beyond their Hebrew schools.

For the next few moments Yussel's cane tapping along the frozen ground was the only sound. Each man lost in his own thoughts, they approached the synagogue, the largest building in the Jewish quarter of Svechka.

To call a backward village "The Candle" was a contradiction. Arel supposed at some point in time the Russians considered it a place of enlightenment.

Hershel ran ahead and dropped to his knees beside something heaped on the doorstep of the men's entrance. "Oy. A fine kettle of chicken soup this is!"

"What is it?" Yussel cocked his head to one side.

There on the steps lay a girl, her black hair splayed out under her head like a glossy veil. Long dark lashes edged her eyelids. Her lips were full and scarlet against her porcelain complexion. The curves of her narrow hips and round bosom were visible through her torn nightgown. Arel turned his head and mopped sweat from his forehead.

"God be thanked! She's breathing. A dead body on the synagogue steps on Sabbath would certainly create a stir." Hershel removed his overcoat and covered her. "Arel, put your eyes back in your head and carry her inside. We must warm her or she will surely die."

Even with the added weight of Hershel's coat she was feather light in Arel's arms. His breath came out in short puffs between twinges of guilt. He had not so much as held hands with Gittel Levine, his intended.

The core of the Jewish community, the synagogue or *shul* was the linchpin that held them together. The scent of musty books and the aroma of linseed oil met Arel's nose when Hershel opened the door. The solid oak woodwork was polished to a warm sheen. Elaborate carvings of plants, birds and animals, including a half-lion, adorned the Holy Ark, an ornate cabinet which contained the sacred scrolls. It sat behind the *bema*, the central platform. Four columns and railings surrounded it.

The balcony where the women observed the Sabbath made a circle close to the canopy of the high ceiling. A stairway led to the door on the west side of the sanctuary. Sun streamed through the high windows and bathed the women's gallery.

Tables had been arranged side by side like stalwart soldiers, around the bema. They stood ready for the men to study, discuss and argue points of law.

A fire blazed in the stone fireplace on the north side.

Yussel felt his way to the hearth by sliding his cane along the floorboards and warmed his hands. "*Gut Shabbes*, Feivel. I see you've already started a fire. Thank you. You're a good sexton, my son."

A spindly man with frizzy red hair, Feivel Resnick bore a dour expression and squinted at them through his thick glasses. His forced smile looked more like a grimace. "Good Sabbath, *Papa*."

He spat out the last word as if it were something unpalatable.

Sparks and ashes erupted as he jabbed at the logs in the fireplace with an iron poker. "What is this you carry, Little Brother, your laundry?"

"A little bundle left on our doorstep. I'm surprised you didn't trip over her when you arrived this morning." Arel made no attempt to hide his disdain.

"I came before sunrise. I saw nothing on the steps but my own feet."

"Have another fight with Tova? How many times did you strike her?"

"Your sister's a miserable hag." Feivel hung the poker on the hook beside the fireplace and snarled.

"Seventeen years married to you would make anyone miserable, my 'brother.'"

"Arel, squabble later, warm the girl now." Yussel waved his hand and gestured toward the fire. "She must have escaped from one of the attacked villages."

Arel sat on the ledge with the strange girl on his lap. Her bare feet were torn and bleeding.

"Give me your handkerchief, Ari. Let's wrap her poor feet until they can be properly bandaged." Pulling his handkerchief from his breast pocket, Hershel knelt and dabbed at her feet.

She stirred and mumbled something Arel could not quite hear.

Yussel's mouth dropped open. "Listen! Can this be? Arel. Hershel. Do you hear it?"

"*'Yees g'dahl, v'yees g'dash, sh'may rahbah.'* Magnified and sanctified be His Great Name.*" The girl's voice grew louder with a familiar melody. *"In the world which He has created."*

Eyes wide, Hershel stumbled and leaned against the wall, crossing his arms across his chest. "How can this be? She's a mere wisp of a girl. How would she know the Kaddish?"

Feivel scowled "She's a demon child."

Her eyes opened. "Mendel?" She snuggled against Arel's shoulder and closed her eyes. "I thought they killed you."

With a single glance, her large brown eyes captivated him. He trembled, fearing she would shatter into a hundred pieces like the delicate china his sisters kept for special occasions.

When Hershel dug his fingers into his shoulder Arel flinched. "Take her to my house. We have an extra room. Fruma Ya'el will know how to care for her."

"She always knows what to do. If she'd been born a Christian man I'm sure she would've been a doctor." Yussel rose from the hearth and hung his coat on a peg beside the fireplace.

"Or if it hadn't been for me," Hershel muttered.

"You want I should carry her on the Sabbath?" Arel looked first at Yussel and then at Hershel and then at the unconscious girl.

"You've carried her this far, haven't you? Ari, my boy, it's a *mitzvah*, a good deed," said Hershel. "This, on *Shabbes*, is allowed."

"Hurry, my son. Don't let the weeds grow under your feet."

Although blind as a burrowing mole at midnight, Yussel could always find the most vulnerable spot between Arel's shoulder blades to poke with his cane.

With the girl in his arms he stumbled toward the entrance. He stooped and fumbled for the handle. Pushing the door, he held it open with his foot and stepped outside.

An icy gust blew off his hat. It rolled along the ground, driven on the wind like a sparrow in a storm. If he stopped to pick it up he would surely drop his charge so he let it go. Perhaps a beggar would find it and make good use of it. It would be his second *mitzvah* of the day.

It was a mile and a half to Cantor Levine's home and all during the long walk her warm breath stirred the hairs on his neck.

*"Extolled and honored, magnified, and lauded be the Name of the Holy One. Blessed be He."* She repeated the prayer over and over, her voice as melodious as Cantor Levine's.

For a moment Arel entertained a thought and then chuckled. "Ridiculous. Who ever heard of a woman cantor?"

With a hefty shove of his foot, he pushed open the crude wooden gate and entered the Levine's yard, navigating around Fruma Ya'el's chickens which pecked at his ankles as he plodded up to the two story house. It was no easy matter to maneuver the unconscious girl to free his hand so he thumped at the door with his foot.

"Auntie Fruma! *Gut Shabbes!*"

The girl moaned and squirmed. His arms protested. "Open the door…please!"

The door swung open and a woman with flowered kerchief framing a pleasant face smiled up at him. "*Gut Shabbes*, Ari. And what have you brought to me this fine morning?" Her brown eyes twinkled. She placed her hands on her hips.

Heat traveled from the back of his neck to his forehead. "I…that is we…she was…she's unconscious."

"This I see. Come. Bring her inside. Put her in the guestroom. Gently, Arel, *gently!* She's not a sack of meal."

Savory *cholent* simmered in a pot on the hot stove. The stew had been made the day before so no work, such as cooking, would be done on the Sabbath. The aroma of meat and beans teased his nose as he followed Fruma Ya'el through the door and up the stairs to the bedroom.

"Ari, shouldn't you be at shul preparing for the Sabbath?"

Arel did not hear Gittel enter the room, so intent was he on lowering the wounded girl to the bed. When he saw his intended, he flushed, straightened and cleared his dry throat. "Reb Hershel thinks she escaped a pogrom and found her way here last night."

"Is she dead?" Gittel fixed her eyes on the stranger.

"Would I let Ari lay a corpse on my bed?" Fruma Ya'el spat between her index and middle fingers to ward off evil spirits. She peeked under Hershel's coat and gasped. "Only a nightgown this child is wearing!"

Words refused to come from Arel's mouth. His feet felt like stones. Diverting his gaze to Gittel, his intended since he was thirteen, his mind swirled like leaves on the wind. Tall and slender, she had an innocent beauty that emanated from the depths of a tender soul. Her auburn hair made a silken cape around her slim shoulders. He had, heretofore, enjoyed the prospect of making her his wife.

"One can only imagine what she's suffered!" Gittel knelt and covered the girl, tucking the soft blanket around her neck. Again, Fruma Ya'el spat. "The Czar, he should go home to his fine house tonight and be found dead in every room."

\*\*\*\*

Cold hands held to Havah's flaming brow prevented her from moving her head. The tip of a glass bottle bumped against her teeth. Another pair of hands pried apart her lips. The liquor scalded her raw throat. The hazy room swirled with shadow and color. She tried to focus on the woman and the girl hovering over her like ravenous vultures. The glare from a lamp seared Havah's eyes.

"Drink, Little Sister." A woman's voice whispered. "Schnapps. To dull the pain."

"Mama," cried Havah. "Don't make me drink it. It tastes awful."

Another hushed voice, a girl's, gentle and full of compassion, spoke. "She thinks you're her mother."

"She thinks nothing. Her mind's simmering with fever."

*"Why did the Almighty make honey bees?" Five-year-old Havah held up her stung hand.*

*Papa's onyx eyes glistened and his beard tickled her nose. "As a reminder. So we don't forget."*

*"Forget what?"*

*"The good things in life are made sweeter by affliction."*

"Gittel, hold her down. We must be quick about it."

Hands grasped Havah's shoulders. Lamplight glinted with wicked brilliance off a short-bladed saw the woman waved through the flame. The bed tilted beneath Havah and she turned her head.

*Twelve-year-old David chased her through Mama's vegetable garden, dangling a dead rat by its tail. "Here, Kitty, Kitty."*

*Six-year-old Havah squealed and pinched her nostrils closed to block the odor. "Make him stop!"*

*Mama caught his shirttail and beat the small carcass from his hand with a straw broom. "David Cohen, take that filthy thing and bury it. Then march yourself to the bathhouse."*

A foul stench, like rotting meat, turned Havah's stomach. Quenchless fire consumed her right foot. She struggled to sit up.

"Don't look." The woman pushed her back.

She wrestled against the woman's hands. Rising up on one elbow, she searched the end of the bed. A mass of black and yellow ooze met her eyes like a serpent slithering from the ground. When she moved her leg, the snake followed. Its dreadful fangs devoured her.

"You'll be all right, little sister. A real doctor taught Mama everything she knows." The younger woman's voice was feathery as butterfly wings. Havah calmed for a moment until the girl jammed a rolled up cloth between her teeth. "Bite hard. It will help."

With panic choking her, she threw her head from side to side, spit out the rag and clamped her teeth down on the girl's finger. The girl yelped and crammed the rag back into Havah's mouth.

"Do you have to, Mama?" asked the girl.

The fiery blade inched closer and closer. "She's dead if I don't."

## Chapter Two

Havah's crusted eyelids scraped her eyes. She moved her hand to cover them, blinked and sniffed her nightgown sleeve. It was clean and crisp and smelled of cinnamon and lye soap.

The cold air nipped at her face so she snuggled down under the thick comforter.

From another room she heard laughter. The aroma of oniony eggs and potatoes frying in chicken fat permeated the cheerful room. Fresh coffee teased her nose.

Bright sunlight shone through the window framed by muslin curtains and reflected off the tin ceiling above her. Mama always made sure the windows sparkled, Havah noted with pride. A kerosene lamp sat on a carved oak stand beside the bed.

Any minute, David would burst through the door. He would tickle her feet until she smacked him with her pillow. He would laugh at her when she told him about her nightmare.

"I'll be late for school." She stretched and swung her legs over the side of the bed. "Mendel will be upset."

Her right foot seethed. She screamed, dragged it back under the blanket and dug her fingernails into the mattress.

This room was not hers, after all. No David. No Mendel. Visions flooded her and her leg hurt. She saw them as fragments of a dream, a woman wearing a colorful kerchief, a girl with orange braids.

Had it not been the night before that her papa tucked her in bed with a kiss?

*His voice, low and soothing still rumbled like distant thunder in her mind.*
*"So my little student, you have decided to put the books away for one day and rest?"*
*"I will have plenty of time tomorrow to study. I love Shabbes; it's my favorite day of the week."*
*"Well, then, I shall let you sleep so that brilliant head of yours will be sharp in the morning."*

A lump formed in her throat as she remembered how she threw her arms around his neck.

*"I love you so much it hurts, Papa!"*
*"What's this? Is something wrong, Havah?"*
*"I just had to tell you. What if I never have another chance to tell you? I would sorrow all my days!"*
*"Such profound thoughts for one so young! Gut Shabbes, my precious daughter.*
*Sleep well. I'll see you in the morning."*
*"Tell Mama I love her, too."*
*Mama peeked around the corner and winked. "She knows."*

"Good morning, little sister!" Startled by the unexpected voice, Havah jumped. A girl with a thick bandage around her index finger carried a tray into the room. Her auburn hair hung over her shoulder in a long braid ending at her slim waist.

"I see you're finally awake! I thought for certain you would sleep through the winter like a bear. I remember that nightgown. I outgrew it. Good thing for you Mama doesn't throw anything away. You won't have to go naked. Here's breakfast."

"I'm not hungry."

"Oh, but you must eat. You've been asleep for three days! Why, you'll shrivel up and blow away. You're skinny enough as it is, little sister."

"I'm not your sister."

The girl frowned and set the tray on the bed stand. "Of course you're not. I meant no harm. I'm Gittel. I'm named after my mother's sister, my aunt of blessed memory. Of course I never knew her so I don't have any memories of her, blessed or otherwise. My mother is Fruma Ya'el. She's the midwife here. I only call you little sister because I don't know your name."

"It's Havah." She rolled over and faced the wall. "Now go away."

Gittel sat next to her on the bed and rubbed her back. "I understand how you feel."

"*You* understand how *I* feel? You…you ignorant half-wit!" Havah sat up and flung the pillow in Gittel's face. She fell back and curled up into a tight ball. "Leave me alone."

Without a trace of hurt or anger Gittel bent down and picked the pillow up off the floor. She fluffed it and tried to slip it under Havah's head. "We saved some chicken soup from last night." Taking a spoon from the tray she dipped it into the soup and brought it to Havah's lips. "Try it. Mama makes the best noodles you've ever tasted."

"Don't you listen? Are you just plain stupid? I'm *not* your sister and I am *not* hungry." With every ounce of strength left to her, Havah seized the bowl and hurled it across the room. It crashed to the floor and shattered.

She pushed back the comforter and slid off the bed. Pain shot through her foot and she collapsed in a puddle of soup.

The door burst open. Fruma Ya'el rushed to Havah's side. "Gittel what is this child doing out of bed?"

Hysteria mounting, Havah scooted away from her. She drew her knees to her chest and huddled in the corner. "Just let me die."

Fruma Ya'el followed her. She pressed her nose against Havah's. "No one is dying in my house today, do you hear, little sister?"

"I'm no one's little sister anymore and I'm not a child. I'm sixteen."

Tears spilled over in Gittel's guileless eyes as she knelt to clean the mess on the floor. "You're such a tiny mite I thought you were much younger."

"You talk too much."

"Let's get her back to bed. I'll take her arms and you take her ankles." Fruma Ya'el reached for her.

"I can walk."

"So I see. But I'd rather you didn't."

"You cut off my foot." Havah stared at the blood seeping through the bandage and remembered the bite of the knife slicing into her flesh.

"Only part of it. Frostbite. Better to lose the toes than the life."

Too weak and weary to fight, Havah allowed them to carry her back to bed. Once under the covers, she cuddled her head against the pillow, rubbed her puffy eyes and blinked back bitter tears.

Fruma Ya'el held out her arms. "Come to Mama."

"My mother's dead."

"I understand. Better you should call me 'Auntie Fruma'." She stroked Havah's hair, smoothing it away from her face. "You are home now."

"You butcher. I hate you."

"I know."

"You're not my mother. You're not my aunt. I don't even know you. Don't *want* to know you." Havah swatted the older woman's hand. "My home's a pile of cinders."

Hunger gnawed at Havah's stomach which betrayed her with a loud growl.

With a self-satisfied grin, Fruma Ya'el tucked two pillows behind Havah. "Gitteleh, go to the kitchen and prepare another bowl of soup. This time our little sister will eat it rather than pitch it, yes?"

****

Tree shadows swayed along the wall like old men at morning prayers. The wind rattled the window. Sleet clattered on the tin roof magnifying Havah's emptiness.

*"You're a fighter, Havaleh."* Her father's voice resonated in her mind. *"Hold your head high, my child, no matter what."*

She huddled under the comforter. *"I can't fight alone, Papa."*

"You're not alone."

Startled by the soft female voice, she opened her eyes and gazed up at Gittel standing beside the bed with a quilt over her arm.

"For a minute I thought you were a ghost," said Havah.

"I'm just a girl." She leaned down to spread the quilt over Havah who relished the added warmth.

"Sit with me. I promise not to bite." She patted the bed beside her.

"I'd have bitten me, too." Gittel wiggled her bandaged finger. "It doesn't hurt."

"You're lying." Havah pulled the covers around her.

"You still have a fever, little sis—I'm sorry— Havah. Let me make some of Mama's special tea for you." Gittel laid a cool hand on Havah's forehead.

Something crashed against the side of the house. Havah screamed. "Hide! They'll kill us all!"

Gittel pushed the curtain aside. "There's nobody out there. See? It's only a tree branch broken off in the wind." She patted Havah's back and stood. "Now for that tea—"

"Don't go...please. I don't want to be alone. And...and I'm sorry I called you stupid. I didn't mean it."

"I know." Gittel gave her a gentle shove. "You need your rest."

"I'm afraid." Every muscle in her body ached. Uncontrollable despair wracked her. She turned on her side and buried her face in the pillow.

"Would you like for me to lie next to you to keep you warm?"

With a nod, Havah said nothing but held up a corner of the blanket. Gittel slipped in beside her. Havah rolled over and nestled her head against Gittel's breasts.

Gittel's whisper was soothing and musical. "I always wanted a sister. I had a little brother but he passed away when he was small."

The door creaked open and Hershel peeked around it, candle in hand. "Gittel? Is that your voice I hear? Your little sister needs her rest."

"I'm keeping her warm, Papa. She's shaking."

At the sight of his only child, his eyes brightened like topaz stars. Setting the candle on the bed stand, he sat on the edge of the bed and tapped her knee. "We have more blankets."

"I gave her another and she's still cold."

"You're very ill, child." He brushed his fingertips across Havah's forehead. "You need sleep, not my daughter chewing your ear all night."

"Please, let her stay." Havah lifted her head off the pillow.

"Hershel, the back door's stuck again." Fruma Ya'el's voice traveled from downstairs.

His back stiffened and his lips formed a thin line. He looked up at the ceiling. "Who can win an argument with a woman? Now I'm surrounded by three. *Oy vey is mir.*"

He stood and walked to the doorway. The door shut behind him.

"Tell me about your brother." Havah let her head sink back into the pillow.

Gittel spoke in a low whisper. "I was six when he was born. Benjamin. A sweet little boy. He came down with cholera right after his second birthday. My poor Mama nearly died of a broken heart. Papa, too." She wiped her eyes with the back of her hand. "They wanted a houseful of children, but all they have is me."

For a moment Havah forgot her own grief. "Your parents seem nice, especially your mother. My mama, of—" she paused, "—blessed memory, would have liked her."

"I don't know what I'd do if I lost my family the way you did. I couldn't run barefoot through the woods in the cold at night. I'm not as brave as you."

"I should have stayed and died with them instead of running away like a frightened squirrel."

"Papa says it takes more courage to live a good life than to die a hero's death."

"My papa said the same thing."

"What would *he* want you to do?"

A cold draft whistled between the wall planks. Fear that the evil ones who murdered her family would break into this house, too, niggled at Havah. She trembled and scooted all the way under the blankets.

"You're right, Havaleh. I talk too much. I should go back to my own bed and let you have some peace."

Some of Havah's loneliness dissipated. She squeezed the other girl's arm. "No. Stay. I always wanted a sister, too."

## Chapter Three

No matter how hard Arel tried to focus his attention on the page in front of him the words only taunted him. For as much as he tried to concentrate on his studies, the letters might as well have stood and walked off the paper.

What if Feivel spoke the truth? Havah's face occupied his every daytime thought. What if she was a demon child after all and had bewitched him? Her eyes haunted him. He saw them at night as he drifted off to sleep, dark and almost too large for her face. She leaped through his dreams, her long gown fluttering behind her. When he awoke to the cold light of dawn his mind would repeat the cycle.

"Arel!" Yussel's cane thumped him back to the Torah study.

"Papa?"

"You haven't answered Reb Pinkas' question."

"I'm sorry, I didn't hear it."

"The man sits beside him and he didn't hear."

Arel cheeks heated with embarrassment. "I was studying the last passage. Could you repeat the question, Reb Pinkas?"

"My son Orev could take lessons from you." The village printer and postmaster of the Jewish sector of Svechka, Pinkas Rabinovich was a large man with an imposing presence. "I asked this group of scholars whether it's right for a woman to study Torah like a man. What say you, Reb Arel?"

"I say…,"Arel rubbed his hands together and blew on them for warmth. "…why not?"

"The world is changing around us." Pinkas clicked his tongue. "Shameful things. In America women study Torah and even appear in public with their heads uncovered like the *goyim*."

"Why shouldn't a woman study Torah like that?" Yussel stroked his beard. "You've said yourself, Hershel, that no one, be they man or woman, in Svechka has been blessed with as much wisdom as your own Fruma Ya'el."

A thin stream of smoke issued through Hershel's pursed lips. "Practical wisdom is one thing, Rebbe, but study of the Holy Writings is quite another. Some things are not meant to be. I ask you, if we start sending our daughters to *Heder*, who will cook and take care of the home?" He wagged his finger under Arel's nose. "Would you want your wife studying at your side instead of raising your children?"

The strange girl's voice, as fresh and tender as grass in springtime, chanting the Kaddish in perfect Hebrew trilled through Arel. "Why couldn't she do both? Itzak's always busy with his cabinetmaking, yet he finds time to study."

"We're talking about *women!*" Half-spewed smoke and laughter nearly choked Hershel. "Can you imagine your future wife, my Gittel, pondering the mysteries of Torah? Discussing Rashi or Rabbi Akiva?"

"She has a mind, doesn't she?"

"Like a flittering bird." Closing his book, Hershel sat back in his chair with a distracted smile. "The sweetest of birds."

Finally, and to Arel's relief, Yussel stretched his arms over his head. "We should be going home, Arel. The hour grows late and your sister Shayndel will have dinner waiting for us. With her being in a family way it's good not to upset her. Hershel, she wants to know if there's anything she can help with. But to tell the truth I think she's curious to meet your new daughter."

"Why don't you join us for Sabbath dinner week after next? We'll have a little Hanukkah celebration, unless, of course, Havah's not strong enough for company. Don't be late or I'll never hear the end of it."

Chapter Four

The bed quaked with Hershel's coughing. He grabbed a napkin off the bed stand and held it over his mouth, his furrowed cheeks turning crimson. Finally the hacking subsided and he lay back against the pillow, folding his hands across his stomach. "Good night, Wife."

Through the casement window a shaft of moonlight illuminated snaking smoke trails stubbornly hanging in the air above the ashtray. Fruma Ya'el nestled her head in the crook of his neck and shoulder and planted a loud kiss on his ear. Slipping her hand under his nightshirt, she gave his chest hair a playful tug.

With a grunt of near disgust, he pushed away her hand. Rolling over on his side with his back to her, he mumbled something she could not quite understand. In less than three minutes his unintelligible mutterings gave way to muffled snores.

"Good night…Husband." Disappointment engulfed her. She scooted to the other side of the bed and burrowed her face in her pillow.

She had almost succumbed to sleep when a sound from the bedroom above, something between a scream and a groan, roused her.

Hershel's snoring stopped with a gurgle followed by a wheezing cough. "Go tend to her."

"Maybe you should go. She hates me."

"I'd hate you too if you'd cut my foot in half. Go to her anyway. She needs you."

Sitting up on the side of the bed, Fruma Ya'el took her shawl from the headboard. She wrapped it around her shoulders, rose and slid her feet into a pair of slippers.

Halfway up the stairs, the crying stopped. She paused in the doorway of what had once been her son's room. Curled up on her side, Havah appeared to have fallen asleep after what must have been a hard fought battle.

Careful not to wake her, Fruma Ya'el tiptoed to the bed and brushed her fingers over the girl's pallid cheek. She sat on the end of the bed and lifted the blanket. Unwinding the bandages, she examined the right foot where she had sawed off a good quarter of it along with the two inside toes. The massive wound had begun to scar over.

What else could she have done? Did she do the child more harm than good? The questions nagged at her.

The flame in the lamp on the night table went out.

Havah groaned in her sleep and then bolted upright. "Run, Mama!"

Fruma Ya'el struck a match and relit the lamp. "I'm here." She held out her arms.

Shrinking back against the pillow, Havah frowned. "I'm sorry I woke you."

"Your fever's broken." Fruma Ya'el stroked the girl's damp forehead. "Forgive me for causing you such pain."

"You saved my life."

"My mother's name was Havah. It's a sign perhaps."

The light reflected in the girl's eyes like glowing embers ready to ignite into a wildfire. "I'll never be your daughter."

"I know." Fruma Ya'el picked up a hairbrush from the bed stand. "May I?"

Havah nodded and sat up.

"Relax." Fruma Ya'el pushed her back. "Close your eyes."

With exhausted obedience Havah rolled onto her side and laid her head in Fruma Ya'el's lap. Shifting her hips under Havah's weight, she leaned back against the tall wooden headboard, kicked off her slippers and stretched out her legs on the bed.

Brittle fragments of leaves and thistledown fell from the girl's hair fell onto the bed as she drew the soft bristles through it. At last all of the snarls and tangles smoothed out under the rhythmic flow of the hairbrush.

"Mine was as black as yours. It hung all the way down to my knees. So heavy it gave me headaches." She curled one of Havah's long tresses around her fingers.

"Why did you cut it?"

"Since when does a rabbi's daughter need to ask such a question?"

"Did you want to or did they force you?"

"Full of questions, aren't you?"

"Papa says—*said*—" Eyes wide with realization and grief, Havah sat up and then collapsed against Fruma Ya'el's breast.

The hairbrush fell from Fruma Ya'el's grasp. She cupped one hand around the girl's head and rubbed her quivering shoulders with the other. "Let it out, Little Sister."

Havah's sobs wracked Fruma Ya'el's chest and soaked her nightgown. Little by little, her tears subsided to sniffling whimpers and her body grew limp against Fruma Ya'el's shoulder.

Closing her eyes, Fruma Ya'el relaxed into a guarded sleep. She dreamt of a tiny boy with auburn hair and green eyes. Pudgy arms raised, he squealed. "Mama. Up. Benny up."

"Did you love him?"

Benjamin vanished and she snapped open her eyes. Rubbing the grit from them, she shook herself awake and focused on Havah. "What? Who?"

"Uncle Hershel. When you got married, did you love him?"

"He was a handsome young cantor with a voice to drive a songbird insane with envy. What girl wouldn't love him?"

"You?"

"I was your age when a doctor came to visit Svechka—Dr. Rosenthal—all the way from New York, America. He claimed it was his mission to recruit Jews to become doctors so we wouldn't always be at the mercy of the *Goyim.* He stayed for two years and filled my head full of knowledge and dreams. Begged me to marry him and go back with him."

"Why didn't you go, Auntie?"

Amber light bathed the room. In the yard below, roosters crowed. Fruma Ya'el arched her stiffening back and stretched her arms. "Where has the time gone?"

Chapter Five

"So the Professor says to the Cossack, 'Itzak Abromovich is the best cabinet maker in all of Moldavia. I'll vouch for him.' Before you can say, 'Adoshem lives,' my travel permission papers are signed and I have more customers than I know what to do with."

To punctuate his words, the stout carpenter waved his short arms as he walked beside Arel.

Although he barely noticed the cold, through sheer force of habit, Arel pulled his coat collar around his ears. His brother-in-law always returned from his travels with stories to tell of his encounters in Kishinev and surrounding villages. Usually, Arel would listen with rapt attention. Today Itzak's conversation faded into the wind.

"Havah." Arel whispered her name under his breath. "Havah." It sounded sweeter than *Kol Nidre,* his favorite prayer sung only on the eve of the Day of Atonement.

"Why, I'd wager Professor Dietrich doesn't even know how much money he has. Can you imagine, Little Brother? What I wouldn't do for just a fraction of it."

*Havah, the name of the first woman in the Torah. Mother of all life.*

"Arel? Have you heard a word I've said?"

Where did she learn to chant? She called him Mendel. Arel's heart raced. Could Mendel be her intended? Arel's jealousy burned for a man who was probably murdered. Guilt riddled him for his barbarous thoughts.

"Anybody home?" Itzak thumped the side of Arel's head with his stubby forefinger.

"Professor Dietrich. Cossacks. Furniture."

"Is something or some*one* on your mind?"

"It's that obvious?"

"Do chickens have beaks?"

"It's wrong, Itzak. I'm betrothed." Arel kicked a rock and watched it tumble down the hill like a drunken acrobat.

"Take it from an old married man. You and Gittel, you're like Shayndel and me. You've known each other since you were babies. It's a solid arrangement and meant to be."

"How can you be so sure? The harder I try not to, the more I think about Havah. I even dream about her."

"Have you actually talked to her?"

"When would I have talked to her?"

"There you have it. You're infatuated. That's all. It will pass. Besides, you might not even like her once you meet her."

"I hope you're right."

"Of course I'm right. I'm always right." He slapped Arel's back. "Hurry. Shayndel's making potato latkes."

As they approached home they passed Feivel and Tova's house. Itzak whistled. "How on earth they manage to cram six people into that three room hovel is beyond me. I wish I could do something for them."

"You've tried. Feivel refused your help. Yet he does nothing. The greatest *mitzvah* he could do is drop dead."

"If your father heard you he'd—"

A shrill scream pierced Arel's ears. It sounded like a wild animal caught in a hunter's trap. He quickened his pace. Not an animal. A child.

"Papa! Stop! I won't do it again! I won't. I won't. *Stop! Stop! Stop!"*

Through the bushes, Arel saw Feivel, swinging a buggy whip, his face contorted with maniacal fury. His nine-year-old son, Lev, groveled in the dirt, desperate to escape its lash.

"You little *momzer*. I'll teach you!"

Trembling with rage, Arel threw off his coat and hat. He raced Itzak down the hill. Without hesitation Itzak grabbed Feivel from behind. Arel butted his head into Feivel's stomach. Feivel grunted and doubled over, clutching his whip.

Like a rabid wolf, he howled and wrenched out of Itzak's grasp. Again he cracked the whip. This time it struck Arel's neck. In turn, undeterred by the pain, Arel balled his fists and struck Feivel's chin. The whip fell from his limp fingers. Itzak picked it up and snapped it around Feivel's leg.

"*Khazer*! Pig!" Feivel spat in Arel's face and bared his teeth at Itzak as he staggered away from them. Halfway down the road he turned, kicked a pile of rocks and waved his fist in the air.

Spittle that reeked of stale schnapps ran down the side of Arel's face. He shuddered and wiped it off with his sleeve. "What I wouldn't give to—"

"Save it for later." Itzak dropped the whip. "The boy."

Snow dusted Lev's bright red hair where he lay sprawled on the frozen ground. A deep gash ran from his right cheek down through his lips and ended at the point of his chin. Mud smeared his wet cheeks. A soft whimper escaped his lips. "Mama. He killed Mama. I tried to stop...stop him."

The ground lurched beneath Arel. He flew to his sister's door and banged on it with his fists. When she did not answer he kicked it. "Tova! Tova! Open up!"

The door slowly opened. Tova, her once beautiful face mottled with gray and purple bruises, blinked up at them with a wooden smile. Great with child, her threadbare blouse stretched tight across her belly. She covered her shorn curls with her ragged shawl. "I…I was taking a nap with Reuven. Stay out. Please. I haven't had…a chance to clean."

With Lev gathered up in his bearlike arms, Itzak pushed past her. Arel fought to catch his breath as he followed. Broken dishes, potato peelings and a discarded liquor bottle littered the dirt floor. The odor of stale urine and spoiled food hung in the air like a curse. Two-year-old Reuven, wide awake, sat amid the debris sucking on Tova's kerchief.

"Where are the girls?" Itzak laid Lev on Tova's bed.

"They went to market with Gittel. I expect them back any minute." With obvious difficulty Tova squatted and hefted Reuven into her arms. Then, with equal difficulty she stood. The child clung to her neck, his chubby legs straddling her stomach. All the while Tovah kept her eyelids lowered.

Grasping her shoulders, Arel kissed her forehead. "Come home with us, Big Sister."

"That's all Papa needs. Four, almost five more children, Little Brother." Finally, she raised her eyes. They were red and puffy and Arel did not need to ask why. She lowered herself onto her bed. "And Shayndel's baby would make six."

Still subdued from the beating, Lev whined and tugged at her skirt. "I'm scared, Mama. Can't we please go live with *Zaydeh*?"

With her big toe protruding from a hole in her worn shoe Tova drew a line in the worn dirt floor and squared her narrow shoulders. "Such as it is, this is my home."

Chapter Six

Although he could well afford to have his suits tailored by the Czar's clothier, Ulrich Dietrich would have none of the aristocracy. The wealthy heir of a German banker and a successful musician in his own right, he baffled his colleagues by choosing to enlist the services of a poor Jewish tailor. When criticized, he would merely shrug and thank the critic to mind his or her own business.

In anticipation of his upcoming concert he hummed Chopin's *Grand Polonaise*. He danced his fingers over an imaginary keyboard until the stab of a pin brought him back to the dusty tailor shop.

"Ouch!" He rubbed his smarting wrist. "Aren't you finished yet, Herr Abromovich?"

"Stand still, Professor, only a few more to go. You're as fidgety as my little Tuli." The slender tailor, crouched at the musician's feet, grinned around a mouthful of pins. "You'll never attract a wife with ill-fitting clothing."

"I'm already married."

"Nine years widowed isn't married."

The tailor's prying eyes left him bereft of a rebuttal. Instead he concentrated on his disjointed reflection through the cracks in the full-length mirror. "What do you think the new century holds for you, Evron?"

"More of the same I suppose. If Adoshem smiles on me and mine, the Czar and his henchmen will let us live for another year."

With a good-natured grin he tilted his face toward the pitted tin ceiling. He slid the pins from his mouth and poked them into the cushion on his wrist. A pained grimace momentarily shadowed his expression when he stood and brushed dirt from his threadbare trousers.

Ulrich frowned. "I spoke with your brother Itzak a couple of weeks ago. He told me about the stir over the new little fraulein. Senseless tragedy."

"This will be ready for you in time for your concert next Sunday." Evron draped the coat over his sewing machine. "Any special instructions? You want I should move the seams? Shorten, maybe, the sleeves?"

"I have the utmost confidence in my tailor." Ulrich pulled his wallet from his trouser pocket, fished out a couple of bills and pressed them into Evron's hand. "He's the best in Kishinev."

"This is too much. More than we agreed on."

When Evron tried to return the excess, Ulrich curved his fingers around Evron's hand. "The tailor needs a new suit of clothes."

"You're a generous man, Reb Professor." Evron stuffed the money into his pocket. "My girls need new dresses."

"Speaking of your beautiful children…Why don't you bring your family to my concert as my guests?"

"*Nu?* My brood of 'Christ Killers' in a cathedral? Could set off another 'tragedy'."

The shop door swung open and the bell, tied to the knob, clinked. Identical twin girls with slate-black eyes and midnight braids to their knees skipped into the shop. Between them a little boy held their hands.

Evron's thick brows knit into a scowl. "Ruth. Rukhel. I've told you, never go out alone. It's not safe for *shayneh maydelehs* like you."

"We pretty girls are not alone, we brought Tuli." The twins giggled and spoke almost in unison.

"Papa!" With an excited squeal the boy jerked from his sisters' grasps and scurried to his father, arms raised.

At once Evron bent to catch him but, instead, clutched his side and dropped to his knees.

Brown eyes wide, Tuli stuffed his finger in his mouth and stumbled backward. One of the twins ran to Evron and threw her arms around his neck. The other hurried to the door that led to their apartment behind the shop. "I'll get Mama."

"No!" Evron struggled to his feet. "I'm all right, Ruth. It's just a twinge."

Unable to ignore the obvious any longer, Ulrich pointed to the glass shards littering the floor under the shattered window. An overturned chair with a splintered leg lay in pieces nearby. He squeezed the tailor's arm. "Who did this?"

"Stay out of it, Reb Ulrich. It's not your problem."

"Isn't it?"

Chapter Seven

Tova's weary reflection stared at her from the dusty mirror above her dresser. In spite of the added weight of her unborn child, her bruised cheeks were sunken and her arms looked like sparse winter branches. Her once bright teeth had begun to turn gray. The back ones had crumbled and fallen out altogether. Fruma Ya'el called it malnutrition. She scolded her for not drinking enough milk and urged her to eat more meat.

It did no good to moon over lost beauty. There was only the matter at hand. She turned away from the mirror. Her eldest child and confidante, sixteen-year-old Leah, curved her arms around her shoulders. "Mama, come with us to Zaydeh's house. He's expecting you. And what if…I mean Papa could—"

"Yes, Papa could kill me. In which case, I'm counting on you to take care of your brothers and sister."

Leah's horrified expression should have filled Tova with remorse for her hasty words. But it did not. Exhaustion, constant beatings and belittling had robbed her of all caring. Only the children's safety mattered.

"I'll protect you, Mama." Lev wrapped his arms around her expansive midsection.

Tova kissed the slash marks on his face. "Haven't you protected me enough for one day, Little Man?"

Thirteen-year-old Devorah stamped her foot. "I don't want to go, Mama. Aunt Shayndel always makes us help with the housework."

"Good for her! Shoo!" Swatting the girl's backside, Tova shoved her out the door. "All of you. It will be dark soon."

"Snow! Snow!" Two-year-old Reuven scampered over the threshold, sticking out his tongue to catch snowflakes.

"Thank God Papa's house is close," whispered Tova under her breath.

Even though fear threatened to choke her, she could not, *would not* be deterred. She watched the children chatter and argue until they disappeared around the bend. After she shut the door she picked up the whip leaning beside the wall. "If I die. I die."

Her children were the only worthwhile things Feivel ever gave her. In them she had her being. She toiled with a single purpose, to make a better way for them. If she had anything to say about it they wouldn't spend the rest of their lives in squalor. Rubbing her sore back, she dragged the whip to her bedroom. She laid it on the floor under the iron-framed bed.

From her top dresser drawer she lifted out a stack of folded diapers. Under them she had hidden a cloth bag. She untied its drawstrings and shook it. Four coins tumbled to the dresser. Barely enough for flour and kasha.

A pittance was all she earned for taking in laundry and mending jobs. After the baby came, if the birth went well, she would not be able to work for at least a month. Where would the money come from then?

Through a crack in the greased paper she peeked to see if Feivel might be coming up the road. Her husband, her provider, he brought home a small salary from taking care of the synagogue but she never saw much of it.

"Sexton of the shul? Ha! Caretaker of the tavern is more like it."

After she returned the bag to its hiding place she went to the front room that served as parlor, kitchen and, at nightfall with pallets on the floor, Lev and Reuven's bedroom. She set a pot of water to boil on the stove for tea and then took two cups from the cupboard. On the table she set a bottle of vodka between them.

The baby flailed its arms and feet within her. She traced its movements with her finger. Her stomach tightened around it for a moment then eased.

"Soon little one. But not tonight."

From her sewing basket under the table she took a pair of shears and a length of rope which she cut into four long pieces. Then she took the pot from the stove and poured hot water into her cup, tossed in a few tea leaves and lowered herself onto a chair. Her stomach hardened again. The clock's ticking pelted her ears. Propping her elbows on the table, she nodded off.

Stomach cramps woke Tova. Her neck ached from sleeping hunched over the table. She raised her head and looked at the clock. Two hours since the last but this one seemed harder.

"Not tonight, Little One." Messaging her belly, she rose from the straight-backed chair. The baby had dropped. She could feel its little head twisting from side to side between her thighs. Hands pressed against her stiff back she paced back and forth. "As if a peasant like me can tell a baby when it can or can't be born."

Through a crack in the wall, she peeked outside. Feivel staggered down the hill. She pulled on her shawl and grasped the door handle. He hollered, his voice thick from a night's drinking. "Open the door, you rotten witch."

With a whispered prayer on her lips, she swung open the door just as he tripped on a rock and tumbled head over heels and landed with his face in the snow. She bit her lip and ran to him. "Come inside where it's nice and warm, my darling, before you catch your death."

"What?" He rolled over and glowered at her. "You drunk?"

"Let me help you up." It took no small effort to make her frozen lips curve upward. She extended her hand.

Grasping her arm, he rose to his knees. She tugged at him to keep him from falling. He wobbled as he stood.

"It's been a long time, my husband." The stench of alcohol gagged her. Holding her breath, she kissed his lips and spoke in a seductive whisper.

"Nine months." Drool and rasping laughter issued from his mouth. He balled his knobby hand into a fist and jammed it into her stomach with astonishing force. She doubled over. The baby somersaulted and kicked.

"You…you must be…exhausted after such a…hard day." When she managed to catch her breath and steady her feet she grabbed his hand. "Come inside and rest…husband." She spat out the last word.

His head wobbled and, with shuffling steps, he followed her inside. She shut the door and led him to the table where he plopped down in the chair. She poured a cup of vodka and set it in front of him.

With a snap in her arm, she lifted her cup. *"L'khaim!* To life!"

In one swallow he downed his cup and then held it out for more. "You know, Tova, with the candle glowing in your face…" He drained the second cup, wiped his mouth on his sleeve and belched. "…you're uglier than ever."

"May you choke on every sip, my love."

At last he emptied the bottle. How much could one scrawny man put away before passing out? Finally his eyes drooped and he slumped over, laying his head on the table.

Rubbing his neck and shoulders she whispered in his ear with a kiss. "Let me tuck you in, my sweet."

In his drunken stupor he slid off the chair. Pulling up on it in an attempt to stand, he tumbled backward, chair and all. She grasped his shoulder, helped him to his feet and shoved him toward the bedroom. He tottered and weaved until he collapsed on the bed.

"Feivel?" She poked him. He groaned but did not open his eyes.

Another cramp seized her midsection as she waddled to the kitchen. She picked up the four pieces of rope she had cut earlier. By the time she returned to the bedroom Feivel's snoring rattled the walls.

She hummed as she wound the first rope around his right wrist and tied it to the iron bedpost. "For Leah, your firstborn."

Spinning on her heel she moved to the end of the bed and tied his right foot to the rail. "For Devorah."

Next she secured his left foot. "For Lev."

When she bent to tie his left hand, he curved it around her leg and muttered something she did not understand. She held her breath until his hand went limp. Heaving a sigh, she roped it to the bed. "For Reuven."

She knelt and reached under the bed to retrieve the buggy whip Feivel had used to beat Lev and then struggled to stand. "This one's for me."

Nausea surged through her. She gripped the whip with both hands, raised it over her head and stared at him. He looked like a ragamuffin child, helpless and pathetic. A shriek started in her throat and exploded through her mouth. She brought the whip down across his back.

The knots held tight. He screeched and struggled against the ropes. Tova's heart thumped against her chest with each strike. "You beast! You animal!"

"Tova, please…"

Again she raised the whip and cracked it across his shoulders. "Touch me or my babies again and—"

His screams turned to sobs.

"—as Adoshem lives I *will* kill you!"

Chapter Eight


One by one Fruma Ya'el cleaned and polished the already immaculate set of nickel plated surgical instruments Dr. Rosenthal had left behind. He had been diligent in teaching her simple techniques, hoping, he said many times, that she would accomplish more in the future. Somewhere along the line the future had become the distant past.

The most significant operation she had performed in twenty years was to extract a well-deserved bullet from Pinkas Rabinovich's backside after a tavern brawl. Never had she imagined she would be called upon to perform such grisly surgery as she had on poor Havah. She ran her finger along the edge of the amputation blade and laid it in the mahogany case between a pair of scissors and a scalpel. What else could she have done? Sometimes life left one no choices.

She shut the lid and opened the oaken silverware chest on the table beside it. The velvet lining had faded and the wood was chipped in a few places, but the silverware it contained, when polished, was still a sight to behold. The pieces were every bit as lovely as they had been when Papa gave them to her on her wedding day.

"Gittel, my precious sister," said Fruma Ya'el, "these should've been yours."

Setting down the tattered diaper she used as a polishing cloth, Fruma Ya'el reached into a concealed pocket in the wooden box's lining and pulled out an old tintype. Lean, with black hair, bushy moustache and olive skin, to this day, Charles' image held the power to quench her arid heart's thirst if only for the briefest moment. The memory of his lips pressed hard against hers still lingered in her mind like sweet cream and honey.

*"Charles. I can't."*

*"You'd rather rot in ignorance because of a narrow minded old man and a piece of paper than come with me?"*

*"I'm all my father has left."*

*Charles' dark eyes filled. He grasped her face with both hands. "I beg of you, Ya'el. Think. There are schools cropping up all over America for women. You'll be a brilliant doctor, a medical pioneer."*

*"What about Papa's honor?"*

*"Damn 'Papa's honor'!"*

Feather light footsteps behind her woke her from her forbidden reverie. Hastily Fruma Ya'el slipped the photograph back into its hiding place. Her tongue fumbled as she struggled for composure and forced a smile for her daughter.

"Your...your...Aunt Gittel would be so proud of her namesake." She lifted out a spoon from the chest and held it up. "A little tarnish hasn't diminished their beauty has it?"

"Is something wrong, Mama?" Gittel's green eyes darted from the secret pocket to Fruma Ya'el.

"Why do you ask?"

"You have the oddest look on your face." She walked to the window by the back door. "It's snowing harder. Maybe there'll be enough for sledding Sunday. Do you think Havah would like that?"

"It's too soon." The house shuddered in the wind. "I hope your father dries himself well before he leaves the bathhouse."

"Me too. He's a bear when he has a cold." Gittel waltzed back to the table. "It hardly seems like Hanukkah this year with Havah coming and her being so sick and all. Why, we haven't lit the menorah or anything." She picked up a butter knife. "Let me help. The work will go faster with two of us."

"No!" Fruma Ya'el grabbed it and dropped it back into the box. She hunched over it, fixing her eyes on the piece she had in her hand. "I mean, you need your rest. Take extra blankets with you. Make sure your little sister's warm."

"Are you sure you're all right, Mama?"

"Good night, Gitteleh. Pleasant dreams."

"Good night, Mama." Gittel kissed Fruma Ya'el's cheek, her eyes still questioning. She turned and left the room.

The back door slammed. Fruma Ya'el turned and forced a smile. "Did you have a good bath, Husband?"

With an indifferent grunt Hershel dropped a pile of dirty clothes and towels at her feet. "Eh, water could've been hotter."

Chapter Nine

Sunlight beat against the thin curtains covering the window over the bed. Havah yawned and rose up on one elbow, pulled back the flimsy material and blinked at bright light reflecting off the snow.

In the enclosure below, Gittel tossed scraps from a bowl to the chickens. Squawking and scratching, they surrounded her. Some pecked at her skirt while the rest fought for the food on the snow-covered ground.

After she emptied the bowl, she crouched down and crawled into the wooden coop that looked like a miniature cabin. A few minutes later, she emerged with feathers in her hair and a bowlful of brown eggs in the crook of her arm.

Two boys scampered across the yard. One flung a snowball at the other.

Hershel burst from the house wielding a wooden spoon. "Scat!"

When the second boy retaliated and the snowball exploded in Hershel's face. Chortling with fiendish glee he stooped to gather a handful of snow and shaped it into a ball. Then he chased the boys, arm raised. He made a direct hit that knocked off the boy's cap. With loud squeals, the boys raced each other over the hill.

"Oh, I almost forgot. Our future son-in-law and family are coming for *Shabbes* dinner." Hershel called over his shoulder to Fruma Ya'el who stood on at the back door.

She ran after him and took the spoon. "Tonight? And just now you're telling me? Am I a magician? Can I make dinner for eight people fly out of the air?"

"If anyone can, you can." He tapped the end of her nose with his fingertip. Turning, he walked down the snowy road and whistled a tune.

The glass chilled Havah's forehead as she pressed it against the window pane and watched him disappear into the distance. Twisting her nightgown collar between her fingers, she ran her other hand through her grimy hair. Then she lay on her back, stretching and wriggling her seven toes. Her maimed foot still throbbed but the pain had lessened quite a bit. Rolling over, she slid backward off the bed and eased her feet to the floor.

With halting steps she hobbled from one side of the room to the other. Putting most of her weight on her left foot, she walked on the outside edge of her right foot to compensate for the missing toes.

She sat down in the rocking chair beside the bed and pulled up her gown. With eyes tightly shut she laid her damaged foot across her left knee. Layer by layer, she unwound the strips of cloth binding and then opened her eyes.

"I'm a freak, a monstrosity."

"You're beautiful, Little Sister. It's just your foot that's not so pretty." Her cheeks glistening, Gittel stood in the doorway with an armload of clothes.

"When did you sneak in? How long have you been gawking at me?" Havah tucked her foot under her gown. "What's all that?"

Gittel set the clothes on the bed. "You wouldn't want to meet the rabbi naked would you? I guess it wouldn't matter to him. He's been blind ever since I can remember." She fished a bathrobe from the pile. "But, on the other hand, everyone else can see so you'd best be getting dressed. Of course, we need to clean the *schmootz* off you. Mama doesn't want you walking to the bathhouse so she filled the washtub in the kitchen. It's nice and warm by the stove."

From her apron pocket she pulled a pair of knitted slippers. "Mama just finished these for you last night. Hope you like green. It's her favorite color. She says it must be Adoshem's favorite color, too, because he put so much of it on the earth."

Havah wrapped the thick robe around her shoulders and put on the slippers. They were soft and warm on her feet and ankles. "You can't see the hideous thing through it."

"Ready?" Gittel held out her arm.

Grasping Gittel's elbow, Havah stood, leaning on her for balance. "I'll have to get used to it. I've never heard of toes growing back, have you?"

"Arel's brother-in-law Itzak does amazing things with wood. I'll bet he could make a cane for you."

"I'm not a cripple."

Recalcitrance, Papa used to say, would be either her triumph or her undoing. Havah let go Gittel's arm and pressed her hands against the walls on either side of the narrow staircase. Hesitantly she lowered her injured foot onto the first step and gingerly transferred the weight of her body onto it, then quickly brought the good foot next to it. Repeating this process took a few minutes, but eventually she found herself in a large kitchen with polished wooden floors. In the center of which sat a steaming brass washtub.

Fruma Ya'el stood at the foot of the stairs with a thick towel draped over her forearm. Her brown eyes twinkled as she gestured toward the washtub with a dramatic wave of her hand.

"Breakfast first or bath, M'Lady?"

Shedding robe, gown and slippers, Havah stepped into the warm water. She settled into the cramped tub relishing the steam and the scent of soap.

"Lean back so I can wash your hair." Gittel took a pan from the stove. She continued to chatter as she sloshed water over Havah's head and worked the soap into a lather. "You'll like Rabbi Yussel. He's the wisest man in the world. His son Arel is my intended. Arel Gitterman. Oh, you've met…well not really. He carried you here. You probably don't remember, do you? Of course not! You were unconscious. What am I thinking? And his sisters, Shayndel and Tova…"

Gittel's prattle faded to a faint background noise. Havah saw Arel as if in a dream remembered long ago. His hair and beard, inky shadows, framed a face as pale as dawn. Like silver clouds, his prolific eyes spoke with silent words.

*Arel. A strong name. Lion of God.*

## Chapter Ten

"There. That should be enough food to last until Sunday." Fragrant jelly doughnuts, flaky and hot, nested in a tin pail lined with a linen napkin. Shayndel covered them with a second napkin and set them in a small wooden pushcart already loaded with potato pancakes, braided *Hollah* and a kettle brimming with *cholent.*

"Hurry up. Mama needs me." With the sole of one foot pressed against the wall, Lev balanced on the opposite foot. Rolling his eyes, he folded his arms across his chest.

Shayndel tapped his leg with a spatula. "No footprints on my whitewash."

"Ooow!" He dropped to the floor, hugging his knees.

"Oh, stop it. I barely touched you."

"Papa whipped him." Leah knelt beside him and pulled down his stocking. Angry red abrasions marked the back of his leg.

Resisting the urge to lose her breakfast, Shayndel swallowed. "I'm sorry, Lev." She took a doughnut from the pail and held it out to him. "Can you forgive me?"

His swollen lips stretched into a lopsided smile as he took it from her. "Guess so." Pulling up his stocking with one hand, he stuffed the whole doughnut into his mouth with the other. "Can we go now?"

"Wait. We need a man here for protection until your uncles and grandfather come back from morning prayers."

With a wet cloth Shayndel wiped his sticky mouth and forced a smile. How could she tell him the truth?

Despite her best efforts to be cheerful, her stomach tangled itself into a knot. She peeked out the window over the sink, hoping for a glimpse of her sister. All the while she could not stop herself from imagining Tova a dead heap in the snow, murdered by Feivel's whip. No. She dare not share that possibility with her nephew. Not yet.

Without a word Tova's children exchanged tense glances. Lev's brows knit and he looked more like an old man than a nine-year-old child. "Don't you mean after they get back from finding out if Mama's–?"

The door popped open. An icy gust whipped through it as Arel and Yussel entered the kitchen. Itzak followed, shaking the snow from his beard. With both of his hands, he fought to shut the heavy door. His wide grin answered all questions.

"Where's my breakfast, Woman?"

Chapter Eleven

From the first glance at Fruma Ya'el's kitchen anyone could tell she loved light. A multitude of sparkling windows, all framed by colorful curtains, bore witness to the fact. Afternoon sunlight bathed the generous kitchen with a comfortable glow.

Above all else Fruma Ya'el valued cleanliness. Havah chuckled. Woe to the poor unfortunate who dared to track mud across her wooden floors. Not even a mouse would find so much as a cracker crumb under her table. A gnat would starve to death in this house.

On the stove a kettle of chicken soup bubbled. Its savory aroma helped lessen Havah's loneliness if only just a little. At least Auntie Fruma allowed her to make the Hollah for the special dinner which was no small thing. After all, she was still a stranger and Auntie's kitchen was clearly her sanctuary.

On a generously floured board, Havah kneaded the bread dough, folding and stretching it until it felt soft and pliable. She divided it into two mounds, and then divided each mound into three equal pieces. Rolling them under her palms she elongated them into strands. "It's a good batch. I can tell. I put raisins in it for Hanukkah."

While Havah braided the strands Gittel pinched the ends and held them to keep them from slipping. "Havaleh, you'd put raisins in the chicken soup if Mama would let you."

"Hmm, might taste good." Havah popped a handful into her mouth. "My papa used to say, 'As raisins are sweet to the tongue so is the reading of the Torah sweet to the ears of the listener.' He used to let me sit on his lap and hold the book of psalms while we—"

"While you what?" Gittel tilted her head.

"Um…while he sang to me." Fruma Ya'el's raised eyebrows told her to swallow her words. This wasn't Natalya and she was no longer the rabbi's daughter.

With a suppressed sigh she covered the braided loaves with clean towels and set them on the back of the stove to rise. "The last time I baked Hollah, I couldn't put raisins in it because my brother David ate all of them. I wish I hadn't gotten so mad. I said horrid things."

"Were they the last words you spoke to him?" Fruma Ya'el unfolded a linen tablecloth. She snapped it so it billowed and dropped to cover the table.

"No." Gathering the bowls and utensils, Havah hobbled to the sink. "I can still see him with Mama's clean dish towel over his head, walking bent over. He sang all raspy like an old lady, too. 'Little Bubbe Fuss Bucket. All astir over a raisin. A raisin. A shriveled little raisin. Oy, yoy, yoy.'"

She took a kettle of hot water from the stove and poured it over the dishes. "I could never stay mad at him. If only I'd known—"

Gittel grabbed a dish towel. "Would you have done anything differently?"

A soap bubble floated up from the water. Havah popped it with her finger. "No."

"Havaleh, let Gittel finish those dishes. You need your rest." Clucking her tongue, Fruma Ya'el took a stack of dishes from the oak sideboard and set them on the table.

"You two have waited on me for weeks. It's not right."

"Youth is always so impatient. Give yourself time to heal, Child. You're nothing but skin and bones. When you're well enough, I'll work you so hard you'll think you're my slave."

With a deep curtsy, Fruma Ya'el pulled a chair from under the table. The legs scraped the floor. She waved her hand over it. "Your throne, Your Highness."

"In a minute." Limping to the stove, Havah peeked under the towel. The loaves had doubled their size. "They're ready to bake."

She brushed the tops of the loaves with beaten egg yolk. "Now for the crowning touch."  Frowning, she searched the countertop. "What happened to the raisins? They were here a minute ago. The gray bowl. Auntie, did you move it?"

"Not I."

Havah's foot buckled underneath her as she opened the cabinet. "They're not here."

"Forget about the raisins. Into the oven with the Hollah and onto the chair with you. Sit!" Fruma Ya'el took the pan from her.

Grateful to be off her throbbing foot, Havah stretched her legs out in front of her and admired her brown and shining leather shoes. "I'm not used to them, my foot or the shoes."

Kneeling, Fruma Ya'el unbuttoned them. "You really are a tiny thing. Gittel outgrew these two years ago."

"Are you saying I have big feet?" Gittel crouched behind Fruma Ya'el's and mischievously untied her mother's apron.

"Oh, I wouldn't say they're big, but if we ever lose the chicken coop we can move the hens into your dainty booties."

Gittel pressed the back of her hand against her forehead in mock distress. "I've never been so insulted. I shall run away from home this very night."

"Before you do, tie my apron and not in a dozen knots like the last time." Fruma Ya'el removed Havah's shoes and replaced them with the knitted slippers from her pocket. "I thought you might need these. Save the shoes for outside."

A small twinge of guilt niggled at Havah. She leaned back and watched mother and daughter scurry about in preparation for impending guests while she enjoyed the delightful scent of fresh bread.

"The beds are made and floors swept." Gittel set the *Shabbes* candlesticks on the carved oak table. "And these you can use for mirrors." She sucked in her cheeks and puckered her lips. "That is if you don't mind looking like this."

Humming a tune, she picked up a feather duster and dusted the chairs around the table, stopping briefly to brush Havah's nose with the feathers. "Oh, silly me. I thought you were part of the chair, Little Sister."

Fruma Ya'el snapped Gittel's behind with a dish-towel. "Goose! Back to work, Miss Chatterbox."

"Ouch!" On her toes Gittel pirouetted and lofted her duster in the air. "This means war!"

She chased Fruma Ya'el into a corner and tickled her until she sneezed and grabbed the duster. "Enough already. Our guests will be arriving before you know it."

Havah stood. "At least let me set the table."

"Sit." Fruma Ya'el pressed her nose against Havah's and pushed her back into the chair. "Why, you're like ice. Even with all this baking." She made her way to the potbellied stove in the corner of the room. "Gittel, bring me some wood."

When she opened the stove's cast iron door, a crockery bowl fell out and landed with a thump. Raisins peppered the floor like black hail. "What on earth were these doing in here?"

With a sly grin, Gittel shrugged. "Keeping warm?"

Chapter Twelve

The metronome's pendulum waged war with the young woman at Ulrich's grand piano. His ears ached with each dissonant note and miscarried beat. He pressed his hand over hers. "Fraulein Petri, have you practiced this piece at all?"

"Oh, yes, Professor Dietrich. I practice every night for at least two hours. Sometimes less when Papa begs me to stop."

"He begs you…to stop?" Ulrich swallowed hard. "Why?"

"You know how fathers are. He's afraid I'll injure my delicate hands."

The lace dress she wore enhanced her generous curves while giving him more than a glimpse of her ample breasts and her perfume added its own discordant note to the room.

He cleared his throat. "*Fraulein*, far be it from me to hurt your feelings, but I must be honest. You're wasting your money and my time with these lessons. After three months you should have, at the very least, mastered the simplified arrangement of *Brahm's Lullaby.*"

Instead of the tears he anticipated, she shrieked with laughter, lifted her hands from the keys and clutched his cheeks between them. "My poor, poor lonely professor." Letting her shawl slide off her shoulders, she wrapped her arms around his neck and pressed her lips against his.

Ulrich writhed from her grasp, sprang off the bench, then took his handkerchief from his waistcoat pocket and dabbed his lips. He pushed his disheveled hair from his perspiring forehead and bent to retrieve her shawl. "I'm…flattered…but I—"

A snicker reminded him of the other person in the room. Seven-year-old Zelig Abromovich, sitting with a book in front of the fireplace, peeked around the wings of a high-back chair. "Uncle Ulri, is it time for my piano lesson yet?"

"Uncle?" With the same contempt she might have shown a cockroach, Miss Petri glared at the boy and, then, at Ulrich. Stamping her feet, she snarled. "The rumors are true, aren't they, Professor? You do keep company with *them*."

Ulrich stood, clicked his heels together and bowed with a flourish. "Happy Hanukkah."

When she stomped from the room, Zelig's huge brown eyes filled with hurt and confusion. "Did I do something wrong?"

"No, son. Nothing at all."

Chapter Thirteen

*"Gut Shabbes!"* Having lit the Sabbath candles, Fruma Ya'el removed her lace scarf and sat down beside Havah. Then, as he had done every Hanukkah since he was a small boy, Arel lit the candles on the family menorah. No matter where they celebrated the holiday Papa insisted on bringing it. Arel could not remember anyone ever being offended. He canted the blessing over the candles and then took a seat between Yussel and Shayndel, his eyes on Havah. "Happy Hanukkah, everyone."

Shayndel smiled at Havah across the table. "I'm glad to finally meet you. I saw Gittel at the butcher shop two days ago and all she talked about was her little sister."

Itzak winked. "If talking could cure the plague, think of all the lives she'd save."

"It's true. If my Gittel ever loses her voice she can find it in my ear." Hershel's green eyes lit with a mixture of adoration and amusement.

Gittel's freckled cheeks flushed as red as her hair. "Papa!"

"Do I lie?"

"Husband, stop embarrassing our daughter in front of our guests." Fruma Ya'el slid the bread platter to him.

His smile dissolved and he glowered at her. "Wife, you'll do well to hold your tongue."

Tense silence descended until Havah whispered, "When is your little one due, *Froi* Abromovich?"

Her voice was gentle on Arel's ears. Not at all harsh or nasal as it tended to be with some pretty girls who destroyed a man's perception just by opening their mouths.

"Please call me Shayndel. *Froi* is much too formal." His sister pressed her hand against her burgeoning midsection. "Auntie says he'll be here sometime in March."

Using his fork to navigate, Yussel found and speared a potato. "And you're certain it's a boy?"

"It might be a tomboy like our sister Bayla, may she rest in peace." Arel forced himself to avert his gaze from Havah.

Shayndel's blue eyes flashed. "Oh, it's a boy. He kicks too hard to be a girl."

Itzak's booming laughter echoed to the rafters. "It's no use arguing with her, Little Brother. If she says it's a boy, it's a boy! And the way he kicks my back in the night I think it may be two boys."

"Itzak!" Shayndel's mouth dropped open.

"Your name, 'he shall laugh' is perfect for you, Reb Itzak." Havah set down her fork and smiled.

"You're quite right, *Fraylin* Cohen. But how does a little *girl* know the meaning of names?" Arel found himself powerless to divert his attention from her black-diamond eyes.

Her shoulders stiffened and squared. "Let me tell you, Reb Gitterman, maybe you don't—"

"Arel, eat more. Talk less." Fruma Ya'el pressed her fingers against Havah's mouth and shoved a plate of roasted potatoes under his nose.

"My compliments to Havah on the Hollah," Hershel broke off a piece of bread and passed the loaf to Itzak. "She's a good cook and with a pretty face, wonderful qualities for a wife. Why, when the time comes, a husband will hardly notice her infirmity."

Havah's lips turned white as if someone had delivered a blow to her stomach. Arel's own stomach churned. Infirmity or no, a sudden urge to take her in his arms seized him. He tucked his sweaty hands under his legs.

"As the Talmud says, 'examine the contents not the bottle.'" Yussel's rumbling voice sliced through the tense silence that had once again fallen over the group. He pointed to his sightless eyes. "In other words, infirmity is in the eyes of the beholder, yes?"

With a scathing frown at Hershel, Gittel wrapped an arm around Havah's shoulders. "Pay Papa no mind. He's had too much wine."

Havah smiled a tenuous smile. She skimmed her hand over the base of the regal menorah in the middle of the table. "Rebbe? Why did you bring this? Isn't Uncle Hershel's good enough?"

Hershel frowned. "Havah! Don't be rude to the rabbi!"

Yussel put his finger to his lips. "*Shah*, Hershel. It's a good question she asks. How many people take their own menorah to their host's home? Arel, tell *Fraylin* Cohen the story of your grandfather's menorah. Like a member of our family for three generations."

"Oh yes, Ari, tell her." Gittel clapped her hands.

Crafted to look like a tree in the wind, the main stem curved with nine branches arcing in opposite directions. The candle cups sat upon them like majestic crowns. Between seven of the branches and the trunk an opening hosted a pair of doves, positioned breast to breast, and perched on a flower covered vine, spreading their graceful wings. The vine twined around the trunk, ending at the wide base.

Proud of its history, on most occasions Arel was usually more than willing to recount the story. Tonight his tongue turned to dust. "My grandfather...of blessed memory...was a rabbi as was his father before him."

"Mine, too." Havah leaned forward, elbows on the table, and propped her head on her hands.

*Did Adam feel this way in the Garden of Eden when he brought the succulent fruit to his hungry lips?*

Arel found his voice again, though not without a struggle. "Zaydeh...Papa's father...an artist. After my grandmother died he made this menorah in her memory. She was very young"

"What did she die of?"

"Christian poison! Tell her Arel." Yussel's bony hands curled into fists. "A pogrom. In the street like an animal. Fifty-three years ago. Like yesterday I remember."

"You must've been a boy."

"Five years old. Her Yosi, her heart, she called me."

Tears quivered in Havah's eyes. "You can tell how much he loved her by the verse he chose to engrave on the menorah, *'Behold, you are lovely. Your eyes are like doves.'* It's from Song of Songs."

"Havah!" Hershel's fork dropped from his hand and it clanked against his plate.

"End of story." Yussel grasped Arel's arm. "Itzak, what do you hear from your brother in Kishinev?"

Itzak took a crumpled envelope from his vest pocket, removed a letter and smoothed it out. "Came today."

"It was steamed open of course." Shayndel rolled her eyes. "I hope Reb Pinkas enjoyed it."

"Enough about Pinkas." Fruma Ya'el spooned drippings over the meat on Havah's plate. "What does Evron say about his children?"

"They're growing like four hornbeam trees." Itzak turned the letter around to show off a stick figure sketch. "As you can see from Tuli's artwork. And..." He squinted and jutted his teeth over his lower lip. "...his bride's as lovely as ever."

"Stop that," said Shayndel. "Katya's a dear person. She's just not very pretty and—"

The back door swung open and Devorah burst into the room. Her shoes clicked with fervor across the floor.

"*Gut Shabbes*, Devorah," said Yussel.

"*Gut Shabbes*, Zaydeh." She tugged at Fruma Ya'el's sleeve. "Please, Auntie Fruma. Mama. The baby. Come quick!"

Itzak leaned back in his chair and folded his arms across his chest. "Doesn't that baby know it's *Shabbes?* He's a rebellious child already!"

Shayndel pushed her plate and stood. She hurried to the kitchen, followed by Devorah, and took her shawl from a peg by the door. "Where's your father, Devorah?"

"He's at home."

"Home? Not at the tavern?"

"He hasn't taken even one drink all day. He just sits and stares at the floor." Devorah leaned her head on Shayndel's shoulder. "He's different. I'm scared, Auntie."

Arel fingered the tender welt on his neck. "Maybe I should come with you."

"Stay put, Ari." Fruma Ya'el rose and bustled about the dining room. "Gittel, bring me my birthing basket. Then go home with Devorah. Help Leah pack the children back to our house. You will all stay here for the night." She wrapped a shawl around Havah's shoulders. "Come, Little Sister. Help me welcome Tova's *Shabbes* baby."

Havah hobbled behind Fruma Ya'el and Shayndel, her bandaged foot cramped in her new shoe.

She dragged her toes through the floor's loose dirt as they entered Tova and Feivel's musty shack.

Two months ago she lived with Mama and Papa in her safe haven. Now, like Moses she was a "stranger in a strange land", her secure world leveled to a pile of silt and ashes. What terrible sin did she commit to deserve such punishment?

"*Gut Shabbes*, Reb Feivel." Fruma Ya'el whispered to the emaciated man with dirty red hair hunched over the kitchen table.

With a slight lift of his head and a curt nod he glared at her through his eyeglasses' thick lenses.

Shayndel scowled with unmasked disdain. She hissed and spat on the floor just missing his stocking foot. Feivel responded with a sneer, his rheumy eyed glare falling on Havah. "You."

Stale liquor and days, possibly weeks, without a bath made the odor around him intolerable. Shuddering, she slunk behind Fruma Ya'el and clung to her skirt.

A woman's cry shrilled from the next room.

The ground tipped and swayed beneath Havah. "Auntie, I'll…I'll wait for you and Shayndel in the wagon so—" She grappled for an excuse, any excuse. "—so…the horses don't get lonely."

Fruma Ya'el chuckled and flapped her free hand over her head like a bird wing. "'Lonely horses,' she says. I should let you freeze to death so four legged animals have company?"

The ramshackle door to the bedroom loomed ahead of her like the sinister entrance to a dungeon. At Fruma Ya'el's urging, Havah pushed it open. The hinges' somber creak sent chills up her spine.

A candle on the night table cast a dull glow over Tova. Her midsection bulged like a small mountain under the comforter. Sweat drenched her face, rolled off her forehead; it dripped off her nose and chin. Dark hair clung to her cheeks beneath a ruffled nightcap. "Where are my children?"

"They're safe with Gittel and Leah." Fruma Ya'el took off her scarf and shawl, slinging them over the end of the cast iron bed. "Shayndel, get the lamps. Havah, take off your shoes."

Unbalanced by her added weight, Shayndel ambled from the room. In a few minutes she returned with an oil lamp in each hand. She set them on the bed stand, used the candle to light them and then scooted the small table toward the end of the bed.

Fruma Ya'el placed her hands on Tova's belly. "How close are the pains?"

"Three, maybe four minutes."

"Why didn't you send for me sooner?"

"I had an important matter…to…attend to." Grasping her stomach, Tova writhed and moaned.

The moan intensified into a scream and Havah backed into a corner with her hands pressed against her ears. After a few minutes that seemed like hours, Tova quieted.

"Where do you think you're going, Little Sister?" Fruma Ya'el grasped Havah's arm. Leading her to a chair, she gave her a gentle nudge. "Sit! Watch. Learn."

One at a time, Fruma Ya'el pulled the tools of her trade from a basket. "Pay attention, Havah. Everything must be cleaner than clean." She took out a strange instrument with curved loops at the end of twin handles. "These are forceps to grab a stubborn baby's head with and help him out."

Havah's tongue stuck to her teeth and she cringed. "Help him out of where?"

Next Fruma Ya'el took out a pair of shears. "These are sacred. For childbirth only. Use your teeth before cutting anything else with them, understand?"

"I'll wash them for you." Havah sprang up from the chair.

Before she could take a step Tova seized her hand and screamed. Havah's tortured fingers reeled from the crushing grip. Sinking into the chair, she struggled to free them.

Shayndel took the instruments and scurried through the door. "Sit tight, Little Sister. I'll boil these."

"Boil them for at least five minutes." Fruma Ya'el seemed unconcerned about Havah's plight and the fact she would probably have to go through life without a hand as well as a foot.

Finally Tova let go. "Did I hurt you?"

Havah flexed her throbbing fingers and forced a smile. "No."

"You're the new one everybody's talking about, aren't you?"

"*Shah!* There'll be plenty of time for chitchat later." Fruma Ya'el pushed back the blanket at the end of the bed. Tova spread her legs apart as the older woman reached between them. "Not long."

When Fruma Ya'el withdrew her slimy hand and dried it on a towel, Havah's stomach churned.

Tova's pallid face contorted. She grabbed the bed's iron bars behind her, arched her back and shrieked.

Havah slumped to the floor, drew up her legs, tucked her head between her knees and closed her eyes.

She heard footsteps clomping on the dirt floor, felt skirts rustle over her head and heard middle-age knees crack as Fruma Ya'el crouched beside her. "Stop it!"

Grasping Havah's chin between her thumb and forefinger Fruma Ya'el raised Havah's head. "Look at me. If you want to go outside then go. I've no time for this."

Shayndel burst through the door with the instruments bundled in a towel in one arm and a bowl of hot soapy water on the other.

Fruma Ya'el sprang off the floor and whisked the bowl away from her. Setting it on the bureau she scrubbed her hands, climbed on the bed and straddled the mattress. "Sit up Tova. Shayndel, you and Havah get on either side of her."

Dropping the towel wrapped bundle on the bed stand, Shayndel scuttled to her sister's side. "Isn't it exciting, Havah?"

Havah blinked back apprehension and clamped her chattering teeth on tremulous lips. Bracing herself by grabbing the bedpost and climbing onto the chair she managed to scale the tall bed.

Tova's face turned purple. Havah feared it would burst open like an overripe grape. Straining forward, Tova hiked her gown, grasped her bare knees, tilted back her head and yowled.

Once more Fruma Ya'el thrust her hand inside of Tova. "One more push."

Havah's heart thumped. A gray and blue face appeared between Tova's thighs. Havah held her breath and watched the wet baby slide into the midwife's waiting hands.

Tova fell back with a relieved groan and closed her eyes. "As Adoshem lives; never again."

"You say that now." Fruma Ya'el hummed a lullaby while she snipped through the umbilical cord with her "sacred shears". "Blessed be He. It's a girl."

For a closer look at the newborn Havah climbed down from the bed and move to the end of it.

"It's your first time, Little Sister, you do the honors." With a flushed smile on her perspiration soaked face, Fruma Ya'el handed Havah a wet cloth and laid the flailing baby in her arms. "You may give this little one her first bath. I'm sorry I yelled at you."

Hardly aware of anything but the newborn, Havah took the cloth and rubbed in circular motions from the infant's downy black cap of hair to her infinitesimal toes. With Shayndel's help she bound the little one in a frayed blanket.

Calmed, the infant opened her murky blue eyes and curled her lips into an "O" reminding Havah of an ancient rabbi pondering a great mystery.

No doubt she had lived her entire life for this moment. She harbored the baby in the crook of her arm and skimmed her finger over the feather soft cheek. *"Adoshem gives and Adoshem takes away. Blessed be the name of Adoshem.'"*

With hungry desperation the baby wrapped her mouth around Havah's finger and sucked.

Fruma Ya'el chuckled as she gathered her things and headed out the door. "Havah, she needs something you don't have to give."

The baby opened her mouth and bawled. Shayndel lifted her from Havah and kissed her tiny cheek before laying her in Tova's arms. "Looks nothing like her—" Shayndel turned her head and spat on the floor. "—father."

Unbuttoning her nightgown, Tova cradled the infant who nuzzled and suckled at her breast. She nestled against the pillows, a weary half smile on her gaunt face. Fingering the baby's damp curls, she whispered, *"Gut Shabbes*, little Bayla, my bright one."

With a gentle tug, Havah closed the bedroom door behind her, her mind spinning with little Bayla's image. When she turned and saw Arel, Yussel and Itzak sitting with Feivel in the front room she started. When had they come in? She did not remember hearing voices or footsteps.

Hanging back in the shadows she watched them. She did not relish her mission to announce to Reb Feivel his daughter's birth.

A few feet away, Itzak and Arel sat next to the stove engaged in a lively discussion. Their elaborate hand gestures reinforced the intensity of their words.

Itzak reminded her of a bear cub, short and stout with black, curly hair. His beard seemed to be as unruly as the young man himself. His dark eyes shimmered like midnight stars.

Her curiosity besting her, she tiptoed closer to hear their conversation.

"Surely she only parrots her father who was a rabbi. What would a mere girl know of the Holy Books?" Itzak leaned forward in his chair.

"I heard her with my own ears, Itzak! In her *sleep* she chanted Kaddish." For emphasis Arel hit his fist against the palm of his other hand. "I'm telling you she's been taught. I'll bet you five kopeks she's studied Torah. There's more to that tiny—"

"Come in, Havaleh. We heard the cry already. You have news for us?"

The rabbi's welcoming smile warmed her more than the fire in the potbellied stove. Already, he recognized her footsteps.

Like a boy caught stealing eggs, Arel blushed. The look in his gray eyes made her forget her mission.

Itzak whacked his hand on the arm of his chair. "The news! Tell us, Havah! Is it a boy or a girl? Or perhaps our Tova had a litter of puppies!"

Flames of embarrassment scorched her face. "Oh, forgive me. She had a beautiful little girl."

Still hunched over the kitchen table, Feivel snarled at her. "Has my 'dear wife' given this 'beautiful girl' a name?"

He rose, limped to the stove and poured a cup of coffee.

"Feivel, your walk sounds labored. Have you recently injured yourself?" Yussel cocked his head.

Leaning back in his chair, Arel pointed. "I'd say he has, Papa."

Pulling his shirt sleeves down over his bandaged wrists Feivel approached Havah. "Has the chanting demon child lost her tongue?"

With dread rising in her chest, she backed away from him. "Froi Resnick is calling her Bayla. She's a beautiful—"

"You said that already!" His cup slipped from his hand. Hot coffee splattered her ankles. Shoving her, he stumped to the door.

A bolt of pain shot through her foot which buckled under her. Arel sprang from his chair and caught her. To steady herself she clutched his forearm and stumbled into his unwitting embrace.

Shayndel's eyes kindled with unmasked hatred as she entered the room and carried the baby to Feivel. "Greet your daughter, my 'brother'."

With little more than a glance at the baby, Feivel grabbed his coat from the coat tree by the door. It toppled. He kicked it aside and then opened the door with his foot.

"Where do you think you're going?"

"A house should collapse on you." A menacing sneer on his lips, he glowered at her, then at Yussel, next at Itzak and finally at Havah. "All of you!"

The door slammed behind him. The top hinge snapped off. Havah shuddered and huddled against Arel.

*A scalding wind whipped around Havah. She raced from the monster. His yellow fangs snapped at her neck. Hollow laughter echoed from the depths of the sepulcher of his throat. Copper eyed serpents slithered from his mouth. He vomited black ash. She choked on it.*

*Striking her toe on a rock, she tumbled down the steep hill and stopped at the edge of a high precipice. Thick steam purled from the bubbling waters below. The monster fell on her, his claws digging at her neck. His eyes spun in their sockets behind dirty spectacles.*

Heart thumping in her ears, she opened her eyes and pulled the threadbare blanket up around her neck. The greased paper covering the window did little to block out the frigid wind. She snuggled close to Shayndel who snored beside her in the feather bed usually shared by Tova's daughters.

Tova and her newborn rested in the next room with Fruma Ya'el keeping vigil.

Loath to fall back to sleep, Havah counted the cracks in the roughhewn walls. An animal, probably a squirrel, clawed at the roof with such ferocity she feared it might dig a hole and fly through the thatched ceiling to join her in the bed below. A mouse in the corner scratched the log wall with his tiny claws.

Throwing off the covers she slipped out of bed and grabbed a broom leaning against the wall. She hopped after the mouse and whacked at it until it no longer moved. Then she picked it up by the tail. thrust it through a tear in the window paper and whispered, "Take *that*, Feivel, you ugly monster."

"Havah, you'll get no rest chasing mice."

"Shayndel, you're awake?"

"Who can sleep with all the noise?"

Havah plopped down on the bed. Flinging her arms over her head she lay back across Shayndel's ankles. "Why did Tova marry him? He's the rudest, most ill-tempered man I've ever met."

"She had no choice. You know how it is." Shayndel sat up, struck a match and lit the lamp by the bed. "Enough about them, what about you, Havah Cohen? My father and brother have done nothing *but* talk about you since the day they found you on the steps of the *shul*."

A pleasurable thrill shot through Havah. "Arel talks about me?"

"They say you were chanting prayers when they found you. Is it true?"

"I don't remember."

"And what you said when you held the baby."

" *'Adoshem gives, Adoshem takes away. Blessed be the name of Adoshem.'* It's from the Holy…I…I heard my father say it."

"Tell me about your family."

"Mendel wanted to be a rabbi like Papa but David preferred to do things with his hands. He could paint a flower to look so real you'd swear you could almost smell its perfume!"

"What about your mother?"

"A lily of the valley. A queen among women. With thick hair so long it touched the floor."

"She didn't cut it when they married?"

"Papa insisted *her* hair was *his* crowning glory and rabbinic tradition meant nothing to him."

"Havah, can you keep a secret?"

Shayndel slid off her kerchief. Underneath it a cap made from hosiery fit tight over her head. She removed it and two golden braids cascaded over her shoulders past her waist.

Havah wrapped a flaxen lock around her finger. "It would have been a tragedy to chop it off."

"Every night Itzak brushes it." She tucked her hair back under the cap and retied her kerchief, snuffed out the lamp and lay back against the pillow. "We call it our sweet secret."

Lulled by the wind and the sound of the baby's suckling in the next room, Havah curled up beside her, burrowed her head in the pillow and let the pleasant feeling of oncoming sleep embrace her. "Maybe in the morning I'll tell you mine."

Weak from giving birth, Tova leaned back against the pillow and studied the shabby room. She tried to keep a tidy home but how could one scrub a dirt floor?

The dilapidated house begged for repair but Feivel had little inclination for filling cracks in the wall or repairing broken windows.

"Perhaps when I've recovered I'll save some of my sewing money to buy a length of cloth to make curtains, something bright and colorful. What do you think, Bayla?"

Bayla stretched one arm over her head, made squeaking noises and opened her eyes. Tova nuzzled against her face. The infant sucked on her chin, filling her with delight.

"How will I feed you when you need more than milk, little one? There's barely enough to feed and clothe your brothers and sisters."

Like excited squirrels, her other four children pushed and shoved through the door. All of them resembled their father with brown eyes and bright red hair. Gittel, Havah and Fruma Ya'el followed them into the room. They gathered around the bed.

"Mama! Mama!" Reuven climbed onto the bed and scowled at the newborn.

Once he settled beside her, Tova laid Bayla across his legs. "You're a big brother now, Little Apple. You must take very good care of your baby sister."

A proud grin replaced his frown and he puffed out his little chest. "Me big brother."

After waiting a moment for him to get acquainted, Leah lifted the baby. "She looks like you, Mama."

Reuven slid off the bed and jumped up and down. "Me too, up, Leah."

"You're not the baby anymore. It's Bayla's turn." Devorah grabbed him around the waist and tickled him.

He giggled and wrapped his arms around her neck.

Gittel peeked over Leah's shoulder. "I think she looks like her Uncle Arel, don't you, Havah?"

With a frown, Lev pointed a finger at Havah. "I know who you are. You're the demon girl. The one they found on the steps."

"Such things should not be allowed to come through your lips." Fruma Ya'el gave his backside a gentle swat with her spoon.

"Come here, Son." Tova's tenuous strength began to ebb. Lev sat on the bed and leaned his head on her breast. His kinky hair smelled like snow and wind. She kissed the scabbing welt on his cheek. "There are no demons here, understand?  Havah helped me with the baby. Now, apologize to our guest."

His scowl faded. He sat up and mumbled. "Sorry."

Fruma Ya'el pointed toward the kitchen. "Come children, I have hot kasha and coffee. Then it's off with you to my house so your mother can rest."

"Leah, stay here with me." Tova watched her eldest daughter stroke the baby's cheek. It would not be long, Adoshem willing, before she held babes of her own. "Have you seen your papa?"

"No, Mama. Do you want me to send Lev to find him?"

Lev stamped his foot and folded his arms across his chest. "Why should I? I hate him."

Fruma Ya'el pinched his ear. "That's no way for a son to talk about his papa."

"I hope he's dead."

"Lev Resnick, do you want to tempt the Evil Eye?"

"There's no eye more evil than his." He sprang from the bed and ran out of the room.

Tova listened to the front door bang shut. "He's right, you know."

Chapter Fourteen

After aimlessly tramping through the woods for most of the night Feivel's legs ached. His patched coat did little to keep out the frigid air. The cold exacerbated the rope burns on his wrists and ankles. He sank down on a gnarled beech tree's exposed web of roots.

Three days without drink had taken their toll. His head pounded with longing for a taste of Schnapps. "All she knows how to do is have babies and whine. 'Feivel, the window's broken. Feivel, the children need shoes. Feivel this and Feivel that.' He regretted ever marrying the nagging crone."

A light snow began to fall, stinging his eyes and blurring his vision. He took off his spectacles, wiped them on his shirt and looked up at the moon shining between two clouds. Its light shocked him into realization. With a clarity he had not had in many years, he leaned against the tree and wailed. "I'm the monster. Adoshem forgive me! I don't deserve to live."

Filled with self-loathing, he dropped his glasses and fell prostrate on the frozen ground.

The crime he denied for seventeen years crashed in on him. At fourteen, Tova Gitterman was a beauty. Her gray eyes sparkled like quartz. Tall and supple as a willow, her black hair shone almost blue in the sun. How could a sixteen-year-old man resist her?

He pleaded for her hand but her father, the rabbi, betrothed her to another. Feivel went insane with rage. Her image plagued him. Night after night he dreamed of nothing else.

One afternoon by the river he seized his opportunity. He wooed her from her laundry into these same woods. The more she begged him to let her go the more it fueled his frenzy.

When she was found to be with child—his child—the marriage was quickly arranged. Feeling like a small animal whose leg is caught in a trap's iron teeth, he drank himself into a stupor on their wedding night and beat her senseless.

A vicious boot kick to his ribs shot him back to the present. "Jew!"

Raising his hands over his head, he rolled over. Two men with clubs loomed above him. One of them took a swig from a bottle and then grinned. "I know this *Zjid.* He's at the tavern every night but Friday, this good religious man." Feivel's spectacles crunched under the man's foot.

Sweat froze Feivel's thin shirt to the not quite scabbed over sores on his back. "Please…Your Honor—"

"You want a drink? Of course you do."

The man planted his heavy boot in the middle of Feivel's chest, pinning him to the ground. Tipping his bottle, he poured the liquor over him. Desperation shuddered through Feivel. He lapped at the splashing liquid with his tongue like a mongrel dog.

"Look at this repulsive *Zjid.*" When the bottle was empty the man smashed it on a nearby tree. Waving the jagged top half, he slashed it across Feivel's cheek. He removed his foot from Feivel's chest and tossed the bottle into a clump of leaves.

Warm blood trickled into Feivel's ear. The other man grabbed him around the neck, forced him to sit and spat in his face. "Any last words, Christ killer?"

What could he say? How many times had he struck Tova? Had he listened when she pleaded with him for mercy? He envisioned her lying unconscious on the dirt floor with little Reuven sobbing and clinging to her breast. Why should these Christians listen to him?

Snowflakes stung the gash on his cheek and he recalled words from the Torah, Adoshem's law. An eye for an eye... *" 'If he pushes him out of hatred...' "*

"Shut your filthy Jew mouth!" The first club slammed into the middle of his back.

*" '...or in enmity...he strikes him with his...hand so that he...dies—' "* Feivel fought for breath.

Deep red drops spattered the white ground with each savage blow. His knees snapped like brittle twigs. Again and again the clubs slammed his skull against the rocky ground. His left arm shattered.

He welcomed pain like a bridegroom embraces his bride. *" 'The...the avenger of...blood...shall put the...murderer to death when...he meets...him.' "*

Through a crimson haze, he saw one of his attackers slip a dagger from his belt. The gray dawn light glinted off the blade. In one swift motion, cold steel seared into Feivel's midsection. Blood gushed from his throat and filled his nose and mouth. Grasping the knife's handle with his right hand, he choked and whispered, "Thank you."

## Chapter Fifteen

"Up. Up." Without waiting for an invitation, little Reuven, climbed up onto Havah's lap. He snuggled against her chest, popped his thumb into his mouth and closed his eyes.

His round face, ruddy complexion and scarlet curls reminded her of the fruit for which he was nicknamed. Little Apple fit him better than the handed down four times nightgown he wore.

Grateful for the toddler's warmth, she leaned her cheek against the top of his head. His rhythmic breathing comforted her. Thrust into this foreign town, she sat in a room full of strangers supposedly mourning Feivel's death. She returned curious stares and longed for home.

According to *Halakhah,* Jewish law, they buried his body within twenty four hours. After the funeral, family and friends squeezed into Tova's dingy hovel to sit *Shiva,* the initial seven days to pay their respects to the widow.

With relish, Feivel's less than grief stricken daughters wolfed down the food the ladies of the village had brought. Leah and Devorah giggled as if it were a wedding celebration until Fruma Ya'el cast a disapproving glance in their direction.

In a rocking chair by the stove, Tova rocked her newborn, her sunken eyes glazed as if in a trance. She seemed unaware of the crowd around her until the baby cried. Only then did she excuse herself and go to the bedroom.

Plate in hand, Fruma Ya'el followed her. "You've got to eat or you'll have nothing to feed your daughter." She shut the door behind her.

Although Havah tried not to eavesdrop on the many conversations spoken in hushed tones she could not help but hear Shayndel who sat in the chair beside her.

"Itzak, I'm worried about Tova. She shouldn't be out of bed so soon. And she hasn't cried."

He responded with a loud whisper. "Why she should squander tears on such a waste of skin?"

"He shared her bed."

"If she shared her bed with a viper would she cry when it was put to death?"

Determined not to laugh, Havah diverted her attention to the *minyan,* a quorum of ten men clustered in a corner of the room chanting *Kaddish* and prayers for the dead man's soul. The group included Uncle Hershel, Reb Yussel and Arel. Each man had his own way of *shokeling* or shaking, bobbing and weaving as he prayed.

Arel reminded her of a swaying poplar tree, head and shoulders above the rest like King Saul. She studied him until he returned her gaze briefly. Feeling the heat of her own blush, she quickly looked away.

Her thoughts returned to her family. Had anyone been left alive to perform the *mitzvah* of *Shiva* or even burial for them or did their bones litter the charred ground that had once been Natalya? The psalmist had written that the death of the righteous ones was precious in Adoshem's sight. Who could be more precious than Papa and Mama? She sang softly.

*"He who makes peace in the heavens, may He in His compassion make peace upon us and all Israel, and all say, 'Amen.'"*

## Chapter Sixteen

To Ulrich's delight, the little ballerina slid down the banister of the theater's elegant staircase into the entry-way. It was what he himself would have done were it not for the aristocracy gathered in the great hall. Sailing to the end, she stopped just short of the statue perched there. Then she flipped in midair and landed on her feet.

With an exaggerated curtsy, she tilted her head, making her curls bob. "Professor, your piano this evening was simply divine."

"It would've been nothing without your brilliant performance, Clara." He bowed and kissed her hand.

"My name's not really Clara, you know. That's just the name of the girl in the Nutcracker."

Still clutching her hand, he knelt on one knee and pressed her palm against his chest. "In my heart you will forever be Clara, my prima ballerina. I've always held a fondness for the name."

"I'll miss you."

"I'll miss you, too."

"Do you have to go back to Kishinev?"

"It's where I live."

"Can't you live here in Odessa?"

"What would my students do without me?" He pressed the back of his hand against his forehead.

"You're silly." She skipped off to join the rest of the children gathered around a candlelit Christmas tree on the other side of the lobby.

For a few moments he watched them tear open beribboned packages with joyful exclamations. Instead of enjoyment he felt hollow and empty for soon he would be back in his mansion to celebrate another holiday alone.

"I should move back home to Vienna." Pulling his overcoat collar around his face and his hat over his eyes, he navigated through the milling crowd.

This evening a hot bath and a soft bed awaited him in his hotel room. He did his best to make a straight line to the theater exit. Bits of conversation in Russian, Romanian and, occasionally, in German or English swirled around him.

"Beautiful music."

"Adorable dancers."

"Pity Tchaikovsky's gone."

A breathless voice with a wheeze and a buzz saw giggle made him stop short of the doors. "It's one thing to carry on trade with them. But to invite them into your home is quite another."

Her partner, a tuxedoed gentleman, shrugged his shoulders. "He's just eccentric. Rich people often are, you know."

"It's no excuse. Hasn't he read about the heinous crimes they've committed against good Christians?"

Ulrich held his breath and let it out, looking up at the arched ceiling. He slipped off his hat and bowed. "Fraulein Petri, what an unexpected displeasure."

A predatory smile spread her sputtering lips, her face flushing deep crimson. "Why, Professor Dietrich, how nice to see you."

"Even after my, shall we say, 'indiscretions?'"

Her lace fan sped to a frantic pace. "Forgiveness is the hallmark of my creed, particularly for a man of your talent and good looks."

"In other words, money covers a multitude of sins."

## Chapter Seventeen

While it was still dark, Fruma Ya'el slipped out of bed to brew Hershel's morning coffee. Since the early days of their marriage he insisted it be waiting for him before he left the house for *Shakharit,* morning prayers. There had been few exceptions to his rule.

Unlike most mornings, this particular morning he poured two cups and offered one to her. Grasping her hand he led her to the table. "Sit, Wife, I mean, please, Fruma."

She pulled back her hand, reached over the cups and pressed her palm against his forehead. "Are you ill?"

"No." He slipped his pipe and tobacco from his coat pocket. Then he took a pinch of tobacco and stuffed it into the pipe's bowl. *"I'm not ill."* Taking a match from a box on the table he struck it on his sole and lit his pipe. He took a long drag and coughed. "It's Havah."

Fruma Ya'el jumped off her chair. "She's ill*?"*

"No, no, no." Another hacking cough wracked him. When he finally caught his breath, he grabbed her arm. "She's…it's her mind…it's brilliant like yours. She challenges me." He took his watch from his pocket, opened it and then snapped it shut. "So I'm thinking. Maybe I'm wrong." He stood, walked to the back door and took his overcoat and hat from the peg. "Tell her that for me, please."

"You tell her." Fruma Ya'el followed him.

"You have a better way with her."

He kissed her temple and then turned to make his way to the synagogue. For a few moments she stood in the open doorway and watched him. With smoke streaming behind him he trudged down the path, a shadow against the growing light of the amber sunrise streaked horizon.

Two hours later her mind still swirled with his words. Never had she heard him admit a mistake. She bent over the open oven. At the same time Gittel bounded into the kitchen. The hot pan slipped and burned Fruma Ya'el's bare forearm. Bagels rolled across the floor like chubby wagon wheels.

Tears in her eyes, Gittel dropped down on all fours and gathered the bagels into her empty egg basket. "I'm sorry, Mama. I should watch where I'm going."

After dumping the rolls onto a plate on the table, Gittel ran back to the doorway and called upstairs. "Hurry, Miss Sleepyhead. We have eggs to gather."

"You go collect the eggs. I need to talk to Havah." Fruma Ya'el held a cold cloth over the blistering burn on her arm.

"She hasn't done anything wrong has she?"

"No, of course not. Now go."

"I love you, Mama." The door slammed behind Gittel.

A fragrant spring breeze through the open windows mingled with the aroma of fresh baked bread. Yawning, Havah stumbled into the kitchen and limped to the back door. "She didn't wait for me?"

Sitting at the table, Fruma Ya'el slathered a hot bagel with butter which melted into creamy liquid. With her finger she indicated an empty chair. "Come. Sit. Eat. Let's talk."

More than the burn festering on her forearm, it hurt Fruma Ya'el to see one so young suffer such heartache. But they lived in a harsh world at a cruel time and the children endured the worst of it.

Taking a small bite of the roll, Havah looked down at her plate. "What's the matter, Auntie?"

Fruma Ya'el tucked her hand under Havah's chin and raised her face so their eyes met. "How long have you been with us?"

"Four months. Why?"

"Havah, I can't replace your mama of blessed memory, but I have ears to listen."

"I've nothing to talk about."

"You don't look well."

"I feel fine."

"What are you hiding? I heard crying and pages rustling last night. It sounded like it came from Uncle Hershel's library. Was it you?"

She nodded, but said nothing, jerking back her head. "I only wanted to—"

"We know exactly what you wanted to do. It's all right. Uncle Hershel said to tell you, you needn't sneak around like a thief. You may read any book you like."

"You mean it?" A smile spread across the girl's face and she threw her arms around Fruma Ya'el's neck. "Thank you. Thank you. Thank you."

The back door opened. Itzak entered with a cheerful smile and a loud greeting. "I smell Auntie Fruma's famous bagels. We're just in time for breakfast."

Fruma Ya'el squeezed Havah's knee. "We'll continue this conversation later." She stood to greet Shayndel, who waddled behind Itzak, her cheeks flushed and drenched with perspiration. "My services are needed, yes?"

"Is it your time, Shayndel?" Havah jumped off her chair.

Unbalanced by her unborn child's weight, Shayndel lowered herself into it. "Not for at least another month, you goose."

After slicing four more bagels, Fruma Ya'el placed them on a plate and gave them to Itzak. "Havah bring some milk. Leah brought it this morning, fresh from the cow. *Nu*? Shayndel? If not for the baby, why are you here?"

"Itzak is going to Kishinev today to make a delivery. He said I can go with him but only if you approve. It's only fifteen miles. Itzak says we can make the journey in five hours."

"Shayndeleh, five hours of bumping in that wagon in each direction isn't a good idea. That's ten hours. What if the baby decides to come? Who'll deliver it? Cossacks?"

"I've never felt better. I'm really just a little uncomfortable."

"A *little* uncomfortable, she says." Itzak put his hands on his back and arched it to make his stomach stick out. He waddled around the kitchen, his face scrunched into an exaggerated grimace. "I've seen bears walk with more grace than she does.All night she complains and whines. 'Rub my ankles, Itzak.' 'My poor back hurts. Oy. Oy'."

Shayndel blushed scarlet. Havah shook so hard she spilled the milk.

"Some friend you are, Havaleh. Someday you'll be great with child and it will be my turn to laugh. Besides you're not helping me persuade Auntie Fruma."

Shayndel continued to beg. "Arel is coming along to help so I won't have to lift anything heavier than a fork."

"And you see how well my little pumpkin lifts her fork." Itzak finished the last few crumbs of his bagel and wiped his mouth. "We'll be spending the night with Evron so she can sleep in a soft bed."

As if her entrance had been rehearsed, Gittel burst into the kitchen and set the full basket on the long wooden table. "Look how big these eggs are this morning! Even the chickens are enjoying this beautiful morning! Mama, I have an idea. Why don't Havah and I go along with them to Kishinev? Then if anything should happen we will be there to take care of Shayndel. Havah and I have helped you deliver two more babies since Bayla." She dropped to her knees, clasping her hands as if in prayer. "Please. Please say yes, Mama. *Pleeeease.*"

"All right Fraylin Chatterbox, take a breath before you choke." Fruma Ya'el raised her hands in surrender. "Did you ask Havah if she wants to go?"

Havah knelt beside Gittel. "Oh yes, please, Auntie."

"So you think you're ready to be a midwife?"

"I am seventeen now."

"'I'm seventeen' she says. My shoes are older than seventeen."

## Chapter Eighteen

"Evron, open up. It's your baby brother." Itzak pounded his fist on a wooden door that looked like it might split in half at the slightest touch.

While she waited between Gittel and Shayndel for someone to answer, Havah rubbed her sore neck. She had slept in the back of the wagon most of the way to Kishinev in a most uncomfortable position.

Finally the door swung open and man who looked like Itzak, only taller, beckoned. His laughter even sounded like Itzak's. "You we've been expecting, Little Brother. But we had no idea you'd be bringing all of Svechka with you."

Havah followed Gittel and Arel over the threshold into the small house. Although not much larger or better constructed than Tova's shack it was warm and welcoming. Garlic and onion aromas made her stomach grumble.

After the brothers embraced and exchanged back slaps, Evron pulled back and winked at Shayndel. "We haven't seen your lovely wife since she was a little girl with yellow braids. And now look at her. She's a rose in full bloom."

Evron's wife Katya, a bony woman with buckteeth, slits for eyes and beak-like nose, hugged her blushing sister-in-law. "Never is a woman more beautiful than when she carries life inside."

"Don't tell me this is the rabbi's son Ari." Evron grasped Arel's shoulders. "You weren't even old enough for bar mitzvah last I saw you. You look so much like your papa I'd know you anywhere."

"And this can't be Auntie Fruma's baby girl, can it?" Katya ran her spindle-fingered hand through Gittel's auburn hair. "It won't be long until you're Froi Gitterman."

Sudden jealousy seized Havah. Who was left alive to remember Miriam Cohen's baby girl? She stepped backward, fell over Shayndel's basket and landed on her back.

"This is Havah." Gittel dropped to her knees beside her, grabbed her arm and helped her to her feet. "She's an orphan."

Orphan? Havah stared at the floor. She wished she could turn into water and disappear between the boards. Papa used to remind her it's a *mitzvah* to be good to widows and orphans. Orphan. The word reverberated like wolf's lonesome howl in the night. Orphan. Motherless. Fatherless. Orphan.

"I don't see any orphans here. Do you?" Katya embraced Havah like a long lost friend. "I see only *mishpokha,* family."

****

At best, Evron's apartment, a large room behind his shop, would have been cramped for three people, let alone six. Nonetheless, it was a welcoming place with smooth wooden floors and cheery curtains framing two sparkling windows. At the center a cast iron stove served for heating and cooking. Beside one of the windows sat a hand carved desk piled high with papers and books. A large table where the family shared meals was by the other. With ten chairs it took up a third of the room. The bedrooms were merely three corners of the main room separated by quilts strung on clotheslines for privacy.

After a filling meal of thick potato soup and fresh baked bagels Arel ate his last bite of sponge cake. It melted on his tongue. He licked his lips and dabbed them with a napkin. "I don't mind sleeping in the wagon if it will make room for someone else."

"Did I invite you or not?" Evron scowled. "What kind of host makes his guests sleep outside like livestock?"

"No one sleeps outside." Arms full of dishes, Katya motioned her head toward the window on her way to the sink. A streak of lightning followed by thunder punctuated her words. "Can you swim and sleep at the same time?"

Once the dishes had been washed and put away Evron motioned for everyone to join him by the desk. "It's time to show our guests how the Kishinev Abromoviches end their day."

"Tell us a story, Papa!" With identical smiles, nine-year-old twins, Ruth and Rukhel, folded their dishtowels and hung them on a peg over the sink. They took chairs from the table and set them in a half-circle around Evron. "These are for Aunt Shayndel and Aunt Gittel."

Arel carried two more chairs, one for himself and the other for Itzak.

"You sit here, Auntie Havah." Three-year-old Tuli scooted a rocking chair into the circle.

"That's Mama's chair." Rukhel frowned.

"*Shah.*" Katya's kind smile made Arel forget her homeliness. She set a stool beside the rocker and perched on it. "Havah's our guest."

When she eased herself onto the rocker, the boy climbed up onto her lap. Arel envied him.

The other three children gathered around their father and uncle who had already begun to play a lively tune, Evron on clarinet and Itzak on his fiddle. Legs straddling Havah's knees, Tuli clapped in time to the music while the twins hopped in place, their long braids bouncing.

After two fast songs the music slowed. The gentle tune carried Arel back to bedtimes when his mother would hold him on her lap. He would lay his head on her bosom and listen to her sing.

Drowsy from a satisfied stomach and a day of travel, he leaned his head against the high backed chair. He had almost fallen asleep when his ears thrilled to the most beautiful voice he had heard since his mother sang the same lullaby.

*"'In dem bais ha meegdash*
*In a vinkle heder*
*Zitz de almoneh vos seeyon alayn...*
*In the room of the temple,*
*In a cozy corner*
*There sits a widow all alone.*

With a rapt grin on his face Tuli snuggled against Havah. Ruth and Rukhel laid their heads on her lap from their places on the floor on either side of the rocking chair.

"Our young sister is a song bird. Even my son has gone to sleep." Shayndel stroked her rounded belly.

Evron laid his clarinet in his lap and whispered, "Little Rabbi, bring me the book."

A fragile looking boy, seven-year-old Zelig most resembled his mother. His teeth protruded over his lower lip in a wide smile. He retrieved a leather bound volume from the top of the pile on the desk. As if he held the tablets from Mount Sinai, he lifted the book in both hands and then gave it to his father.

Adoration for his children radiated from Evron's dark eyes. "Who wants to read the first line of tonight's psalm?"

Tuli slid off Havah's lap. He hopped up and down. "I do! I do!"

Hoisting him onto his lap, Evron held the book for him. "Our little rooster always reads first. He just started *Heder* and hasn't learned to read as many words as the rest of us. The first line of the psalm is usually the shortest."

After Tuli sounded out three words Zelig read his portion. Ruth and Rukhel read the next two lines together. Their pronunciation of the Hebrew words and understanding amazed Arel. "Your daughters read the Holy Books?"

Evron, beaming with pride, kissed each of his children before they returned to their places on the floor. "Why not? The Almighty has blessed them with sharp minds. Why shouldn't they have the same opportunities as their brothers?"

"Evron?" Havah slowly rose from her chair and limped to him. Kneeling beside him, she touched the book. "May I read, too?"

In the dim lamp light her face glistened. She read verse after verse without error. This was no parrot. Eyes aglow with unspoken triumph, her moonlight smile sent flames through Arel.

When she finished he glanced over at Itzak whose mouth gaped. Arel thrust his hand, palm up, under his brother-in-law's nose.

"You owe me five kopeks."

****

"These are goose down. They're special for company." With two pillows in her arms, Ruth stopped at the end of the bed, her eyes wide and mouth agape. "What happened to your toes?"

Heat creeping from her neck into her cheeks, Havah quickly drew her exposed foot up under the covers. "I...I had an accident."

"What kind of an accident?" Ruth crawled in next to her sister who had already nodded off between Havah and Gittel.

"A great big ferocious bear bit off her toes for asking too many questions at bedtime." Gittel growled.

"You're making up stories."

"Am I? Ask another question and see what happens." Gittel shrugged her shoulders and batted her eyelashes. Opening her mouth in an exaggerated yawn she stretched her arms over her head. Nestling her head into her pillow she pressed her nose against Ruth's.

"Good night. Sweet dreams." The child wrapped her arm around her sister and snapped her eyes shut.

Havah's embarrassment eased as she let her head sink into the down pillow's cool softness. The rain's steady rhythm on the roof soothed her. Her dreams took her to Natalya where she skipped rope with familiar playmates.

*The sky grew dark and Mama's voice echoed in her ears. "Havah! Run!"*

*She tried but her feet turned to stone. No matter how hard she tugged and pulled she could not budge them.*

*Flames engulfed her. When she opened her mouth black smoke choked her screams.*

*From amidst the smoky fog two hands dripping with blood pulled at her nightgown. Two more grabbed her ankles. Gunfire exploded in her ears.*

Thunder shook her back to the tiny house in Kishinev. To keep from going back to sleep, she sat up.

Whispered male voices came from the kitchen on the other side of the wall. She strained to hear them.

"We're living in precarious times," said Evron. "Every day I hear the lies they write in their newspapers. Can you imagine anyone believing we would kill children in our rituals?"

Her heart rang like a hammer in her ears as Arel spoke. "History itself tells us the *Goyim* can and do believe them. Why don't you move to some place safer?"

"Is there such a place, my young friend? It's not so simple this thing you suggest. I have six mouths to feed. Where would you have us go?"

"The boy makes sense." Itzak's voice sounded sad. "You're an excellent tailor, Evron. You could move to America like Shayndel's brother-in-law Wolf. He's doing very well in a village they call Kansas City. Besides, I know for a fact Professor Dietrich's offered to pay your way."

"I don't need his Christian charity."

## Chapter Nineteen

"What kind of irresponsible husband would allow his expectant wife to make such a long journey? I should've insisted you stay home. You're my bride, my greatest treasure. I should've listened to Fruma Ya'el." Itzak wagged his head as he helped his wife into the wagon.

"Stop it. I'm fine and I'm glad I came." She settled into the back of the wagon on a blanket.

Even though Evron and Katya had given up their bed the night before, Shayndel had not been able to sleep. Her face was pale with exhaustion.

"Here's something to sustain you on your safe journey." Katya handed Itzak a basket filled with food then gave Shayndel a large cloth bag. "I think you'll need these."

"Oh, no, I couldn't. I have diapers already and clothes from my sister's children. What if you should need them again?"

"Hold your tongue. You shouldn't wish such a thing on me. And if I should need them again I have a husband who sews and Adoshem Who provides. Yes?" She patted Shayndel's swollen stomach and winked. "You might need more diapers than you think."

After embracing Evron, Itzak climbed up onto the wagon seat next to Arel. "Be well, Big Brother."

Evron's dark eyes misted. He reached up and grasped Itzak's forearm with a firm grip. "Write and tell us when your child is born."

"I will."

When Itzak clucked his tongue the horses jerked the wagon forward. Holding tight to the reins, he whistled a tune as he maneuvered the horses along the muddy road. Last night's storm made travel a challenge. Surveying the clouds, he silently prayed they would reach Svechka before encountering another downpour.

Two hours later his hopes for an early return vanished when Havah stood up behind the wagon seat and leaned over his shoulder. "Could you stop, please?"

It was the last thing he wanted to do. Anxious for his wife's safety he opened his mouth to refuse. But the desperation in Havah's voice pierced him.

After bringing the wagon to a halt, he stepped down and helped her climb out. She pulled back her hand and trotted through the wet grass like a lame colt. With a shriek, she tore her sleeve and collapsed in a pile of rubble.

"Shouldn't we go after her?" Gittel hoisted one leg over the side of the wagon.

"No."

Although he had noticed the row of charred houses on the way to Evron's Itzak had made a point of not calling attention to them. Mercifully she had been asleep when they passed what was left of the synagogue. He bowed his head and whispered to Arel, "Welcome to Natalya."

\*\*\*\*

Sprawled face down on the ground, Havah begged the angel of death to stab her through the heart. What difference would it make? Her chest already ached. She burrowed her head in the dirt between two mounds.

Gittel's compassionate voice and tender hand upon her shoulder brought her to. "Itzak. Ari. Come quickly. She's fainted."

They sloshed through the mud to Havah's side. When they stopped she rolled over onto her back. "No, I didn't."

"Your...family?" Gittel pointed to four mounds surrounding her.

"Yes." Sitting up, she wiped her mouth on her torn sleeve.

"How can you be sure?"

Unconstrained tears rolled down her face. She opened an oval locket that she had found on one of the graves and gazed at the photograph inside. Her parents, Shimon and Miriam Cohen on their wedding day, smiled at her. She held up the necklace for Gittel to see along with a muddy rag doll and a book.

Someone had taken the time to bury her family and wrap these small treasures in a singed towel. She could not imagine who might have done such a *mitzvah,* but she trembled with gratitude.

Cautiously, Gittel took the locket from her hand and opened the clasp. "May I?"   Without waiting for an answer, she fastened it around Havah's neck. The sun glinted off the golden chain.

Havah fumbled the locket shut. "Mama never took it off."

"It's a sign." Gittel pressed her palms together.

"May I see the book?" Arel extended his hand. "I'll be careful with it."

Havah hesitated, and then turned it over to him.

With reverence, he opened it and flipped to the first page. He read the handwritten note aloud.

*"'Friday, 21 February 1896 To my dear sister Havah on her day of becoming Bas Mitzvah, a daughter of the covenant. May yours forever be a shining name in the house of Yisroel!*

*With love, your brother Mendel'"*

**\*\*\*\***

Huddled between Havah and Arel in the back of the wagon, Shayndel pressed her spine against the wooden panel and admired the photograph in Havah's locket. "You look like your papa."

Shayndel's stomach cramped and pain traveled from her hips to her knees. She bit her lip to keep from crying.

Havah grabbed her hand. "You're not—how long?"

Holding her breath as pain ripped through her back, Shayndel looked from Havah to Arel and whispered. "Since we left Natalya."

"We should never have stopped there. Shouldn't we tell Itzak?"

The cramp eased. "I don't want to have this baby in the middle of the wilderness."

"It's all my fault. If I hadn't made Itzak stop we'd be home."

"No tears." Shayndel's finger made a streak across Havah's muddy cheek. She pointed to the locket. "We had to stop."

"At least lie down. If he asks I'll tell him you're tired and wanted to take a nap."

Her unborn child did two somersaults as Shayndel attempted to find a comfortable position. Arel took off his coat and folded it under her head.

Itzak stopped whistling. "I hear a lot of whispering back there. Is everything all right?"

Shayndel shook her head and gave Arel and Havah warning looks. "Yes, my husband. All is well back here. Will we be home soon?"

"I would say another hour or so."

Gittel turned around and opened her mouth to exclaim.

Moving her fingers and thumb up and down to look like a chirping bird Havah motioned for her to engage

Itzak in conversation. Gittel winked. An easy assignment for her. She leaned forward in the wagon seat and pointed. "What kind of tree is that pretty one with little white flowers, Itzak?"

"That, my girl, is a hornbeam tree. It's pretty enough, but not good wood for furniture."

"Do you think it's going to rain again?"

With Itzak's attention averted, Shayndel relaxed as best she could with her unwieldy stomach and intermittent pain. She as sure he had not missed a single rock or bump since they left Kishinev.

"What a nice watch. My papa had one just like it! May I see it?" Havah raised her voice as she took Arel's watch from his pocket.

Cruel bands of pain gripped Shayndel's stomach. Arel hovered over her, but she pushed him away. No man should have to see a woman in labor and certainly not his sister.

"Fifteen minutes since the last," said Havah. "You'll make it."

Havah's reassuring smile soothed Shayndel. How different she was from the girl who cowered on the floor during Bayla's birth. Auntie Fruma had trained her well.

"Tell me about this…um…Bas Mitzvah. Who ever heard of such a thing?" Arel thumbed through Havah's prayer book.

The way her brother's face lit up when he looked at her friend did not escape Shayndel's notice. While she understood his infatuation she hoped it would end soon. Reserving her strength for the next labor pain, she rested her head on Arel's coat and listened with wonder to Havah's reply.

"I read a portion from the Torah and the books of the prophets just like my brothers only not at the synagogue. It was Papa's idea to have a private ceremony at home. He didn't think the congregation was quite ready for such a thing."

At last the wagon lurched to a halt. Itzak jumped from the seat and made his way to the back of the wagon. Havah stood. "I'll go find Auntie Fruma".

With Arel's help Shayndel struggled to her feet and grasped Havah's hand. "No! Stay! Gittel, you go!"

As she stepped down between her brother and husband another pain seized her. She dug her fingers into their shoulders. The water inside her burst and ran down her legs, soaking her skirts, pooling around her feet.

****

No longer repulsed by the sight, Havah watched Fruma Ya'el thrust her hand between Shayndel's straddled legs. She held her breath in anticipation of the new baby's appearance.

"I quit! I can't do this!" Shayndel's face glistened and flushed. She grasped her bulging abdomen. "Just cut me open and take it out."

"Remember, Havah, when a woman in labor rattles off nonsense the time is at hand." Fruma Ya'el pushed her nose against Shayndel's "You can and you *will.*"

"This will soon be a memory, Shayndeleh." Gittel stroked her forehead. "When you look at the face of your sweet little baby—"

"This 'sweet little baby' is tearing me apart!"

"I see the head." Fruma Ya'el positioned herself at the end of the bed and raised her voice to be heard over Shayndel's shrieking. "Sit up before the next pain. Then push him out."

Red faced and dripping with sweat, Shayndel gripped Havah's arm and struggled to sit. With a series grunts she held her breath and strained until a dark haired baby, wet and blue faced, slid out into Fruma Ya'el's hands. She grabbed his ankles, held him upside down and then slapped his bottom several times until he bawled.

Falling back against the pillows, Shayndel grinned and closed her eyes. "What did I tell you, Havah?"

With her birthing scissors Fruma Ya'el snipped the cord. Eyeing Shayndel's stomach, she shook her head and raised an eyebrow. "You still look swollen to me."

Shayndel sat up and grasped her knees. "There's another one! And it's coming."

"Your turn, Havah! Wash your hands. Now!"

There was no time to argue. This baby would not wait. A mixture of excitement and raw terror shot through Havah as she plunged her trembling hands into the basin of soapy water on the bureau. She scrubbed and hastened back to the bed.

With one last push, Shayndel let out a cry somewhere between a grunt and a yelp. Havah grasped the baby's head on each side and gave it a gentle tug until the face appeared. Next came a shoulder and, a moment later, she held a slippery, howling newborn.

In one glorious moment everyone and everything disappeared except for the child who quieted in her arms.

"Havah, what is it?" Shayndel nestled against the pillows, suckling the first baby.

"What's what?"

"Is the baby a boy or a girl?"

After cleaning the infant with a wet cloth, Havah wrapped it in a blanket and laid it in the crook of Shayndel's free arm. "You have a golden-haired son."

\*\*\*\*

Satisfied that all was well with Shayndel and her newborn sons, Fruma Ya'el allowed entrance to the men who had been waiting in the next room for a over five hours. Lifting one of the tiny bundles from the bed she placed him in Itzak's trembling arms.

"My bride. She's so pale." With unashamed tears he dropped down on the bed and kissed his slumbering wife. "She's…she's…alive?"

Shayndel opened her eyes and smiled. "I'm just sleepy. They're beautiful, aren't they?"

"Does the Czar eat roast pork?" Itzak beamed. "Of course they're quite beautiful. Good looks run in the Abromovich family."

"This one looks like Shayndel." Fruma Ya'el took the other baby and held him out to Arel. "Greet your nephew, Uncle."

At first he put his hands behind his back and shook his head. Finally, at her insistence, he gingerly took the baby. His gray eyes shone as he ran his finger over the child's cheek and then touched his tiny fist. Fruma Ya'el smiled. He would be a good father to her grandchildren.

"Look at that! He grabbed my thumb!" Arel grinned.

Itzak's laughter boomed. Shayndel put her finger to her lips then pointed to Havah who slumped beside the bed in a straight backed chair with her head on one of the pillows on the bed. Her matted hair begged to be washed and her filthy blouse was torn beyond repair.

Reluctantly laying his son in Shayndel's arms, Itzak stood. "I'll take her to Sarah's room for the night."

"Not yet. I need to talk to her." With a sigh Fruma Ya'el shook Havah's shoulder. She hated to wake her for she had never seen such peace on her face.

With a start Havah opened her eyes. Fruma Ya'el took her hand. "Come with me."

Half awake, the girl slid off her chair and hobbled down the hall behind her. When they reached the kitchen Fruma Ya'el poured two cups of tea. She watched Havah's reflection in the brass samovar as she sank into a chair.

"What's wrong, Auntie?"

Over the next few moments Fruma Ya'el studied the faded photographs in the open locket around the girl's neck and deliberated how to answer. How much could she expect of Havah? After all, as she had reminded her on numerous occasions, she was not her daughter.

"Shayndel's had a difficult birth."

"She's not going to…to die, is she?" Havah's lower lip quivered.

"No, but she's weaker than she'll admit. The rabbi needs someone to look after his house and I don't want her doing too much." Fruma Ya'el rubbed her sweaty hands together. "I have no right to ask since you're not my daughter…but Shayndel loves you so…and Gittel wouldn't really—"

With a smile spreading across her dirty face, Havah shut the locket. "I'll be happy to stay with them—*Mama.*"

****

Aside from an occasional infant's cry Havah woke to a quiet house. Since Feivel's death Itzak had agreed to take on the job of synagogue caretaker. With two new mouths to feed a few extra kopeks came in handy. Every day before sunrise he put a pot of strong coffee on the stove before leaving. Yussel and Arel left soon after for morning prayers.

The rabbi's house was bigger than the Levine's home, boasting two extra bedrooms and a parlor. Havah's favorite room, the library, was filled with volumes that beckoned her. It was hard for her to resist a short read before beginning her duties for the day. Would Rabbi Gitterman be angry if he knew? She imagined him, a young man like Arel with a soot-black beard, seated behind the carved oak desk preparing lessons for *Shabbes.* A pair of spectacles on top of a stack of books told her that he must have needed them before he went blind.

Reluctantly she pulled herself from the study and continued on to the kitchen. Throwing open the backdoor she stepped outside and drank in the sweet smell of grass and flowers. White and yellow jonquils surrounded the house. Arel told her that his older sister Sarah had sent some of the bulbs from America. Havah knelt to sniff one.

"They were my mama's favorite flower."

Shayndel's voice startled her. She jumped up. "You shouldn't be out of bed!"

"You've been waiting on me hand and foot for three days. I'm bored. All I've done is feed babies and eat."

"We can't let your milk dry up, can we?" Havah spoke in her most authoritative tone. "Now back to bed with you while I fix breakfast."

"Let me help."

"No."

"Fine. But I'm sitting at the table. One more minute in bed like an invalid and I'm going to run away from home."

Shayndel's knee length hair shone like honey in the sun and her round cheeks glowed. Havah felt shriveled and pale next to her.

Once she had finished scrambling eggs, Havah buttered the last of the bread she had baked the day before. She loaded two plates, set them on the table and sat across from Shayndel. "They're beautiful boys. Itzak's spirits are so high the birds in the sky are having trouble keeping up with him! He's almost finished with the second cradle."

"I told him we could borrow a cradle." Shayndel rolled her eyes. "He's made enough of them around Svechka! But you know by now how Itzak is. He wants everything to be perfect. He insists that the cradles have to match."

"But the babies don't match! Have you and Itzak decided on names for them?"

"Itzak and I had a long talk last night. He thought perhaps we could name one after my grandfather and the other after his father, may they rest in peace." Shayndel took a long drink of milk. "But we finally agreed, but only if you agree—"

"It's done." Itzak entered lofting a cradle over his head. He set it on the floor with a proud grin. When he noticed Shayndel sitting at the table, he frowned and scooped her up in his arms.

"You shouldn't be up yet," he said.

"Shayndel, tell me their names." Her curiosity aroused, Havah followed them to the bedroom.

"You haven't told her?" Itzak sat his wife down on the bed.

"I was trying to when I was so rudely interrupted by 'Itzak the Cabinetmaker.'" Her blue eyes twinkled.

"If we may have your blessing, Havaleh..." A somber expression replaced his effervescent smile. He straightened and cleared his throat like a rabbi giving a speech. "We'd like to name them after your brothers of blessed memory...Mendel and David."

****

Most of Svechka had turned out for eight-day-old Mendel and David's circumcision ceremony. The rabbi's yard teemed with well-wishers. Havah watched the party through Shayndel's bedroom window. Jewish law prevented her from taking part in festivities of any kind for it had not yet been a year since her family's passing. It did not matter to her. Celebrations only served to intensify her grief.

The women had set up tables and loaded them with sponge cake, fresh baked breads, apples, honey and more.

Fruma Ya'el piled food onto a plate and gave it to Gittel. "When you've eaten, take a plate to your sister."

Some of the ladies gathered around them.

"Fruma. Is it true? Your new daughter delivered Shayndel's second baby?"

"A credit to you."

"A charming girl."

"She'll bring a good bride price."

The men gathered around Itzak.

"Mazel tov!" Hershel raised his glass. "Two sons! Quite an accomplishment!"

"May you have many more sons!" Pinkas Rabinovich drank from a bottle.

"Perhaps next time you'll have *three* sons! May you and Gittel be as prolific, Arel!" Hershel slapped his future son-in-law on the back.

"Be careful what you wish for our Ari." Itzak wiped his mouth on his sleeve and hiccupped. "If his children turn out to be magpies like their mother, his ears will fold in on themselves."

"Look at those ridiculous men. You'd think Itzak had given birth himself and without a midwife." Havah stamped her foot for emphasis and turned to Shayndel who curled up on her side under a quilt.

"Oh, Havah, let them have their time."

"As if I could stop them. It doesn't seem right to me. You're the one who did the work."

"Itzak's a tender husband." Shayndel yawned.

"He's better than most I suppose. The way they think about us. Who decided women should be ignorant housemaids? Surely it's not written in the Holy Book. Miriam was a leader in Israel beside her brother *Moshe Rahbeynu*. Deborah was a judge in Israel. But we're reduced to illiterate subservience, not allowed to study, to learn the Holy Language. Doesn't this ever bother you,

Shayndel? Don't you ever have a longing for something more?"

Shayndel's faint snoring and sleepy grin answered her. Sinking into the rocking chair beside the bed, Havah watched the babies. "Promise me you'll grow up to be good men who know how to treat women."

A knock on the bedroom door interrupted her thoughts. She opened the door, making as little noise as possible and whispered greetings to Leah and Devorah Resnick.

"May we see the new babies?" Leah peered over Havah's shoulder.

Although Havah had not had a chance to spend much time with them, she liked them. They looked enough alike to be twins themselves with their bright red hair and freckled faces. However Devorah stood a good two inches taller than her older sister.

"You must be very quiet. Mendel and David are sleeping."

To associate the names with life again made Havah happy. Itzak and Shayndel had given her the honor of assigning the names. It had not been a hard decision. Like her brothers, David was fair and Mendel dark.

Her eyes welling up, Leah dropped to her knees beside the cradles. "They're beautiful babies."

"Soon you will have pretty ones like these, Big Sister." Devorah knelt beside her and leaned her head on Leah's shoulder.

Shoving her sister, Leah snapped to her feet and raced from the room. Devorah ran after her. Havah followed them to the yard. "What's the matter, Leah? Are you ill? Your mother?"

Leah collapsed in the grass.

"Please don't take on so. It's our good fortune. Gavrel's a nice man. He'll be a good husband...and father." Devorah knelt beside her.

Havah crouched down. "Froi Tova's marrying the shoemaker? That's

wonderful news!"

Leah rolled over and glared at Havah with swollen eyes. "Not Mama. *Me. I'm* marrying him."

"But he must be at least forty."

"No." Devorah shook her head. "He's thirty-three."

Before Havah could reply, Lev ran toward them, yelling and waving his arms. "Leah, come quick. Reuven's stuck in the mud by the river. It's all the way up to his waist and I can't budge him."

As she watched the two girls chase after their brother, Havah fumed. "'Gavrel's a nice man.' Devorah should have said, 'Gavrel has money.'"

Picking up a rock, she struggled to her feet and flung it with all her might. An unwitting half-drunk Arel staggered into its path.

"Ow!" He tripped and dropped to the ground, his eyes rolling back in his head.

A lump had already begun to form on his forehead. Removing her headscarf, Havah knelt beside Arel and dabbed at a small cut. "Oh, dear. I've killed you.

He opened his eyes and grasped her wrist. "A most pleasant death, Fraylin Cohen."

## Chapter Twenty

Havah enjoyed the scent of lilacs on the gentle breeze as she carried a basket of soiled diapers to the river to wash. Her mind jumped between the joy of spring and her heart's forbidden desire. No matter how she tried to blot him out, Arel's image plagued her. She wished she had not let him kiss her. How could she have stopped him? It happened so fast.

"Good morning, Havah." Tova carried her own laundry basket.

"Good morning, Froi Resnick."

"The diapers never stop, do they? It's a lovely morning isn't it?" Tova smiled.

"Yes."

"My, my. You're not very talkative this morning are you? Living with Gittel the Chatterbox hasn't rubbed off on you, has it?"

Only the sounds of clothes sloshing through the water disturbed the uncomfortable silence. Havah kept her eyes trained on the diapers until Tova said, "I can't believe my little Leah will be seventeen in two days."

"What a birthday present you're giving her, Froi Resnick. Everyone should have their own shoemaker!"

"So *that's* it. Leah told you about her engagement and you don't approve."

"Devorah told me. Poor Leah couldn't stop crying long enough."

Finally Havah raised her head to glare at the other woman. Under different circumstances she would have pitied her. At thirty-one Tova looked closer to fifty. Years of abuse had worn lines into her face. Childbearing had left its mark on her slight frame, curving her spine and bowing her shoulders.

"Fraylin Cohen, I have five mouths to feed. I make but a few kopeks a month from my sewing. It's hardly enough to buy food, let alone clothing."

"Or shoes?"

"Yes, shoes. Children outgrow *shoes.*" Tova threw a knotted pair of pants into the water so it splashed Havah's face. "Leah is marrying Gavrel the shoemaker."

"Ha! You admit it. You're selling your own daughter into slavery for a pair of shoes. Oh, I'm sorry, that would be *five* pairs of shoes wouldn't it?" Havah threw a wadded diaper into the water, dousing Tova.

"Selling my daughter into *slavery?* Is *that* what you think? How *dare* you judge me! What do you know of providing for a family?"

"I just hope I wouldn't start selling members of my family like cattle to make a living."

"I am not *selling* Leah. I've arranged a marriage for her with a good man."

"A good man who's twice her age."

Once more a tense hush fell over them. Havah scrubbed a diaper, wrung out the excess water and then flung it into her basket. She repeated the process several times until the basket was full.

At last Tova finished with one of Reuven's patched shirts and tossed it into her basket. Picking up the basket, she straightened and squared her shoulders.

"Gavrel is a good man, a scholar and a gentleman. Leah will learn to love him."

"You mean the way you learned to love Feivel?" Havah picked up her basket, stood and glared at Tova.

Tova's mouth dropped open. "I will thank you to stay out of what does not concern you." To punctuate her words, she shoved her basket into Havah's basket, then turned on her heel and trudged up the hill, head held high.

In her fury to chase after Tova, Havah's lame foot turned and she lost her balance on the slippery rocks. Stumbling backward, she plunged into the river.

The basket floated just out of reach and diapers sank around her. As she groped for them she slipped on an underwater ledge. Water filled her nose and mouth. The river rushed over her, the current dragging her deeper and deeper until blackness claimed her.

****

Arel sat under a tree at the top of the hill. Since it was such a nice day he decided to prepare his lessons outside. However, nothing could be further from his mind than bar mitzvah students.

He pulled Havah's kerchief from his pocket and studied the flowered material that had touched her hair. Awash with desire, he held the soft cloth against his cheek and closed his eyes. If only things could be different.

The sound of Tova's voice roused him from his private reverie. He opened his eyes in time to see Havah fall backward into the river. He held his breath as he waited for her to come up. A minute passed and still no Havah. Stuffing the kerchief back into his pocket, he tossed his books aside, stood and ran to the river.

A strong swimmer, he found her quickly, grabbed her around the waist and pulled her to shore. She lay still as stone. He slapped her cheek.

"Breathe, Havah. Please breathe."

She gasped and coughed. "I'm sorry, Papa. I wet the bed."

****

In the stone fireplace in the rabbi's library, embers rose from flaming logs. Havah was curled up in an overstuffed chair, still chilled from her fall into the river. She held out her hands to warm them. Yussel and Arel sat side by side on the sofa next to her.

Arel had told her how, at the age of four he had become his blind father's eyes, reading from the holy books every night. She admired the obvious bond between the rabbi and his son.

To Havah's surprise, on her fifth night as temporary housemistress, Reb Yussel invited her to join them. With eagle swiftness the last four weeks had flown by. It was almost like being back in her own father's study. Although she loved Uncle Hershel and his family, she wished it had been the rabbi who had adopted her.

"What shall we read, children?" Yussel's voice, heavy with emotion, shook her from her thoughts. He patted the sofa. "Come, Havah, sit beside me. Since it's our last night together it's only fitting you should choose."

"Our last night?" Havah tried to blink back the tears filling her eyes.

"Shayndel's quite well and your papa has begged for the return of his daughter."

"My…my papa? How could he beg for anything when he's—oh, you mean Uncle Hershel."

Yussel smiled and nodded. "So what will it be, Fraylin Cohen?"

"Song of songs, my true papa's favorite." Out of the corner of her eye she glanced at Arel as she moved from her chair. Sitting beside Yussel, she looked down at the book on his lap, a dog-eared edition of *K'tuveem,* the writings. Gently she turned the parchment pages.

"Wonderful choice. It's about the love between the soul of a Jew and his Creator between the Almighty and his people. Arel, you read first."

*"'Behold you are fair, my beloved, behold you are fair, your eyes are like doves.'"* Arel's eyes, aglow in the flickering light, were trained on her as he recited from memory.

Verse after verse they each spoke by heart, neither of them bothering to turn a page. Color rose from his neck to his pale cheeks. *"'You have captivated my heart, my sister, my bride, you have captivated my heart with but one of your virtues.'"*

No matter how hard she tried, she could not keep her mind on the Almighty or His people, save one. At last she forced herself to read the final verse of the last chapter. *"'Make haste my beloved, and be like a gazelle or a young stag on the mountain of spices.'"*

Silence permeated the room like early morning mist. She fixed her eyes on her lap, imagining herself on a narrow precipice overlooking a whirlpool. One more look into his eyes and she felt as though she would fall in.

"Arel, there's a book, a small one." Yussel cleared his throat, slicing through the awkward hush. "Black leather. Gold letters on the spine. It should be on the fourth shelf up. At least that's where it used to be."

With a startled flinch, Arel leaped off the couch and practically ran to the bookshelf behind the desk. "It's still here, Papa."

"Give it to Havah."

Arel bounded across the room and bowed at the waist, lifting the book on his upraised palms. "The Psalms, Your Highness."

It looked rich and expensive. "Reb Yussel, it's too much. I can't accept," she whispered.

"And this one I cannot keep." The rabbi waved his hand. "Look around you, Little Scholar. I have plenty of books. Do I look like I can read any of them?"

"I'll cherish this always."

"Indeed you will. Read the note on the first page."

Obediently she opened the elegant volume. Swooping and dramatic, the familiar handwriting danced off the paper.

*" '15 June, 1873*
*" 'Dear Rabbi Gitterman,*
*" 'On this the day of my wedding: I am forever in your debt. May the Psalms be a source of comfort to you as they have always been to me. Shalom,*
*" 'Shimon Cohen."*

"You knew Papa? Why didn't you tell me before?"

"You think you're the only Cohen I've known? I had to be sure."

"What convinced you?"

"One of a kind. Deserving of his headstrong daughter's loyalty. Unruliest student I ever had in my Yeshiva class in Kishinev. Hated traditions. A rule breaker."

"Why was he in your debt?"

"Because I married him to your mother in spite of her betrothal to another."

# Chapter Twenty-one

*Broken glass and burning embers littered the ground everywhere Havah looked. People darted out from behind trees and bushes. Among them were her mother and father. They held out their arms and called her name. She tried to run to them but an invisible barrier blocked her path. A piercing cry rang in her ears. Leah Resnick, tied to a tree, cried for mercy. Suddenly someone grabbed Havah from behind and shoved her. Water and blackness surrounded her. Opening her mouth in a soundless scream, she sank in the water like a stone.*

Sweat soaked Havah's nightgown. She fought to wake up, hoping she had not cried out and disturbed anyone. Listening to the quiet, she decided the only sleep disturbed had been her own.

Through the window over the bed the full moon looked like a silver coin against the clear sky. She watched its reflection on the river, trying to concentrate on the beauty before her eyes. In her mind she saw the way Arel's wet shirt clung to his otherwise bare torso after he had saved her from drowning that afternoon. She heard his voice, alive with passion, as he read from *Song of Songs* that evening. The calm landscape outside her window could not quell her impure thoughts.

Like her father, reading the Psalms always served as a source of comfort for her. Wrapping herself in a blanket, she hugged her new book to her breast and tiptoed to the rabbi's study.

****

Arel's feelings warred against everything he had always accepted as law. He paced back and forth in front of the fireplace. Her glossy hair, which fell in spiraling waves to her knees, enticed him and her deep brown eyes tormented him. The thought of her returning to her home gnawed at him. He felt destitute and forsaken.

There was no denying how much he looked forward to evening study sessions with his father and Havah. She challenged him. She made him think. She even intruded on the lessons he taught at Heder.

*"Reb Arel, wasn't the name of Abraham's wife Sarah?"*

*"Yes, of course. Why do you ask?"*

*"When you read this morning, you said 'Abraham and Havah!'"* A collective titter traveled around the classroom.

Halting footsteps startled him and he turned his head. Havah stood in the doorway, wrapped in a blanket, clutching her book. She looked so small and delicate. Vulnerable. Resisting the urge to scoop her up in his arms and carry her to his bed he wrung his hands behind his back and coaxed a smile.

"You couldn't sleep either?"

"Bad dream." She turned away from him and hobbled to the door to leave but he stepped in front of her and blocked her way.

"Don't go. Please." Quivering, he inched closer and brushed his fingertips along her silky cheek. "When I thought you'd drowned I...I—"

He leaned in closer until their lips almost touched. Suddenly she wrenched back, ducked under his arm and dashed from the room.

His legs buckled and he fell to his knees.

At that moment Itzak walked by, bouncing a baby on each arm. He stopped and smirked. "I'm but an ordinary man. You needn't bow down to me, Little Brother."

Chapter Twenty-two

Over the course of eight months Havah had grown to accept Svechka as home. Carrying three-month-old Mendel who slumbered against her shoulder, she surveyed the ramshackle village while she helped Shayndel run her errands. A blacksmith shop sat on the corner of Zev, the main street, next door to the butcher's shop. Behind that, was a large pen where the *shokhet* slaughtered livestock to be prepared according to dietary law. Unconcerned and ignorant of his ultimate destiny to become a kosher pot roast, a small brown bull chewed his cud.

Their final stop, Reb Pinkas' print shop and post office, sat across the street. Havah limped alongside Shayndel. Even after eight months, her foot ached relentlessly and the baby in her arms seemed to gain weight with each painful step.

Shayndel's scarlet cheeks glistened under her sweat drenched kerchief. She pulled a small wooden cart behind her that Itzak had built to make it easier for her to transport their growing sons. Today, however, it was loaded with bags of flour, slabs of meat and other essentials so she carried David on one arm.

When they entered the dusty print shop, Reb Pinkas flashed a yellow toothed smile. "Havah, that baby's almost big enough to carry you." Tobacco juice oozed from the corners of his mouth and trickled down his crusty beard.

How could someone who professed to be a learned man be so filthy? Havah shuddered and wrinkled her nose. Did he visit the bathhouse more than once a month? She doubted it.

"Here's a letter from your sister in America." From a stack of mail on the counter he took one and held it up to the light coming through the smudged window. "The ugly, runaway witch. If I ever see her again I swear—"

"You won't." Shayndel growled and took the crinkled envelope from his dirty fingers. "Good day, Reb Pinkas." She spun on her heel, almost upsetting the cart.

Once outside, Havah took a deep breath to clear her nostrils of the postman's stench. "Where to next?"

"Over here." Shayndel pointed to a lush hornbeam tree growing beside the blacksmith's shop. "You look like you could use some rest, Little Sister."

"Mama sent lunch. Three's boiled eggs and her delicious bagels."

When they had settled under the tree's shade, Shayndel spread a blanket on the ground and laid the babies on it. Neither of them stirred. She sighed. "I'll bet they'll be awake all night."

To ease her discomfort Havah untied her shoelaces. She stretched out her legs in front of her and flexed her ankles.

"Maybe Reb Gavrel could make a special shoe for you. Look, his new sign's up. Lev painted it. I like the blue letters. Don't you?"

For the first time since they had begun their shopping Havah noticed the shoe shop. She read the sign above the door, "'Wolinsky and Sons Distinguished Shoes?' He doesn't have any children."

"Reuven calls him Papa. He loves those children as if they were his own."

Following her watery confrontation with Tova, Havah had struggled to keep her opinions to herself but the shoemaker's presumptuous advertisement made that harder than ever. "What if Leah decides not to marry him?"

"Shhh!" Shayndel's eyebrows knit together in a warning scowl. Glancing over her shoulder, she pressed her finger against her lips. "Aren't there enough tongues wagging about you?" She shoved a whole egg into her mouth, puffed out her cheeks and crossed her eyes.

"Let's read your letter." Havah took the envelope from Shayndel's skirt pocket.

The strange English characters among the familiar Yiddish intrigued Havah. She wished she could read them. With each passing story of the free land called America her desire to go there grew.

"Not yet." Shayndel nibbled at a second egg. "We'll read it tonight after dinner for the whole family. Why don't you and Gittel and your parents come?" She reached into her pocket and drew out a flowered headscarf. "I almost forgot. I found this under Arel's pillow. Isn't it yours? What on earth was it doing there?"

Havah seized the scarf. It still bore his bloodstains from the time she hit him with the rock on the day of the twins' circumcision.

"He's been acting very strange for the past two months. I've never known him to be so moody." Shayndel leaned into Havah and poked her chest. "Did something happen that I should know about?"

Havah wished for a reason to say yes. At least if she carried his child nothing could stop them. The law would be on their side. Of course it would mean public humiliation for the Levines and the Gittermans. Still, for a brief moment, in her mind's eye, Havah saw him smiling at her under a marriage canopy.

"No, Shayndel. Nothing happened."

"Good. Then I'll expect you for supper tonight."

\*\*\*\*

For two months Havah succeeded in avoiding Arel. When he and his father came to the house for their occasional visits, she would greet Reb Yussel and hastily excuse herself. Reasons were not hard to find. A stomachache would exempt her from supper. A headache warranted an early bedtime. Solicitous of her delicate health, Mama hardly ever questioned Havah until tonight. Although she tried to feign a head cold, Havah's sneezing convinced no one, not even Uncle Hershel.

All through dinner Arel tried to garner her attention. When his winks and smiles failed, he resorted to provocation. "I've missed you, Fraylin Cohen. I've not had a good argument in months."

When she did not answer he gently kicked her shin. She returned his gesture with vengeance.

"Ouch!" He yelped and jumped off his chair. It toppled to the floor.

"Arel! What's the matter with you?" Shayndel's brow furrowed. She gave Havah a perceptive glance.

Arel's ears turned scarlet. He righted the chair and plopped down rubbing his shin. "I…I have a cramp."

After supper the family gathered in the parlor in anticipation of the reading of the letter from America. Havah sat beside Gittel on the sofa and laid Mendel on her lap. He seemed to study her with wise-old-sage intensity with his dark eyes. She touched her nose to his. "So serious. Maybe you'll be a rabbi someday…like my brother Mendel."

"He's definitely the quiet one. His brother is the loud demanding one." Taking a seat beside Itzak, Shayndel pointed to the fair complexioned baby on Gittel's lap.

"Oh, but he's so pretty. Look at his lovely blue eyes" Gittel cuddled him against her shoulder. "I hope we have a whole house full of pretty babies just like David and Mendel, don't you, Ari? Isn't he adorable? Aren't you glad you came now, Havaleh? I don't know why you'd want to stay home all by yourself."

"You wanted to stay home?" Arel's eyes shimmered in the lamplight. Havah quivered.

Gittel continued to chatter. "I'm looking forward to hearing what Sarah has to say. Why, sometimes I can hardly remember her. She was so quiet. It's been four years already since she moved away. Can you believe it has been so long? Havah are you listening? Has your mind flown like a bird to the mountains?"

"No doubt our Havah has her mind on loftier things than our simple country minds can fathom." Tova entered the room with six-month-old Bayla on her hip. The rest of her children trailed in behind her.

Taking Sarah's letter from her apron pocket, Shayndel handed it to Arel. "Here, Little Brother. We're all together now. Read."

When he unfolded it a photograph fell from the envelope.

"Look, it's Sarah and her family." Shayndel held it up. "Aren't her twins cute?"

At that moment Bayla squealed, wriggled and hit Tova's cheek with her head. Reuven upset a china bowl on the end table and it shattered on the floor. To avoid a spanking he scurried to Yussel and climbed onto his lap. Lev stuck out his tongue at his little brother. Devorah ran to the kitchen and returned with a whisk broom.

"I have my own children to worry about. Can we hear the letter now and look at the picture later?" Tova eased herself into a rocking chair and yawned.

Looking as weary as her mother, Leah took Bayla from her. "Mama's been up late every night working on my wedding dress. I tell her it doesn't have to be so fancy but does she listen?"

Although she had made a vow to herself to keep her thoughts to herself, tonight Tova's sarcasm and disregard for Leah irritated Havah. "It's not every day one sells a daughter and buys a shoemaker."

"Havah!" Hershel's pipe dropped from his mouth and clunked across the floor.

Clasping the whisk broom and muffling a giggle, Devorah swept ashes and pieces of bowl into a dustpan, then, covered her mouth with one hand and ran from the room. Tova glowered at Havah but said nothing.

Yussel pounded his cane on the floor. "Arel! Read already!"

With one last look in Havah's direction, Arel cleared his throat.

*" 2 May 1900*

*'My Dear Family,*

*I pray this letter finds everyone in good health. We had a nice Passover. We invited some friends over who are new immigrants from Russia. They remind me of my family who I think of often.*

*Wolf is doing well in his tailor shop. Jeffrey and Evalyne will soon be two years old.*

*I wish I could be there next year to see my baby brother married.'"* Arel paused and swallowed. *" 'Springtime is beautiful here. We have a garden with roses and daffodils. I wish you could come to Kansas City.*

*Love to all,*
*Sarah Gitterman Tulschinsky' "*

"It's a short letter. But that's our Sarah." Itzak chuckled. "If she said more than two words at one time— from her it was a conversation. Right, Papa?"

"I only hope she's forgiven me." Yussel eased Reuven off his lap, rose from his chair and shuffled from the room.

\*\*\*\*

In the darkened study Havah could just make out the rabbi's form slumped over his desk. Unsure of what to do or say, she leaned against the doorjamb. Yussel raised his head.

"Don't just stand there, Havah, come in. But I'll warn you, I'm not good company."

"Why do you need Sarah's forgiveness?" She entered the room and lit the lamp on an end table.

"You ask a lot of questions, Havah Cohen." His cheeks glistened with tears.

"Doesn't the Holy Book say, 'A wise man seeks after knowledge'?"

"You are indeed Shimon's daughter." He sighed and leaned back in his chair, folding his hands behind his head. "Sarah was born two months too soon. Not even enough strength to cry. Fruma didn't think she'd live more than a few hours, if that."

"But she did, didn't' she?" Sinking into a nearby chair, Havah tucked her feet beneath her.

"How else could she be sending letters from Kansas City, America?" With something between a chuckle and a sob, his quick smile fading, he fished a handkerchief from his vest pocket. Yussel blew his nose, crumpled the fabric and stuffed it back into his pocket.

"Sarah…princess…my Aidel names her. When Fruma laid the baby in my arms I could hardly stand to look at her. Shriveled. More like a hairy rat than a child. A father should never say this about his own daughter but she repulsed me.

"As she grew I tried to love her. I did. But she was nothing like her beautiful sisters. Quiet. Scrawny. Easy to ignore." He choked and wiped his eyes with his palms.

"1885, the year Sarah turned eleven, she and her mama came down with brain fever. So frail this child. I knew she'd never recover. One night I went to bed with a sore neck. When I woke from the fever a week later they told me my Aidel was gone. Sickly Sarah? Alive and well."

"Is that when you went—"

"Blind. Can you imagine? Such blackness. I couldn't breathe. Alone. Trapped. I prayed for death. I pleaded. I begged.

"Over time I learned to live with it. All the while, without a complaint, 'Silent Sarah' took care of the house, the cooking and the laundry. She looked after Shayndel and Arel. All this without one word of appreciation from her papa."

"But you were…afflicted."

"Yes. Afflicted…with selfishness."

"Why did Sarah run away?"

"Oy, don't ask. Naturally, as Sarah's papa, it was my responsibility to find a husband for her. The printer agreed to marry her. I called her into my study to tell her the good news."

"Surely you don't mean Reb Pinkas." Havah shuddered.

"The same. A little cleaner in those days."

"What did she say?"

"Say? Smash! Glass breaking. Crash! Dishes hitting the floor. Like a windstorm, papers and books flew past my head. And her words? They haunt me to this day. 'You may be blind now, Papa, but you have *never* seen *me*!'"

## Chapter Twenty-three

Leah's hair gleamed under her lace veil like burgundy colored silk. Gavrel looked younger than his years. His light brown hair showed no strands of gray. His hazel eyes, golden in the firelight from surrounding torches, shone with joy. No one could question their happiness, not even Havah.

From the beginning of the betrothal the shoemaker took full responsibility for the Resnicks by assuming and settling Feivel's debts. But what impressed her most was the way he courted Leah with small gifts and clumsy poetry. Every Saturday he escorted her to and from the synagogue. He treated her with tenderness and respect. By the time the wedding date came there was no doubt she not only accepted the arrangement but welcomed it as well.

After they promised their lives to each other and shared a sip of wine, Gavrel crushed the glass under his foot. Cheers rose from the excited crowd. "Mazel tov! Mazel tov!"

While the bride and groom were hoisted up on chairs Itzak and the rest of the musicians played a brisk tune. A procession carrying flaming torches formed behind the newlyweds and they were paraded among the guests like royalty. As soon as the chairs returned to the ground two dance circles formed around them, men in one, women in the other.

Before Leah and Gavrel could enter their respective circles, three-year-old Reuven rushed toward them waving his pudgy arms, shouting, "Papa! Papa!"

A proud smile spread across Gavrel's face. He swept the child into his arms and then onto his shoulders. "Let's join the other men."

"Just us men!" The boy's giggles and squeals nearly drowned out the music.

Breathless from skipping, Gittel broke away from the circle and tugged Havah's hand. "Dance with me, Little Sister!"

Dance? Had Gittel lost her feathery mind? Havah yanked back her hand. "Cripples don't dance."

Gittel's effervescent smile dissolved and her eyes brimmed. "I'll stay here with you then."

Havah wished she could swallow her hasty words. She kissed Gittel's freckled cheek and then gave her a gentle shove. "You dance for both of us, big sister."

"You're sure?"

"Sure."

Smile returning, Gittel skipped back to the circle linking arms with the other girls.

Something bumped into Havah's knees. She knelt and scooped up Bayla Resnick. A mirror image of her mother with her dark curls and gray eyes, she was the only one of the children who bore no resemblance to Feivel.

Havah carried her to the rabbi's yard where Tova chatted with other women who chose to sit and eat rather than dance. With a true provider in the family the older woman no longer looked like a walking skeleton. Lowering the child onto Tova's lap, Havah nodded her head toward the circle of dancing girls. "A beautiful ceremony. Leah's a lovely bride."

"So you admit you were wrong? I didn't sell my daughter for shoes after all?"

A brisk autumn wind went through Havah. She shrugged her shoulders and pulled her shawl around her, twisting its fringes around her fingers. "Some arrangements work out better than others, that's all."

"I hear Reb Hershel is making one for you."

"You're lying!"

"Am I now? Ask him. You little fool. Who do you think you are?

Havah turned and stumbled toward the river where she could be alone. What if Tova told the truth? Tears blinded her and Tova's laughter echoed in her ears.

Torch in hand, Arel stood in her path. Heart pounding, she shoved him out of her way and continued down the hill. He ran ahead of her and blocked her way once more.

With his free hand he stroked her cheek. "My sweet Havaleh."

"You thick headed mooncalf!" She gritted her teeth and, at the same time, relished his touch. "Tomorrow you and Gittel will sign the marriage contract. The end."

"Since when do you respect marriage contracts?"

"She's my sister and you're the rabbi's son."

In desperation she ducked under his arm and headed for the river, cursing her three toed foot. Heat from his torch beat against her neck. When she reached the riverbank she spun around and faced him.

His eyes, iridescent yellow in the flame's orange light, mesmerized her. She fought for the right words. As he closed in on her their lips met and her resistance vanished. "It would mean shame for both for…for…Gittel…and…"

"I don't care. Be my bride tonight."

Chapter Twenty-four

In the month following Leah and Gavrel's wedding, Havah tried to forget those stolen moments in Arel's arms beside the river. The taste of his lips pressed against hers lingered like honey and raisins. His whispered plea still warmed her ear.

What if she had run away with him? She would never know for the following night he and Gittel signed their *kesubah*. A handshake between Uncle Hershel and Reb Yussel cemented the plan for a spring wedding.

Like a flock of white doves, snowflakes floated passed the frosted kitchen window. Her dreams scattered and melted with them. She leaned her forehead against the chilled glass.

"No fever." Fruma Ya'el's warm hand on her face startled her.

"I'm fine, Mama."

"Good. Sit. Your breakfast is getting cold."

"Yes, Mama."

"You're awfully pale. Are you sure you're not ill?"

"Yes Mama."

"Uncle Hershel has a surprise for you."

"You have a surprise for me, Uncle?" The back of her neck tingled as she slid into the chair next to Gittel, dug a raisin from her steaming porridge and squished it between her fingers. "Is it a new book?"

Pipe clenched between his teeth, Uncle Hershel held her in his intent gaze. His voice sounded flat and his words rehearsed. "Havaleh, this is a joyful occasion. Monday last, Pinkas' son Orev asked for your hand. He's a fine young man and he's paid a handsome price. I've every confidence he'll be a good husband."

"Thank you." The words tasted like gravel on her tongue.

What choice did she have? As her guardian Uncle Hershel had every right, according to their custom, to auction her off like a milk cow to the highest bidder.

After sundown, well-wishers from all over Svechka filled the Levine's living room to celebrate her betrothal. The air swelled with the sweet aroma of fresh baked pastries.

*"This isn't happening!"* Her mind screamed what her mouth dare not utter.

While she went through expected motions her true self traveled to a distant place where Svechka did not exist and no one could not touch her.

Amid the celebrants Itzak played a lively tune on his violin. Over it his brown eyes, trained on her, lacked their usual spark. Devorah huddled in a chair and glared at Havah. Even Reb Yussel's joyful prayers sounded hollow and sad.

The one she longed for was nowhere to be seen. Finally she found Gittel who chatted with Tova. When she saw Havah Gittel grinned. "My beautiful sister will make the prettiest bride. Don't you think?"

"Mazel tov, Havah." The triumphant smile Havah expected did not appear. Tova merely nodded and disappeared among the crowd.

Forcing a casual grin, Havah wrapped her arm around her adopted sister. "Where's your dear intended tonight?"

Gittel pouted. "Poor Arel has a bad head cold. Shayndel stayed home to take care of him."

"Good. I hope he dies."

Gittel's mouth dropped open. "You shouldn't tease about such things, Little Sister. You tempt the evil eye."

"Who's teasing?" Havah slipped her arm from Gittel's shoulder, limped to the table and took her place beside Orev.

Reb Pinkas' slurred voice boomed over the music. His words seared her more than his harsh voice. "She's a bargain this cripple! Not only will she make pretty babies, she can't run far." He slapped his son's back. "What are you waiting for, boy? Sign already."

Who was this stranger with a fountain pen clamped in his fist? The younger Rabinovich must have resembled his mother for, with his pleasant features, he looked nothing like his father. Orev's gaze never left Devorah as he scrawled his name across the bottom of the contract and handed the pen to Havah.

Dazed, she rolled the pen between her fingers and studied the ornate document on the table before her. A border of skillfully drawn flowers surrounded the Hebrew and Aramaic words that sealed her fate. Closing her hand around the pen, she swallowed hard and signed away her life.

From behind her, Tova reached for the pen. She took it from Havah's hand, dropped it on the table and grasped Havah's shoulders. As they stood face to face, Tova tucked her fingertips under Havah's chin and kissed her forehead.

"Now you understand, little girl. We women do what we must to survive."

## Chapter Twenty-five

With nothing but a blanket over his thin nightshirt, Arel slouched on a stump. Shayndel pushed open the back door. "Come in, little brother. You'll catch your death."

"I hope so."

A frigid wind whistled past her ears. She put on her coat, tied an extra scarf under her chin and then slipped on a pair of mittens.

Snow frosted her shoe tops like cake icing as she plodded across the yard. "Doesn't it bother you that we lied?"

"You should've gone to Havah's party." He lifted his head and his red-rimmed eyes pierced her like daggers.

"*A brokh tsu dir!*" Shayndel bent, scooped up a mound of snow, straightened and hurled it. "Damn you! Why didn't you stop her?"

The snowball exploded against the back of his head. He flinched. The blanket fell from his shoulders. Leaping off the stump he whirled around and flung a handful of snow. "I tried."

Wiping her face on her sleeve, Shayndel formed another snowball and lobbed it. Scraping more snow from the ground she threw another and then another. He returned each one blow for blow. Finally her arm ached too much and she dropped to her knees. "*Dumkopf!*"

"It's over."

"You gave up."

"Blame your friend." With a shrug and a growl, Arel pivoted and walked to the house, head bowed. "She refused me." He opened the door and banged it shut behind him.

The countryside echoed her anger. "You...you... *feygeleh!*" Spitting on the ground, she shook her fist. "Little girl-boy!"

\*\*\*\*

The day after the marriage contract was signed Havah locked herself in her room. For a solid week she spoke to no one. Uncle Hershel's idle threats to whip her only strengthened her resolve. And her despair.

Friday afternoon, two hours before sundown, someone knocked at the front door.

"Havaleh, my hands are full." Fruma Ya'el pulled a loaf of bread from the oven. "See who's there, please."

Gritting her teeth, Havah glared at Gittel who shrugged. "I have to stir the stew or it will burn."

With a yank that made her wrist scream, Havah opened the door. There stood Orev. For the first time she noticed his violet-blue eyes and even teeth. Under his cap his brown hair curled over his ears. "*Gut Shabbes,* Fraylin Cohen."

"Daughter, where are your manners? Come in, son!" From behind her Uncle Hershel reached over her and grasped the younger man's shoulder. "Gawk at each other where it's warm."

Through dinner, Havah drank in the men's conversation. Orev was an avid reader. Since he helped his father print newspapers he kept current with world events. He had much to say and did so with eloquence and emotion.

"The time for Jewish enlightenment is now," he said. "It's happening in Moscow and in Odessa."

"Do you suggest we turn from Torah, from our prophets?" Uncle Hershel pushed away his empty plate and lit his pipe.

"Absolutely not. But there's more to life than the Torah. Karl Marx says the philosophers have only interpreted the world. Now it's time to change it!"

"And just how do you and Mr. Marx propose to do this?"

"Take up arms against these Christians. Give them a taste of their own poison."

Although his words frightened her, his passion gave Havah hope. She cleared her throat. "Would you like to go for a walk after dinner, Reb Orev?"

"I'd like it very much," he answered with a shy smile, "if it's all right with Reb Levine."

"Call me Papa." Uncle Hershel winked at Fruma Ya'el.

Every Friday night through the winter Orev came to call. He possessed a quick wit and an easy laugh. Always he treated her with tenderness and respect, showering her with small gifts. Little by little her affection for him grew and her ache for Arel lessened.

Although Orev never discussed social revolution or literature with her there was no doubt in her mind he would once she shared her secret. She imagined cozy nights by the fire reading and discussing. Man and wife, studying as one. And then, perhaps, they would have a daughter. They would turn Svechka upside down by sending her to Talmud Torah School.

One night in early spring, her fragile hope shattered with the literal turn of a page. Arel chose the same evening to call on Gittel. After supper the two couples retired to the parlor where they engaged in superficial conversation. Soon, drowsy from the heavy meal, Gittel excused herself, leaving Havah alone with the two young men.

With his eyes fixed on her, Arel picked up her book of Psalms which lay open on the small writing desk by the window. He read aloud, "'*Kos y'shuat esah, the cup of salvation I will raise…*'"

Cursing her carelessness she grabbed for her book. "I'll put that away for…Uncle Hershel."

Arel snapped it shut and gave it her. For a brief moment he held her hands between his. "Orev, my friend, how do you feel about girls reading the Holy writings?"

Orev laughed. "You're drunk, Reb Gitterman!"

"I'm serious. You profess yourself to be a modern man and a free thinker. What if, let's say, your wife wanted to study Talmud, ponder the words of the Baal Shem Tov?"

Havah's heart cratered to her stomach when Orev jumped off the couch. He stomped his booted foot and shook his fist in her face.

"I'd beat her within an inch of her life!"

## Chapter Twenty-six

For the seventh and last time, Gittel emerged from her bridal *mikveh,* or bath of purification. In twenty-four hours she would be Froi Gitterman. Fruma Ya'el wrapped a blanket around her. All the women gathered to wish her well and took turns combing her auburn hair, adorning it with ribbons and flowers.

Havah turned to leave, but before she could escape the festivity, Devorah caught up to her. Her brown eyes flared and her fingernails gouged Havah's arm. "Soon it will be you, Froi Rabinovich. Aren't you excited?"

"Listen, Devorah. I wish you and Orev—"

"There's no me and Orev, you...you husband thief!"

Havah Rabinovich. The name even sounded cold and dead. Prying off Devorah's fingers, Havah slipped through the bathhouse door and hobbled to the river to add her tears to the water. Despair overwhelmed her. She dropped down and wrapped her arms around her knees, burying her face between them.

Over the past month, Orev's attentions turned from tender to sinister and foreboding. He treated her more like a coveted award than a cherished bride-to-be. When she went to the market he stood in the doorway of the print shop, his gaze followed her until she finished her errands. When she went to the rabbi's house to help Shayndel with the twins, Orev would "just happen by" to say hello and then stay. Every suffocating minute of her time belonged to him.

"Havah?"

"Go away." She could not allow herself to look into Arel's eyes. "If Orev catches us…"

"Forgive me, my love." His footsteps rustled the wet grass.

"No, wait!"

As she struggled to her feet he stopped and whirled around, arms beckoning. She melted into his embrace and relished his warmth against her. His lips traveled from her forehead to her eyelids, then to her cheek and, finally, to her mouth.

With reluctance she pulled back and gazed into his shimmering gray eyes. "Tonight, Arel. Just like you said. Let's go to Kishinev."

"It's too late."

"You don't love Gittel. It's not fair…to anyone!"

"What's done is done. We'll remember this moment all our lives. It must be enough."

Tears choked her. "Enough?"

"Gittel's your sister."

"Enough?"

"I'm the rabbi's son."

She sent her hand across his face with a resounding slap that sent bursts of pain all the way to her shoulder. "Drop dead!"

\*\*\*\*

Arel pushed open the front door. He tried not to make any noise as he stepped over the threshold and took off his shoes. Removing his coat, he shook the grass from it. He buried his face in the folds and savored a deep breath. It still held the scent of Havah, wildflowers and roses.

Hanging it on the coat tree, he turned and tip-toed down the hallway to the stairs. As he put his foot on the first step he heard a familiar tapping sound on the floor behind him.

"I trust you had a good walk in the cool night air, my son."

"Papa? I woke you."

"Dawn's light shining in my eyes won't let me sleep."

"It's late and I'm too tired for riddles."

"Come with me. Let's talk" Yussel grasped his arm and led him to the study. "You've been with Havah."

"How did you know?" Feeling his way in the dark, Arel bumped his shin on the desk. A burst of pain sent him to his knees. He bit his lip to keep from crying out and plopped down on the floor. He sat cross legged and braced himself for a tongue lashing.

The floorboards creaked as Yussel went to his favorite chair and sat. It squeaked. "How could I not know?"

"You're angry with me."

"I should be angry at you for following your heart?"

Outside a wolf's mournful howl punctuated the silence. Arel's cheek still smarted from where Havah had struck him and her voice blew through the cavern of his mind like a whirlwind. It echoed and repeated. *"It's not fair. It's not fair. It's not fair."*

Moonlight illuminated Yussel's glistening eyes. "What have I done? To my own children? Tradition. *Feh!"*

"Gittel will be a good rabbi's wife."

"She deserves better than half a husband."

Arel stood and walked to the open window. The moon mocked him. Even the wind accused him. He would never forget Havah's kiss. She was right. It would never be enough.

*"Zai nisht dum."* Yussel's chair squawked as he rose and followed Arel. "Even a blind man can see it. If you disappear with Havah tonight my blessings will go with you."

"No, Papa, I have to honor the covenant. The agreement *you* signed."

"My hand should shrivel and fall off. With an agreement I condemned Tova. With an agreement I drove Sarah across the ocean. And *you.* Like a *schlemiel,* you honor this 'covenant' you'll regret for the rest of your life."

"A covenant is what has preserved our people for centuries." The stiff words tasted like stale bread to Arel even as he spoke them.

"Now the son presumes to teach the father. So you've made your decision?"

"Yes."

"I hope you can live with it. *Fool.*"

\*\*\*\*

"Mama?"

White satin gleamed in the lamplight. Fruma Ya'el bent over her needle and thread. Straightening to ease the ache wracking her spine, she set down her sewing and looked up.

"What's troubling you, child?"

"It's a mistake." Gittel sat on the floor and laid her head in Fruma Ya'el's lap.

Fruma Ya'el's heart ached for her girls but what could she do? Combing her fingers through her daughter's damp hair, she picked out a wilted flower and crushed it between her thumb and forefinger. "Some things cannot be changed just because we wish it. Arel's love for you will grow over time, as will yours for him. You believe this don't you?"

"Do you?"

"I'd like to hear the answer to that question myself." Hershel emerged from his study, pipe in hand. "It's time for bed, Daughter. You wouldn't want to scare your bridegroom with dark circles under your eyes."

"Good night, Papa." Gittel rose, pushed her hair out of her face and kissed Hershel's cheek. With her head bowed and shoulders drooping in her long flannel nightgown, she reminded Fruma Ya'el more of a reprimanded six-year-old than an almost married woman.

For a brief moment she relived her own wedding. Even then Hershel smelled like pipe smoke and Witch Hazel. Her heart recoiled with the memory of the horror of the moment. The dutiful daughter who always did what was expected without question. Love denied into the next generation.

A smoke ring floated from Hershel's lips to the ceiling. He squeezed her shoulder. "I'm going to bed. Join me."

"I will, just as soon as I finish here." She held the dress at arm's length. "I had to add a ruffle to the hem for Gittel's height."

"You'll have to tear off the ruffle and shorten it for the other one next month."

His eyes seemed brighter green than usual. Why had she not noticed how thin he had grown? He took a last drag from his pipe and then laid it in an ashtray on the table beside her.

"Havah's wedding so soon?"

"Why wait?"

He lifted the dress into his arms and cradled it like a favored son. "This has seen its share of canopies. My Gittel of blessed memory wore it. You wore it. And, now, *our* Gittel will wear it." Dropping to his knees, he laid the gown back on her lap. He grasped her hand and held it to his lips. "Dear wife. I wronged you—*and* Charles."

Pressing her palm against his cheek, she brushed a tear from his nose with her thumb. "Dear Husband—I chose my lot. I'm content."

The front door opened and closed. Havah limped into the room. Her eyes darted from Fruma Ya'el to Hershel. "Mama...Uncle Hershel. I...I went for a...a... walk."

"You went for a walk? It's neither safe nor proper for a young lady to be out alone at night." Hershel's knees cracked as he stood with a painful groan.

Instead of the tongue lashing, or worse, the whipping Fruma Ya'el feared, he wrapped his arm around the girl. "Will I never be Papa to you?"

With a defiant shake of her head, Havah freed herself from his embrace and squared her narrow shoulders. "No words of wisdom for me...*Uncle*?"

"None."

\*\*\*\*

"Little Sister, is that you?" Gittel called from her room.

Havah hobbled in and sat down on the bed. She tried to force her quivering lips to smile. "You should be asleep so you can be rested for your...wedding...day." The words stuck in her throat like cold porridge.

"I'm freezing." Gittel pushed back the comforter and motioned to Havah to join her.

The lamp on the chest of drawers went out. Havah slipped into the bed beside her and nestled her head against Gittel's shoulder. Why must it end this way? Both love and loathing filled her for the girl who would tomorrow night lie with Arel.

"Remember how you threw things at me? You called me a half-wit and said I talked too much."

"You still do." She tugged a strand of Gittel's hair. "You'll let them cut it, won't you?"

"It's *Halakhah,* the law."

"Says who? Where's it written in Torah?"

"I don't know."

"Just once in your life...fight! Ask questions. Read."

"Are you going to marry Orev?"

"I have a choice?"

"I'll miss you, little sister."

"We'll still see each other."

"No, we won't."

In the yard below a dog barked and the hens in the coop cackled. Footsteps on the stone steps preceded a broom's swish and Fruma Ya'el's muffled voice. "Scat, you mangy cur."

With a yelp, the dog skittered away, its paws pounding the dirt.

Gittel sniffled in Havah's ear. "I can't take your place."

"Arel *does* love you."

"Like a sister."

Chapter Twenty-seven

Ulrich sipped a steaming mixture of rum, honey and lemon. For a moment the vapor cleared his clogged nose and the hot liquid soothed his raw throat. He eased his achy head into the down pillows on the massive four poster bed. "Doctor, you may very well have saved me from death by pneumonia."

"It's nothing more than a common cold, hardly worth paying a messenger boy to come across town." A slight man in his early thirties, Dr. Nikolai Derevenko tied a robe around his waist. "In any case, thanks for the use of your bathtub. It beats waiting in line."

Nikolai lifted his threadbare suit jacket from the high back chair next to the bed. After that he fished a button, a needle and a spool of thread from a pocket and sat. As he threaded the needle he peered over his spectacles with a raised eyebrow. "You could've mixed your own hot toddy and diagnosed yourself. What's your ulterior motive?"

Ulrich fingered Nikolai's fraying coat sleeve. "When are you going to come to your senses and move out of that infested tenement house?"

"I can't afford it."

"You could if you accepted currency instead of potatoes and chickens for your services."

"At least I'm well fed."

Under a fringe of pale blond hair, Nikolai's gaunt face told another story. Ulrich curved his fingers around one of the other man's rawboned forearms.

"Move in, Kolyah. My new cook will fatten you up in no time."

"I don't need your damnable charity."

"Charity be damned. I'm offering you a position as my personal physician." A burning cough wracked him. Several moments passed before he could catch his breath. "Heaven knows I need one."

"Ha. You need a wife." With a scowl, Nikolai jerked from Ulrich's grasp and resumed his mending. "And what of my other patients?"

"Open a clinic here if it pleases you. The east wing's perfect. It's practically untouched. What've you got to lose?"

"Privacy."

"You call sharing a bathtub with twelve strangers, privacy? The rats will never miss you." Ulrich took the doctor's trousers from his lap and poked his finger through a small hole. "Lay this poor patient to rest, Dr. Ragamuffin, before he exposes your assets. I've just the tailor for you, the best in Kishinev."

"Who?"

"Evron Abromovich."

"Abromovich? Your Jewish cabinetmaker?"

"His brother. I wager he'd clothe you for, say…ongoing medical care of his four children. I'll pay for the yard goods. Everybody wins."

"If I choose to accept your generous offer, which room should I claim for my living quarters?"

"Whichever one suits your fancy."

"Any room?"

"Except *that* one."

"Sell this place. It's a mausoleum."

"Valerica loved this house. I built it for her."

"Let her go."

The door burst open. Ulrich's housekeeper, a middle aged woman with ruddy cheeks and blazing eyes stomped into the room. Even through his congested nasal passages, Ulrich smelled vinegar and peppermint oil exuding from her rustling skirts.

"Professor Dietrich, this is positively the last straw. Isn't it enough you open your fine house to Jewish vermin? Now you go and hire one."

Nikolai stood and bowed, his robe falling open to the waist. "Good afternoon, Mrs. Dragomir." He then straightened and scratched his bare chest. "How rude of me."

Her face darkened to brick red. She pointed a sausage-round finger at him. "And *you,* Dr. Derevenko, I know all about you. You take medicine from good Christians and give it to those…those—"

"People?"

With a hissing growl she flounced to the bed and shook her feather duster under Ulrich's nose. "What do you have to say for yourself?"

His neck ached and his sore throat tightened. In a sneezing fit, he grabbed the duster, seized with the overweening desire to smash it across her mouth. He gagged on dust and gall. "My house. My rules. If this displeases you, get out."

She turned and tripped to the door. "I hope that *Zjid* poisons you!"

The door slammed behind her. Bolting upright, Ulrich flung the feather duster. It cracked against the wall and fell in pieces, to the floor.

Nikolai grasped Ulrich's wrist. "Rapid pulse and profuse sweating. Compelling case. Expect your personal physician's arrival in less than a fortnight."

# Chapter Twenty-eight

Guests gathered around Arel and his bride as they took their places beneath the wedding canopy. A sea of candle and torch flames offered him no warmth just as honor offered him no comfort. Arel repeated the marriage litany in all the proper places by rote.

If only some careless guest would set fire to the canopy. In the ensuing chaos he would find Havah, sweep her into his arms and flee Svechka for good. He searched the crowd and found her on Gittel's right side. She was close enough to touch. He ached with desire.

"According to tradition, as Joshua circled Jericho seven times, so the bride circles her groom, causing any wall of division between them to crumble, bringing unity to their souls."

After Yussel finished his recitation he squeezed Arel's shoulder in a pincer grip and lowered his voice to an angry hiss. "No matter how miserable the union may be."

Flanked by Fruma Ya'el and Tova, Gittel kissed Havah on the cheek through her veil before beginning her circle. "Adoshem go with you, little sister."

"Stand strong, Havah." Tova hugged Havah and kissed her forehead.

As his bride made her fourth time circle he noticed Fruma Ya'el's smile seemed painted on her pale face. Her eyes looked puffy and swollen.

Finally Gittel returned to her spot beneath the canopy.

"Blessed are You, Adoshem, King of the universe, creator of the fruit of the vine." Even Hershel looked sad as he recited the blessing over the wine. He shoved a silver goblet into Arel's hand and some wine sloshed over the rim.

The wine had no taste. No life. He handed the silver cup to Gittel. She took it under her veil, sipped and glowered through the lace. "You should've gone with her."

"Behold, you are betrothed to me with this ring according to the Law of Moses and Israel." Even as he recited the words, he looked past Gittel's shoulder only to see Havah scowl and turn. She said something to Devorah who smiled. Swallowing the rock in his throat he slid the gold ring onto his bride's slender finger.

"May you rejoice forever together as did Adam and Eve in the Garden." Yussel paused and then continued with a heavy sigh. "May the names of Gittel and Arel Gitterman be shining names in Jerusalem one day when the temple is restored."

To end the ceremony, Itzak placed a glass wrapped in a linen napkin under Arel's foot. He stomped. The glass and his heart shattered in unison.

****

Heart and foot throbbing, Havah limped up the stairs to her room. She had to hurry. The newly married couple would return soon. Lighting the lamp on the bed stand, she indulged in one last look, infused with poignant memory and sorrow.

From the wardrobe in the corner she pulled a wicker suitcase. She laid it on the bed and opened it. The few things she packed included her books and her doll. Traveling on foot to Kishinev necessitated carrying as little as possible.

As she gathered her clothes she spied a white handkerchief with tatted lace trim on her pillow. "Where did this come from?"

Folded into a neat square it had familiar embroidery on the corner. Purple flowers surrounded the Yiddish words. *"'For Havah my little sister in her travels. Be safe. Remember me.'"*

Havah sniffed the handkerchief. It smelled of vanilla and cinnamon. It smelled like Gittel. Dabbing her eyes with the edge of it, Havah noticed something more than cloth between the creases.

She unfolded it and stared at a pile of raisins in the middle. Refolding it with care, she tucked the little bundle between stolen bagels, boiled eggs and books. Closing the suitcase, she smoothed the bedcovers and placed a note on her pillow.

"Please forgive me, Mama."

By leaving and reneging on the marriage contract with Orev, she would put Uncle Hershel in an awkward position. Pinkas, not the sort to let things go, would no doubt demand remuneration. Worst of all, Fruma Ya'el would feel betrayed.

Each thump of the suitcase on the stairs pounded against her temples in baneful singsong.

"Arel and Gittel."

"Husband and wife."

"Havah."

"Orphan."

The suitcase slid from the bottom step with a mournful thud. "Alone."

With one final glance around the kitchen she heaved a ragged breath, opened the back door and stepped outside. She closed the door behind her, turned, and bumped headlong into Shayndel who stood before her, arms folded. "Were you going to leave without saying good-bye?"

"Just let me go."

"You're my best friend. How can you hurt me this way?"

Shayndel's plump arms surrounded her and she buried her face in her bosom. "I...I ...can't stay..."

"It's too dangerous for you to travel on foot, especially *your* poor foot. Itzak will take you to Kishinev in our wagon."

"How can I repay you?"

"Don't ever try to cut me out of your life again."

# Part II

## *EXILE*

Chapter One

The night sky faded to an amber haze striped with lavender and golden bands. Havah's eyes were swollen and full of grit. She pulled her shawl around her to stave off the early morning chill. The wagon's wooden seat was rough and cold against her backside.

"Wouldn't you be more comfortable lying down in the back? It will be at least another hour before we get to Kishinev," said Itzak.

Havah shook her head. "Are you sure Evron and Katya will let me live with them? They have so many children and not much room."

"It's not in their nature to turn anyone away. Besides, they've been preparing for your arrival for months."

"But…but…how?"

"Gittel."

"Gittel asked them?"

"Not exactly. Right after you signed the marriage contract she came to Shayndel and me and asked if we'd find a place for you *when* you ran away."

"Does she know where I'll be?" Sudden longing for her sister filled Havah. She wished she could slip under the covers beside her and share her fears, triumphs and secrets. But now Gittel shared her bed with Havah's deepest secret.

"She begged us not to tell her. You know how she is. She's afraid she might let it slip to the wrong person." The sun, an orange circle low on the horizon, bathed

Itzak's ruddy cheeks with light. "Katya will welcome an extra pair of hands with a new baby on the way."

"She's with child? She said she wasn't having any more!"

"Some things just aren't so simple, are they Havaleh?"

The idea of caring for an infant cheered her a little. "When's the baby due?"

"Any day now I'd say."

The horses' hooves clopping on rocky ground lulled her and she fought to stay awake. In the distance she saw a strangely familiar child with dark curls flying behind her on the wind. She turned a cartwheel and then skipped toward the wagon, calling, "Come play with me, Havah!"

"Stop. That child's going to catch her death playing in the grass wearing nothing but a nightgown." She grabbed Itzak's arm.

"What child?" He shielded his eyes with his hand.

"Over there. Don't you see her?"

"No."

Nonetheless, he stopped. Before he could walk to her side to help her she had already jumped down. She limped off to where she had seen the girl. Where had she gone? Her hair danced across her scalp. Voices, long silenced, called, laughed, wept and sang.

> *"Magnified and sanctified..."*
> *"Havah, will you help me with my lesson?"*
> *"...is His great name..."*
> *"No more raisins, Bubbe Fuss Bucket!"*
> *"...in the world which He has created..."*
> *"David, stop teasing your little sister."*
> *"...according to His great Name."*
> *"Don't look back, Havah. Run!"*

There was no synagogue or houses or people but she recognized the landscape.

Itzak touched her shoulder and led her to a rock walled enclosure. "Would you like to visit them?

Someone had set a headstone before the four mounds. Tripping on something half buried in the dirt, she knelt to dig it out. She trembled. How could it have survived a fire and two winters? A carved cylinder inscribed with *Shin,* the first letter in the Hebrew word *Shaddai,* 'Almighty'. It was the *mezuzah* David made when he was only eleven.

"Someday, when I have a house of my own, this will go on my front door."

As she read the inscription on the headstone her vision blurred. "'Revered Rabbi Shimon, Beloved Wife Miriam, Honored Sons: David and Mendel. The Cohen Family. November 1899. May Their Memories be Blessed.'"

She gathered up four stones and placed them on the marker then traced the words and carved Star of David with her finger. Leaning forward she kissed each name, then turned to Itzak who stood behind her whistling and twirling the fringe of his prayer shawl under his vest. "Who performed this *mitzvah*?"

"Angels?"

"Thank you, 'Angel'." She stood, brushed dirt from her skirts and rose on tiptoe to kiss his cheek.

"It wasn't my idea. It was Arel's. He came to me over a year ago. *Noodged* me something fierce until it I finished it."

"He always does the right thing, doesn't he?"

"No, Havah. Not always."

## Chapter Two

News of Havah's disappearance spread faster than a swarm of locusts throughout Svechka. The day after she left Orev fumed and hollered for the entire town to hear. He threatened to find her himself, drag her back by her hair and force her into submission. Shayndel shuddered, never doubting for a minute he would do just as he said and more.

A week later Fruma Ya'el and Hershel came to the rabbi's house. Shayndel opened the door for them. The sadness on their faces was almost more than she could bear.

"May I get you some tea?" She led them to the parlor sofa.

"No, please. Nothing." Fruma Ya'el buried her face in her husband's shoulder.

Side by side they slumped down on couch. Yussel slouched in a chair across from them, tapping his bony fingers against his cane. Shayndel took a seat on a stool beside him. Hershel whipped a handkerchief from his pocket and blew his nose with a loud blast.

"Rabbi, her note says not to search for her. How can we not? She's such a tiny thing and…and…crippled. Why, she's hardly a mouthful for a bear."

"Crippled? Havah?" A slow smile spread across Yussel's face. "A little inconvenienced perhaps."

"She trusted you, Rebbe. We thought maybe…"

Smile fading, Yussel shook his head. "Have you asked Gittel?"

"I'm certain she knows more than she'll tell us. But what can we do? Beat it out of her?" Hershel leaned forward, his eyes so swollen he could hardly keep them open. He lowered his voice to a choked whisper. "Should we say *Kaddish* for Havah?"

"No. She's not dead." Shayndel shrieked.

All conversation halted and two pairs of eyes bore down on her. She bit her lip and swallowed. "I mean...I hope she's not...I don't know."

With a sigh that was more of a groan, Yussel whispered, "Daughter? Just what *do* you know?"

The next morning when Shayndel went to the post office for her mail, Reb Pinkas confronted her, waving his ink encrusted finger in her face. "It's no coincidence Itzak left the same night *she* ran off. I'll bet your husband has the little harlot tucked away somewhere. This is what comes from allowing a girl to study like a man!"

Wadding her letter in her clenched fist, Shayndel snarled and opened her mouth to say that a herd of wild boar could not make her betray her best friend. Gittel pushed past her before she could utter a word. With cheeks as red as her cropped and covered hair, Arel's wife stomped her foot and slapped her palms on the counter.

"You stupid fool. Don't you see? We drove her away." She collapsed into Shayndel's arms. "*I* drove her away."

Chapter Three

Just one week after Havah's arrival, Katya's water broke as the family sat down to eat. With her hand on her swollen belly she rose from the chair and giggled. "My children come hard and fast, little midwife, so be ready to catch!"

Midwife? Havah choked on a potato. Although she had assisted Fruma Ya'el and Gittel many times since Bayla's birth two years ago, she never considered herself a midwife. The title both pleased her and filled her with apprehension. Fortunately there was no time for her to fret.

True to her word, Katya labored less an hour when the baby's head crowned. She sat up, yelped once and pushed. The wet baby slid into Havah's waiting hands and the room echoed with its squalling cries.

"A son!" As Fruma Ya'el had taught her, she snipped the cord with a pair of scrubbed and boiled sewing shears. She bathed the black haired newborn in a basin of warm water. He quieted as she swaddled him in a blanket and laid him in Katya's arms.

"The twins had their hearts set on a sister." The child wrapped his tiny mouth around Katya's breast. She cupped her hand around his head and lay back against the pillows, her buck-toothed smile lighting up her narrow face. "A child is Adoshem's greatest gift. May you be blessed with a houseful of your own, Havaleh."

"I'm never getting married."

"You'll change your mind. You'll see. Perhaps our matchmaker—"

"The children heard the cry and couldn't wait." Evron burst into the room, followed by his children. He flashed a sheepish grin, reminding her of a little boy caught pilfering eggs from the henhouse.

Grateful for the interruption Havah gathered her tools and dumped them into the water basin. She backed toward the door while she watched the children greet their new brother.

Ruth and Rukhel hopped up and down, holding hands. Touching his cheek at the same time, the girls' disappointed frowns turned to smiles. "Ooooh, he's so sweet. May we change his diaper?"

"He hasn't been here long enough to fill one, you silly geese!" Evron lifted his new son into his arms.

Tuli curled up in the washtub lined with blankets beside the bed. He stuck out his lower lip. "I'm the baby."

"Not any more. Now you're the wiser and much stronger big brother." Kneeling beside the tub, Evron laid the swaddled infant next to Tuli.

"Big brother?" The boy's scowl faded and he kissed the infant. He sat up and then climbed out of the washtub. "Like Zelig?"

"Like Zelig." Evron stood. "What does everyone think of the name Velvil?"

"Yes. Yes." Ruth clapped her hands. "After Zaydeh Velvil!"

Rukhel sniffed. "I miss Zaydeh. Remember how he used to hold us on his lap and tell stories about when he was a little boy in the olden days?"

Evron took both of his daughters into his lanky arms. "None of that, my girls. You have a new brother, and your grandfather has a namesake! So be happy!"

Chapter Four

"I can't wait to see Katya's baby!"

Shayndel's eagerness made Itzak smile. He clucked to the horses. "*You* can't wait to see Havah."

"Oh yes, her, too." She turned in her seat beside him and bent over the wagon bed where Mendel and David napped. "Does Evron say anything about her in his letter?"

"You know better. We agreed nothing could be written concerning her. Remember Pinkas, the snoop? That's why I address all of her letters to Evron with a little star by his name so she knows it's for her."

"Halt, *Zjid*! Jew Dog!" Four Russian soldiers on horseback, one of them who was obviously in command, surrounded them.

Itzak yanked the reins. The horses whinnied in protest and the wagon lurched to a stop. He did not allow his smile to dim as he stared down the captain's rifle barrel and raised his trembling hands.

"It's a beautiful day for a ride through our great countryside of Moldavia, Your Honor."

Three of the soldiers dismounted while the captain barked commands. "Down from the wagon! By order of Czar Nicolas II Jews are not to leave their villages."

Hair standing at attention on the back of his neck, Itzak obeyed, and then bowed. "Begging your pardon, Sir, I'm a humble carpenter by trade. I'm...I'm my way to Kishinev to deliver chairs to a customer who is not a Jew."

"Liar."

A fist slammed into his lips and bursts of colored lights danced before his eyes. The ground swirled like a speeding carousel. A rifle butt rammed into his gut and sent him to his knees. Blood filled his mouth.

Two soldiers sauntered to the wagon. Itzak tried to shout but could not catch his breath. One man curled an arm around Shayndel and dragged her off the seat. Another caressed her cheek and fingered her kerchief. "Is it true these Jewish cows shave their heads when they marry?"

When the first man tore off her scarf with vicious force her tawny hair cascaded over her shoulders. "This one didn't."

Itzak spat and stared for a moment at the crimson puddle in the grass. Had he condemned his bride by flying in tradition's face? Would the forbidden mane he delighted in be responsible for her ravagement?

*"A brokh tsu dir!"* Shayndel yanked back her hair and spat in the soldier's face. She scraped a long gash across his neck with her nails. "A curse on you!"

"Ha ha! She's a little spitfire." He grabbed her wrist, punched her cheek with a balled fist, kicked her to the ground and planted his foot on her stomach.

For a moment she lay very still and Itzak feared the worst. Finally she fought her way from under the soldier's boot and bit his calf. He smashed his open hand against her face and, tugging at his trousers, he dropped down and forced her back into the grass with his body.

"Please…please…kill me but let her go." Itzak tried to stand but another rifle butt slammed him back to his knees. Again he struggled to his feet and staggered toward the captain, sputtering through blood and bile. "Your… your Honor, I have…have papers."

The captain pressed his rifle against Itzak's forehead and tightened his finger on the trigger. Itzak closed his eyes and waited for death.

"Mama? Can me wake up now?"

Itzak snapped open his eyes to see David peek over the wagon and rub his eyes. His golden curls shone in the sunlight. He blinked and flashed his eight teeth.

"Stop!" The captain, his eyes intent on the child, laid his rifle across his horse's back and held up his hand. He turned to Itzak, lowering his voice. "Show me your papers."

Shayndel rolled out from under her disappointed attacker, stood and hurried to the wagon. She retrieved an envelope from under the seat. Glowering, she thrust it into the captain's hands.

With imperious solemnity he fished a pair of spectacles from his breast pocket. He placed them halfway down his nose and skimmed all three pages. "Impressive. You have some influential customers. Dietrich? The pianist?"

Itzak's swelling lower lip made it hard to speak, so he nodded.

"I heard him in concert in Moscow once. He's a passionate musician." The captain folded the papers and returned them. "Everything seems to be in order."

The other three soldiers mounted their horses while the captain shoved his rifle back into its scabbard. As they trotted away, the captain looked back over his shoulder and waved. "Good day."

"'Good day,' he says." Tousled hair obscured the red lump on Shayndel's cheek. She spat in the dust. "*Khazers.*"

"Not all of them. That captain's a father."

## Chapter Five

Havah's hopes of finding employment dwindled. Disappointed to find the same backward thinking in the city as in Svechka she limped along the stone sidewalk in the Jewish quarter. Most of the many shop proprietors preferred not to hire women. The butcher offered to sell her a choice pot roast to cook for her supper. The watchmaker refused to talk to her and, worst of all, the bookseller laughed at her.

*A learned woman? Preposterous.*

So lost in her despair, she failed to see four young men blocking her path until they surrounded her. One reached out and pinched her cheek. "Who is this pretty Christ killer? I don't think I've ever seen this one on our streets before."

"Please, don't," Havah whispered.

"'Please, don't.'" Another man's leering falsetto mocked her. He put his arms around her shoulders and pushed her into an alley. With a painful grip he seized her breasts. "There's hardly a mouthful here."

Pinning her against the wall he pressed his mouth against hers. His stench gagged her. She clamped down her teeth on his lower lip and he reared back in pain. With all her might she kicked him where men tended to be most fragile and he fell to his knees shrieking curses. She turned to run.

Someone grabbed her long braid and she fell, hitting her head on the stone pavement. Dazed and helpless she lay on the ground as her attacker pressed his body against her, tearing at her blouse. Sharp rocks poked her back while cruel hands bruised her bare chest.

"Help!" She writhed and screamed as loud as she could.

"Shut up, you *Zjid* witch!" He punched her cheek, sending jagged pain from one side of her face to the other.

An umbrella handle from nowhere crashed against his head and sent him reeling. "Hoodlums! Rats!"

In a daze, she watched the gang flee like roaches down the alley. Rolling over, she pressed her face to the ground and tried to cover her exposed breasts. Gentle hands draped a scratchy woolen coat around her and helped her to her feet.

"Are you hurt?" He spoke to her in Yiddish with an accent she could not identify.

"Take me home. Evron…Abromovich."

"As you wish, Fraulein Cohen."

Fixing her gaze on the ground, her face flushed with embarrassment and her knees buckled. Then, enfolded by the man's arms, her feet left the ground and the aroma of bay rum filled the encroaching black void.

Chapter Six

Shayndel's voice sounded strained and angry. "Are you sure she's going to be all right, Doctor?"

Awake but not ready to open her eyes, Havah listened to the hushed conversation around her. The scrapes on her back smarted and the down pillow offered no relief to the knot on the back of her head. Who had brought her home? His voice was soft and deep like spring rain. And how did he know her name?

A small hand patted her forehead. "Wake up Auntie Havah. Don't be dead."

"Tuli. Shoo!" There were tears in Katya's command.

"Let him stay." Havah managed to croak.

"The Almighty be thanked!"

"She has a mild concussion," said an unfamiliar voice in formal Russian. Fingers pressed gently against her sore cheekbone. "She has a few minor abrasions and some bruising. I expect her to make a full recovery in less than a fortnight."

"What do you care?" asked Shayndel.

"Shayndel, Dr. Nikolai's our friend." Evron's chiding voice answered.

"Friend? Look what 'friends' did to us. To *her*."

"They're not all bad men." Itzak's voice chimed in. "The soldier…"

"He would've gunned you down had it not been for David."

"But he didn't, did he? And what about Professor Dietrich?"

"He's just using you."

"I apologize for my esteemed countrymen," said the Russian voice. "For it to happen twice in one day is most regrettable."

The same fingers that had prodded Havah's face moved to her scraped knees. Sliding down her right leg, the hand stopped at her bare foot. "What, in God's name, happened here?"

Jerking her foot back, Havah opened her eyes. "Get your filthy hands off of me you pig!"

"I understand." The doctor's blue eyes behind his spectacles misted and his square jaw rippled. He tucked a quilt around her legs.

"No you don't." She sat up. "How could you?"

"Rest now, Mademoiselle Cohen. Pound me later."

The room seemed to spin and the bed tilted beneath her. She fell back against the pillow and noticed the silent children around the bed. Even little Velvil, in Zelig's arms, looked like a little old man who understood. One by one she smiled at them until she came to Shayndel and Itzak's banged up faces. She gasped.

"What do we owe you, Dr. Derevenko?" Itzak grasped his hand.

"No charge. Just take it easy for a while so those bruised ribs have a chance to heal." The doctor put on his coat. Havah recognized it as one Evron had been sewing buttons on a week ago.

"Dr. Nikolai, won't you stay for supper? We have plenty." Katya picked up his bag and hat and followed him to the door.

"As you can see, my little brother went to extra lengths to bring us a chicken." Evron curved his arm around Itzak's shoulder.

Glancing in Havah's direction, Dr. Derevenko donned his hat and gave his head a slight shake. "Ulrich's made dinner plans for us. Another time perhaps." The door shut behind him.

"I'm such a burden." Havah's eyes teared up.

*"Feh!* Nonsense." Katya eased down on the bed and pressed a cool cloth against Havah's tender cheek. "You're a blessing."

"Indeed." Evron lifted the baby from Zelig's arms. "Time to study, my young rabbi."

With a buck-toothed grin, the older boy followed him to the table by the window. He sat and opened his book, licked the tip of his pencil and hunched over his lessons.

As the women and girls dispersed to the kitchen, Itzak took a seat at the end of the bed and whittled. Breathing in the onion-laden aroma from the kitchen, Havah pulled the blanket around her neck and watched a block of wood change into a lioness.

"Remind you of anyone we know?" He winked. "Little Sister, let me make a walking cane for you."

"I'm not a cripple."

"Suit yourself. But it would make a dandy weapon." Although his swollen lips tried to smile, his dark eyes reflected unspoken anguish. "Why do you think you need a job, little sister? Don't they keep you busy enough here?"

In the corner by the window Zelig squinted and pressed his nose against his book page. "Papa, the words are furry. I turned up the lamp wick as far as it'll go and the light's still too dim."

"I'm afraid it's not the light, little rabbi. It's your eyes." Evron frowned.

With a sense of triumph, Havah rose up on one elbow. "There! Zelig needs glasses. When I'm better I'll ask at the tobacco factory."

"A factory's no place for a young lady."

Itzak snapped his fingers. "Has Professor Dietrich found a housekeeper yet?"

"You want me to work for a *goy?*" Havah folded her arms across her chest and scowled.

"Nu? For whom do you think you'd be working at the tobacco factory? A rabbi?"

Chapter Seven

"Ari, aren't you finished yet?"

Without looking up he pried Gittel's arms from his neck. "I have to complete tomorrow's lesson. Now be a good girl and let me work."

"But that's all you ever do. Come! Walk with me. It's such a beautiful day. I'll make a picnic lunch. We'll eat by the river like when we were children."

"Not now. I'm so far behind and I promised Papa I would read to him tonight."

"I cleaned all morning. A person could eat off the floor. I milked the cow, fed the chickens and gathered the eggs. There's nothing left to do. I am so bored!" Pouting, she flounced from the room, slamming the door behind her.

A little while later she returned carrying a steaming cup. "I brought you some tea, my husband. Rest already. If you don't your eyes will fall out of your head and the cow will trample them underfoot. Then, I ask you, who'll read to Papa Gitterman? I can't and Havah's gone."

Sudden anger bubbled up in his chest. He slammed his book shut and swung around. The teacup flew from her hand. Scalding tea sloshed over the papers on his desk and into his lap.

"Are you stupid? Just once do as I ask." He bolted from his chair and pulled off his soaked trousers. "All day long you chatter, chatter, chatter. Can't I have a moment's peace?"

Huge tears welled up in her green eyes and she sank, forlorn, to the floor. Wet papers surrounded her.

"I'm sorry. I'm sorry. I can't be her. I wish I could. But I can't…I can't…I can't…

"I married you, not Havah." He knelt, pressed his palms against her cheeks and brushed away her tears with his thumbs. Then he pressed his index finger to her lips.

Next he closed her in the circle of his arm. Her breasts were soft and warm against his chest. On a sudden whim he slid off her scarf and studied her shorn hair. It stood up in tufts and, at the same time, fell in tiny ringlets close to her scalp.

"It looks like Moses' burning bush." He wound one of her red curls around his fingertip. "Never cut it again."

"But it's the law…"

"Where does it say?"

"You're not mad at me?"

At that moment he forgave her for not being Havah. Sweeping her into his arms, he stood and carried her to their room. He lowered her onto the bed. "Froi Gitterman, let's discuss the matter of your stupid husband."

## Chapter Eight

Fruma Ya'el swaddled the baby girl and laid her in Tova's arms. Nothing compared to the sight and sweet scent of new life. "Mazel tov, Bubbe."

"Imagine me a grandmother." Tova kissed the baby's forehead. "She favors her papa, I think."

"Yes, yes. Of course she does." Gavrel's cheeks shone in the lamplight. He sat beside the bed, clutching Leah's hand, his eyes trained on her. "You're sure my wife's all right, Auntie Fruma?"

"She's as strong as a horse. It was a quick and easy birth. What more can you ask of the Almighty?"

"You're disappointed." Pale and weary from her labor that had ended just moments before, Leah twined her fingers between Gavrel's. "I failed. I didn't give you a son."

"Lev and Reuven are already sons to me."

Had it really been almost twenty years since she placed baby Leah in Tova's arms? Fruma Ya'el smoothed her kerchief and slipped off her apron. Gathering her instruments into her birthing basket, she heaved a happy sigh.

"You're a *mensch,* a good man, Gavrel." She tapped her foot against the wooden floorboards of the cozy home he had built.

He fished a bill from his pocket and pressed it into Fruma Ya'el's hand. "Thank you for taking such good care of my bride."

"Save it. You have another mouth to feed." The money fell on the bed.

"At least have some tea before you go."

"The tea I'll take."

"Let me get it for you, Auntie. Sit." Tova handed the slumbering infant to Leah and turned to go to the kitchen.

Just inches from the doorway she pitched forward and crumpled to the floor.

Leah's screams ringing in her ears; Fruma Ya'el dropped beside Tova. She pressed her hand against her forehead. "No fever."

"Li'l head...ache," Tova whispered through lopsided lips and her speech slurred. One of her eyes bulged while the other eyelid drooped. Suddenly she wheezed and her head flopped to one side, weighing heavy against Fruma Ya'el's legs.

Pressing her fingertips against Tova's neck, Fruma Ya'el's heart pounded "Please, please, let me feel a beat, a flutter." Nothing. Only her own throbbing pulse.

*"Can I help make biscuits?"*
*Twenty six years ago the little girl with black curls and deep dimples peeked over the flour-dusted table. Her grey eyes darted back and forth, following Fruma Ya'el's rolling pin.*

The same grey eyes stared at nothing. Fruma Ya'el closed them and then cradled Tova in her arms. Rocking to and fro as she had the day they made biscuits together, her melody sliced through the pall.

*"Ay li lu li lu...shluf jhe yiddele shluf, sleep, little one, sleep."*

## Chapter Nine

Although Arel tried to keep his mind on prayers, the starchy aroma of lentil soup, traditional mourning fare, whelmed him with memories. His own mother died when he was only four, the same age as Reuven who had cried himself to sleep in Gittel's arms. Lonely tears leaked from under his swollen eyelids.

Finally Yussel ended *Kaddish* with a resounding and tearful "Amayn!" Arel heaved a relieved sigh. His empty stomach grumbled and his back ached.

"Has anyone seen Lev?" Fruma Ya'el ladled soup into a row of bowls on the table.

"I've an idea where he might've gone." Arel went to the front door.

"You should eat first." Shayndel helped Fruma Ya'el distribute soup and dense chunks of brown bread to the men who had spent the past three days reciting prayers to honor the dead. Shayndel followed him to the door and tried to put a bowl into his hands.

"Later, Shayndel, after I find the boy." He shoved open the door.

"You tell him Leah's worried sick," said Shayndel. "On top of everything else, she needs his *mishegoss* like a hole in the head. I'm afraid all this trouble is going to curdle her milk."

"Keep the soup warm, big sister." Arel grabbed the bread, crammed a piece into his mouth and stepped outside.

\*\*\*\*

The moon shone like a pearl against the velvet sky. Grateful for the light it cast on the path, he kicked a pebble and plodded toward the synagogue. Under his hat, his sodden hair stuck to his scalp. Summer humidity clung to him like a heavy coat.

A high pitched voice, half sobbing, and half singing, wafted from the cemetery enclosure.

"*Magnified and Sanctified be His great name.*'"

Beyond a clump of weather beaten headstones Lev gathered a handful of dirt and sprinkled it in his hair.

"*From the world which he has created.*'"

Suddenly he stopped singing and collapsed on top of the fresh mound. "Why, Mama? Why?" Balling his hands into frantic fists he pummeled the grave. "I hate you."

Arel pushed open the wrought iron gate and made his way through the maze of graves, markers and gnarled brambles. Kneeling, he laid his hand on the boy's shoulder. "You don't hate her."

Flipping over onto his back, Lev snarled and kicked him. "Leave me alone, everyone else does."

Arel sat down next to Lev. "How old are you?"

"You should know." Lev sniffed and wiped his nose with the back of his hand, smearing mud like paint across his perspiring forehead. "I'm eleven."

"You know you're not supposed to sing Kaddish without a *minyan.*"

"Zaydeh wouldn't let me pray with them. He says I'm too young."

"Be grateful you're not yet saddled with the burden."

"But she was *my* mother." Lev sat up, his dark eyes glistening in the moonlight. "What about that strange girl Havah? When she sang Kaddish by herself you and Zaydeh acted like it was the most amazing thing since Moses parted the Red Sea."

Arel's heart leaped. "This has nothing to do with her."

"Do you miss her, Uncle Arel?"

"Right now I miss your mother, my sister, more than anyone. Why do you hate her?"

"She abandoned me."

"It's not as if it was her idea you know."

Chapter Ten

Far from being the crotchety old man Havah expected, Professor Dietrich had thick sandy hair and a friendly smile defined by deep dimples.

"My friend Itzak tells me good things about you. The job is yours if you want it. You may start whenever you like, today if you desire." He clicked his heels together, bowed and held his hand out to Havah, speaking Russian with a slight accent. Then he pointed to the shorter man beside him. "But it's only fair to warn you that picking up after two cranky old bachelors may be a difficult task."

"Dr. Derevenko?" She bit her lip. "You live here?"

Without the slightest hint of a smile, he bowed. "Mademoiselle Cohen, a pleasure to see you're feeling better." He indicated a doorway to his left. "My surgery and apartment are through those double doors. I do my own cleaning, thank you. Unless you need medical attention, stay out. *Doh Svedanya.* Good day."

The doors shut behind him and Havah whispered to Itzak in Yiddish. "I don't like that man."

"Give him time, Fraulein Cohen," said Professor Dietrich. "Once you get to know him you'll find Kolyah to be every bit as disagreeable as he seems."

At the sound of Yiddish from the tall German's lips, she started. Where had she heard that accented voice? His sparkling eyes were the most amazing color. They were bluer than summer skies yet iridescent as rain.

"What do you think Havah?" Itzak whispered. "Can you lower yourself to work in a shack like this?"

The dining room, with its high ceiling, boasted an elaborate chandelier dripping with crystal tear drops. A fringed Indian rug covered only part of the highly polished floorboards. High backed chairs surrounded the oak table.

"It's like a fairy tale." She tightened her fingers around a cloth sack filled with food. "I brought my lunch."

"Fraulein Cohen, we have more than enough—" Professor Dietrich stopped and slapped his forehead. "Ach! What a *dumkopf.* Kosher. As a matter of fact, my kitchen *is* Kosher. My cook, Anzya, is also Jewish. I hope you'll be happy here. Feel free to acclimate yourself."

"Try not to get lost, Havaleh." Itzak turned to leave. "I'll be back for you at four o'clock."

"When you return, Reb Abromovich, bring your family and your music." The professor grasped both of Itzak's hands. His voice sounded lonely and pleading. "I'll have Anzya make her famous noodle kugel. You brought your fiddle?"

Itzak's slightly swollen lips spread into a grin. "Is the rabbi Jewish?"

****

In all of her eighteen years, Havah had never seen so many books in one place or so grand a room as Professor Dietrich's library. The bookshelves stretched from floor to ceiling. An oak desk with intricate carvings sat in one corner of the room. It looked just like the one in Reb Yussel's study. Both of them, no doubt, were Itzak's handiwork.

A sofa flanked by two chairs faced a marble fireplace framed by an ornate carved granite mantel. The matching chairs fascinated her. Their frames were carved wood with scrolled armrests. The seats and oval shaped backs were upholstered with patterned crimson brocade.

Perhaps King David had chairs like these in his palace. She wished she could curl up in one and read the hundreds of books, starting with the top shelves and working her way to the bottom ones.

The grand piano where the professor gave lessons took up the corner opposite the desk. She tapped one of the gleaming keys. A low note resonated in her ears. She ran her fingers across the other end of the keyboard. The succession of high notes put her in mind of clear water in a stream.

When she was a young child, there was a Russian spinster near Natalya who owned an upright piano. She made her living giving lessons to Christian children. One day Havah garnered the courage to knock on her door and ask for lessons.

"Do you seriously expect me to let Jewish paws on my piano? Go away you mangy *Zjid* cur."

Although it was more than ten years ago the woman's high pitched laughter still sounded in Havah's ears. She never forgot those sparse and jagged teeth. Nor could she forget, no matter how hard she tried, warm spittle splattering her forehead and dripping into her eyes.

"Do you play?"

Startled, she whipped around. Professor Dietrich leaned against the wall behind her. Wringing her hands, she backed away. "No! I didn't mean to touch it. I mean—I mean I don't play, Sir."

"Would you like to learn?" His dimpled smile was nothing like the old spinster's.

"Yes, I would love to, Sir."

"You're staring at me. Do I have a dead mouse on my head?"

"It was *you*—in the alley."

"Guilty as charged."

"Why?"

"I never could resist a damsel in distress."

"You speak Yiddish. I've never known a Christian who did."

"Well, now you do!" He sauntered to the piano and with aristocratic mien, sat on the bench. Then with a faraway smile on his lips he played the lullaby Havah's beloved mother sang to her when she had trouble falling asleep. "Yiddish is a sweet language, so expressive. I had to learn it to communicate with my Jewish grandmother who lit the *Shabbes* candles every Friday night until the day she died."

"How could she marry a—"

"—a Christian? *Goyisheh* scum?"

"That's *not* what I was going to say!" She stamped her foot and then lowered her eyes. "I'm sorry. I didn't mean to lash out at you. It's just that Christians are murderers and thieves."

"Now it is my turn to apologize. But I urge you, Havah, not to confuse the word 'gentile' with the word 'Christian.' A *true* Christian could never do the things these beasts do."

His cerulean eyes glittered with compassion. Unsettled, she turned from his gaze to the bookshelves. "Have you read all of these, Professor Dietrich?"

"Most of them. Some are gifts from my students, Fraulein Cohen."

"Oh, please, call me Havah."

"I will but only if you call me Ulrich."

"But I'm your maid, Sir."

"And I'm your employer." He cocked his head to one side and crossed his eyes. "And never, but *never,* call me 'Sir'."

"If you insist, S—Ulrich." She pursed her lips.

"You like to read, don't you, Havah?"

"Oh yes!"

"So did my wife. She used to spend hours in those red chairs. You can still smell lavender between the pages of her favorites. I can see her, Queen Valerica on her throne, reading Tolstoy or Dostoyevsky. Have you read them?"

"No. Mostly I've read Psalms, Talmud and Torah." She pulled her book of Psalms from her apron pocket and held it out to him.

"Ach! I envy you."

"Me? Why?"

"To read King David in his own tongue, what could possibly be any better than that?" Reverence and awe shone on his face as he took the book from her. Opening it, he fingered the pages with the tenderness of a father stroking his child's face.

"You may borrow my books if you like. Any language you fancy. Russian, German, English."

"English?"

"Do you speak it?" He gave her back her book.

"No, but it's what they speak in America, yes?"

"Indeed they do, although the British might take exception to the colonies' claim. Why do you ask?"

"I'm going to live there someday...America. I mean...could you...would you..."

"...teach you? I will have to give the matter some thought."

With his eyes shut he set his slender fingers on the piano keys and played. The music engulfed her. Her heart thumped in time while she waited for his answer. Had she angered him? Was her employment ended before it began? At last the final chords resounded in her ears and he opened his eyes.

"It will cost you, Fraulein."

"I...have no money...I..." Her lips trembled.

"*Geld verdammt!*" He slid off the piano bench and knelt before her. "Your wealth is greater than mine for you read the language of the prophets. I will gladly teach you English but only if you agree to teach me Hebrew."

## Chapter Eleven

Wind gusted through the back doorway, whisking Nikolai's newspaper off the kitchen table. Havah burst into the room with a broad smile. "Good morning, everyone!"

"I've told you to use the front door. You needn't come through the back door like some kind of servant." Ulrich rose from his chair.

"But I *am* your servant."

"*Nein.* You're my employee and my employees don't use the back door."

Her raven hair cascaded over her shoulders when she took off her shawl. After she hung it on a peg by the door she dropped to her hands and knees to pick up her fallen hairpins. Once she had recovered them she stood and twisted her hair into a knot on top of her head.

"It just won't stay up."

"Magnificent hair like yours should be left down."

For a moment he imagined his fingers lost in those midnight waves. Plopping back down in his chair, he reprimanded himself. She was just a child.

"Shut the door, Princess." Anzya scowled from the cast iron stove where she stood taking muffins from a pan.

The door banged shut. Havah stuck out her tongue as she picked up a broom and dustpan. "Pardon me, Your Majesty." She curtsied with an exaggerated flourish and disappeared.

"I see they're getting on well," said Nikolai's with a wry smile. He bent to retrieve his paper.

Anzya slammed a plate of muffins on the table. One rolled into Ulrich's lap. Catching it, he dropped it onto his plate and looked up at her only to catch a stare that would have curdled cold milk. She turned and dashed from the room.

"She's a wonderful cook. But is it worth the aggravation to keep her on?" Nikolai smoothed his paper and spread it on the table. "Have you ever considered hiring men instead?"

"I like a woman's touch."

"That woman has the gentle touch of an angry badger."

"She's never missed a day's work."

"I suppose there is something good to be said for reliability. At least the new one has a better attitude. She's pretty, too."

"I hadn't noticed."

"Is that so?" Nikolai raised an eyebrow.

When Anzya returned she struck a match and lit a fire under a kettle on the stove. As she picked up a coffee pot the flame licked her hand. She flinched and yelped.

"Let me look at that." Nikolai sprang from his chair.

"Don't touch me!" She jerked away from him. The pot fell from her grasp, splattering the floor and Nikolai.

Grabbing a towel, she fell to her knees to sop up the spilled coffee. She then regained her disdainful composure and stood. "I'm sorry to have spoken to you with disrespect, Dr. Derevenko. I will understand if you dismiss me, Professor Dietrich."

Ulrich's mild annoyance at the chaotic morning intensified to stern irritation. "Don't be absurd. Your employment's secure. Take the rest of the day off. With pay. But first tell me why—"

Lips pinched into a tight knot, she lifted her shawl from its peg and hurried out the door.

Pulling the curtains aside, he looked out the window and watched her walk down the street. He slapped the wall. "Damnable woman."

"Aren't they all?" With a painful grimace, Nikolai dabbed at his wet trousers.

"I wonder how Havah would feel about making dinner."

"According to you, she does everything but fly."

Not wanting to pursue the topic of women any longer, Ulrich picked up Nikolai's paper. "What are you so intent on reading this morning?"

*"The Bessarabitz."*

"By Pavel Krushevan?"

"The same."

"Kolyah, why do you read such rubbish?"

"'Know thine enemy.'"

"Touché."

"There is an amusing article this time. He printed an apology for something he wrote prior to Easter. He accused the Jews of murdering a Christian boy through their ritual, making unleavened bread from his blood. It seems the true murderer has been apprehended. The child's own relative."

"There's nothing amusing about it. One day this town's going to witness a pogrom like Eastern Europe has never seen because of the outrageous garbage he writes."

Chapter Twelve

Havah felt desolate and alone as she watched Itzak help Shayndel into the wagon. Over and over Havah's life had changed. Like Moses she was always a stranger in a strange land. Nowhere could she call home.

"Do you really have to leave?"

"You know the answer to that," said Itzak.

"As it is, we've stayed longer that we should have. I'm not sure what we'll tell Papa." Shayndel took Havah's hand and squeezed it.

"Tell him the truth. Cossacks attacked you and Itzak needed time to heal from his cracked rib." Havah pointed to Itzak's injured lip.

"I'm sure Katya and Evron will be happy to sleep in their own bed for a change. We'll be back when it warms up. By then I should have the constable's headboard finished. And there's the cradle I'm working on." Itzak gave his horse a sugar cube, patted her flank and climbed up onto the wagon seat.

"Cradle?' Havah trembled. She locked her knees and braced herself for the dreaded news. While she had expected it at some point she did not think it would happen so soon. Arel and Gittel had only been married a few months. "When?"

"Sometime in the spring."

## Chapter Thirteen

The hot iron hissed against Havah's wet fingertip. Bending over a large wicker basket, she pulled a fine linen shirt from the damp pile. She draped it over the wooden ironing board and, taking care not to scorch the fabric, she skimmed the iron over it, smoothing out every possible wrinkle.

Somewhere in the house a flute played an ethereal melody, like nothing she had ever heard. Ulrich never mentioned playing anything besides piano other than organ or harpsichord. Enthralled, she stopped ironing until, to her disappointment, the music stopped.

A cool breeze riffled the kitchen curtains, offsetting the heat emanating from the stove and iron. She put the pressed shirt onto a hanger, laid it over a chair back and mopped sweat from her forehead on her sleeve.

"Stir the stew every ten minutes, Princess. Don't let it burn." With a threatening scowl Anzya shoved past her, nearly upsetting the laundry. Her mouth made a thin line under her narrow nose. She secured a black shawl over her kerchief.

The sour woman seldom spoke and never smiled. Perhaps she had no teeth. When Havah asked Ulrich about her he said she was as much of a mystery as when she first came to work for him a year ago.

The backdoor slammed behind Anzya. Then, like an exclamation point, a thunderclap rattled the windows. Havah pulled open the door, stepped outside and watched Anzya trudge down the sidewalk. A sudden downpour did not make her walk any faster.

"What did I do to make her so mad? I hope the old hag falls in a drain and drowns." Havah stood in the rain, letting it cool her face, until she remembered the ironing under the open window. Hurrying back inside, she berated herself for the drenched shirts left dripping over the chair.

"Drat! Now I have to start all over."

One by one she slipped the shirts off the hangers. She tossed one on the ironing board and the other into the basket. To her horror when she skimmed the iron over the white shirt it left a brownish streak.

If that was not enough, the kettle on the stove bubbled over, splattering the floor and the other shirt. Once she extinguished the fire, Havah grabbed a spoon and stirred the stew. Too little, too late. The fragrant beef and potato mixture had been reduced to sludge at the bottom of the pot.

"I hope Ulrich and that doctor person like chicken sandwiches." She limped to the icebox and pulled out a plate of leftover chicken.

After she set the plate on the table she searched the many drawers for a knife. Before she could cut into the crusty bread on the counter, a masculine hand reached around her and took the knife. "Allow me. You're liable to slice off your fingers."

"Must you always be so rude?" She whirled around and glared at Dr. Nikolai.

With surgical precision he cut the bread into even slices and stacked them on a platter. He peered at her over his spectacles with one raised eyebrow. "Or so gentile?"

## Chapter Fourteen

Five hours of thumping on a hard wagon seat left Shayndel's backside tender and sore. Flexing her stiff shoulders, she sliced potatoes and onions and dropped them into hot chicken fat called *schmaltz*. After a day of traveling, it was simple to prepare scrambled eggs and fried potatoes for supper. A little toasted bread smeared with cold *schmaltz* and they had an acceptable meal.

Yussel's cane made tapping sounds along the kitchen floor. "I see you've returned safe and sound from Kishinev."

"Yes, Papa. Did Leah come over to look in on you while we were gone?"

"She's a faithful granddaughter."

"Her hands are too full for someone so young."

"She's had to grow up too soon, just like her mama. But unlike her mama, she's married to a good man."

"That's true. But Devorah is old enough to help and she hardly lifts a finger." Shayndel turned the potatoes. "Papa, are you sure betrothing her to Orev is a good idea?"

With the end of his cane Yussel found a chair and sat. "To tell the truth, the boy's been sweet on her as long as I can remember."

"She's only fifteen."

"How old were you when you were betrothed to Itzak? It's not as if they're getting married this week."

"They spend too much time together. It's not proper. And that father of his...ugh!"

Yussel's shoulders sagged and an uncomfortable silence fell between father and daughter. The potatoes and onions sizzled in the pan. Shayndel flipped them over and breathed in the pungent aroma.

"Zaydeh! Zaydeh!" The twins burst through the back door, raced to Yussel and clambered up onto his narrow lap.

"The horses are fed and bedded for the night." With his usual cheerfulness Itzak followed the boys. In one long stride he crossed the kitchen and grabbed Shayndel around the waist. Leaning over her shoulder, he growled like a bear and nibbled her earlobe. "My turn."

His hot breath excited her. "Itzak….Papa…the children."

Giving her a firm squeeze, he kissed her cheek with a loud smack. "Papa can't see."

"But he can hear." Yussel's voice turned singsong and he wagged his finger.

Color rose above Itzak's bushy beard and he let go of her. His laughter erupted and caressed her ears. Desire for him made it hard to concentrate on supper.

Suddenly loud and demanding, Yussel's voice startled her. "Nu? Evron and his family, they're happy?"

"As happy as a Jewish family *can* be in Kishinev." Itzak sat down and took David from his father-in-law.

Grateful for the diversion, Shayndel broke eight eggs into a bowl and whipped them with milk. "Velvil is growing like wheat in fertile soil. And such beautiful brown eyes. Just like our Mendel."

"I imagine he looks very much like you, Itzak." Yussel smiled. "Evron was just eight years old when we came to Svechka and twelve when you were born. I said the blessings over your circumcision. Such a chubby fellow. I could hardly resist pinching your little—"

"Papa!" Shayndel stirred the eggs harder.

"I really don't remember, Papa." Itzak's face flushed crimson.

"Of course not. So tell me more about your visit to Kishinev. Your customers? They're pleased with your work?"

"Of course."

"They pay good wages?"

"Always."

After a short pause, the rabbi whispered, "And Havah, she's well?"

## Chapter Fifteen

Pounding on the back door below her bedroom woke Shayndel from pleasant dreams. She burrowed her head in her pillow's softness. The banging refused to stop.

"Aunt Shayndel! Uncle Itzak! Zaydeh!"

"Who on earth could that be this late? It sounds like Devorah." Beside her, Itzak threw off the covers, grabbed his robe and leaped out of bed. Taking her robe from the bedpost, she wrapped it around her shoulders and lit the lantern on the bed stand. Lamp in hand she hurried downstairs, hoping the twins would not wake.

As she reached the kitchen, Itzak swung open the door. He gasped. There at his feet huddled Devorah, her red hair disheveled and her nose bleeding. Tears made rivers through the dirt caked on her face. She held her hands over her torn blouse and partially exposed chest.

"Who did this to you? *Goyim? Cossacks?*" Tossing his robe over her shoulders, Itzak swept her up in his arms.

"No." Her voice was a mumbling whisper. "Auntie, I'm sorry…my monthly hasn't come and Orev…"

"He beat you?" Shayndel shuddered. As a child, Orev was a bully. Bigger and stronger than most, he enjoyed intimidating the other boys. She would not put such a thing past him for she had heard him threaten Havah more than once.

"As Adoshem lives, I'll tear him apart." Itzak's eyes flashed with menacing vengeance.

In the circle of his arm, Devorah wailed. "Not Orev…Reb Pinkas."

## Chapter Sixteen

The door opened a crack and Orev pushed his nightcap off his forehead and peered through the sliver of an opening. "Rebbe?"

Itzak stood beside Yussel in the pouring rain. To Itzak's other side, Gavrel scowled and cracked his knuckles.

"Good evening, Reb Orev." Yussel pressed his hand against the door. "May we come in?"

"It's late." Orev's face paled.

"We'd like to see your father."

"He's sleeping."

"Wake him." Itzak, impatient with the rabbi's feigned courtesy, pushed past Orev with a growl. Yussel and Gavrel followed him into the shack's front room.

The malodor of rancid chicken fat assailed him from an iron skillet on the stove. Dishes caked with grease were piled on the table in the corner. Rain dripped through holes in the rotted roof. Itzak guided Yussel around mud puddles forming on the dirt floor.

Yussel groped for Orev's shoulder. When he found it he squeezed. "Before we talk to your father, Orev, I need to know if you're prepared to accept responsibility for the child my granddaughter carries?"

Orev hung his head. "I...I'm sorry. I never meant for it to happen."

"My son's not marrying that little *harlot!* You can't trust her kind!" Pinkas barged into the room looking more like a rampaging bear in a nightshirt than a man.

"And just what kind would that be, Reb Pinkas?" Itzak stomped through the puddles to Pinkas and seized his collar.

"Itzak." Yussel held his finger to his lips. "Remember a soft answer turns away wrath."

"Papa, I love her." Orev laid his hand on his father's shoulder.

"You may love a dog but you don't marry it." Wrenching out of Itzak's grasp, Pinkas swung around and punched his son's stomach.

With a groan, Orev doubled over and dropped into a nearby chair.

"Be reasonable, Reb Pinkas." Yussel's voice lowered to a whisper. "The children have already signed the marriage contract. When Devorah has recovered from the beating, I'll marry them. A nice quiet ceremony."

Orev's eyes darted from Yussel to Pinkas. "Recovered from the beating?"

"You expect me to agree?" Fists balled at his sides, Pinkas leaned toward the rabbi. "Just like that?"

"Soft answer be dammed!" Itzak had restrained himself as long as he could. The time for reasoning with this madman had passed. He gave Pinkas a rough shove and wedged himself between him and the rabbi.

"Recovered?" Orev repeated and leaped off his chair.

"Why don't we take him outside for a little convincing?" Gavrel rolled up his sleeves and then grabbed Pinkas' arm.

With a grin, Itzak took hold of Pinkas' other arm. "Yes, Orev, when she has recovered. Ask your papa what gave him the right to beat a helpless fifteen year old girl with child?"

"Papa? You *hit* Devorah?"

"I did it for your own good, Son. You don't want to be matched up to a harlot."

"Stop calling her that, Papa!"

Together, Itzak and Gavrel dragged Pinkas from dilapidated house. Screaming threats and curses, he writhed in their grasp.

Once they reached the woods, Gavrel let go and kicked Pinkas to his knees. Itzak threw the first punch to Pinkas' nose. It crunched under his knuckles. Gavrel followed his lead with a right to Pinkas' left eye.

Orev's drenched nightshirt clung to him. He stood back, mouth agape, making no move to rescue his father.

Itzak and Gavrel continued to pummel Pinkas.

"Enough," shouted Gavrel as he caught Itzak's fist in midair.

Itzak stopped and stared at his own bruised knuckles. "I'm no better than a Cossack."

Exhausted and heart sore, he allowed Gavrel and Orev to drag Pinkas back into the house. They dropped him on his back in the mud.

With gentle calm, Yussel rubbed his palms together. "My sons, perhaps Reb Pinkas is ready to agree to a wedding. Yes?"

"I know the authorities." Pinkas wiped blood from his nose on his sleeve. "I'll see to it you are punished for this crime."

"It's your word against ours. We saw you fall down a flight of stairs. We tried to help you but it was too late." Gavrel winked. "Right, Reb Itzak?"

"So drunk he couldn't keep his balance." Clasping his brother-in-law's hand high in the air, Itzak grinned.

"Orev?" Pinkas looked to his son.

"You should be more careful on those steps, Papa."

"Rabbi?"

"To tell the truth, Pinkas, I never saw a thing."

## Chapter Seventeen

The fragrance of fresh baked bread filled Evron's tiny home. Potato latkes fried in chicken fat added a buttery aroma.

Ulrich's stomach gurgled with anticipation. Sitting cross-legged on the floor with Tuli and Zelig, he spun a clay top called a *dreidel* between his fingers. He read off the Hebrew letters inscribed on each of its four sides. *"Noon, gimmel, hey, sheen.* Did I pronounce them right, Teacher?"

"Perfect." Cheeks flushed from working over a hot stove, Havah set two loaves of Hollah on the table. "I'm so glad you could stay and celebrate Hanukkah with us."

The quintessential rabbi, Zelig pointed to each letter on the dreidel. "'Nes *gadol hayah sham.* That means 'A great miracle happened there.'"

With arms full of plates and cutlery, Ruth and Rukhel followed Havah. As they set the table, they fluttered around it, cooing like excited pigeons. It was difficult for Ulrich to tell where one left off and the other began. Even their voices were identical.

"Hanukkah is all about the Macaroons' victory over their enemies in ancient days…It was a miracle…The oil in the temple menorah burned for eight whole days…That's why we light the candles for eight nights."

"It's Maccabees not macaroons!" Zelig rolled his eyes.

"We're lighting the second candle tonight." Ruth, or maybe Rukhel, held up two fingers.

"I wish we had a piano." Havah folded cloth napkins and set them by each plate. "What's Hanukkah without music? Did you bring your flute, Professor?"

"What flute?"

"The one I've heard you play. It was like an angel's song. It would sound nice with Evron's clarinet, don't you think?"

"Havah, rest those weary feet. The twins can finish here." Katya emerged from the kitchen with a huge platter of latkes balanced on her palm.

Her teeth clamped over her lower lip, Havah grasped the back of a chair for support and then sat. Untying her high-top shoes she rubbed her swollen ankles.

"Little Sister, you should let Itzak make that cane for you."

Although Havah did not give a verbal reply, her frown said it all. Ulrich wished there was something he could do for her. If only he could hire a specialist who could restore her foot. Alas, there were some things his ridiculous wealth could not purchase.

"It's sundown," announced Evron, "time to light the *Shabbes* candles. And we have a special treat. Havah's singing the blessings tonight." Over his shoulder, Evron looked out the window, set his mending aside and clapped his hands.

"I get to light the Hanukkah menorah." Zelig raced Tuli to the food laden table. In the midst of scurrying children, Ulrich rose off the floor and found a place between the twins.

Illuminated by candlelight, her hair covered with a lace scarf, Havah stood at the head of the table. She reminded Ulrich of a haloed Madonna. Three times she passed her hands over the flames with the fluid grace of a prima ballerina. Her voice, filled with passion and innocence, caressed his ears.

When she finished he whispered, "Amen."

## Chapter Eighteen

Poised to knock on the door, Ulrich thought better of it. Instead he tiptoed past a cabinet full of apothecary bottles and entered the surgery. Mesmerized by the music and the tableau before him he found a chair and sat, careful not to disturb the musician. Nikolai reclined in a bentwood rocker, his feet propped on his treatment table, eyes shut, a flute pressed below his smiling lips.

When he finished playing, he set the flute on his lap. "What can I do for you, Ulrich? Did you scratch your finger? Your knee? My office hours are clearly posted on the outside door."

"I'm your landlord and dinner's served."

"Is there anything else you wanted?" Nikolai opened his eyes.

"That was Bach's Sonata in A minor. I see you still play as well as ever. I feared the fire might've gone out after all these years."

"Never."

"Havah heard you. She thought it was me."

"Who cares what she thinks?" Nikolai dismantled his flute and laid the sections in a velvet lined case on the treatment table. Clasping the lid shut, he picked up his spectacles and slipped them on.

"You disappeared without a trace after your wife left you. I thought we were friends. You could have at least told me you where you were going. Now, after five years, you return to Kishinev? And at that I would not have known had I not happened upon you on the street."

"I left you a note."

"'Farewell. Will write soon.' You never did. After all we'd been through together. Why?"

"I couldn't let that witch kidnap my son like that. I had to find him."

"Did you find him?

"No."

Chapter Nineteen

Ulrich's house had so many rooms it was impossible to clean it all in one day. After the first month of trying and frustrating herself Havah developed a system. Each day she chose a wing of the three story mansion and cleaned it from top to bottom. Thursday was her favorite, for that was the day she spent in the library.

Sun poured through the long windows on either side of the bookcases that flanked the fireplace. The magnificent chandelier glittered and cast sparkling rainbows on the high ceiling. She took her feather duster from her tool bucket. The sooner she finished her appointed tasks the sooner she could cuddle up to a book in one of the red chairs.

At the piano, hunched over a pile of sheet music on his lap, Ulrich greeted her with a warm smile. "If I'm in your way, I'll move. I can always sort through this later. My concert's not until next week. Do you like Chopin?"

"What's that?"

"What's Chopin? *What's* Chopin?" With a sudden frown, he slapped the piano bench. "Sit, Fraulein!"

"You're angry with me." Never before had he raised his voice to her. Trembling, she went to the bench.

"Forgive me. I didn't mean to frighten you." His voice softened and he chuckled.

Still clutching the feather duster, she sat beside him. "My work…I'm not finished…I should…"

"*Blödsinn!* Remember, Havah, I'm your boss and I say that your education is of the utmost importance." He seized the duster and flung it. It bounced across the polished wood floor and stopped under a chair.

"Sir." With a look of disdain directed at Havah, Anzya peeked around the double doors. "How many should I plan on for dinner?"

"Twelve."

"As you wish, sir." As she shut the doors she muttered something about *meshuggenah goyim* and spoiled princesses.

"Now, where was I? Your education...Frederic Chopin." Ulrich cleared his throat and poised his hands over the keys. "He was one of the world's greatest composers. His life was short but his influence great. Nocturne in C-sharp Minor was my Valerica's favorite. Her life was also short. She said this piece took her to far off places. Close your eyes and see where it takes you."

From the first resounding chords a flood of emotion flowed through Havah like a river current. In a moment she was both callow child, alive with anticipation, and wizened matron, bone weary and full of years. Her mother's voice lulled and comforted her with a song about raisins and almonds. She saw her father's face, half illuminated by candle flame as he poured over volume after volume of Talmud. Arel approached from the shadows, tall and thin. His gray eyes devoured her. His tender lips kissed her.

The doorbell interrupted the last few bars. Arel's image dissolved. Havah blinked, open her eyes and sprang off the bench.

"They're early." An odd half smile on his lips, Ulrich rose from the bench and hurried to the front door.

"They?" Her curiosity mounted as she followed close behind. He swung open the heavy door.

"It's cold out here! If I have to wait much longer I'll turn into a block of ice!" Itzak trotted in place on the porch, rubbing his hands up and down along his arms.

"My good friend!" Ulrich embraced him. "Come in! Come in!"

"You were expecting maybe the Czar?"

A familiar tapping sound came from behind him. Havah held her breath when the rabbi shuffled to the door. He tilted his head and smiled. "My little scholar. Is there, perhaps a greeting for an old blind man?"

Chapter Twenty

From the beginning Havah learned two things about her employer. One was his propensity to throw a party for any reason at a moment's notice. The other was his unusual love and respect for Jewish people. There was more to it than his claim to a Jewish grandmother. Havah suspected her to be a fabrication. Nonetheless he studied Hebrew and Midrash with a rabbinic student's passion.

Three weeks in planning, Yussel's arrival in Kishinev to visit with Havah, gave Ulrich the perfect opportunity to honor Yussel and to have a celebration with both Abromovich families. Anzya served a meal fit for aristocracy on Ulrich's finest china. All the while she eyed his guests with disdain even after he invited her to join them.

"Wonderful dinner, Professor Dietrich." Yussel sipped wine from the crystal glass. "Who'd ever believe the best Kosher meal I've had in years would be in a Christian's home?"

"Anzya's a marvel." Ulrich winked at Havah.

Earlier that day the marvel threw a saucepan at her. It missed Havah by inches only to hit Ulrich when he entered the kitchen for his breakfast. Why he did not fire the old crone baffled Havah.

With a shrug, Havah put Anzya out of her mind and turned to Shayndel. "You told your father I was here, didn't you? Did you tell anyone else?"

"My daughter told me nothing." Yussel leaned back in his chair. "I listen to what isn't said. Since when does Itzak take his wife and children on dangerous journeys just to deliver furniture? Not just once, but many times in the past year."

"Havah, come home." Shayndel's blue eyes pleaded across the table. "It's safe now. Orev and Devorah moved to Odessa to work in his uncle's print shop."

"What about Reb Pinkas?"

"He's gone." A grimace shadowed Itzak's face. "The day after Orev left Gavrel found his body in the river."

Shayndel grabbed her hand. "Auntie Fruma misses you so much and Uncle Hershel doesn't look well these days."

"Reb Yussel, Itzak says you've stepped down as rabbi." Havah wound her shawl fringe around her pinkie finger.

"I'm old and tired. It's time to make way for a younger man."

"Arel?"

"Who else?"

"I can never go back."

****

After dinner Ulrich led his guests to the ballroom. Itzak and Evron helped him push the sofas against the walls so the children could play or dance without obstacles. Havah plopped down on the sofa closest to the piano so she could watch the professor's elegant hands.

Once the furniture was moved Ulrich sat at the piano and ran his long fingers over the keys, making them trill from low to high notes. "Shall we?"

Itzak raised his violin and tucked it under his chin. "Do one legged ducks swim in circles?"

Evron held his clarinet to his lips. "At the ready, Professor."

With an arm slung over the piano's rim, Dr. Nikolai leaned back in his chair, one foot resting on his opposite knee. Havah blinked and pointed to the flute in his lap. "So it was *you*!"

"Surprised?" He pursed his lips.

"Allow me to explain." Ulrich grinned at Nikolai. "You all know Kolyah as a physician but what you don't know is that he is a highly trained flautist and my closest friend since our Heidelberg University days. I hope you don't mind my inviting him to join us tonight."

"A tailor with a clarinet, a cabinetmaker with a fiddle, a doctor with a flute and a professional pianist, we're the perfect quartet." Itzak plucked his violin strings.

"Gentlemen, Kolyah's not used to our music so we might have to slow it down for him. Shall we begin with *Khosid Dance*?"

"It just so happens I know that one." Nikolai sent Ulrich a sidelong glance. "I can keep up with you any day of the week."

"*Eyn und Zvay und Dray!*" Itzak counted and they began to play the lively folk music.

True to his claim, Nikolai kept up with no problem. Ruth and Rukhel were first to leap to the center of the room. Shayndel stood and tugged Havah's hand.

"Let's dance, Little Sister!"

"I can't." Tucking her foot between the cushions and yanking back her hand, Havah pressed her back against the sofa.

To her surprise, Yussel grasped her shoulder. "If I can. You can."

Reluctantly, Havah rose and followed him with halting steps. Shayndel took her hand and Tuli took Yussel's. The twins' braids bounced over their shoulders as they twirled and hopped.

Their eyes twinkled like the crystal chandelier above them. "Auntie Havah! You're dancing!"

Although far from graceful with her hobbling attempts to skip, Havah felt almost whole until she tripped over Velvil. He began to cry. The music stopped and a circle of concerned faces hovered over her.

"I'm all right."

"Let your physician be the judge." Dr. Nikolai swept her up in his arms and lowered her onto the nearest sofa. He untied her shoes and squeezed her ankles. "Does this hurt?"

"No more than usual."

Once satisfied there were no substantial injuries, he turned and took the crying baby from Katya. Sitting back in his chair, the doctor pressed Velvil's pudgy cheek against his own. His square jaw softened and his eyes focused on something beyond the immediate.

"You're okay, *Solnyshko.*"

Havah could not help but stare as Dr. Nikolai laid the child across his lap. Taking off his spectacles, he set them on the piano, pressed the flute to his lips and played the opening notes of a Yiddish lullaby. Violin, clarinet and piano joined in, rounding out the melody. Velvil's cries subsided.

## Chapter Twenty-one

The relentless sun beat against Fruma Ya'el face. She reached out her arm for her husband but found only an empty bed. He was probably up rereading Havah's letter which had came in Itzak's mail only the day before and already Hershel had read it to her eleven times. The last time he put a tune to it and sang it as a lullaby. "Havaleh's alive, alive, alive, lai lai lai lai live."

Stretching her stiff arms and legs, she arched her back, coaxed open her eyes and placed her feet on the cold floor. "Reb Yussel will be so pleased to hear about Havah when he returns from Kishinev."

She put on her slippers and padded to the kitchen to put on a pot of coffee. No sign of her husband. Perhaps he went to the bathhouse. She slapped her forehead with her palm and shook her head.

"How could I forget? It's Friday. He has an early meeting at the synagogue." She grinned and returned to the bedroom to change out of her nightclothes.

Once she finished the outside chores, Fruma Ya'el set about her daily dusting and sweeping. Humming a tune, she opened the study door. Her voice stuck in her throat like thick porridge. Books and papers littered the floor. Her husband, known for his loud snoring, slumped over his desk without a sound. With trembling fingers she poked his shoulder several times. It felt like cold stone under his nightshirt.

"Hershel?" She raised her voice. "Hershel, wake up!"

The silence roared in her ears.

Sinking beside him, she dug her fingernails into his arm and tugged. He fell sideways off the chair and landed with a thud, Havah's note crumpled in his hand. Fruma Ya'el sat on the floor and cradled his head in her lap, her tears splashing into his glazed green eyes.

## Chapter Twenty-two

"Floh-versh…fla…Ooooh." Havah slammed her English primer shut and flung it to the floor.

"The word is pronounced much like 'plow-er' only with an 'f.' Ulrich took a rose from a vase on the mantel and waved it under her nose. "Flow-er."

"Who am I fooling? I'm never going to America."

"What's really vexing you?"

"Nothing."

"Talk to me. I won't move until you do. I'm a good listener. Just ask my dog, Franz. I listen to him all the time when he tells me his troubles. It's tough to be a dog. He's a Romanian sheepdog you know and he's fallen madly in love with Gigi, a French Poodle down the way. Alas, she doesn't return his affection." Ulrich dropped to the floor and sat cross legged in front of her, propping his elbows in his lap.

"You don't have a dog."

"No, but I made you smile." He fished a white handkerchief from his waistcoat and dabbed her cheeks.

"I'm all alone."

"You hurt my feelings."

"Quit teasing me."

His smile faded. "Forgive me. Heartache should not be the subject of jest. And I know just what you need." He stood and nodded toward the piano. "'Music has charms to soothe the savage breast, to soften rocks or bend a knotted oak.'"

"What does that mean?"

"It means we're finished with your English lesson for today. It's ime for your first piano lesson."

Her fingers tingled with anticipation. Momentarily forgetting her grief at Uncle Hershel's passing, she followed the professor and sat beside him.

"This one is middle C, where it all begins." He positioned her hands over the keys and pressed her index finger down. The note rang sweet in her ears.

He propped open a book on the piano and showed her how the dots and lines on the page corresponded to the ivory keys. Within minutes music became a new language for her. She followed the notes on the page up and down the staff with her fingers. "C-E-G-B-D, C-A-F-D I did it. Now teach me Chopin's Nocturne, please."

"Not so fast, my little prodigy. Practice your scales, bass and treble clef, every day until you can whip through them, then..." He turned the page. "...I'll teach you this simplified version of 'Brahms' Lullaby.' Havah? Are you listening?"

Although she had dusted it many times, a faded photograph in a silver frame caught her attention. A woman with pale curls around her face smiled at her from under a lace bridal veil. She lifted the picture from the table beside the piano.

"What was she like?"

"My Valerica." He took the picture from her. Then, holding it to his chest, he propped an elbow on the piano and rested his head on his hand. "Kolyah introduced us."

"Dr. Nikolai?"

"She was his wife's best friend. Do you believe in love at first sight, Havah?"

Not waiting for an answer, he continued. His spirit seemed to travel to a distant time and place. Tears shimmered in his eyes. "Valerica Dietrich. She was always the picture of fashion. But, if you ask me, she could've worn flour sacks and still have turned heads.

"After I graduated from the University of Heidelberg I went to teach at the Royal College of Music in London. She detested England and never could grasp the language. She missed her family. So I resigned my position and we settled here.

"She was with child by then." He hesitated. "She labored for several hours before…she was too small, Kolyah said. My daughter would be eleven, the same age as Ruth and Rukhel Abromovich, had she lived.

"She had music in her eyes." He kissed the photograph and returned it to the table. "I keep her beside me for inspiration."

Unnerved by the depth of his sorrow, Havah counted the knots in the carpet beneath the piano. "Did Mrs. Derevenko die too?"

"Why do you ask?"

"Dr. Nikolai's never mentioned her."

"Nor will he. As far as I know she's still alive. That one had a roving eye. She left him for another man and took their six-year-old son with her."

"That's why he dislikes women, isn't it?"

"You're very perceptive, Havah."

"But *one* woman hurt him. He shouldn't hate all of us."

"Sometimes that's all it takes." He stretched his arms over his head, lowered them to his sides and stood. "If you'll excuse me I have other matters to attend to."

Stooped like a weary old man he walked from the room. Havah shook her head. "It's as the Holy Book says, *'The rich and the poor meet, the Almighty is the maker of both.'*"

## Chapter Twenty-three

*"Do you think we will be happy together forever, Ari?" Eleven-year-old Gittel grabbed thirteen-year-old Arel's cap and tossed it in the air.*

*"Silly little girl!" He picked up his cap and pulled one of her red braids. "You had better learn to mind your manners or I shall have to spank you!"*

*"You will not spank me, Arel Gitterman! If you do I'll tell and your papa will take a strap to your own behind!" She laughed and ran from him.*

*Watching her run down the hill, he called after her. "You can run away now, Gitteleh! But one day you'll be my wife and then you'll find out how hard my hand is!"*

"Ari?"

Arel woke with a start. Gittel's angelic face glowed in the golden light suffused the bedroom. A soft breeze blew through the open window and ruffled her shoulder length curls.

"I'm glad you're letting it grow." He wrapped a scarlet lock around his finger, pulled her down and kissed her lips.

"You were laughing in your sleep." She snuggled against him. "You were dreaming about Havah weren't you?"

Arel followed his unborn child's movements with his fingertips. Then he threw his arm around her bulging stomach and pressed his lips to the base of her fragrant neck. Desire overwhelmed him.

"*You* have ravished my heart, my sister, my bride."

## Chapter Twenty-four

"Why is this night different from all other nights?" Five-year-old Reuven recited the traditional four questions asked by the youngest child at the Seder, the celebratory meal of Passover.

"On all other nights we eat leaven and *matzo*, unleavened bread. On this night we eat only *matzo*." After Yussel gave the traditional answers he tapped Reuven with his cane. "Well done, Grandson. You've been studying."

Reuven grinned at Gavrel. "Papa helps me."

"How many times do I have to tell you? He's our brother-in-law, not our papa," said Lev.

Yussel poked Lev with his cane and patted Reuven's head. "He's a good man, your *papa*."

The lengthy ceremony continued with Yussel telling the story of the Israelites' flight from Pharaoh's tyranny in Egypt and how they were saved by the outstretched arm of the Almighty.

Arel's stomach growled in anticipation of the meal the women had spent an entire day preparing. He fidgeted like a child. Roasted chicken and savory potatoes tantalized him.

He remembered Papa spanking him for sneaking a piece of chicken during the Seder when he was only three. His mother scolded Yussel, saying a young child should not have to sit and listen to the rabbi drone on and on.

Beside him Gittel let out a soft cry. Her white face contrasted her crimson wig. "Is it supposed to hurt this much?"

"How long have you been having pains?" Fruma Ya'el stopped Yussel's recitation in midsentence.

"Since this morning."

"Forgive me, Rebbe." Fruma Ya'el rose from her chair and took Gittel's hand. "This child is impatient."

With a broad smile, Yussel raised his wine glass. "Nu? The Red Sea will have to part after my grandchild's born. *L'Chaim!*"

****

"Mama, something's wrong." Gittel clutched her stomach while Shayndel helped her out of her clothes and into her nightgown.

"Nonsense, Gittel. How many babies have you had to make you such an expert?" Fruma Ya'el pulled back the blanket. "Into bed with you."

"Mamaaaa." Gittel wailed and doubled over. Liquid splattered the floor.

"Your water's broken."

"Soon then." With a tenuous smile on her pallid lips Gittel settled into bed.

Shayndel's face blanched. She grasped Fruma Ya'el's forearm and pointed to blood seeping into the cracks of the floor. She sat and squeezed Gittel's hand. "Yes, little sister. Soon you'll hold your little one to your breast and you'll forget the pain. Trust me. I had two at once."

Fruma Ya'el swallowed hard to keep her fear at bay. "Do...do you and Arel have names picked out for my first grandchild?"

"If it's a boy we're going to name him Hershel."

"Papa would like that. Now let's see how close we are." She reached inside Gittel's body, held her breath, and then forced a smile. "Your baby wants to kick his way out."

"Am I going to die?"

"Of course not!" Shayndel mopped Gittel's forehead with a wet cloth. "Reuven was born feet first and Tova didn't die, did she?"

Gittel's scream ravaged Fruma Ya'el's soul. How could she tell her daughter the truth she would learn for herself all too soon?

****

His wife's painful cry from the upstairs bedroom tormented Arel. He covered his ears and laid his head on the table. Yussel's soothing voice did little to comfort him.

"These things take time. Gittel's young and strong."

Again she cried out. A strained hush settled over the men when her cry escalated to a shrill scream.

Itzak's forced laugh sounded like a lost lamb bleating for his mother. "It's nothing, Arel. Remember how Shayndel carried on when she had the twins? Gittel will be—"

At that moment Arel caught a glimpse of Shayndel rushing down the hallway with an armload of blood-soaked sheets. He leaped off his chair and followed her out to the yard. When she spun around to face him he read the verdict in Shayndel's eyes. He turned, bolted up the stairs and burst into the bedroom with Shayndel close behind begging him to stop.

"Out!" Fruma Ya'el shook her finger at him.

"No, Ari. Stay." Gittel's colorless face glistened with sweat. He shuddered to his knees beside the bed and grasped her hand.

"The baby! He's coming!" With Shayndel's help Gittel sat up and leaned forward. At the same time she gouged her nails into Arel's wrist leaving a bloody trail.

"Push hard!" Fruma Ya'el hollered.

Arel's fingers throbbed in Gittel's grip. She grunted and shrieked. Suddenly she let go and fell back against the pillows.

At the end of the bed, Fruma Ya'el bent over a still infant. She unwound the cord coiled around its neck and clipped it with her birthing shears. Then she held her ear to its mouth.

"Cry, baby boy. Please, please cry." Grabbing him by his ankles she held him upside down and slapped his bottom again and again. The sound rang hollow in Arel's ears.

In a final act of desperation she shook the pale blue infant and slapped his face. And again. Only ear-splitting, devastating, excruciating silence answered.

Arel felt empty and helpless. He had a son, a son who would never know the joy of Torah and Talmud, a son who would never kiss his father or hear his mother laugh.

Gittel's voice was barely audible. "Give him to me."

"No, Gitteleh, you mustn't. You'll tempt the evil eye." Fruma Ya'el dropped to her knees still clutching the lifeless baby.

"Nonsense." Arel took the tiny body from her and laid it in Gittel's arms.

"Promise me…" She struggled to speak. "…you'll find…my sister. Give her a…good life."

"I don't want her."

"Promise!" She grasped his collar, her green eyes wide.

"I promise." The words choked him.

Her limp hands slipped from his shirt. With his fingertips he closed her vacant eyes. She was his chatterbox—never gave him a moment's peace.

## Chapter Twenty-five

Fruma Ya'el's dining room table overflowed with food. Her house teemed with people who came to offer condolences and sit *shivah.* Just four months before the same well-wishers filled her parlor to honor Hershel. The pungent lentil and onion odor threatened to choke her.

"Won't you eat something, Auntie?" Shayndel curved her arm around her shoulder.

"Maybe later."

A round loaf of bread to signify the circle of life sat in the middle of the table. Fruma Ya'el backed away from it. Circle of life? What life? Her Benjamin's life spanned a few months beyond two years. Gittel's only nineteen.

"Auntie, I haven't seen you take a bite in three days."

"Shayndel, leave me be! Go tend to your children, your *living* children."

The women surrounded Fruma Ya'el. Their kisses, like insect bites, stung her cheeks. Their faces blurred into one. Their mouths became open empty caves that echoed nonsensical, albeit, well-meaning words.

"Poor Gittel. So young."

"A tragedy."

"Is there anything I can do?"

"At least you have Arel."

Hunched over with elbows resting on his knees and his head propped between his hands, Arel looked much older than his twenty years. Refusing even to pray with the *minyan,* he had not spoken or slept since his wife's death. The angry scratches on his wrist appeared to be fresher than four days ago.

Like a tree full of starlings, the women continued their chatter.

"A good son."

"A good husband."

"We should all be blessed with such a man."

"I heard he took up with that crippled girl before the wedding."

"She had some strange ideas."

"Good riddance."

Swallowing the acid rising from her empty stomach, Fruma Ya'el stumbled from the room. Unable to see through the mist in her eyes she staggered through her bedroom door. Collapsing on the bed she shuddered and choked on her grief until no more tears would come.

Her wedding gown, like a shroud, hung in the open wardrobe in the corner. Three generations had worn it.

"There's no one left." She rose and went to the closet. Slipping the dress off the hanger she cradled it in her arms and burrowed her head in the lace folds of the bodice. Gittel's scent still clung to it.

Kneeling beside the bed, she pulled her shears from her birthing basket. They still bore her daughter's bloodstains. She curved her fingers through the handle loops and slid a dress sleeve between the blades.

*Snip.* It fell to the floor. "My sister Gittel. My right arm."

*Snip snip.* The other sleeve dropped beside the first. "Charles. My dreams."

*Snip snip snip.* She sliced through the bodice. "Hershel. My husband."

The gleaming shears sliced through the satin sash with ease. "Gittel. My daughter. My consolation."

She cut the skirt in half. "Benjamin. My angel."

Her chest constricted. She cut the pieces into still smaller pieces until there was nothing left but a pile of satin and lace scrap. "Havah. My heart."

With both hands she poised the shears over her breasts and shut her eyes. One plunge into the right spot and it would be over.

Someone knocked on the door. "Auntie, are you all right?"

Her hand jerked. "Fine, Shayndel. I'm fine." The shears slit her blouse and gashed her skin. She gazed at the spreading stain. "A scratch. Nothing but a scratch."

Despair enveloped her like a thick blanket. She turned and hurled the scissors at the mirror over her dresser. It shattered beneath the mourning drape.

"Oh God, kill me now!"

## Chapter Twenty-six

Enthroned on one of the brocade chairs, in the library Havah pulled Itzak's letter from her pocket. Although Evron gave it to her early that morning she waited until late afternoon when she had finished her work to read it. Here she would not be interrupted by nattering children or fussy babies demanding to be held.

If she calculated correctly the letter announced the new Gitterman baby. She tried to prepare herself for what it might say. "Arel and Gittel have a son. He's beautiful, he looks just like his father" or perhaps, "The baby is a lovely girl with red hair, she's so sweet and looks just like Gittel."

There might even be a note from Gittel herself. Every so often she would insert little cards and sketches into Itzak's envelope. Havah missed her constant chatter that sometimes irritated her. She yearned for a time when Arel did not matter.

She ripped open the envelope and unfolded the note. Itzak's scrawled handwriting came into focus. She felt paralyzed,. Surely she had misread his chicken scratches. She read the letter again. After she reread it three times more she crumpled it and let it drop to the floor.

Sliding off the chair, she stood and went to the piano where she sat on the bench and mournfully picked out the scales Ulrich had taught her. The notes echoed hollow and sour. Unable to focus on music she stared at a crystal vase filled with fresh cut lilacs on a nearby table.

They were Gittel's favorite. Varied shades of lavender blurred before her eyes.

A moment later flowers littered the hardwood floor. She screamed and collapsed amid the glass shards, pounding the floor with her fists.

"Havah, what on earth is the matter?" Ulrich rushed through the door and dropped to his knees beside her.

In a burst of frantic energy, she picked up pieces of broken glass. "Oh, dear! What a mess I've made. I broke your vase. I'll pay for it. Look at your clothes. They're ruined and it's my fault."

"Stop it! You're raving."

"Go away." Suddenly weak and drained, she huddled under the piano.

"Must I beat it out of you?" He gently grasped her shoulders.

"I dare you."

Releasing her, he picked up the crumpled letter and smoothed it out. His eyes misted as he read. "Let me take you home. You should be with family at a time like this."

"What family? I have no family."

"You may stay here tonight if you wish."

"Yes. Please."

"Anzya, please put fresh linens on the bed in Frau Dietrich's room."

Havah lifted her head. Anzya stood in the doorway, a pasty scowl on her drab face. How long had the old biddy been watching?

"With all due respect, Sir, I'm your cook." Her pale eyes bored through Havah. "If your precious chambermaid's going to sleep in your wife's bed, let *her* fetch fresh linens."

## Chapter Twenty-seven

Loath to awaken, Havah nestled her head against the goose down pillow. Finally she opened her eyes and shielded them with her hand from the bright light pouring through windows. Framed by pink lace curtains, they stretched from floor to ceiling. Patterned Indian carpets graced the burnished hardwood floors. Pink flowers festooned the wallpaper. A daybed piled with a folded quilt and pillows sat beside the four poster canopy bed.

Were it not been for her throbbing headache she would have enjoyed the luxury of having an entire feather mattress to herself. She glanced at the grandfather clock in the corner by the window. Eight o'clock.

Familiar footsteps clicked out an angry beat across the floorboards. "So you're awake, Princess."

Anzya loomed over her with her usual churlish expression, Havah's dress draped over her arm. "When you are up to it there's coffee and biscuits in the kitchen. I'm going home now. Professor Dietrich's letting me take the day off since I stayed with you all night."

"Thank you, Anzya. That was very kind of you."

"Kindness has nothing to do with it. It's improper for a young girl to spend the night in a man's home without a chaperone. Besides, he paid me."

"Oh." Havah sat up and swung her legs over the side of the bed. She walked to the full length mirror and looked at her reflection. "Valerica must have been my size. Her nightgown fits perfectly. She certainly liked pink, didn't she?"

"I wouldn't know. I never met her." Anzya tossed Havah's dress on the bed.

"Ulrich said this used to be their bedroom but after she died he couldn't bear to sleep in it so he moved to another room." She pressed her hands against her face but could not squelch her tears.

"I'm truly sorry about your sister. But she's better off than the rest of us. At least she had the good fortune to die *with* her baby." Anzya turned and left the room.

Havah rubbed her eyes, dressed, and braided her hair. She stared at her reflection again. Her puffy eyes matched the pink décor. She pinched her wan cheeks to bring some color to them and finally decided she was presentable.

Opening her locket as she did every morning, she kissed the picture.

"Kissing her picture won't bring her back." Anzya appeared in the doorway and glared at her.

"I thought you left." Maybe someday she would explain the locket to the old harridan, but not today. She snapped it shut.

"How can you be so friendly to him? How can you let him touch you?"

"Ulrich? Why don't you like him?"

"He's a *goy*. Isn't that reason enough?"

"Anzya, what happened to you to make you so bitter?"

"Do you really want to know?"

"Yes." Havah turned from the mirror and sat on the bed.

"I was young and pretty like you. I had a husband who would have made the sages blush with his insight. Such a scholar he was. And I had children. Beautiful children. My son, seven years old and just like his father. My daughter, not yet a year old with eyes as bright as candles at midnight.

"One night they came, those monsters! They ripped my baby from my breast and robbed me of my womanhood. They beat my children and my husband to death with clubs and crowbars. If that wasn't bad enough, if that was not cruel enough, they let me live."

Anzya's lashless eyes flashed and she poked Havah's chest with a scarred finger. "I hope you never see what I've seen, Princess. May you never know what it is to be dead while you live."

## Chapter Twenty-eight

"Higher! Higher! Let me soar with eagles."

Fresh spring air ruffled Havah's hair. As the swing arced through the air she almost believed if she slid off she would sprout wings and fly.

"Any higher, my dear, you'll vault over the fence and I'll have to search every street in Kishinev for you." Ulrich seized the ropes and brought her to a halt. He fished his watch from his vest pocket. "Katya will serve my head on a platter if I'm late taking you and Tuli home. And you, my glassy-eyed Fraulein, are tipsy."

"I am, too." A loud belch erupted from her throat and out her mouth before she could stop it. She pressed her fingertips over her lips and giggled. "You promised me one more mug."

"So I did."

She followed him to one of the many park vendors who sold kvass, a drink made from brown bread, mint and raisins. He purchased two mugs and handed her one. Anything made with raisins had to be good.

*"L'Chaim!"* Thirsty from the heat, she gulped it down and gave the mug back to the vendor.

*"Prost!"* Ulrich did the same.

The bright colors of the city park danced before her. Red, pink and yellow roses, like royalty, sat on their well pruned thrones. Ivy twined around and through the ornate iron fence. Taking deep breaths, she sniffed sugar laden sweets, fruits and various ladies' perfumes. Somewhere beyond a grove of trees an accordion player entertained a boisterous crowd. She waggled her head and tapped her toes in time to the lively folk tune.

"What a perfect day for a festival. I haven't seen that gorgeous smile of yours for weeks."

"I wish the other children could've come. 'Rabbi' Zelig would rather read and Katya insisted the twins stay home to help with laundry."

"Next time I'll make my invitation farther in advance."

"Oh dear, I'm dizzy," said Havah.

"Allow me." Ulrich crooked his arm.

Anzya's words came back to Havah. *"How can you let him touch you? He's a goy..."*

"No! It's not proper."

"Suit yourself." Stuffing his hands in his pocket, Ulrich shrugged.

"I'm sorry I snapped at you." She hobbled beside him, fixing her eyes on the stones along the path.

"You're forgiven. Pity I couldn't convince Anzya to join us. Some fresh air and sunshine might do her some good."

"I'm glad the old grouch stayed home."

"After all she's been through I'd think you of all people would be sympathetic."

"It doesn't give her the right to be hateful and selfish."

"It's easy to love those who love you back."

"Love? How can you speak her name and the word 'love' in the same breath? You've shown her the highest form of charity and she's repaid you with scorn. You treat her like a queen and she practically spits in your face. Even Ram Bam would say you carry forgiveness too far."

"How far is too far, Havah? Seventy times seven?"

Behind them childish squeals split the air. She turned in time to see two boys racing toward them, rolling wooden hoops. Ulrich reached for her arm to pull her out of the way but he was not quick enough.

In a headlong flurry of hoops and colliding children, she tumbled to the pavement. Dazed, she sprawled on the sidewalk in a most unladylike fashion. Grabbing their renegade toys, the boys mumbled faint apologies and disappeared around a cluster of bushes.

"Rapscallions!" Dropping down beside her, Ulrich shook his fist.

Sitting up, she smoothed her skirts over her torn stockings and stinging knees. "How many times seven?"

He blushed like a reprimanded child. "Are you hurt?"

"Only my pride." She brushed sand and pebbles from her skinned palms.

"Our doctor friend can rub some salve into your wounds but your pride will have to heal on its own."

As she struggled to stand a searing pain seized her ankle. She pitched forward and fell to the ground. "Oooow."

"Pardon my impropriety, Fraulein." Scooping her up in his arms, Ulrich carried her to a nearby bench. He laid her on it and then sat, propped her feet on his lap and unhooked the top button on her right shoe. "This one?"

"The other one." She chewed her lower lip. "The good one."

When he unbuttoned and pulled off the left shoe, he grimaced. "I'd better find Kolyah. He and Tuli are probably still on the merry-go-round."

"They're having such a good time. Now I've spoiled the day for everyone."

"Rubbish." He leaned down and kissed her forehead.

His mint and kvass breath on her face stirred her. Bay rum engulfed her like a spicy mist. Her heart somersaulted and pulsated its way to her throat.

"I can't leave the two of you alone for a minute, can I?" Nikolai's voice wedged in between them.

Both relieved and disappointed, she jerked back, clipping her head on the arm of the bench. "Dr. Nikolai. I—I tripped and Ulrich—the professor—he—"

Like a man with a chicken bone lodged in his throat, Ulrich coughed and bolted upright. "It's about time. We were ready to send out a search party."

"So I see." Nikolai raised one eyebrow. "You were sick with worry."

"Look at me! I'm a Derevenko bird." Tuli, perched on Nikolai's shoulders, a huge lollipop in one hand, flapped his arms. The doctor's hat and spectacles all but eclipsed his round face. "Can we ride the merry-go-round again?"

"Twelve times is enough for one day." Nikolai's wide smile and flushed cheeks made him look more like a schoolboy than a staid physician. Had it not been for the omnipresent medical bag in his hand, Havah might not have recognized him.

Kneeling beside the bench, he reached back over his head and lifted his eyeglasses from Tuli's nose. "Dismount, General Rooster."

The boy slid off Nikolai's shoulders. "What happened to your foot, Auntie? It's all puffy and purple."

Dr. Derevenko pushed back his disheveled hair, he curved his hands around her ankle and prodded. Havah grimaced and bit her tongue.

"It's not fractured. It is a nasty sprain, though. You may wish you'd broken it."

He pulled out a roll of gauze bandages from his bag.

"Can I help?" Tuli's brown eyes glittered.

"Wind it tight, Dr. Abromovich." With a father's tenderness, Nikolai guided the boy's hands.

"When I grow up I'm going to be doctor just like you, Dr. Nikolai." Tuli grinned.

With brimming mugs of kvass in hand, two men strolled by. One took a swig and wiped his mouth on his sleeve. "Dogs."

The other waved his glass, sloshing his drink on the pavement. "The world would be a better place without them."

"Christ killers. Lice. Exterminate them all."

Tuli's smile vanished. He huddled against Nikolai. "Can we go home now?"

Chapter Twenty-nine


*Tall and slender, her hair a scarlet avalanche, Gittel chased after a toddler with red curls. When she placed a firefly on his pudgy hand he shrieked with delight. It left his palm, its lambent light lingering in the darkness.*

Suddenly mother and child melted like ice in the summer heat. Outside the lonely house he shared with his mother-in-law, Arel slouched on a chair between Itzak and Yussel. Shayndel and her two-year-old sons took Gittel's place. She shoved a jar into Arel's hand.

"Come catch fireflies with us, Uncle."

A cloth over the mouth of the jar kept the captive insects from suffocating. In frantic desperation two of them thrashed their wings against the glass. Arel felt as though he, too, would suffocate and flung the jar on the rocky ground and watched it shatter.

While Mendel and David raced each other to catch the liberated fireflies Shayndel knelt and swept up as much of the broken glass as she could.

"You couldn't just say no?" she asked.

"This letter says the new rabbi will be here two Sabbaths from now from Yeshiva in Kishinev with his wife and two children." Itzak held a piece of paper up to the light shining through the kitchen window.

"May the Almighty grant them safe travels." Fruma Ya'el settled into a chair beside Yussel. "Sitting outside was a good idea, Itzak. Gittel loved the summer night air. She claimed it helped her digestion after a heavy meal."

Arel dropped his head into his hands.

"Nu?" Yussel turned his face in Itzak's direction. "Does the new rabbi say anything else?"

"Only that he and the new *rebbetzin* are looking forward to meeting their congregation. They are also expecting a third child. They have two little girls and are hoping for a son."

"It seems like only yesterday another rabbi and *rebbetzin* came to Svechka with two little girls," said Fruma Ya'el. "It will seem strange not to have a Gitterman leading the congregation." Yussel poked Arel with his cane. "Are you sure this is what you want? And more important, is it what the Almighty wants?"

Arel grabbed the tip of the cane and pushed it away. "I'm half a man. My heart's just not in it anymore."

"Give yourself some time. Gittel has only been gone three months."

"What difference does it make? The new rabbi's on his way. What's done is done."

The twins, bored with fireflies, leaped into a huge puddle. Mud and water splattered Shayndel's skirts. "David! Mendel! Stop it!"

"Shah!" Yussel laughed. "Let them have their fun. Nobody knows better than little boys how to cool off on a hot summer night."

For a while the children's laughter and splashing of water were the only sounds. The twins filled their hands with mud and plopped it on each other's heads. When David screamed because water dripped into his eyes Itzak dropped the letter and jumped off his chair. He scooped them up and tucked a boy under each arm.

"Let's wash the *shmutz* from you two little *Hassids*."

"Wait, Itzak. Let me bathe them." Fruma Ya'el stood and reached for the boys.

"Are you sure? They're a noisy pair."

"Good! Without Gittel, the walls are talking to themselves." She held out her hands. "Come children. Auntie Fruma will wash you so clean your own mama won't recognize you."

As she disappeared with the twins silence descended like a shroud.

Finally Yussel cleared his throat. "I think it might rain again tonight."

"I hope it cools things down." Itzak sat back down, picked up the new rabbi's letter and folded it into a fan.

Shayndel sat on his lap. "We could use a break in the heat. Don't you agree, Arel?"

Arel looked up and scanned the clear sky as a cursory gesture. Why should he care if it ever rained again?

After what seemed like a fortnight to Arel, Fruma Ya'el returned. "Shayndel, your little men are sound asleep. Bless them. I never met a little boy who could resist a mud puddle. It's a good thing I didn't give Gittel's little nightgowns away, isn't it?"

Arel could stand Fruma Ya'el's chitchat no longer. He jumped from his chair and ran into the woods. Ripping a low branch from a tree he thrashed it until his strength gave out. Exhausted, he dropped to the ground. Over and over, he hit the back of his head against the rough bark of the tree.

"It won't help." Itzak crouched beside him.

"She talks about Gittel as though she's alive."

"It's her way of making peace with her grief. You might feel better if you followed her example and didn't keep so much to yourself."

"I loved her." Arel picked up a large rock, stood and flung it into the night. "But I was unfaithful to her."

"Unfaithful? No one could've been a more devoted husband, not even me!"

"In my head. In my heart. She never had all of me. She knew it and, still, she gave me all of herself."

"Life goes on, little brother. You're young. Almost handsome when you're cleaned up." Maybe it's not too late to find—"

Falling to his knees, Arel clapped his hands over his ears and howled. "Noooo! Don't speak her name. God help me. I've lost them both."

## Chapter Thirty

"I've never been so hot in my life." Fruma Ya'el's scalp itched under her sopping kerchief. She mopped her cheeks with her apron and then stared at the sweat stains. She wished modesty did not demand so many clothes in summer. Her stockings clung to her legs and her petticoat tangled around her ankles.

"Yussel, I'm worried about your son. He does nothing but mope about the house day and night. He doesn't talk. He doesn't laugh. In three months he hasn't even cried."

"He cries." Yussel pointed to his ears and out to the woods where Arel and Itzak had gone moments before.

"Why didn't you stop him, Papa?" asked Shayndel.

"Stop him? Does this old blind man look like he can chase after a young man like your brother?"

"I mean why didn't you stop him from resigning as rabbi?"

"Arel's a grown man."

"After all those years of preparation he throws it all away and you say nothing. He's thinking with his heart now and not his head."

"I agree with his heart."

"How can you say that?"

"Ever since your mama, of blessed memory, left us, Arel has been both my eyes and my shadow."

"He never questioned his calling."

"Exactly." Yussel stamped his cane on the ground, punctuating his strident words. "He never questioned. If

Papa said, 'Arel you will be the rabbi,' Arel said, 'Yes, Papa, anything you say.'"

Conversation stopped when Mendel climbed onto Shayndel's lap. "Mama, Mama. Bad dream."

David followed. "Mama, me hot."

"Why don't I sing you back to sleep?" With Mendel in one arm Shayndel stood and took David's hand.

"Such treasures." Fruma Ya'el followed them with her eyes. She bowed her head and covered her eyes with her hands. "I've never known such loneliness."

Yussel's hand closed around hers. "May I say something? As a friend?"

"Yes, of course."

He coughed, his voice wavering. "We've known each other for a long time, yes?"

"Thirty years."

"Thirty years. I know it's only been six months since Reb Hershel, of blessed memory, has been gone. He was my dearest friend. I miss him so I mean no disrespect."

Although his black hair had turned white years before and his lucent gray eyes no longer saw, he was still strong and handsome. His cheeks reddened and his grip tightened.

"You're lonely. I'm lonely. I'm an old man."

"And I'm so young?"

"I've always admired you, Fruma. My children and my children's children adore you. It's...it's been a long time since I've been with...a...a woman."

"Rabbi, enough with the speech making already! Yes, I will marry you."

## Chapter Thirty-one

"Havah, could you take over for a while?" Katya turned away from the kettle on the iron stove that took up half of the tiny kitchen. She slumped down in a chair, her face as pale as her white cotton blouse.

"Let me send Zelig for Dr. Nikolai." Havah grabbed the long wooden spoon from her hand and stirred the porridge made of kasha and milk so it would not scorch. She took a pinch of cinnamon and threw it into the bubbling cereal. Her empty stomach growled at the sweet aroma. "I wish we had some raisins."

"I'll be fine after I sit for a while. I'm just a little dizzy this morning."

"Up." One-year-old Velvil, dragging his blanket, climbed onto Katya's lap and wrapped his arms around her neck.

"You're hardly a baby anymore." She hugged him and pressed her beaklike nose against his tiny one. "My monthly visitor hasn't visited for almost two months. You tell *me*, little midwife, what does *that* mean?"

"Are you sure?" Havah spooned cereal into eight bowls and set them on the table.

While her children scampered into the kitchen to take their seats Katya winked at Havah with a crooked smile. "I've given birth to five children and she asks if I'm sure!"

"When?"

"Next spring, close to Passover I think."

When Havah left Svechka a year before, she made a pact with herself. Never again would she attach herself to another family. Alas, her plan failed within the first hour of her arrival in Kishinev. Katya and Evron treated her like one of their own, but with another child it would be too crowded. Once more the word 'orphan' beat a somber rhythm against her temples.

"I'll find another place to live as soon...as I...can," said Havah.

"You'll do no such thing. We need you more than ever." Evron burst into the kitchen. Bending down to kiss his wife, he swept Velvil off her lap and hoisted him up onto his shoulders.

"May we have a sister please? There are too many boys in this house." Ruth and Rukhel chattered like excited squirrels, their words tumbling over each other. "Twin girls like us."

"Having a baby is not like ordering a new suit from the tailor. We can't tell the Almighty how many stitches to make or how many buttons to sew." With his youngest son still perched on his shoulders Evron sat down on the chair next to Katya and kissed her cheek.

"My precious bride, you've made me a wealthy man. As wise old King Solomon said, " *'Behold children are an inheritance from the Almighty, the fruit of the womb His reward.'"*

Chapter Thirty-two

*"You are altogether fair, my love."* Arel read the words on the page, but could not concentrate on them.

With its ancient books and its walls stained with the soot of fire and lamplight, his father's library had always been a place of succor. Closing the Bible, he leaned back in his chair and raised the front legs off the floor. He propped his feet on the desk, careful not to kick the oil lamp which gave the room a warm glow.

Tonight he found no solace. He saw only Havah. Her eyes, dark as pitch and round as wagon wheels, teemed with passion. Protracted desires, held at bay for two years, provoked him.

"Arel Gitterman, there you are. Itzak was right." Shayndel entered the room. Nudging his feet off the desk, she set a plate in front of him and clucked her tongue. "You missed supper. The boys are in bed and the dishes are washed. Have you been in here all this time? Papa thought maybe you were over at Gavrel's helping Lev with his Bar Mitzvah readings. Why didn't you come when I called?"

"You know where she is, don't you?"

"She who?" Tucking a napkin into his collar, Shayndel pointed to a thick sandwich piled with roast chicken. "Eat."

Arm in arm, Itzak and Yussel sauntered into the room. Itzak waved a parchment envelope between two fingers. "From Sarah. Came today. Fancy."

Yussel reclined in his overstuffed chair, grasping the armrests. "Read my daughter's letter already."

With a good-natured frown, Fruma Ya'el bustled into the room, her hands on her hips. "You were going to start without me, Old Man?"

He held out his arms. "Old habits. Forgive me, Wife."

"Just this once, Husband." Her smile radiated a joy Arel had never seen on her face.

Although happy for his father's marriage after seventeen lonely years, Arel battled his own emptiness. A solitary man in a room full of couples, he swallowed a lump. "Itzak, please read."

With an exaggerated cough Itzak cleared his throat. "Ahem. *'3 December 1902*

*"'Dear Family,'* That's us. What do you suppose it's like in Kansas City?"

Yussel stamped his foot. "*I* could read it faster."

"Sorry, Papa." Itzak flashed a grin that said he was anything but sorry. "Sarah goes on to say, *'We are looking forward to Hanukkah. Every year I tell Jeffrey and Evalyne about their Zaydeh's special menorah. I hope one day they will see it and him with their own eyes.'"*

"Every time she writes she invites me to come to America."

"Maybe someday you will."

"How? Sprout wings and fly? Keep reading."

*"'We are all well. Jeffrey is a busy boy. When he grows up he wants to play professional baseball. Evalyne loves to climb trees with her brother. She says when she grows up she wants to be a trapeze artist in the circus.'"*

"Baseball? What's that?"

"She doesn't say. Some kind of American musical instrument maybe? Listen to this, *'Not long ago Wolf caught his assistant with his hand in the cash drawer. Now he has more work than he can handle and is looking to hire someone else. What about Arel? It would be a fresh start for him. We've saved enough to pay his way.'"*

"No!" Shayndel sprang off the sofa.

Arel fiddled with a button dangling by a thread from his vest. "A tailor? Me?"

"Why not?" Itzak curled a lock of his beard around his finger. "It's an honorable trade. My brother Evron makes a fair living at it. He's told me more than once how much he needs help and is willing to teach an apprentice. His house is pretty crowded, though, and he can't pay more than room and board." He winked at Shayndel. "It's not nearly as far away as America."

She plopped back down and jabbed her elbow in Itzak's side. Tucking a long strand of hair back under her kerchief, she licked her lips. "Remember how you used to help Sarah with the mending, Arel? When you were ten you were almost as good at it as she was."

"It was a game."

The loose button popped off in Arel's hand. He rolled it between his fingers. Maybe he could be a tailor at that. It would be something to take his mind off Havah.

"Itzak!" Yussel whistled. "Read the letter now, plan Arel's future later."

"*'Love, Sarah!'*" Itzak sang in a falsetto voice and waved the letter like a flag.

"That's it?"

"That's it."

Arel bit into his untouched sandwich. "Mind if I tag along next time you go to Kishinev, Itzak? I'd like to talk to Evron about this tailor business."

Yussel patted Fruma Ya'el's knee. "We should all go."

"Old man, have you lost your mind? If the journey doesn't kill us, the Cossacks will!"

"Wouldn't you like to see Evron and Katya again?" Shayndel picked up a half knitted stocking from her basket beside the sofa. "It's been ten years since they left Svechka to seek their fortune."

"Some fortune." Itzak laughed. "They have very little money with five children and one more on the way."

Yussel smiled and tilted his head. "To some men this *is* a fortune."

Fruma Ya'el's horrified expression softened into a wistful smile. "I brought those two girls into the world, you know. Tiniest babies I've ever seen. Honestly, I didn't think they'd live more than an hour, if that. I've never seen two babies as determined to thrive or more attached to each other. If they weren't in the same cradle they howled. Why, I even caught them sucking each other's thumbs!"

"It's as if Adoshem gave those girls two bodies and one heart." Shayndel's needles gleamed in the lamplight. "What do you say, Mama?"

# Part III

## *MARRY ME*

Chapter One


In Itzak's letter he said that Yussel had married a beautiful widow, but refused to say whom. Itzak only promised that Havah would love her at first sight which ruled out most of the widows Havah remembered in Svechka. Surely not Naomi the seamstress who was a sour woman with an eyebrow that stretched over both of her slits for eyes. Nor could Havah imagine her sweet rebbe with Reyna the watchmaker's widow. Havah had been the victim of the old gossip's rapier tongue more than once.

For Ulrich it was the perfect excuse to throw an extravagant party. His long dining room table had been set with Austrian crystal, fine china and polished silver. Anzya had been cooking for a week. Not only was there a beef roast, but baked chicken and goose as well. A large bowl of potato kugel and more fruits and vegetables than Havah had ever seen in summer, let alone winter, were part of the fare for the evening. Her mouth watered in anticipation.

At Ulrich's invitation, Evron and his family had arrived the day before and slept over so they would be rested for the festivities. They gathered in the ballroom to wait for the guests of honor. Zelig, enthroned like a king on one of the red chairs, had been reading all day. Reuven sat on the floor with Velvil as they rolled a ball back and forth.

Havah paced in front of the sofa where Evron sat beside Katya and asked, "Evron, did Itzak tell you who Rabbi Yussel married?"

"Do you think I would tell you? You know how my little brother is. He'd never forgive me if I divulged his precious secret."

Ulrich sat at the piano between Ruth and Rukhel and showed them where to place their fingers on the keys. "You'll have to take turns," he told them.

Havah leaned over and tapped the center key causing the note to echo throughout the spacious room. "That's middle C. The professor says that's where it all begins."

"Auntie Havah, this is our lesson, not yours." Ruth stuck out her lower lip.

Ulrich's eyes twinkled. "She's been like this all day, as restless as a kitten with a ball of string. I fear any minute now our Havaleh will climb the curtains and hang from the chandelier!"

"Perhaps a sedative is in order." Beside the piano, Dr. Nikolai tuxedoed, for the wedding celebration, polished his flute.

Although Ulrich exaggerated a little, it was true. Excitement and curiosity made it hard for her to sit still. She could not imagine Reb Yussel with a wife.

She crossed her eyes and made a face at the doctor and spun on her heel. Half hobbling, half skipping she went to the parlor and pulled back the long velvet drape. The street was empty.

As she turned to go back to the ballroom someone rapped the brass knocker at the front door. With great effort, she swung it open. "It's about time! I've been waiting for—"

Instead of Yussel and his bride, a strange boy clutching an envelope scowled at her. "I have a letter for Professor Dietrich."

"I'll give it to him."

"*Nyet!* It's for the professor only."

The boy's unmasked disdain frightened her. Would he pull a gun from his pocket and shoot her like the Cossacks who shot her brothers? To her relief, Ulrich, Evron and Dr. Nikolai walked up and surrounded her.

"Is there a problem?" Ulrich took the envelope from the boy, tore it open and read its contents. He frowned and handed it to Nikolai who, in turn, skimmed it, his mouth a taut line over clenched teeth.

Evron reached for it.

Nikolai hesitated. "I don't think—"

Plucking it from his grasp, Evron's perpetual smile faded.

Ulrich's face turned red and his voice rose to a wrathful shout. "Do you expect a tip for delivering this rubbish to my door? Leave now and never show yourself here again!'" Havah feared he would strike the boy. Instead he slammed the door in his face with a ringing crash.

A few moments later another knock sounded at the door. Stuffing the letter into his pocket, Ulrich seized Havah's arm. His flashing eyes sent lightning bolts through her chest.

"Never, never, *never* open this door again. Do you understand?"

The pounding at the door grew louder. Havah huddled against Ulrich. He grasped the knob with one hand and balled his other into a fist. Then with a forceful jerk and a threatening scowl he opened the door.

When Itzak and Shayndel entered the foyer, he peered around them, craning his neck to the right and then to the left. "No one followed you did they?" Satisfied only friends were present his brow relaxed. "You brought the newlyweds?"

"May I present the Rabbi Yussel Gitterman and his dear wife Fruma Ya'el?" Itzak and Shayndel stepped aside in opposite directions, raised their arms and twined their fingers to create an arch. The newlyweds ducked under it. Mendel and David crawled between their legs and raced to the library to find their cousins.

"I don't know why we couldn't have waited until spring, Husband. It's so cold I won't thaw out for months. You—Havaleh!" The bride's brown eyes brimmed. She leaped forward and drew Havah into an embrace. "Itzak and his secrets."

The aroma of cinnamon and homemade soap filled Havah's nostrils. Pulling back she studied Fruma Ya'el. Sorrow had taken a toll, leaving new lines around her mouth and eyes.

"Just like I said, it's love at first sight." Itzak's laughter echoed off the high tiled ceiling.

With a dramatic wave, Ulrich pointed to the spiral staircase leading to the second story. "Havah, show our honored guests to rooms of their choosing. After they've had time to freshen up, a fine wedding dinner awaits, replete with their daughter's delicious Hollah."

Clutching Fruma Ya'el's hand, Havah walked toward the stairs until a familiar voice whispered her name and turned her feet to stone. She let go of Fruma Ya'el's hand and turned to face the door where, arms folded across his chest, Arel stood.

"It's good to see you again...Arel." His name sounded foreign. She forced a smile.

"Is it?" He glowered at Ulrich.

"Herr Gitterman. I've heard so much about you." Ulrich's smile disappeared. He clicked his heels, bowed and turned. "If you'll excuse me, I will leave you to your...reunion." His shoulders sagged as he walked down the hall and slipped through the double doors of the library.

Fruma Ya'el curved her hand around Havah's arm. "Show me the way to our room already. I might get lost in this grand palace."

"So you approve of my…arrangement, little scholar?" Yussel placed his hand on his wife's shoulder.

Torn between wanting to follow Ulrich and wanting to spend time with the mother she had longed for, Havah slipped her arm around Fruma Ya'el's waist. "Very much, Rabbi."

"Tut, tut. To you, my bride is 'Mama'. At least you could call me, maybe, 'Uncle.'?"

"No." She kissed his cheek. "I shall call you Papa."

"You have a new sister, Little Brother." Itzak grabbed Arel's hand and pumped it up and down. "Mazel tov!"

Chapter Two

Fruma Ya'el's mouth ached from smiling. What a night it had been with music, dancing and children. To see Havah, her beautiful daughter, clad in pink silk and fine lace filled her with pride. Fruma Ya'el stacked the serving platters from dinner and carried them to the kitchen.

"May I help you with the dishes, Anzya?"

Steam rose from a kettle boiling on the stove. Hunched over the sink, the other woman grunted. "It's your party. Do whatever you like."

Approaching the sink, Fruma Ya'el set down the dishes. "Dinner was wonderful. I'm only sorry you didn't share it with us."

"I don't eat with their kind." Anzya kept her eyes trained on the soapy water.

"I see." Fruma Ya'el dried a crystal goblet and placed it in the cabinet. "Why do you call my Havah 'Princess'?"

"She's too comfortable with him as if he were a human being and not a *goyisheh* pig."

"He seems nice enough."

"Nice enough to marry your daughter?"

"Havah would never—"

"Wouldn't she? She wears his dead wife's clothes, doesn't she? Furthermore, she has no idea what it is to suffer, other than her handicap of course. Certainly that's why you've pampered her. And, nu? Look at the thanks you got for your troubles. She ran away."

"You don't know her very well, do you?" Fruma Ya'el hurled the towel angrily. It landed in the sink, dousing the other woman, from head to waist, with hot water.

"What's to know?" Anzya's dripping cheeks flushed. Fruma Ya'el shoved her into a nearby chair.

"Sit. Let me tell you about my 'pampered' daughter.'"

Chapter Three

Flames in the fireplace cast dancing light on the walls. The empty ballroom loomed larger than ever. Like arbitrary phrases scribbled on paper scraps and released to the wind, Havah's thoughts flew.

Since the near kiss at the city park she saw Ulrich in a new light. Their fifteen year age difference mattered less and less. What more could a peasant girl want? Both handsome and rich, he treated her like royalty. She would never lack for anything. But there were other things to consider.

Setting her fingers on the ivory piano keys in front of her she peered at the page on the music stand. Chopin's Nocturne in C-Sharp Minor. Even though Ulrich told her the piece was much too complicated for a beginning student she was determined to master it.

Masculine footsteps thumped the hardwood floor and stopped behind her. The familiar scents of Witch Hazel and old books wafted over her. She stopped playing and folded her hands on her lap. Had she not dreamed of this moment every night for two years? Why, Arel? Why now? Her heart galloped like a runaway horse.

There was so much and, yet, nothing at all to say. "Is your bed not to your liking?"

"Gittel's last words were of you." He sat on the bench beside her. "She begged me to find you."

"You found me. Now go away."

Maybe if she ignored him he would leave. She positioned her hands on the keyboard and then pounded out the beginning chords. In spite of her clumsy playing, the faltering music soothed her.

When she finished he inched closer. "You've changed, Havah. The girl I knew would never serve a Christian master."

What gave him the right to accuse her? "It's called employment not slavery. Ulrich and I are friends."

"Friends?" Arel stood and walked to the fireplace. He stared at her and then gave her a wry smile. "Are you sure friendship is *all* he wants from you?"

"How dare you?" She sprang off the bench and stomped to the door.

With long-legged strides he beat her to it and blocked her path. He grasped her shoulders and shook her. "Do you love him?"

"What's it to you?" She tried to writhe from in his grip.

His breath brushed her cheeks. "I love you," he said.

"I hate you."

His lips met hers and, like a hungry woman offered nourishment after a long fast, she devoured them.

Chapter Four

Sleep refused Havah. By turns she giggled and sobbed into her pillow. The week's events boggled her mind. Every time she closed her eyes she felt Arel's kiss with crystal clarity. Everything happened so fast. Had she really signed the betrothal agreement or was that just one of her vivid dreams? Sometimes they were so real that she confused them with reality. Was this one of them?

To Havah's amazement Ulrich ordered Anzya to prepare a celebratory feast. Instead of the expected dissension the dour cook smiled and congratulated her.

For a solid week the professor's house bustled with activity. Children scampered up the spiral staircase and slid down the bannisters. Dr. Nikolai, who usually kept to himself, wrestled on the floor with Mendel and David, drew pictures with Tuli and taught Ruth and Rukhel a simple tune on the flute.

Tomorrow Itzak would return to Svechka with his family and Mama and Papa Gitterman. Havah would go back home with the Kishinev Abromoviches where Arel would be Evron's apprentice. There were so many details.

The bedroom door creaked open and a candle flame floated across the room, stopping at her bedside. "Mama? Is Papa's snoring keeping you awake?"

"That's just it. He doesn't snore at all." Fruma Ya'el eased down on the bed, setting the candle in its silver holder on the bed table. She slipped under the covers next to Havah. "How's a body supposed to sleep in such quiet?"

"It's going to be hard to go back to sharing a bed with two little wiggly worms." Havah stretched her arms over her head and yawned. "But poor Arel will have to share his with three."

"Come home with us, Daughter. It's not proper for you to dwell under the same roof during your betrothal. You'll tempt the Evil Eye."

Before she could answer, Tuli climbed up and wedged himself between them. "I had a bad dream. Can I sleep with you, Auntie Havah?"

"Won't Zelig protect you?"

"He laughed at me and said there's nothing to be afraid of. Please, please, can't I sleep in your bed?" Tuli's voice filled with desperation and he cuddled his head in the crook of her arm.

"Tell me about your dream."

"Monsters…they came to our house. They hurt us. You and me. All of us."

"Were they bears or lions?"

"Men. Bad ugly *men*."

"They're gone now." She stroked his dark curls and tucked the down comforter around him. "I'll keep you safe, Little Rooster."

A sleepy smile replaced his quivering pout and he shut his eyes. "When I grow up will you marry me?"

## Chapter Five

As far as tempting the evil eye went Fruma Yael need never have worried. After the marriage contract was signed Arel did not even allow his fingertips to brush Havah's. In fact, because the tiny Abromovich home was so crowded, Arel opted to sleep on a pallet in the tailor shop.

However, Havah doubted he slept much. His eyes were always bloodshot. A tape measure became his necktie. Thread spools and needles crowded his vest pockets. One morning over breakfast Evron remarked that if Arel could cram a sewing machine into his coat pocket he would.

When she voiced her worry he shrugged. "What kind of husband will I be if I can't support my wife?"

"Couldn't you go back to being a rabbi?"

With a muffled answer about inseams and shirt collars, he grabbed a piece of bread and bolted out the kitchen door.

Arel agreed that she should still work for Ulrich. He paid her well and, until Arel could make a proper living as a tailor, they needed the money.

In less than a month's time everything changed. Most baffling to her was the change in Anzya. Every morning she greeted Havah with a pleasant smile and a cup of coffee and raisins. Although she still called her Princess it was said with tenderness.

Ulrich, too, had changed. Gone were the jokes and infectious laughter. However, he insisted her lessons continue as long as she desired.

"'Oh my poor…lit-tle feet…I won-der who will put…on your shoes and shtock-stockings…for you now…dears.'" Havah read haltingly from *Alice's Adventures in Wonderland* and then stopped. Although she understood them, the English words still sounded strange and foreign to her.

"You've made amazing progress in just two years." Ulrich took the book from her and closed it gently. "You're practically fluent in English and have surpassed all of my other piano students. But what good will any of this do you as a *hausfrau* in Svechka?"

As if they were curdled milk he spat out the words *"hausfrau"* and "Svechka". His tense jaw rippled and his eyes flashed blue fire.

"Arel and haven't told anyone yet but we've made arrangements with Arel's sister Sarah. After Passover and our wedding, we'll go to America. He's going to work in his brother-in-law's shop."

"Good." Ulrich's jaws relaxed.

"I've hurt you. You should find another maid."

"No! You never kept your love for him a secret."

\*\*\*\*

A week later a loud bang jarred her from her sweeping.

"Anzya! Havah! Kolyah! Somebody!"

The broom fell from her hands. Although Ulrich had cautioned her about opening the door, she rushed it and jerked it open. Stumbling over the threshold Ulich held out his hand to steady himself, leaving a scarlet handprint on the wall. Blood streamed from a long gash above his eyebrow and stained his collar. He wore no coat and his linen shirt was torn beyond repair. One eye was almost swollen shut.

"Ulrich! Who did this to you?"

"No one. It's just an unfortunate accident. I'm such a clumsy *dumkopf.*" Shaking, he leaned on her and almost fainted before reaching the daybed in the parlor.

She took off her apron and laid it under his head to protect the furniture. "Dr. Nikolai just left. He can't have gone far."

Before she could make a move, Ulrich seized her hand, pulling her to her knees. "Don't wait!" Pressing his lips against her palm, he tightened his grip. "Go to America! Now!"

His eyes rolled back. A rumpled piece of paper fell from his pocket. She recognized it as the one delivered by a hateful Russian boy. She smoothed it out and read.

The words leaped and blurred before her. *"'Beat these low immoral bastards, these blood suckers, sucking Russian blood.'"*

"This is because of me. Ulrich, your 'accident' had nothing to do with clumsiness, did it?"

## Chapter Six

The gash above Ulrich's eyebrow pinged with each snip of Nikolai's scissors. "Eleven stitches. You could've lost your eye, Professor."

Camphor and iodine permeated the air. Over the past few weeks Nikolai's clinic business had picked up. They were mostly Jewish children. Cuts and bruises for the most part.

"No one's going to tell me who I can have as a friend or whom I can or cannot employ!" Ulrich clutched a schnapps bottle in one hand and waved a glass in the other. His shadow on the paneled wall mimicked his furious movements. "How can you be so calm, Kolyah?"

"I've always held to the belief that a soft answer turns away wrath."

"Do you really think a soft answer will turn away the wrath of those bloodthirsty vigilantes?"

"I meant *your* wrath, my friend." Nikolai dabbed Ulrich's injury with iodine and then capped the bottle. He washed his hands in a water basin and dried them.

After that he moved about the surgery, returning instruments and medicines to their places. "You're not a popular man in this town. Surely a musician of your caliber could find employment elsewhere. Germany? England? What about the philharmonic in St. Petersburg?"

"This is my home and Valerica's home. I'll not be driven out by a pack of rabid wolves, claiming to be Christians."

"The next blow could be fatal."

Ulrich slugged back the contents of his glass. The liquor burned his throat. He turned the bottle upside down and slipped off the examination table. "Empty. Let's go to the tavern to drink a toast to the happy bride to be and her groom, the rabbi turned tailor, Arel Gitterman."

"I've a better idea. Let's stay here and make a pot of coffee. You're drunk enough."

"Not yet." Ulrich set the bottle and the glass on the counter.

Nikolai took his coat off the rack by the door. "Count me in. Someone has to protect you from yourself."

When they reached the tavern the sound of men singing songs proclaiming their love for "Mother Russia" welcomed them. Nikolai maneuvered him to a corner table.

The waiter brought them a bottle, two glasses and a piece of paper. "Here is a letter that all who come here are required to read."

The familiar words hit Ulrich like a slap in the face.

*'Remind them of the Odessa pogrom, at that time even the army was on the side of the people and surely they will stand with us this time, the workers party, the true Christians. All of your guests must read this, otherwise we will destroy your tavern.'"*

"I've already had this piece of excrement delivered to my door." Ulrich crumpled it and threw it at him.

The waiter snickered and walked away.

"Lower your voice," whispered Nikolai.

"This man, Krushevan has the right idea." A man, two tables away, pounded his fist to punctuate his words. "We must band together to protect our land against these vermin before they take over."

Black eyes almost hidden under his bushy eyebrows gave the man an ape-like appearance. What little hair he had was clipped close to his square head. An unforgettable face. The kind that sent children scurrying to hide under their beds

"Sasha speaks the truth." A thin man with scraggly hair swigged Vodka from a bottle and slapped the man's back. When he smiled the teeth in his mouth could be counted on the fingers of one hand.

Repulsed by the notice's threat and insidious lies, Ulrich shuddered with rage. He doubled up his fist. "Someone should pound some morality into these cretins, Kolyah."

"Don't look at me. I took the Hippocratic Oath. What wounds I inflict I'm duty bound to treat." Nikolai hunched over the table and sipped his drink. "Please, Ulrich. Let's just leave."

Sauntering over to their table, Sasha placed his massive hand on Nikolai's shoulder. "And you, my good friend, you will stand with us and do your Christian duty as a loyal Russian?"

"Kindly remove your hand before I amputate it, 'friend.'" Nikolai peered at him over his eyeglasses.

With something between a laugh and growl, Sasha turned to Ulrich. "Professor, you're looking better than the last time I saw you."

"No thanks to you, you filthy snake."

"I'm surprised to see you'd show yourself again amongst good Christian men."

Ulrich emptied his glass and slammed it down. "Good *Christian* men? You're not even *human*."

"Do we need to teach Professor High and Mighty another lesson?" Sasha's friend sidled to the table to join them.

"It's time to vanish." Nikolai rose and reached for his coat. "Let's go home, Professor."

"I wouldn't dream of leaving such charming company." Ulrich pressed his nose against Sasha's and snarled. "What kind of lesson will these 'good Christian men' teach me?"

"Don't you see, Professor?" Sasha's greasy lips under his heavy moustache curled into an ingratiating smile. "These Christ killers must be driven from our land."

Ulrich seized his collar and shoved him against the wall. "You stinking sack of garbage! Good thing my friend's a doctor. You make me sick!"

He balled his fist and punched Sasha squarely between the eyes. Dazed, the burly man toppled like a felled tree. The other man lunged at Ulrich but Nikolai restrained him by coiling an arm around his neck.

Meanwhile, Sasha came to with a groan. Ulrich hovered over him with a triumphant smile. "Bring the bottle, Dr. Derevenko. It's time for us to leave."

Sasha's crony broke free from Nikolai and charged Ulrich, grabbing him around his waist. Together they crashed to the floor. Ulrich reeled around and managed a well-placed punch.

Clapping his hands over his face, the skinny man shrieked. "My nose! It's broken! Kill him!"

Dizzy from too much liquor, Ulrich laid back on the floor. Before he could rally, Sasha, fully recovered, curved his lips into a smile and his hand into a fist. He dropped down and grasped Ulrich's collar.

Ulrich closed his eyes and braced himself for the inevitable. Instead, a chair crashed across Sasha's head and he collapsed in a massive heap.

With a relieved sigh, Ulrich looked up to see Nikolai clutching the remains of a chair. The doctor shrugged his shoulders and wiped his bloody nose on his shirt sleeve. "May Hippocrates forgive me."

Chapter Seven

"Fortunately, your injuries aren't too serious, just a couple of cracked ribs. A few days bed rest for you and you should be recovered from your self-inflicted miseries." Nikolai patted Ulrich's side and pulled a blanket over him.

Ulrich's head pounded and his side throbbed. He pressed his hands over his eyes and groaned. "The entire Russian army is marching inside my head."

"Consider it retaliation. You drank enough last night to give them all hangovers."

"You have a nasty habit of being right."

"I've been thinking, Ulrich. Why don't you consider a holiday with me in Moscow? The Cathedral of Christ has a wonderful Easter celebration every year, full of pageantry. A few days away from here will do you good."

\*\*\*\*

The Russian countryside rushed past the train window and the amber sunset along with the train's chugging rhythm, soothed Ulrich. Trees and flowers melted into a haze until he found himself sitting in the pillared hall of an old church.

*While the priest proclaimed Christ's resurrection his censor swung on its chain releasing sweet puffs of fragrance. Satin robed clergy walked in a procession behind him, their voices raised in a chant. "Christ is risen."*

*Candles illuminated the painted altars under the high domed ceilings. The crowd sang praises to God and Savior. Toward the end of the procession, a priest held a huge brass crucifix on a pole high over his head. As Ulrich raised his head for a glimpse of the Christ, he gasped.*

*Instead of the expected icon, Evron hung, hands and feet nailed to the cross. Blood saturated the priest's white robe and left a trail on the polished floor.*

*A small person clad in a black hooded cloak hobbled behind him. She stopped beside Ulrich and pushed back her hood. Havah's brown eyes pierced him.*

*From under the cloak she presented a wafer and a golden chalice which she raised high overhead and poured. The crimson liquid pooled around his feet.*

*"Eat, Professor. Drink." Her voice, hollow, yet musical, reverberated in his ears. "Our bodies. Our blood."*

## Chapter Eight

After three treks to the outhouse, Itzak hoped this would be his last. He looked up at the moon, a crescent low in the sky. Pulling his coat around his nightgown he trudged back to the house and chided himself for eating a third piece of sponge cake after dinner.

Since Papa married Fruma Ya'el Itzak had loosened his belt at least one notch if not two. He sniffed. Wildflowers would soon be in full bloom.

As he neared the house, he heard hooves clip clopping on the dirt road. They sounded close. Who would be out traveling this late? Cossacks! He walked faster. A horse whinnied.

Sweat broke out on his forehead and ran down his cheeks into his beard. Hiding behind the nearest tree, he watched for soldiers as the horse came into view. Instead he saw only a man and woman who were wearing wedding garments. He let out a long sigh.

Stepping out from his hiding place, Itzak stood in the middle of the road and waved his arms. The man brought the horse to a halt.

One look at the weary couple changed Itzak's mind about making a joke and he grabbed the horse's reins. Blood from a gash on the side of his head ran down the man's face. His bride leaned against him, eyes closed.

"Come into the house and rest, Friend."

The woman woke with a start. She clung to the man, terror in her swollen eyes. Itzak could tell by the bruises on her face and her torn dress she had been attacked.

The man dismounted and his bride slid off into his arms.

Fruma Ya'el met them at the door and wrapped a blanket around the woman. "Itzak, take them up to Arel's old room."

Without a word, Itzak led them up the stairs. He needed no one to tell him what had happened. Why on a wedding day of all days?

When they reached the room the man gently lowered his wife onto the bed. She clung to his arm. "Don't go."

He eased himself down beside her. "I'm never going anywhere without you."

Twenty minutes later, Fruma Ya'el finished winding a bandage around the young groom's head. She handed him a plate. "Have some cake. Fortunately, my son left some for the rest of us."

Itzak blushed, feeling very much like he had as the eight-year-old who had been caught snitching bagels. Fruma Ya'el never scolded him for his crime but she did make him clean out her chicken coop every day for a week.

The young bride, scrubbed and dressed in a fresh nightgown, leaned back against the pillow. "I'm sorry to have ruined your sleep, Froi Gitterman."

Fruma Ya'el kissed her palm. "Sleep we can have anytime. For what they did to you their feet should all be twisted backward and they should have to crawl on their bellies like the serpents they are."

"Do you think it's an omen for a marriage to start this way?"

Spitting between two fingers while pressing her other hand against the bride's lips, Fruma Ya'el hissed. "Hush! Do you want to tempt the Evil Eye?" She leaned forward and lowered her voice. "Did they—?"

"No." The bride smiled at her husband, her adoration evident in her dark eyes. "They would have but my beloved prevented them."

Itzak squeezed the groom's arm. "Good man. I hope you killed the scoundrels."

"I wanted to. There were oo many of them." The man took a sip of tea to wash down the cake. "They beat us with clubs and whips. We did well to escape with our lives. I don't know if anyone else survived. I stole one of the horses and ran." He fixed his tortured eyes on Itzak. "Do you think I'm a coward for not staying to fight?"

Itzak's heart ached for them. What would he have done in the same situation? What *could* he have done? This memory of this night would haunt them for many Sabbaths to come.

"Coward? *Shah.* You did the most valiant thing a man could do. You saved your bride's virtue."

"Come, Itzak. Let them rest." Fruma Ya'el tucked the covers around the woman's neck.

Itzak embraced the man. "Sleep well, my young hero."

"I should've listened to Reb Abromovich." The man crawled into bed beside his wife.

"Evron Abromovich the tailor? A lump formed in Itzak's throat.

"You know him?"

"Yes. What did he say?"

"He said this would be a bad week to plan a wedding."

"Where...where did you say you're from?"

Chapter Nine

A thunderous crash roused Havah from a fitful sleep. She tried to roll over but Arel's arm, tight around her waist prevented her. Blinking open her eyes, she looked up and down his fully clothed form. Why was he there?

Then she remembered. Yesterday pogrom rumors became reality. Evron did not work in the shop. The sounds of shattering glass and screams outside caused a tense hush to fall over the children from oldest to youngest. No one played. No one laughed. No one even smiled. Most of the day and on into the night Evron and Arel stood vigil at the door clutching thick poles to defend themselves.

Finally, after a supper of lentil soup that everyone picked at, Havah gathered the children on her bed. Arel joined her in telling them stories, singing songs and reading comforting psalms. No one spoke of bedtime. At some point, cheek by jowl, they all nodded off.

Thumb in mouth and curled like a puppy, Velvil still slept with his head on Havah's knees. Tuli, his dark hair a tousled bush, sat up at the end of the bed, his dark eyes wide.

"What was that?"

"It's starting again." Arel's grip around Havah tightened and he pressed his lips against hers.

"Arel, not in front of the children. It's not proper."

"Would the Almighty begrudge us a kiss when there may never be a wedding?"

Finally he let go of her and she rolled over.

At the desk beside the window, Zelig peered over his new eyeglasses that made him look more like a rabbi than ever. "Aw, it was just the dumb old washtub. My clumsy sister dropped it."

"I'm sorry, Auntie Havah. Mama said to be quiet so you could sleep." Ruth, peeking around the stovepipe, blushed. "Good thing there wasn't any water in it. Papa says we would've all floated away."

Giddy with relief, Havah wanted to leap and twirl. Only a washtub. She snuggled against Arel and closed her eyes. Snapping them open she sat straight up. "Ruth, did you say 'washtub'?"

Havah shoved Velvil out of her way. He woke with a sharp cry. She swung her legs over the side of the bed expecting to find Katya writhing in labor.

Instead Katya stood at the stove between the twins stirring kasha into the kettle. Her clothes were rumpled and her gaunt face was pale gray. The washtub at her feet, padded with blankets, said it would not be long until another Abromovich joined the family.

With a tightlipped, bucktoothed grin she pressed one hand over her belly's expanse. "Only a twinge or two. A little indigestion perhaps."

"How far apart?" Havah placed her hand on Katya's hard stomach.

"Fifteen minutes."

"She's...it's...why now?" From crying, lack of sleep or both, Evron's eyes were red and swollen. He hunched over the table clutching his coffee cup in both hands.

"The trouble is over," said Katya. "You said so yourself."

"I lied."

"Listen to this, Papa." Zelig read from his book. "*'Though a thousand fall at your side and ten thousand by your right hand, it shall not come near you.'*"

"There, you have it from our little rabbi's mouth. It's a sign. The Almighty has spared us. Blessed be He." Katya raised her hands toward the ceiling and waved her spoon.

A large rock shattered the window and struck Zelig square in the forehead, knocking his glasses to the floor. Blood spattered the book which dropped from his hands. Mouth agape, he slid off the chair and lay still on the floor. A dark red puddle spread under his head.

Katya dropped beside him and cradled his head. Wailing, she rocked to and fro. The other children gathered around them. Ashen, Evron jumped up from his chair and grasped her shoulders. "Not now. Hide!"

Arel bounded across the room and grabbed the poles propped by the door. He threw one to Evron. Ruth grabbed Velvil who howled in protest. She clasped her hand over his mouth and scooted under the bed. Rukhel and Tuli followed in silence their gazes fixed on Zelig.

"Kill the Jews!" Frenzied shouts came from the tailor shop and fear sent icicles down Havah's back. Sounds of machines toppling and tearing cloth ripped through her. Arel and Evron positioned themselves on either side of the door, poles poised. She grabbed a paring knife from the table and tucked it into her waistband. At her side, Katya doubled over.

"Nooooo, nooo, not now baby. Not now."

Before Havah could get Katya to bed, the door burst open and five men rushed into the room. Evron swung his pole, hitting one of them between the shoulders. Another pulled a dagger from his belt. He grabbed Evron from behind and, with one deft motion, slit his throat.

In that horrific second the world turned sideways then upside down. Havah bit her tongue to keep from screaming as Evron slid to the floor, blood spurting from his neck.

Paralyzed, she could only watch Katya, who, despite, labor pains, scurried to her husband's body. Collapsing beside it she wailed and dropped her head on his chest.

Eyes like black coals, the largest man closed in on Katya with a leering grin. He kicked her side and tugged her into a standing position. Then, with vicious force, he squeezed her stomach.

"This Jew dog had his way with this ugly bitch." He shoved Evron's body with his heavy boot then grasped her face in his massive hand and forced his mouth over hers.

She reared back and spit in his face. Yanking a knitting needle from her apron pocket, she jabbed it into his eye.

"Jew witch!" He shrieked, grabbed her and snapped her neck. Her body crumpled to the floor.

Havah wanted to scream but dared not. Where had Arel gone? As she hobbled backward to the bed where the children hid, she caught sight of his body in the doorway, his clothes torn and his face a mass of shredded flesh. She tried to duck behind the hanging quilt but her lame foot betrayed her and she tripped. Her ankle twisted and pain shot through it.

The ape man with dark blood oozing from his eye socket turned his head and grinned like a wolf on the prowl. Havah's sprained ankle thwarted her attempt to run. Before she could manage two steps, he had her in his grasp, squeezing her so hard she could not breathe. His maniacal laughter echoed in her ears and made her head throb.

Velvil whimpered from his hiding place. "Mama."

"Not the babies." Havah's heart pounded until she feared her chest would burst. "Oh God, not the babies."

"What have we here, a litter of Jew puppies? Come out of there, you little brats!"

Agitated like wild dogs intoxicated by the taste of blood, the feral pack surrounded the bed. They dragged Velvil and Tuli out. The baby's shrieks tormented her until in one brutal moment the monster swung Velvil by his feet, slamming his head into the wall with a hollow thump. She choked and prayed for a swift death.

"I found two of a kind." Another beast held an arm around each of the twins' necks.

Did the Almighty not see? Why did he not send his mighty arm to save them? Havah screamed until her throat burned.

"Dear God! I've brought this curse."

In desperation she managed to reach the knife tucked into her skirt and stabbed her captor's forearm.

With a shrill cry he dropped her.

Her injured ankle snapped. She tried to reach Tuli who huddled on the ground, his hands over his head to protect himself. His pitiful cries tortured her as they faded to a pathetic whimper.

"Forgive me, Little Rooster."

A scabrous hand covered her nose and mouth. She writhed and fought until he wrenched the paring knife from her, slicing her right hand in the process. Searing pain ripped deep into her side and blackness took her.

****

Havah came to in the darkened house and ran her hands through a sticky puddle on the rough wooden floor beneath her. Something poked at her side. Who put Katya's kitchen knife there? She tugged at it but it would not budge. Her right hand burned.

Silence of a tomb, heavy and cruel closed in on Havah like a burial garment. She opened her eyes. Her soul pleaded for a sound. She longed to hear children's laughter.

As though answering her plea, from a distant place, she heard a child crying, calling her name. She had to find him. She crawled toward his voice and answered. "I'm...here, Tuli."

Havah found Tuli in the corner, broken like a discarded toy. When she touched him he cried out in pain. She cried, "Oh, Tuli."

"Don't...forget, Auntie, you promised to...marry me...when I...grow up."

## Chapter Ten

Sunset's amber beauty contrasted with the sight of broken glass, paper and other debris littering the streets. Bile rose in Ulrich's throat and gagged him. Jeremiah the prophet's words swirled through his mind like a bitter wind.

> *"A voice was heard in Ramah,*
> *Lamentation, weeping, and great mourning,*
> *Rachel weeping for her children,*
> *Refusing to be comforted,*
> *Because they were no more."*

"Professor Dietrich!"

Although bruised and bloody there was no mistaking the man who ran toward them. "Arel. The Abromoviches, Havah are they—?"

"The police. They stood there…did…nothing."

Ulrich's heart pounded. He lit the lantern he carried, afraid of what it might illuminate and continued the funeral march to the tailor's house.

The door hung by a single hinge. The odor of decaying flesh assaulted him. He tripped over the bodies in the entrance. Evron's vacuous eyes stared out from a face bearing a look of eternal surprise. Katya lay face down in a crumpled heap beside him.

Nikolai knelt and turned her over. A blood-covered infant still attached to the umbilical cord curled up beneath her skirts. He cradled the baby, curved his hand around her tiny neck and shook his head.

"Dead before she had a chance to live." He kissed the child and laid her beside Katya's body, then took off his coat and covered their faces.

Overturned chairs littered the cramped apartment. Looted cabinets hung open, empty save a few broken cups and saucers. Feathers, like little rafts, floated on crimson ponds. Ulrich staggered through the house, his mind reeling.

Ulrich lifted Evron's desk and found Zelig. He took one of the hanging quilts from its clothesline to cover the boy. When he did so he gagged. Ruth and Rukhel lay on the bed. Hand in hand. He fought not to imagine the horrors visited upon them, robbing them first of their innocence and then their lives. He pulled the quilt from its clothesline 'wall' and covered their naked bodies. Had Havah met a similar fate?

With dread stabbing his temples he searched until he found her sitting in a corner behind the bed, her head drooped to one side. She clutched a mass of flesh that had once been a child. Nothing but Tuli's shoes was recognizable.

Afraid to touch her, he choked and held his breath. "Kolyah…is she…?"

Nikolai dropped down beside her and pressed his thumb against her neck. "No, thank God."

"Thank God for what?" Ulrich clenched his teeth.

Arel dropped to the floor, took Havah in his arms and tried to dislodge the knife from her side.

"Don't." Nikolai grasped his hand. "She may die if you do."

Her eyes snapped open. "Do it, Arel."

Dim light from Ulrich's lantern cast macabre shadows on the blood spattered walls. He looked down at Tuli's battered face. What could reduce men to such bestial acts? What possessed them?

His stomach shuddered and emptied itself. He wiped his mouth on the back of his sleeve. "You bloody bastards! Christ died for you and you use Him as an excuse for your bloodletting! Why? Why? Why?"

# Part IV

## *LIVE AND REMEMBER*

Chapter One

In Kishinev's Jewish quarter corpses wrapped in prayer shawls littered the street while the living stood vigil. Some wept while others stared with the glazed eyes of dead men.

Seized with the urge to vomit, Itzak put his arm around Shayndel. "If you want to stay here in the wagon I'll understand."

"No, I'm going with you." Her voice trailed off and her lips trembled.

"Mama. Papa. Would you prefer to stay here?" Itzak turned to the two in the back of the wagon. "It has been a long journey, perhaps you should rest."

"We're family. We stay together." Yussel tapped his cane on the floorboards.

After descending from the wagon they walked toward Evron's home in solemn silence.

"Evron Abromovich? The tailor, have you seen him?" Itzak asked of people as they passed, hoping for a good word.

A man with one of his arms in a sling whom Itzak recognized as one of Evron's customers motioned to him. "Walk with me."

By his expression Itzak could tell the short trek to his brother's house would prove to be the longest and most torturous journey of his life.

When they stopped in front of the shop, the young man pointed to six bundles lined up on the sidewalk like fish in a marketplace. Itzak wailed and tore his shirt then knelt and moved a corner of the quilt around the first bundle. Ruth and Rukhel, inseparable to the very end, even in death.

One by one, he identified each member of his brother's family. He recognized Dr. Derevenko's coat enshrouding Katya and her tiny infant, the sister the twins prayed for.

No one needed to identify the last corpse in the row for it was draped in his father's *tallis*. Itzak took off his hat, scraped a handful of dirt from the street and sprinkled it over his bare head. With a muffled sob he fell beside Evron's body, clutching the prayer shawl's fringes. Then he uncovered his brother's face for one last goodbye, kissed Evron's cold forehead and replaced the cover.

At last Itzak stood. His throat constricted. "The house."

"I will leave you alone now," whispered Evron's customer.

"Did your family survive?" Itzak grasped the man's good hand.

"All living, thank the Almighty, but our house is gone and my wife—" He bowed his head. "My wife will never be the same." The man turned and kicked his way down the littered street.

The glass from the shop windows lay in shards on the ground and the door hung by a single hinge. Inside, tattered fabric, thread spools and broken machines were strewn on the floor. As he led his wife and parents through the doorway single file into the apartment behind the shop Itzak choked back bitter gall.

In the three corners the beds had been shredded and the pillows gutted. The only thing in the one room apartment undisturbed was the cast iron stove. The looters had not wasted any time. What few valuables the Abromoviches owned, such as Katya's few pieces of jewelry and silverware, were gone.

As she swept through the debris, Fruma Ya'el's haunted eyes asked the question that no one dared to voice. She sank down on the girls' bloodstained bed where she found Havah's rag doll which she clutched to her breast. Her mouth opened in soundless cries and she rocked back and forth.

Havah's psalm book in one hand and Arel's bloodied cap in the other, Shayndel looked around and asked, "Itzak, do you think there's any way they could be alive?"

"There's always hope."

His own words did little to convince him. How could anyone survive such a massacre? Still, their bodies were nowhere in sight.

Stepping over and between rubble he kicked Katya's frayed knitting basket. A ball of yarn, a half knitted sock and a blue velvet sack tumbled out onto the floor. It was the bag Evron had made from scrap to store his clarinet until he could afford a proper case. Itzak removed the instrument and cradled it in both hands like a baby. How many weddings and bar mitzvah celebrations had heard its melodies?

A low rumble started in his chest and erupted in laughter, uncontrollable, ridiculous and maniacal laughter. Tears rolled down his cheeks.

"Itzak Abromovich, have you lost your mind?" Shayndel scowled. "What can you possibly find to laugh at?"

"The Almighty's…wit and mercy."

"Mercy? Wit? What do you mean?"

"I pitied my brother his ugly wife…yet…he…he…could not have lived without her."

## Chapter Two

A warm gust of wind blew through Ulrich's hair. He leaned against the wall by the open window overlooking the cobblestone street below where two small boys using sticks for guns pretended to be Cossacks in battle. A few feet away a girl with beribboned curls sang a lullaby to her doll.

"In the name of our Father the Czar, down with the *Zjids!*" One of the boys held his stick aloft.

The other boy raised his high pitched voice. "Save Mother Russia from the blood sucking Jews!"

"Kolyah, do you hear that?"

Ulrich turned from the window. Havah's colorless face, if not framed by her raven hair, would have been indistinguishable from the white bed linen.

"They're babies, five or six years old at the most. They're parroting what they've heard." For two days Nikolai had kept vigil in the bedside chair. His disheveled hair hung in front of his inflamed eyes.

"Teach a child to hate when he's young and when he's old he'll snuff out a life without conscience."

"Change the world tomorrow, Professor. Get some rest."

"Methinks the doctor should follow his own prescription." Ulrich eased himself into a chair beside Nikolai.

On the other side of the bed, head bandaged, arm in a sling, Arel slept in the chaise lounge. Although Ulrich offered the young man a room and a bed he refused to leave Havah's side. When awake, he stood and, with stubborn dedication, chanted traditional prayers for the sick.

"He'll be a good husband to her."

"If she lives." Nikolai lowered his voice to a whisper.

"Are you saying—?" Ulrich refused to voice the unthinkable.

"She's lost a lot of blood and—"

Havah's voice, weak and raspy, broke in. "I...can't...breathe."

Nikolai hastily put his stethoscope's earpieces in his ears, leaned forward and pressed the bell against her chest.

"It's cold," she murmured.

"It's supposed to be cold. First thing I learned in medical school."

"You lie."

"Never, I'm a doctor."

"You have a...nice smile." She stopped to cough. "No...wonder Tuli...loves...loved you." Her cough turned to sobbing. "I...promised to...keep him...safe."

"No more talking." A frown replaced Nikolai's smile as he moved the stethoscope. "Dammit. I took every precaution."

"What is it, Kolyah?" Afraid of the answer Ulrich held his breath.

"Complications. Post-operative infection."

Through another coughing fit Havah wheezed and fixed her gaze on the doctor. "Let me die."

## Chapter Three

Ulrich's house with its pillars and ornate stone carvings cast a shadow across the wagon as Itzak reined in the horses. Shayndel raised her head and gazed up at the tall second story windows. She huddled close to him, trembling more from exhaustion than cold.

"What if they're not here?"

"If they're not, Ulrich knows where they are."

"How can you be so sure?"

"He and Dr. Nikolai left their coats to be buried with the dead. A man like that wouldn't leave Arel and Havah stranded. Well, Arel maybe."

Shayndel opened her mouth to reprimand her husband for such a tasteless comment but stopped. It had been days since he had slept more than an hour at a time. Silver strands had appeared in his black beard overnight. Yet he still smiled and winked at her as he helped Yussel down from the back of the wagon.

Two stones flew through the air. One crashed through the front door's stained glass window. The other hit Yussel who cried out and collapsed on the sidewalk.

Shayndel dropped beside him and dabbed the gash on his forehead with the hem of her skirt. She held her breath, fearing the worst. To her relief, he opened his eyes.

Behind them a child, who could not have been older than ten, shook his fist. "Dirty Christ killing Jews."

The door flew open. Ulrich burst through the doorway and charged at the boy, brandishing a broom. "Away, you miserable little viper!"

Nikolai raced after him. "Ulrich, have you gone mad?"

Stumbling into the street, the boy picked up another rock and hurled it. It struck Ulrich with a loud thud. "Zjid lover!"

"There's one of your 'harmless babies,' Kolyah." The professor rubbed the red mark swelling on his stubbled cheek.

"How many windmills have you slain today, Señor Quixote?" Nikolai seized the broom and tossed it to the ground. "That, my friend, is merely a symptom of the disease."

****

Pain wracked Havah from head to foot. It thumped out a steady rhythm against her forehead. No matter how she moved, it refused to subside. The goose down blanket covering her failed to warm her.

Like figures on a merry-go-round, people moved through the air about her. Shayndel, Fruma Ya'el, Anzya and Dr. Nikolai by turns bound her wounds and forced soup or ill flavored medicines through her lips. Their heads floated without bodies and their voices spoke from the depths of a dense fog.

*"Havaleh, wake up, sleepyhead. You're late for Heder."*

*"Mama? I had a bad dream. You and Papa and Mendel and David were all dead."*

*"We are."*

Arel's voice intoned prayers for the sick. But how could that be? She saw the monsters kill him with her own eyes. It must be a dream.

Somewhere in the haze Itzak's lonesome violin wept for Evron's resonant clarinet.

*"Auntie Havah? Where are you?"*

*"I'm here."*

*"I can't see you. I'm afraid!"*

*His pitiful sobbing pierced her heart. Through the murky darkness she searched for him but his voice trailed off into hollow silence. "Forgive me, Tuli."*

"Don't cry, Havah. You'll make your cough worse." Ulrich's hair hung in his eyes and his face was as gray and flat as cardboard.

"Ulrich…I let the fire go out and…and forgot to mop the floor. Blood's everywhere."

"Forget my floor. You must rest." He tucked the covers around her neck.

"Who's that lady?"

*Behind him a petite woman clad in a pink dress stood beside the window, her translucent skirts billowing on the breeze. Her golden ringlets bobbed around her ageless face and her outstretched hands beckoned.*

"Valerica, take me with you." Havah raised her hand and tried to sit up.

"Fight her!" Ulrich clasped her wrist and pushed her back against the pillows.

Like morning mist rising from a brook, Valerica floated to the ceiling and dissolved.

*"Magnified and sanctified be His great name in the world which He created according to his will."*

*"Papa, is it really you?"*

*"Hush, Havah, you know better than to interrupt the mourner's Kaddish."*

*Nine more men wearing prayer shawls gathered around her bed with Papa, including Uncle Hershel, Evron and even Feivel Resnick. But how?*

*"Who are you praying for, Papa?"*
*"You, my daughter."*
*"But I'm not dead."*
*"Are you sure?"*

"Drink, Havah. Let's lower this fever before your head turns into a boiled egg. Shayndel hold her still."
"Ugh. It stinks. What is it?"
"Willow bark tea."
The bitter mixture gagged Havah and seared her raw throat. She fought to free herself from Shayndel's grip. "Let me go."
Icy against the fire blazing in her cheeks, Fruma Ya'el's hands held firm. Adamant and desperate, her voice sounded Havah's ear. "You are *not* going to die, do you hear me?"

*"Come along, Daughter."* From the porch of a familiar wood-frame house, Miriam waved. *"Your brothers are waiting for you."*
*"Where?"*
*"On the other side, of course."*
*Daffodils surrounded the house like a row of pretty maidens with yellow bonnets. Their fragrance enticed Havah to pick them and gather them into a bouquet for Mama.*

"You have to get well, Havah. You must."
The voice annoyed her. What right did Shayndel have to bloom with health while Katya and her children lie beneath the earth? Havah flinched. "Don't touch me!"

*As she inched toward the tidy house on the hill, a two story building grew out of the ground. Its stained glass windows sparkled. With a velvet-adorned Torah nestled in his arms Rabbi Cohen stood in front of the polished door.*

"No change. She's drowning. Her body can't take much more." Dr. Nikolai's face looked haggard.

"Peppermint Schnapps." Fruma Ya'el's worried face hovered over her like a faded balloon. "It will break up the congestion in her lungs."

"Why not? I'll try anything short of witchcraft."

*Everything was just the way she remembered. The rabbi opened the door and greeted the line of people who appeared from nowhere. Each of them was a villager she recognized, from the Heder boys who teased her to Tabitha, the oldest person in Natalya. She grasped the woman's withered hand.*

*Papa touched the fringes of his prayer shawl to the Torah and then to her lips. Raisins never tasted sweeter.*

*"Hurry, Daughter. Services are about to begin."*

"We're losing her." Dr. Nikolai's voice was a weary rasp.

*From the balcony separating men from women, Ruth and Rukhel leaned over the railing. "Auntie Havah, come join us!"*

*With an inviting grin, David glanced at her over his desk in the front row. "What are you waiting for, Bubbe Fuss Bucket?"*

*On his lap, Tuli held out his pudgy arms. No evidence of the savage beating remained. "Come marry me!"*

*Looking down at her bare feet she counted five perfect toes on each. So this was death. No pain. No sorrow. The voices inside the synagogue welcomed her. She raised one foot to step over the threshold.*

*Suddenly Tova Resnick, with a basket of bloodstained laundry perched on her shoulder, blocked her path. "Once you enter there's no turning back."*

"Get out of my way."

*"Is Havah Cohen, champion warrior of learned women, going to lie down and die without so much as whimper?"*

"'Even though I walk through...the valley...of the shadow of...death...'"

"No Havah! Don't give up!"

Although she was aware of someone's hand holding hers she could not feel its warmth. Her arms and legs sank into the bed. *Thump...thump...thump...*her heart pulsed slower with each beat.

"...I ...will not...fear."

*Weightless, she floated between the synagogue and the stuffy bedroom where a stone-pale Havah reclined on the bed.*

Like a defeated soldier Nikolai dropped his head into his hands. "There was nothing I could do."

"Don't leave me." Arel's bandaged head drooped forward and he collapsed on the still woman's stomach.

*"It's not your time." Tova shoved her.*

*"I have to stay."*

*"If you do the bastards win."*

*"They've won already."*

*"Have they?" Lightning bolts flashed from Tova's luminous eyes and she laughed a shrill, earsplitting cackle. The synagogue exploded into flames. "Have they really?"*

Once more black smoke devoured Natalya, taking everything and everyone she ever loved. Valerica's bed sucked her back into her ravaged body. The weight of Arel's head on her stomach made her wounded side hurt.

"Get...off...of me."

The people who had been obscured by dream mist and shadow came into focus. Their agonized wailing changed to exclamations of joy.

*"His name be praised!"*

*"Blessed be He!"*

*"Gott in Himmel!"*

With a look of disbelief, Dr. Nikolai pressed the stethoscope bell against her chest. "Strong and steady. The congestion's breaking up."

"I've never seen anything like this!" Fruma Ya'el brushed her palm across Havah's forehead. "Her fever's broken."

"Adoshem has spared us one more sorrow." Itzak swept Shayndel up in his arms and spun her around. His raucous laughter echoed and grated in Havah's ears.

*How dare they celebrate when there was nothing left to laugh about?* Summoning every ounce of strength, she rose up on her elbows. "Go away! All of you!"

## Chapter Four

Arel's reflection in the dark window panes shocked him. He hardly recognized himself without a beard. His broken nose was swollen to half again its normal size and the bruises around his eyes looked like a death mask.

Outside a spring storm raged. Like the lightning bolts, horrendous images and sounds flashed through Arel's mind; man size animals busting down the door, the stunned look on Evron's face, Havah's scream, the taste of his own blood and coming to on the debris strewn floor surrounded by corpses.

He turned from the window and gazed at Havah. When her fever broke two days before, she drifted off, waking for brief sips of broth. She was so small and frail the four poster bed dwarfed her.

He refused to abandon his vigil, save for the most necessary activities. Determined to be there when his beloved woke, he took all of his meals in the room and slept on the chaise lounge beside the bed.

The door opened and Dr. Nikolai entered the room with scissors and a bottle of iodine. "I waited all day for you to come to the clinic so that I could remove my embroidery." He sat on the couch and patted the cushion beside him. "You leave me no choice. Sit!"

Arel sat beside him. "Doctor, do you have a pistol?"

"No." Nikolai unwrapped Arel's bandages. "Why?"

The gashes stung but not as much as the guilt that tortured him. "Maybe if I'd had one instead of a stick this wouldn't have happened."

"That rabid mob would have taken it and blown your head off." The doctor snipped and tugged at the last stitch. "You're going to have some scars and I'm afraid a full beard's a thing of the past. But it could've been worse."

Worse? Arel's gorge rose. He shook his head and turned back to Havah who mumbled in her sleep.

"Is she going to be all right?"

"It depends on how much fight she has left."

In dry mouthed silence Arel searched the other man's eyes for hidden answers but found only bloodshot fatigue and unspoken anguish.

Outside the storm intensified. Thunder rumbled with increasing frequency and crashed with such force the windows rattled.

"Zelig!" Havah bolted upright. "Watch out!"

In one swift leap from his couch to the bedside, Arel caught her in his arms. "It's all right, my love."

Wrestling out of his arms she laid back, her dark eye wide. "It will never be all right." Then, with a look of panic, she raised her right arm. "I can't feel my hand. The beasts cut it off, didn't they?"

"If they had it would hurt like hell." Sinking down on the bed, the doctor lifted her hand and unwound the bandages. The stitched cut made an angry red line from her thumb to her little finger. "See, one, two, three, four, and five. Can you move them at all?"

Arel watched her fingers and willed them to move, but they did not even twitch.

"What good am I?" she said.

"You're alive." He stroked her cheek. "Things will be better in America. You'll have your own house and—"

"Who will take care of it? I'm a cripple. I can't even hold my own *mop*."

\*\*\*\*

At the bedroom doorway, breakfast tray in hand, Ulrich paused to watch Havah before entering the room. No bigger than Ruth and Rukhel, she did not look much older than twelve. Propped up against three stacked pillows, her hair fell in two long braids. She clutched the torn rag doll which, like its owner, had survived two massacres.

Taking a deep breath, he forced his lips into a smile.

"Good morning, Princess! Anzya sends up some of her choicest delicacies. You wouldn't want to insult her would you?"

Terse silence answered him. He set the tray on the bed table and then tucked a linen napkin under Havah's nightgown collar. Lifting a silver plated lid off of a bowl, he bowed.

"For your dining pleasure, I bring you kasha with raisins." He lifted another lid. "And for the lady's dessert, chocolate truffles imported from Paris, guaranteed kosher."

"Eat it yourself." She pulled off the napkin and dropped it on the floor.

A stray lock of hair blew across her face when a warm gust blew through the open window. She seemed neither to notice nor care. Ulrich brushed it out of her sunken eyes. Hollow and dark, they had lost their song.

How he longed to breathe life into her again and hear the music of her laughter. He curled his hand around her arm almost afraid it would snap in two. "Child, you must eat. Look at you, the slightest breeze could carry you off."

"Let it."

"Don't you want to get well?"

"No."

"What would I do without you?"

"Hire another Jew."

Scooping up a spoonful of the kasha, he held it to her lips. "Please take one bite for your poor old Uncle Ulrich."

"Just for you...Uncle." With an odd twist of a smile she took the cereal into her mouth, then sat up straight and spewed it in his face.

Blinded by sticky gruel, he dropped to his knees, groped for her discarded napkin and wiped his eyes. Before he could rise, with a sweep of her arm across the night table, bowls, plates and lids crashed to the floor. Chocolate and hot kasha spattered the Indian carpets and his trousers.

"Have it your way. I'll sit on the floor." With one finger he scraped some of the chocolate on his leg and popped it into his mouth. "Mm. You don't know what you're missing."

Disappointed he could not even rouse a smile from her, he leaned back against the bed table. He eyed her book of Psalms that had fallen with her breakfast. It lay open. He picked it up and read from the yellowed page in halting Hebrew. *"'Kee m'rey'eem y'careysoon...For the evildoers shall be cut off but those who place hope in the Lord, they shall inherit the earth.'"*

"Who's left to inherit anything?"

"You can't lose your faith in the Almighty. He's all any of us has."

Her charcoal eyes sent daggers through his heart.

"I'll never forgive him. Or *you*."

## Chapter Five

A paint-spotted tarpaulin covered the floor of the empty apartment. Ulrich's shoulders throbbed and his head ached. He dunked his brush into the paint bucket and then with broad up and down motions began to paint the wall.

"Two coats and the stains still show through." Disgusted he dropped the brush into the bucket. Paint splashed out onto his shoes.

From his pocket he slipped a silver flask, unscrewed the cap and took a long swig of peppermint schnapps. How much liquor did it take to blot out horror? A river? An ocean?

"Maybe we should consider wallpaper." Nikolai's paint-dotted eyeglasses partly hid his eyes. He yanked them off and wiped them on his shirt tail.

"Or use red paint." Itzak flung his brush to the tarp.

In the month since the travesty it had fallen to him to put his brother's affairs, what was left of them, in order. Although the shop and adjoining apartment had been rented, he agreed to make them presentable for the new tenants before they took possession in July.

"Let's eat." He walked to the stove where fragrant steam rose over a kettle. "The women made us a meal fit for King David."

*"Professor Dietrich, please stay for dinner. We helped cook."*

Never one given to belief in ghosts, Ulrich rubbed his eyes. He could have sworn he saw Ruth and Rukhel peek around the stove. Their voices, as sweet as birdsong, rang in his ears.

"If such lovely young ladies helped, I've no choice, do I?"

The twins giggled and then vanished like smoke.

Not realizing he spoke his wishful thought aloud, he started when Nikolai took the flask from him. "Ulrich, when was the last time you slept?"

Sleep? It had been at least a month since a night passed without nightmares or insomnia. He plucked the flask from Nikolai's grip and took another swallow before tucking it back into his pocket.

With a ragged sigh, Arel squatted and hunched over a bucket. Black stubble covered one gaunt cheek. On the other side of his face scars ran from his temple to his chin. His uncombed black hair fell from under his cap into his red rimmed eyes.

"We'll all feel better after a little nourishment." Itzak ladled stew into four bowls. He held the first to Arel who dropped his hands to his sides.

"I'm not hungry."

"You're feverish, Reb Gitterman." Nikolai pressed his palm against the younger man's forehead. "After lunch, go home and rest—in bed. Not fully clothed in the chair in her room. Havah needs your strength."

"She won't talk to me. She won't even look at me." Arel slumped to the floor.

"*Nu?* Are you so much to look at?" Bowl in one hand and carving tool in the other, Itzak sat beside him. "Give her time, Little Brother. After you're married she'll have plenty to say."

"There isn't going to be any marriage."

"She'll change her mind."

"I hope you're right."

"Of course I'm right. I'm always right." Itzak's voice had a hollow edge.

Between bites of stew, he carved a thick staff of oak that already boasted an eagle's head at one end. Ulrich marveled at the cabinetmaker's skill as a flowering vine seemed to grow beneath his hand and wound its way around the circumference.

"What's it going to be?"

"It's nothing." Itzak shrugged his shoulders and grunted. "A gift for a friend."

Suddenly Arel blanched, sprang to his feet and bolted from the room. Itzak propped his evolving work against the stove. Stretching his arms over his head, he rose, arched his back and heaved an exhausted sigh.

"See you back at the house. Could you gentlemen bring the kettle with you?" Before he disappeared through the doorway Itzak peered back over his shoulder. "Reb Ulrich, I owe you."

In the ensuing silence, Ulrich's stomach grumbled. Picking up a bowl he sank to the floor. After three half-hearted bites he set the bowl aside. Like everything else, food had lost its flavor. He might as well have swallowed paint.

With a newspaper in hand Nikolai sat cross-legged on the floor. "Mind if I read?"

"Mind if I drink?"

Sunlight glinted off the smooth silver as Ulrich held the flask high in the air. He brought it to his lips and downed the last few drops. The empty container slipped from his hand and clattered across the stained floorboards. Once more he heard the children.

"He owes me? For what?"

"Ulrich, you couldn't have prevented it."

"If I'd not been traipsing off on holiday—"

"Then what?"

"She hates me."

"You're drunk."

"Not drunk enough. What are you reading?"

"*The New York Times.*"

"You and your newspapers." Ulrich leaned his aching back against the wall. "How are our friends across the sea? Have they discovered a new washing powder to save the American woman from her drudgery? Will their president charge up San Juan Hill again?"

"Far from it. According to this article he and his Cabinet are pressuring the Czar to denounce the pogrom."

Nikolai's voice cracked as he wadded the paper and hurled it against the wall. It left a crinkled print in the wet paint. "Condemn it? No doubt our precious leader is behind this madness. It's one of those things that make me 'proud' to be Russian."

"What else does it say?"

"Read it yourself."

Curiosity aroused, Ulrich scooted to where the crumpled paper had landed. He smoothed it, read the first few lines and gasped. "Fifty lives were taken and two thousand left homeless. Kolyah, did you read this?"

Nikolai's abject silence answered him. Bowed, with his head against his knees, the doctor's shoulders trembled.

Ulrich turned back to the wrinkled article and read. With dizzying intensity the words hit his eyes and the print blurred.

"*'The conduct of the intelligent Christians was disgraceful. They made no attempt to check the rioting. They simply walked around enjoying the frightful sport. On Tuesday, the third day, when it became known that the troops had received orders to shoot, the rioters ceased.'*"

"How could anyone call those demons Christians?" Nikolai lifted his head and wiped his eyes on his sleeve.

"You're right Kolyah, it's time to leave this place."

"Where will you go?"

"London, I think."

"Good. I'm leaving as well."

"When?"

"As soon as I'm sure Havah's out of the woods."

"Will you go back to St. Petersburg?"

"No, there's nothing for me there. Either America or London."

Ulrich grabbed his shoulders. "Choose London. It will be like old times in Heidelberg. We'll be two devil-may-care gadabouts."

"Since when were *we* ever gadabouts...devil-may-care or otherwise?"

"Just follow my lead."

Half-digested stew waged war with too much schnapps. Ulrich jumped up and staggered toward the door. Dropping to his knees on the sidewalk he gave in to the inevitable. He collapsed weakly onto his back and looked up.

Nikolai hovered over him, a wry smile on his lips, and said, "'*If the blind leads the blind both shall fall into a ditch.*'"

## Chapter Six

After her first real bath in months, Havah felt alive. The late spring breeze blew through her wet hair and cooled her. Both her hair and her freshly laundered nightgown smelled of cinnamon and vanilla.

With her left hand Havah grasped her locket and with her right index finger traced the engraved floral pattern. Given to her mother by her father before Havah was born, the gold still glittered in the sunlight. Using her left thumbnail to pop it open she studied her parents' faces which were reduced to faded black and white.

How odd that those animals had not ripped it from her neck. They took all of Katya's jewelry and silverware. Why not her necklace, too?

From the rocking chair by the window she watched the children play across the street, imagining Tuli and Velvil in their places. When one of them fell and scraped his knee, he screamed so loud his mother burst from the house. Sweeping the child into her arms she carried him inside.

"Christian brat." Havah turned away from the window and watched Anzya spread a clean sheet on the bed.

Intent on the task at hand, she fluffed the pillows and hummed a tune. Then she stopped and fixed her gaze on Havah. "What on earth did you say to Professor Dietrich the other day?"

"It's none of your business."

"Maybe it is. He hasn't eaten or slept since. The weeping I hear from his study could wrench a dead man's heart."

"What should you care? He's just a *Goy.*"

"Is he?" Anzya leaned over and kissed Havah's forehead. "Be sweet. Don't let the bastards win."

Havah fumed as the older woman loaded her basket with dirty bed linens and left the room. "How dare she preach to me about sweetness?"

Havah stretched her legs and stared at her disfigured foot. "They're killing me one piece at a time. First my foot, then my hand—what's next?"

"I once had a patient who lost both hands. Out of sheer determination he learned to do the most amazing things with his feet," said Nikolai as he entered the room carrying a portfolio under one arm and a small book in the opposite hand. "It's a beautiful day for a carriage ride."

"I don't have any clothes."

"Nonsense. Ulrich's given you a closet full of magnificent frocks."

"They're Valerica's, not mine."

"In other words you'd rather sit and feel sorry for yourself." He laid her prayer book into her lap. "Shayndel found this under the stove."

"Why didn't she bring it herself?"

"She's honoring your wishes, Miss Cohen. You told her to go away and never come back."

The hurt in her friend's eyes haunted Havah. She wished she could take back the cruel things she had said. Perhaps it was better this way and someday Shayndel would thank her.

Havah blinked and returned her attention to the little book. It lay open to the page that bore her brother's note written a lifetime ago—Tuli's lifetime. As she lifted the book a folded piece of paper slipped out. Trembling, she unfolded it and held her breath. A child's drawing of a woman with long black hair made her vision blur. Underneath the sketch, written in crude block letters it said, "Tuli loves Havah."

"He died in my arms."

"It's my turn." The doctor opened his folder and pulled out two similar pieces of paper. With an air of solemn reverence he held them out for her to see. The first one she recognized as the sketch Tuli had given him after their day at the fair.

The second was another child's drawing of two people with pale yellow hair. The figures were identical except for their sizes. At the bottom of the page it read, "*Tatko* and me."

"*Tatko*. It means papa, doesn't it?"

"He was only six the last time I tucked him in." Nikolai's spectacles could not mask his longing. It was the same look he wore the night he comforted little Velvil and called him *Solnyshko.* Havah suspected then that it was his nickname for someone very dear to him.

"Every day I ask myself what I could've done differently." A tear rolled down the stoic doctor's cheek as he tucked the papers back into the folder. "At least if he'd died in my arms I'd know where he was."

Chapter Seven

One at a time, Havah flexed each finger of her right hand. First her thumb, next her index finger and so on. When she finished she balled her hand into a fist. While it was still weak and basically useless, at least she had regained some feeling.

From outside, Itzak's voice boomed through the open window. "What a pity our little sister won't join us."

Although she heard Shayndel's muffled reply, she could not make out her words. After that the carriage squeaked and the horse's hooves clopped along the cobblestone pavement.

Havah lay back on the bed and counted the filigree tiles on the ceiling. She had almost drifted off when Yussel tapped his cane on the door.

"May I come in? Or will you leave me standing in the hall like a stray dog waiting for a pat on the head?"

"Go away."

With a smirk he entered using his cane to navigate around the furniture. "How can I refuse such a gracious invitation?"

"Can't you hear?"

"Better than most I'm told." He found a chair by the bed and lowered himself into it.

"Leave me alone. Just go away and leave me be."

"You'll have your wish soon enough. We're leaving in a few days. Dr. Derevenko says you are on the mend and Anzya will look after you. However, Arel insists on staying until you're well enough to travel. You do remember Arel?"

"He doesn't have to. I'm not going anywhere with him."

"Nonsense. Of course you are."

"How can I be an acceptable wife...to anyone? I'm handicapped."

"So am I. Doesn't seem to bother Mama." He grinned like a naughty little boy.

Havah felt the heat in her cheeks. "I'm sorry, Rabbi."

"Rabbi, is it? So formal?"

"It's better this way."

"Better you should treat the people who love you like pariahs?"

"Don't you see? I'm cursed. Everyone I care about dies."

Yussel's smile changed to a deep frown. For a while he leaned back in his chair and tapped his index fingers together. The pregnant silence made Havah squirm under the covers. Then, instead of the rebuttal she expected, he laid his cane across his knees and skimmed his fingertips over it with obvious affection.

"Lovely isn't it?"

Although the carving was crude, she could still see a candle with a disproportionally long flame. "It looks like a child made it."

"Itzak Abromovich. Eight years old. A bright, happy child. But when his mama died of brain fever he changed. Angry. Somber. Wouldn't speak a word to anyone.

"Little by little this slip of a boy turned his grief inside out and comforted others with his music. Finally he discovered his gift for woodcarving and from the ashes of his sorrow he made this cane for his grief stricken, blind rabbi."

"At least he had two good hands." Havah ground her teeth.

Yussel's fiery cheeks contrasted his ice-white beard. He pounded his cane on the floor, jumped from his chair and yelled, "You selfish child!"

## Chapter Eight

*One afternoon Mama and Papa went to visit friends. Havah's brother David who had been left in charge accidentally broke a prize pitcher, an heirloom passed down for two generations. Guilt plagued her. The accident was her fault. Had he not been chasing her he never would have tripped and knocked over the table.*

*When her parents came home, she and David endured a severe paddling. For hours afterward she pouted, refused to eat or speak to anyone and pondered her worthlessness.*

*Later that night David confessed that he and he alone had been responsible. After giving him a second whipping, Papa summoned Havah to his study. He laid his hands on her shoulders. "Why are you punishing us?"*

*Unable to answer, she hung her head. What did he mean? Wasn't it she who still felt the paddle's sting?*

*"Who do you think you are to carry the world's weight on your shoulders...the Almighty?" He tucked his finger under her chin and made her face him. His stern scowl and harsh voice frightened her.*

*Her tongue stuck to her lips. "I..."*

*"Selfish child. Wake up!"*

Havah started and opened her eyes. She kicked off the down comforter, rolled out of bed, hobbled to the window and stared at the empty cobblestone street below.

Her stomach growled, reminding her of the dinner she spurned earlier. Hoping there might be something to eat in the icebox; she slipped into her dressing gown and crept down the back stairs. As she neared the kitchen she heard music coming from the library. Something about the music's urgency beckoned her.

Bypassing the kitchen, she padded to the ballroom and tugged one of the heavy French doors until she managed to open it and slipped through the narrow gap. She tiptoed into the darkened ballroom.

Silhouetted at the piano by a solitary oil lamp, Ulrich played a mournful funeral dirge. The eerie appearance coupled with the intensity of his playing made her quiver and the resounding, yet poignant melody shook her insides. Hunched over the keyboard, his disheveled hair resembled windblown grass. A three day growth of beard covered his chin. Instead of the usual bay rum scent she loved, he reeked of stale liquor and the odor of days without a bath.

"Ulrich?"

Without looking up, he smirked and pounded out the final chords. Then he spoke in a slurred voice. "Chopin, Nocturne in C minor, Opus forty eight and to what do I owe the honor of Her Majesty's visit?"

Her neck and scalp tingled. With caution she reached out and pushed the hair off his forehead. He grabbed her bandaged hand and pressed it against his face. "Does it hurt badly?"

"A little."

"Damn them." He let go of her hand and reached for the bottle beside him.

She gently pushed it away. "Don't drink anymore. Please."

Ulrich lunged for it, upsetting the table. Valerica's picture fell, smashing the glass in the frame. Before he could catch it the photograph landed in a puddle of Schnapps. Ulrich picked it up and dried it on his paint stained shirt. Then he took Havah's wrist.

His fervid eyes sent electric shocks through her. Never had he looked at her that way before. Had Anzya been right all along? Vicious *goyim*—they were all alike in the end.

She jerked back, dropped to her knees and crawled away from him. Huddled under the piano, she covered her head with both arms and waited for the first blow. It never came. She heard only his ragged breathing.

Curiosity won over her fear and she uncovered her head and peered at him around the piano leg. He lolled in the midst of broken glass and spilled liquor, shirt tails hanging over his wrinkled trousers. Eyes closed, head laid back against the bench, Ulrich held the picture to his chest as if it were Valerica herself.

Havah inched toward him on her hands and knees. "I didn't mean to break it. Is...is it ruined?"

Opening his eyes he held it up to the lamplight. "She's a little damp at the corners. Otherwise she's still smiling."

A searing jolt shot through Havah's side and she doubled over. The picture fell from Ulrich's hand. He rose to his knees, scooped her up in his arms then stood and carried her to the sofa. As he eased down on it he gathered her onto his lap.

Candlelight glinted off the tears making narrow streams through the stubble on his face. "If only I'd been there."

"They'd have killed you, too." She shuddered and blinked. "It's all my fault."

"Stop it!" He pressed his palm against her lips and his embrace nearly suffocated her. Then he slipped his hand off her mouth and leaned his cheek on the top of her head. "Havah, Havah, you're too small to carry the weight of the world on your shoulders."

Like rain in the desert absolution washed over her and the tears she had kept at bay for two months fell in a deluge. Little by little her sobs subsided and she relaxed against his chest.

"Breakfast is served." Anzya stood in the doorway clad in her dressing gown. Under her ruffled nightcap she smiled. "Is anybody hungry?"

Embarrassed at having been caught in such a compromising position, Havah jumped off his lap. "How…how long have you been there?"

"Long enough to know the bastards haven't won."

## Chapter Nine

The distinctive Royal Academy letterhead blurred. Ulrich read the letter a tenth time before folding the parchment and sliding it back into the envelope. Had he made the right decision?

While she had gained back weight and the color had returned to her complexion, Havah was still as fragile as hand-blown crystal. At dinner when he announced his plans she burst into tears. It did not help when he reminded her of her own plans to marry and move to America. She only cried louder until Arel escorted her from the table.

Weary of pacing the floor between his bed and bureau, Ulrich put on his dressing gown. He struck a match on the sole of his slipper, lit a small lamp, lifted it off the bed stand and headed for the ballroom.

When he entered the room he padded to the piano and sat down on the bench. Tapping the center key, he whispered, "Middle C. Where *did* it all begin and where will it all end?"

From the newly framed, battered photograph on the end table, Valerica smiled but offered no answers.

"We're moving back to London, dearest." He kissed his fingertip and touched it to her image.

He sighed and skimmed his hand over the grand piano's smooth surface. Alas, it would cost a king's ransom to have it shipped and even then it might be damaged in the process so he opted to leave it behind.

Thirteen years ago the movers had delivered the magnificent instrument. Although he would have been satisfied with less, Valerica insisted on giving it to him for his birthday. Her eyes glistened like sapphires when it arrived.

He swept her up and spun her around. Even eight months with child she was still light as a bird in his arms. Then he sat at the piano with her on his lap. After all this time he could almost feel her warm breath on his neck.

"You murderer."

He turned to see that the warm breath on his neck came not from Valerica but from Havah who held a knitting needle over her head at a threatening angle.

Although her eyes were open she appeared to be in some sort of trance. He reached for her hand. The moment he touched her she lunged at him. The sharp point missed his face by a fraction of an inch.

She screamed. "Touch me again and I'll put out your other eye!"

Being as gentle as possible, he grabbed her wrist and pried her fingers from the needle. It bounced on the hardwood floorboards. Screeching like a feral animal caught in a trap, Havah jerked out of his grip. All at once she silenced and crumpled to the floor. Ulrich dropped beside her and tapped her cheek.

She bolted upright, hitting his chin with her head and jarred his front teeth. Havah scooted backward on her bottom and huddled in a corner. With the same caution he would use to approach a wild dog he crawled to her, crossed his legs and he sat with his back pressed against the wall.

Ever so gently he managed to wrap his arms around her waist and pull her onto his lap. To his relief she snuggled against him. Then, seconds later, she switched around, howled and beat her fists against his chest.

At that moment Arel burst into the room. "I should've known better than to trust you."

"It's not what you think." Ulrich yelled so he could be heard over her cries.

"Liar. I've seen the way you look at her."

"Dammit, Gitterman, shut up and help me rein in your cat. I can't wake her." Her teeth went deep into Ulrich's forearm. He wrenched it free with a shout.

"She's..." The color drained from Arel's face. "...asleep? Are you sure?" He inched toward them and knelt. "Havah?"

With a surprised cry he lurched backward when she hissed and spit in his face.

"Something cold, get me something cold." Ulrich's arm throbbed from her bite but he held her firmly for fear she would harm herself.

Arel ran from the room and returned moments later clutching a wet towel.

"Slap her face gently, boy, but make sure she feels it," said Ulrich.

At first Havah struggled but then she fell limp against Ulrich who stood and carried her to the sofa.

As soon as he laid her down her eyes opened. She looked at Arel, then Ulrich and then to the knitting needle on the floor. "I had the worst dream...but it wasn't a dream, was it? I...I almost killed you, Ulrich, didn't I?"

Ulrich shrugged. "I'll try not to take it personally."

## Chapter Ten

"Mama, Jeffrey took my doll and hid it. Make him tell me where it is!"

"Tattletale!"

Frustrated by her children's constant bickering, Sarah Tulschinsky stood and hurled her sewing basket to the floor. "Can't you two play nice? Don't you know how good you have it?"

Eyes wide, twins Jeffrey and Evalyne backed away from her. Sarah wished she could take back her harsh words. She had always made it a point never to raise her voice to them. After all they were only four. How could she expect them to understand?

While they were outside playing tag and climbing trees, the postman delivered a letter from Arel that had been lost for almost two months. His detailed account tore her heart into pieces.

Before she could explain to her son and daughter what had happened to those poor children in Kishinev, the front door opened. Wolf stepped over the threshold. Evalyne and Jeffrey raced to him. He scooped them up, one on each arm and spun them around.

"Papa, the lights comed back on today and we gots water, too!" Evalyne always had to be the first to share whatever she knew.

After kissing each of them, Wolf set the children back on their feet. His grin dissolved into a concerned frown. "It's still a mess around Union Depot but at least the trains are up and running. The *Star* says as many as twenty three thousand were flooded out of their homes."

"How many Jewish babies died?" Sarah could no longer control the emotion welling up in her chest. She dropped her head into her hands.

"Jewish babies? Sarah, what are you talking about? What's the matter?" Wolf knelt to pick up her spilled needles and thread.

When she managed to stop her tears, she fished the letter from her apron pocket and handed it to him.

As he read it tears welled up in his bulbous, dark eyes. "Suddenly a flood and a few days without electricity seem insignificant." Standing, he crumpled the letter into his balled fist. "Damnation! Let's bring them *all* here. Not just Arel and Havah. I'll turn this place into a boarding house if I have to."

A sober hush fell over the children. Jeffrey squeezed his sister's hand. "Come on, Evie. Lemme show you where I hid your doll."

## Chapter Eleven

More elaborate than Fruma Ya'el's simple brass samovar, Ulrich's enamel and silver one sat like royalty in the middle of his kitchen table. Steam rolled from its chimney. Havah poured just enough strong Russian tea from a china pot to cover the bottom of her cup. Then she turned the samovar's spigot and filled the cup the rest of the way with boiling water. She held a sugar cube between her teeth as she drank. After a few bitter sips, she crunched and swallowed the sugar.

Barefoot but otherwise dressed for the day, Shayndel padded into the room. Since there was no need in Ulrich's house to keep it a secret, her unrestrained golden braid swung behind her. She tugged one of Havah's tousled ringlets.

"Will you chop it all off tomorrow like a pious bride, little sister?"

"What do you think?"

"I think I'm happy that we'll be true sisters. Nothing can separate us now."

Hot tea scalded Havah's throat and tears filled her eyes. She blinked and forced a smile. Until this moment it had not occurred to her that moving to America would mean leaving the people who meant the most to her.

"What are you going to wear?" Shayndel's round cheeks flushed from the hot steam rising from her cup.

Relieved at not having to share her travel plans just yet, Havah smiled. "I'm not sure. Valerica had so many pretty dresses to choose from."

"There's no need to choose. I've something much, much better." Ulrich entered the room with a large box in tow.

"Haven't you given me enough?"

"Just open it," said Shayndel with childlike impatience as she clapped her hands.

"Voilà." Ulrich removed the lid and lifted out the most elegant ivory silk gown Havah had ever seen. He held it up to Havah. Lace and seed pearls trimmed the low neckline. "It's fourteen years out of date perhaps," he said, with a distant look in his eyes. "You'll be a most beautiful bride as was my Valerica."

Shayndel's grin widened. "Arel's eyes will just pop right out his head!"

"I can't accept this," said Havah. "It's too much."

"Of what use is it hanging in my closet, food for the moths? Besides, it's one less thing I have to pack." He handed the dress to Shayndel, then dropped to one knee and took Havah's hands in both of his. "Please, Havah. If I can't be your Prince Charming, at least allow me to be your benefactor."

Chapter Twelve

Itzak and Shayndel escorted Havah to the wedding canopy, beginning to circle it the traditional seven times.

"Such a beautiful bride." Shayndel's eyes brimmed as she linked her arm with Havah's. "The Czarina herself should be jealous."

Itzak held Havah's other arm. "Shayndel, hasn't there been enough crying? This is a happy occasion!"

"And these are happy tears." On the seventh time around, Shayndel whispered, "The time has come, little sister! Are you ready?"

"She's been ready for four years," said Itzak in a stage whisper.

Heat rose from Havah's bare collarbones to her cheeks. The dress's provocative neckline worried her. Although her virtue was for the most part hidden, she did not want to be perceived as a wanton woman at her own marriage ceremony.

*"'Blessed is she who is arriving. He who understands the speech of the rose among the thorns, the love of a bride, who is the joy of the beloved ones, may He bless the groom and the bride.'"* Thirteen-year-old Lev Resnick sang in a melodious alto with an occasional squeak, a boy's voice on the cusp of manhood.

In deference to Ulrich and Nikolai, Yussel translated the Hebrew blessing into Russian. He reached for Arel and Havah's hands and whispered, "Now, my little scholar, you are indeed my daughter."

Her heart danced with angels as Yussel said the blessing over the wine then handed it to Arel to drink.

Arel, in turn, handed the cup to Fruma Ya'el who, as mother of the bride, held it while Havah drank.

Arel slid a gold ring on Havah's right index finger. "'Behold you are fair, my beloved, behold you are fair, your eyes are doves.'"

While Yussel recited the traditional seven blessings, she gazed into Arel's clear gray eyes. His clean-shaven face shone like a boy's.

After vows were said and Arel broke the wine glass under his foot, Itzak yelled, "Mazel Tov!" then tucked his violin under his chin.

Havah's stomach flip flopped with each dip as Nikolai and Lev lofted her high above the crowd on one of her favorite brocade chairs. Gavrel and Ulrich carried Arel who sat on the other chair. After parading them in a circle around the ballroom, to her relief, they were returned safely to the floor.

Yussel and Fruma Ya'el accompanied the bride and groom to the door of the *yikhud*, the room prepared for their first meal as man and wife.

Hand in hand, right feet first, Havah and Arel stepped over a silver spoon in front of the threshold. When the door closed behind them, he locked it and then engulfed her in a breathtaking embrace. With unrestrained passion he caressed her. One by one, he pulled out her hairpins. Her hair cascaded over her shoulders and past her waist to her knees.

In vain she tried to twist it back into a bun. "Not now, Arel. Remember our guests. We have to make our grand entrance in eight minutes."

She trembled with delight when he burrowed his hands beneath her bodice. His breath hot and moist in her ear, he whispered, "Our guests can wait. I've waited long enough."

## Chapter Thirteen

Like a silver waterfall, moonlight poured through the tall window. Havah snuggled next to her husband, her ear against his chest. His heartbeat, slow and steady, soothed her.

Even though they had excused themselves over an hour before, the wedding festivities continued in the ballroom downstairs. Piano, flute and violin played melody after joyful melody.

Curving her arm around Arel, she sang in his ear and tapped her foot against his leg in time to the music.

He rolled over. "Do you want to go back downstairs and join them?"

"No. I just want to stay here with you like this forever."

"You're sure you wouldn't rather dance?"

"Of course not. What a silly thing to ask."

"*You* may not want to dance, but your feet certainly do." Playfully, he grabbed her right foot.

In a frantic attempt to jerk it from his grasp she kicked him. Determined, he held tight and tugged at her heavy sock.

"It's the middle of summer. Are you cold?" He sat up and lit the lamp on the bed stand.

"No."

"Then why the socks?"

"You know why."

"Let me see it, Havah."

"See what?"

"You know what."

"It's hideous. You'll never want to share my bed again."

"Is it worse than this?" He took the lamp from the stand and held it under his chin. "And I can't hide it with stockings."

The weight of his words pierced her heart. While she had seen children stare and point at him, until this moment his embarrassment never occurred to her. Nor had she considered his pain at having been beaten and left for dead.

She sat up and brushed her lips across the scars cobwebbing from his forehead to his chin. "My beloved is pure and ruddy, exalted among ten thousand." Then she laid her leg across his knees.

He slid off her woolen stocking and dropped it on the floor. With rabbinic concentration he studied her gnarled three-toed foot that looked like eagle's talons. Instead of gagging as she expected he cradled it in his hands like a precious jewel and kissed it. "My bride. You are altogether lovely."

## Chapter Fourteen

"I'll miss you." On the platform Shayndel, her eyes swollen and red, hugged Leah. "But Devorah will be glad to have you with her. You've grown up well. My sister would be proud of you."

Fruma Ya'el's eyes filled with tears. Two-year-old Bayla squirmed in her arms. "Want down, Bubbe."

Loath to let go, Fruma Ya'el tightened her hold around the child's waist. "You stay here. Do you want to be run over by a train?"

With a puzzled look in her huge gray eyes, Bayla reached up and wiped a tear from Fruma Ya'el's cheek. "Why you cry, Bubbe?"

The lump in Fruma Ya'el's throat made it hard to speak. Instead she seized Bayla's pudgy hand and pressed it against her lips.

As she watched Leah straighten Reuven's cap Fruma Ya'el remembered when the young wife was a busy seven-year-old who had been Gittel's favorite playmate. Death had stolen her daughter. Soon the cruel train would come and steal Leah away, too.

Bayla popped her thumb in her mouth and snuggled against Fruma Ya'el's shoulder. Twisting the fringes of her shawl around her tiny fingers, she sighed and closed her eyes.

The child's rhythmic breathing comforted Fruma Ya'el. Her mind harked back to a day when she offered to keep Leah and her five-year-old sister Devorah while Tova recuperated from one of Feivel's savage beatings.

Fruma Ya'el gave each of the girls a fabric square and taught them a simple pattern to embroider; a quiet, ladylike task to occupy them while she kneaded her Hollah for Shabbes.

Just as she set the dough to rise, she heard giggling followed by a shriek. She would never forget the sight that met her when she ran to the front room. There sat Devorah looking like a spiny thistle. Gittel and Leah tried to hide the sewing shears behind their backs. Devorah's shorn curls covered the floor like red puffs of smoke.

"Auntie Fruma?" She started and looked at Leah who lifted Bayla from her grasp. "It's time."

Gavrel, with Reuven perched on his shoulders and Lev carrying his one-year-old niece, Pora, gathered around to say goodbye to Yussel and Fruma Ya'el.

Yussel embraced Gavrel. "Have a good life in Odessa. Take care of my grandchildren. Write often."

"I will, Zaydeh."

"Hurry, Papa, let's go ride the train." Reuven squeezed Gavrel's neck.

Itzak grasped Gavrel's shoulders and kissed his right cheek. "My brother." Then he kissed the left. "My partner in justice."

As they boarded the train Bayla peeked over Leah's shoulder and waved. "Goodbye, Bubbe. Goodbye, Zaydeh!"

The vibration from the wheels rumbled under Fruma Ya'el's feet. The whistle's mournful blast intensified the ache in her heart. Over the chugging and clatter she heard Shayndel sobbing.

"What's all the fuss?" With a shrug that convinced no one, Yussel thumped his cane on the pavement. "They're just moving to another place. Gavrel will write. He's a man of his word." Then he added softly under his breath. "We'll never see them again."

## Chapter Fifteen

Nikolai raised his wine glass. "To Arel and Havah!"

"To Arel and Havah!" Everyone repeated with glasses raised.

"To my beautiful wife!" Arel emptied his glass.

Exhausted from a week of activity with little sleep, Havah leaned her head on his shoulder, content to listen.

David pointed. "Uncle Arel looks funny."

Mendel giggled. "His face is all red."

"Has my son had maybe a glass too many?" Yussel slapped Arel's shoulder.

Ulrich leaned across the table and reached for Yussel's hand. "Rebbe, may I ask you a question?"

Obviously giddy from the wine, Yussel chuckled. "You just did."

"*Another* question then. What's the significance of the groom smashing the glass under his foot?"

"I would think a learned man such as yourself would know the answer. The glass is broken to remind us that in the midst of our greatest joy we must always remember God's kingdom is not complete until the Holy Temple is rebuilt."

"It's a fine tradition and a worthy sentiment." Ulrich stood and rang his fork against his glass. "If I may have everyone's attention, I have a gift for the bride and groom."

Itzak poured a glass of wine. "To the bride and groom!"

Shayndel hit his arm. "Let the Professor talk."

"Thank you, Froi Abromovich." Ulrich bowed to her, grinned and continued. "As you probably know, Arel has made arrangements to take Havah to America to live with his sister Sarah."

A collective gasp went around the table. Even Mendel and David ceased from their chatter and giggles. Finally Yussel's strained voice cut through the pall.

"Is this true?"

"Yes, Papa. I think Havah might sleep better over there." Arel squeezed Havah's hand.

Despite four servings of wine, Itzak sobered and set his glass on the table. "That's an awful long way to go just for a good night's sleep!"

With a muffled sob and a glare that would melt midwinter ice, Shayndel scowled at Havah. "When were you going to tell us? When you boarded the train?"

Ulrich cleared his throat with a cough and continued. "As I was saying, for my wedding present I'm paying Arel and Havah's passage."

"How nice for you, little sister." Shayndel's hot gaze continued to sear through Havah.

"I've no one left." Fruma Ya'el rocked back and forth in her chair. "No one."

"Please. Please let me finish." Once more Ulrich tapped his fork against his goblet.

"Go on." Itzak's eyes darkened as he trained them on Arel and gulped down his fifth glass of wine. "Since you're the only one telling us anything."

"As part of my gift I'm offering passage for *all* of you to America!"

Fruma Ya'el's wailing came to an abrupt stop and her mouth dropped open. Yussel choked on his wine.

Itzak roared with laughter. "The wine's gone straight to your head, Ulrich! You can't be serious!"

"I've never been more serious."

"But we don't have passports."

"I thought of that already, Reb Itzak." With aristocratic aplomb, Ulrich set two small folders in the middle of the table. "I believe you'll find everything's in order. There's one for the Gitterman family and one for the Abromoviches."

"You would squander your entire fortune on poor strangers?" asked Yussel.

"On strangers, no. On family, yes."

## Chapter Sixteen

"I hope I didn't disturb anyone." After waking with a loud scream, Havah trembled and snuggled against Arel. Her sweat soaked through his nightshirt.

"'Everyone can simply roll over and go back to sleep."

Almost every night the nightmares tormented her. Arel wished he could do something to make them cease. Often he had to slap her awake to keep her from hurting him or herself.

"What if the others don't accept Ulrich's offer?" she asked. "What if they decide to stay in Svechka? I can't bear to lose another family. I can't."

"Isn't this what you wanted? What you've worked for? Why you've learned to speak English?"

"Do you really think my nightmares will stop in America?"

Even in the dim light he could see dark circles under her eyes. He stroked the side of her head while he searched for the right words. "No, I don't think moving will take those horrible memories from your head. But it's a safer place so perhaps you will feel more secure and maybe the dreams will occur less often. Does this make sense to you, Havaleh? Havah?"

He smiled at his wife, asleep in his arms. "I guess it makes sense."

****

Shayndel sat up. "My goodness! Did you hear her scream, Itzak? Poor Havah!"

"Poor Havah?" He groaned and pulled his pillow over his head. "I just fell asleep. Now I have to start counting backwards from one hundred all over again."

"As long as you're awake, Itzak, what do you think about Professor Dietrich's offer?"

"That's some offer."

"Well? Do you want to move?"

The pillow fell to the floor. Did he *want* to move? He had never known any home other than Svechka. If he agreed to it, he would have to learn a new language and a new way of life.

On the other hand, what did he really have left in Moldavia? His most treasured possession waited for an answer. The streetlight outside the window illuminated the longing in her blue eyes.

He wound a lock of her hair around his wrist and tugged until her head rested on his shoulder. "Surely there's a place in America for a skilled cabinetmaker."

\*\*\*\*

Did Professor Dietrich know he shared his home with a mouse? Yussel lay back on the pillow listening to his surroundings. Comforting sounds…a mourning dove's nocturnal melody floating on the wind, his bride's soft breathing beside him.

"Yussel, answer me." Fruma Ya'el's strident whisper demanded attention.

"If Havah and Arel have a chance at a better life in America, I say they should pursue it." He rolled over and wrapped his arm around her. As he searched her face tears bathed his fingertips.

"And what of our going with them? What will you tell Professor Dietrich?"

"If they go and Shayndel and Itzak go, whom do we have left? What do you *think* my answer will be?"

## Chapter Seventeen

"May I help you make the bed, Mama?" asked Evalyne

"No," answered Sarah.

"May I make lemonade?"

"Not now."

"Do we got company coming, Mama?"

"No."

"But Mrs. Mayer says we do."

With a swipe of her already damp sleeve, Sarah mopped dripping sweat from her eyes. The humid summer air made her impatient with her inquisitive daughter and even less patient with Zelda Mayer, the biggest snob and gossip in the congregation. She punched the heavy feather pillow and then plopped down on the bed.

"And just what else does Mrs. Mayer say?"

"She says we're going to have so many peoples in our house they'll be falling out the windows. Papa says Mrs. Mayer is more 'liable than a telegraph wire."

"That's *re*-liable and, yes, my little tomboy. We are going to have 'company.'" She stroked her daughter's frizzled hair. "Remember when I told you about my family way far away in a village called Svechka?"

"Uh-huh, it's where you got borned. It's why you and Papa talk different. And it's where my Zaydeh, the rabbi lives." Her chocolate brown eyes, round with four-year-old wonder, Evalyne climbed up beside Sarah.

"That's right. Your Zaydeh is my papa. It's been a long time since I've seen him."

"Are you happy about Zaydeh coming to live with us?"

"Of course I am. Why?"

"I dunno. You had a funny look on your face just now."

Sarah hated to admit that the prospect of an actual physical meeting with her father rattled her. Until Arel's telegram came a month ago she never really expected to see him again. Had he forgiven her? It was hard to tell in the few cheerful letters from her brother that read, "Papa says *'Gut Yontif,* Happy Holiday'" or "Papa says, 'give my grandchildren a kiss.'" What would he say to her face?

Chapter Eighteen

The depot building reminded Havah of a palace with its turrets and towers. The elegant waiting room made her feel like a princess. Stopping before a baroque framed mirror she marveled at her reflection. Pink silk roses adorned a wide brimmed hat. She felt like a fashionable lady.

Shayndel, too, wore a new hat with blue feathers that accentuated her ocean-blue eyes. Her golden braids wound around her head were no longer hidden under layers of fabric. Even Mama's short grey hair had been curled and coifed and her hat boasted red plumes.

Ulrich insisted the less they looked like poor immigrants the better treatment they would receive on their journey. Therefore, he had purchased first class tickets and expensive travel clothes for everyone including Mendel and David.

Throughout the morning Havah noticed other first class passengers pointing and smiling at her cane. Carved out of oak, its ornate vines wound their way to the eagle's head at the top. The beauty of it made it easier to accept her need for it.

Someone's acrid cigar smoke irritated her eyes and nose so she stepped outside where the railway station bustled with people. While the magnificent building offered every possible amenity for the upper class there was hardly a decent waiting room for those with second or third class tickets. Wending her way through the crowd, she found Ulrich who had also left the building for some fresh air. She sniffed bay rum and tried to forget how soon goodbye would come.

"I'm glad you and Dr. Nikolai are going with us to Rotterdam," she said.

"We just want to make sure you board the right ship."

"Havah! Professor!"

Accompanied by a thin man with a gray beard, a woman hurried toward them. Havah shielded her eyes from the afternoon sun with her hand. "Anzya!"

Havah's former nemesis glowed. Her partner flashed a broad smile. Anzya blushed. "This is my intended, Shimon. We're to be married Sunday."

With a grin, Ulrich bowed and then clasped Shimon's hand. "Mazel tov! You couldn't have chosen a better bride."

"My Anzya has told me of your kindness, Professor Dietrich, for this, I too am in your debt."

"Shimon's wife passed away two years ago," said Anzya. "He has three children who need a mother."

"Shimon's a good name, my papa's name." Havah embraced her. "Adoshem is restoring to you what the locust has eaten."

"Be well." Anzya kissed her cheek. "Be sweet."

"I have to know. What changed you?"

"You did, Princess." Turning to Ulrich, Anzya smiled. "Thank you, Professor. I will never forget."

Again he bowed. "Godspeed to you both."

****

As Havah watched them walk away, a familiar voice reverberated in her ears like rushing wind through a hollow tree. A demon's voice. Harbinger of death.

"Professor, my friend," said an apelike man with a black moustache. "Surely you and your doctor friend aren't leaving without saying 'good-bye.'"

At that moment Nikolai and Itzak flanked Ulrich on each side. They glared at the man with a crude patch over one of his beady eyes. Then Nikolai spoke as if spewing something unpalatable from his mouth.

"Sasha."

Havah shuddered. "You know this pig?"

"Like I know dysentery."

Ulrich's jaws rippled with tension. He took a step toward Sasha, his knuckles white and his hands balled into fists. As he reared back to deliver a punch, Nikolai seized his arm. "He's not worth it. Save your hands for music."

Hatred consumed Havah. Not sure of what she would do or say she stepped up onto an empty crate and stood face to face with the one-eyed ogre who leered at her like a ravenous wolf.

"Well, well, who is this handsome young maiden?"

The way his lips curled over his rotting teeth nauseated her. Her desire to hack him to pieces, one limb at a time, blotted out all reason. Then, with all the force she could muster, she hit his face with the back of her hand.

His injured mouth dropped open and he stumbled backward, lost his footing and fell. His head hit the sidewalk with a crack. Blood from his wound made little rivers between the cobblestones.

A crowd gathered around her and erupted into applause yet she felt no sense of victory or triumph. She stepped from her perch and picked up the cane that had fallen from her weak grasp.

She raised it high but before she could slam it down across the beast's head, Itzak wrenched it from her. "Not with my masterpiece you don't."

Undeterred, she gathered what strength she had left and delivered a vicious kick to Sasha's ribs.

*"Oof!"* He cried out and grabbed her skirt hem.

Tugging it from his hand she dropped to her knees and spit in his face. "Suffer and remember, you child murdering bastard."

## Chapter Nineteen

To rest her throbbing feet Havah sat down on her trunk. She looked down at her new high buttoned shoes which though stylish, they were far from comfortable.

In her twenty years of life she had never seen a body of water bigger than the river behind Yussel's house in Svechka. Rotterdam harbor was vast and like a floating city, the huge ship called the Ryndam that would carry her to a new life was moored against a wharf at its edge. Already lines of travelers were trudging up the long ramp to the deck. Her heart raced. Soon she would be one of them.

"It's time." Arel offered her his hand.

Excitement mingled with sorrow. She stood beside him as the rest of the family circled around Ulrich and Nikolai. One by one they said their goodbyes.

Fruma Ya'el grasped Ulrich and Nikolai's hands and brought them to her lips. "*Azayht gesundt,* be well."

Next, Yussel wrapped his arms around Ulrich, kissing first one cheek and then the other. "You are an angel sent to us by Adoshem Himself."

"No, Rebbe. It's you and your family who are the angels sent to me by the Almighty to give my life meaning and purpose."

The rabbi shrugged his shoulders. "I've heard it said, 'hell shared with a sage is better than paradise with a fool.'"

At last the only one who had not said her farewells was Havah. As she watched the others walk toward the ship, an odd queasiness in her stomach and tightness in her throat made it hard for her to breathe.

"Mrs. Gitterman, it's been an honor to know you." Nikolai bowed and kissed her hand, his grey-blue eyes brimming.

"I owe you my life." She grasped his hand and kissed it.

"You owe me nothing. Now go turn America upside down."

"You'll find your son, Dr. Nikolai. I'm sure of it."

"Hurry, Havah." Arel tapped her shoulder.

"Please, a few more minutes."

"All right, but I'd hate to sail away without my bride." He placed his hands on Ulrich's shoulders, before pulling him into a determined embrace. "I'll take care of her for both of us."

Together, Arel and Nikolai took the rest of the baggage to the ship, leaving Ulrich and Havah alone. This was the moment she had been dreading. More like a child lost from his mother than a wealthy aristocrat, Ulrich's eyes brimmed.

"Remember what I told you. Speak English every chance." Hands shaking, he tied her hat's ribbon under her chin. "Promise me you'll write."

"In Yiddish or English?"

"I want to know everything that happens in your life."

"Will I ever see you again?"

"Of…of course. Someday I'll do a concert in Kansas City…and…" His voice cracked and he pulled her close.

Engulfed in his arms she did not want to let go. It was yet another safe haven soon to be left behind. The unknown terrified her.

As a brother might, he gave her forehead a discreet kiss. "Farewell, Frau Gitterman. You've written a melody on my heart that will play on forever."

Suddenly his forced smile dissolved. He tightened his embrace and mashed his lips against hers. Then he dropped his arms and stepped back.

Unsure of what to do or say next, she studied his face. She wanted to remember every detail, every line. Taking a step toward him she rose on tiptoe, brushed her lips over his cheek and whispered, "And I...I will miss the music in your eyes."

Chapter Twenty

Every Tuesday morning the women gathered at the Tulschinsky's to make clothes for Jewish refugees coming to Kansas City in increasing numbers. Sarah saw it as a way to repay the Almighty for taking care of her in this new world.

One of the sewing ladies, a handsome woman with dark hair and violet eyes, Zelda Mayer resembled one of the drawings on the cover of *Fashion World*. She seldom missed an opportunity to flaunt her wealth. As far as she was concerned her status entitled everyone else to her opinion.

She wagged her perfectly coifed head from side to side. "You're going to let your daughter sleep in a room with three *boys*? Sarah dear, it's just not proper."

With mild irritation, Sarah looked up from her sewing. "Relax, Zelda. They're babies. Not even five years old. They don't know borscht about the ways of men and women."

"Have you heard any news from your family, Sarah?" Nettie Weinberg, Sarah's best friend, looked up from the button she had been sewing on a shirt.

"I only know they left Kishinev sometime in August." Sarah bit off the end of her thread, took a sip of lemonade and gazed out the window at a cluster of dark clouds.

Zelda sniffed. "I don't see why you feel you have to turn your home into a—a flophouse. With eight more people, it will practically be a *shtetl*. There are other places for people like them to stay."

"What do you mean like *them*?"

"You know—immigrants."

"Where would you suggest?"

Nettie rolled her eyes and spoke in heavily accented English. "Why is it you should care, Mrs. 'Quality Hill'? They won't be moving into *your* house."

With a sidelong glance of haughty disapproval, Zelda flashed an ingratiating smile. "Sarah, dear, I'm only thinking of you, you being so frail and all. Don't you think they'd be more comfortable in McClure Flats among their own kind?"

"I nearly died of typhoid in that pest hole and you want I should send my family there?" Sarah's lemonade glass slipped from her hand and shattered on the floor. Outside thunder rolled. She jumped off the sofa and leaned into the other woman's face. *"Their kind* is welcome in my home. *Yours*, Mrs. Mayer is not!"

## Chapter Twenty-one

Like an impetuous child, Havah hopped from foot to foot. New York City's imposing skyline appeared to be painted against gray clouds.

What kind of life would they have in this unfamiliar place? She wound and unwound the fringes of her shawl around her index finger. Would Americans understand her English?

Yussel grasped her arm. "Is she there, Little Scholar? The Statue of Liberty we've heard about?"

"Yes, Papa. She's standing in the harbor holding her torch of freedom high in the air for the entire world to see. She's wearing a crown and flowing robes like a queen."

"Yes, I see her," he said smiling serenely.

Her eyes burned. Whether from salt sea air or salty tears, she could not tell. She closed them and listened to the wind rushing by her ears, wind that bore the rich earthy smell of land. From all decks she heard people cheering, singing and weeping.

Something tugged at her skirt. "Pick me up, Auntie Havah."

She knelt and scooped David up in her arms.

He waved his plump hands and pointed. "Look Mendel, Stachoo Livertee!"

Beside her, in Shayndel's arms, Mendel did not seem the least bit interested. Instead he whimpered. His head drooped over her shoulder. Shayndel coughed. "Havah, feel Mendel's head. I think he has a fever."

"He was fine yesterday." Havah pressed her hand against Shayndel's hot forehead. "You don't look like you're feeling so well yourself."

"Nonsense, I've never been sick a day in my life."

The ship slowed and, with the help of tugs, was maneuvered to a wharf that extended from a city whose innumerable buildings reached to the sky. Itzak took David from Havah. Arel appeared at her side and offered his arm. "Come along, Mrs. Gitterman. Your new land awaits its most beautiful citizen."

She fell in step with him as they followed behind Itzak and Shayndel, taking in the new sights. Did grass grow in America? So far she had only seen the forests of tall buildings and the hustle and bustle of activity along the pier.

A few feet from the exit Mendel hacked a loud whooping cough which attracted the attention of a ship's crewman. He stopped Shayndel and felt the boy's head.

With a firm hand on her shoulder he frowned. "I'm sorry, Lady, but I hafta send you and your kid to be examined by the docs at Ellis Island before I allow you into the country."

When Shayndel did not respond, he raised his voice. "You deaf?" He slapped his own forehead. "What am I thinking? You don't understand a word I'm sayin' do ya?"

Although he did not speak English the way Ulrich taught her, Havah understood most of what he said. "I speak some. What is problems, officer?"

"What I been trying to tell your friend here is that this boy is sick. She don't look too good neither. They need to go to the hospital on the island to make sure they ain't too sick."

"But she already pass examination on ship. We are First Class. Doctors say we don't need to go to Island of Ellis."

Determined to have her way, Havah folded her arms and scowled at him. He could not have been much older than she. He was a skinny boy with freckles wearing a uniform to make him feel like a big man, just like the Cossacks.

"Don't blame me, I don't make the rules." He shrugged.

"If my sister she don't go then none of us, we don't go!"

"Suit yourself, lady. You can all take the ferry to Ellis Island. It ain't no skin off my nose. Don't make no difference to me what happens to a bunch of greenhorns. You can all go back where you came from for all I care but we don't want none of your diseases in our country. We got enough of our own, hear?"

"Yes, I hear. You are welcoming us *not* to come to America because *you* are sick."

Chapter Twenty-two


Almost every bed in the stark hospital ward was occupied by sick women and children. Shayndel and Mendel lay on two of the beds, still fully clothed, waiting to be examined by a doctor. He would decide whether or not they should be sent back to Eastern Europe.

The antiseptic odor turned Fruma Ya'el's stomach. Nurses milled around speaking a language she did not know. She set her heavy bag on the floor. Rubbing her aching back she almost wished for one of the beds for herself.

One nurse, a stout woman wearing an ankle length gray dress and white apron, wagged her finger in her face. While Fruma Ya'el did not understand her words she needed no translation to understand her tone.

"Havah, what is she so angry about?"

"She says the hospital is for contagious sick only. We must all leave."

"I'll not leave my daughter and grandson alone in this—this dungeon." Yussel thumped his cane on the floor. "You tell this fat crone my family stays together."

David tugged at Yussel's coat sleeve. "How can you tell she's fat, Zaydeh?"

"Listen to the way the floor groans when she walks. It's either her or somebody's stray milk cow."

Shayndel grasped Itzak's hand. "Maybe you should do what she says. I don't want to be in trouble with the authorities."

Defiance flashed in Itzak's dark eyes as he sat beside her on the the bed. "The 'authorities' can beat me senseless. It won't be the first time. My place is with my bride."

"Please, Lady, don't hurt Papa." Mendel slid off the bed, followed after the nurse, pulled on her skirts and whimpered.

The nurse grabbed Mendel's collar and pointed to the bed. His whining intensified until his shrieks echoed and the other children responded in kind. The nurse picked him up. His screaming grew even louder and he kicked against her ample hips. Clapping her hand over his mouth, she threw him back down on the bed.

Fruma Ya'el did not know what the English words "kike" and "brat" meant but she felt certain they were not words of comfort for a frightened child. She sat on the bed and took Mendel in her arms, stroking his dark curls. His screaming turned to hacking sobs.

Itzak rose, fists clenched and lunged at the nurse who backed away, her hand over her face. "Havah, you tell her if she touches my son again I'll forget she's a woman."

In English, Havah said something to which the nurse replied in a brusque voice. Then the nurse turned on her heel and walked down the aisle to the door.

"What did she say?" asked Fruma Ya'el, certain it was nothing nice.

"She's going after someone to throw us out." Havah's eyelids drooped and her cheeks blanched. She lowered herself onto Shayndel's bed.

"You don't look well, Little Sister. I wonder if you shouldn't be lying down in one of these beds."

Havah's otherwise pale face shone. She pointed to where the ship's doctor had chalk marked her coat with a large "Pg". "What I have isn't contagious, Mama."

Fruma Ya'el felt Mendel's forehead. "No fever. No rash. This one's not contagious either. It's certainly not Too—Too—what was the word the inspector used?"

"He wrote it down for me." Havah reached into her bag and pulled out a torn piece of paper. "Ugh. If it's not bad enough it's in English, his handwriting is terrible. Too-burk-yoo-low-sis. Tuberculosis."

"Bubbe, am I bad? David says I am." Mendel curled up on the bed. "He says if we have to go back to Svechka it will be my fault."

David stuck out his tongue.

"No one's going back." She smacked his backside. Taking her handkerchief from her coat pocket she wiped Mendel's runny nose.

He sniffed. "Promise?"

"Does Bubbe ever lie to you?"

Making a face at David, he popped his thumb into his mouth and closed his eyes.

Tears slid down Shayndel's cheeks. "What if it is what the inspector says? What if we are too sick?" She sneezed.

As though she swatted a bothersome fly, Fruma Ya'el waved her hand. "*Feh!* A cold. That's all."

"How can you be sure?" Shayndel's eyes widened. She pointed and whispered. "Here's that horrid nurse again and a man. I think he's a doctor."

"Good. He'll examine you and he'll tell you I'm right."

"Right." Gentle hands squeezed Fruma Ya'el shoulders and a man spoke in Yiddish. "If this dear woman says it's a cold, rest assured that's all it is."

Although his voice had deepened with age Fruma Ya'el still recognized it. Quivering, she turned and blinked. His smooth head glowed under the electric lights. What remained of his dark hair and full moustache had turned to silver. But his coffee-brown eyes had lost neither their zest, nor their sparkle.

"Ya'el," said Dr. Rosenthal "you're still a beauty."

## Chapter Twenty-three

Still unaccustomed to the feeling of wind in her hair, Fruma Ya'el secured her hat and shielded her eyes from the sun with her gloved hand. From the lawn in front of the Great Hall, she looked across the water at New York City.

"Charles, after all these years, I can't believe it's really you."

"In the flesh…wrinkled though it may be." Charles Rosenthal, clad in as fine a suit as she had ever seen, leaned against the flag pole in the middle of the yard, a stethoscope draped over his neck like a scarf.

"Pity you chopped off your beautiful curls." He held up his hand. "I know. I know. You couldn't fly in the face of tradition. I'm just happy to see you've come to your senses." Brushing his hand over his glossy pate, he winked. "Unlike mine, yours will grow back."

"Thank you for what you did for us back there at the hospital."

"How all of you managed to stay together and worm your way into the clinic in the first place is beyond me. But, I couldn't allow my revered colleagues to torture such a *shayna maydeleh* and her child for a simple cold, could I?"

"Our Shayndel is a pretty girl, isn't she? And you. Are you still trying to change the world, Dr. Rosenthal?"

"Only my small part of it."

Her shawl slid off and landed in a heap at her feet. Charles scrambled to retrieve it then stood and groaned. "I'm not as spry as I used to be."

He wrapped her shawl around her and then slipped his hands to her forearms. "I'm sorry you and your family have to put up with the rigmarole they put you through at the registry. On the other hand, had it not been for the health inspector's error in judgment we wouldn't be here."

A sudden gust made the flag above them snap and ripple, red and white stripes bright against the blue sky.

"Are you married, Charles?"

"Twenty-five years this past June."

"Do you love her?"

"Of course."

"Is she a doctor, too?"

"No, she's a teacher at Normal College, a *women's* college."

"You have children?"

"Three daughters. My eldest just blessed me with a grandson last year. My son-in-law, the doctor, is a good husband and father. They married for love."

Even after all these years, Charles' eyes still had the power to bring her to her knees. "I…I should go back inside."

"They'll hold your place in line. No one would dare cut in front of your spitfire of a daughter." He seized her hand. "She reminds me of a certain young woman I once knew."

"*Feh!* I was nothing like Havah."

"Ah, but you *were*…with one notable exception. I'll wager she'd never have allowed her father to make her decisions."

His grip tightened around her wrist and his scowl deepened the crease between his dark eyebrows. Memories never too far from the surface of her mind swept her back through time.

*Returning from market, she sat on the wagon seat next to her older sister Gittel. The air was redolent with* the fresh aroma of newly hung laundry drying in the sun. She breathed in lilac and cinnamon which Gittel always added to her lye soap.

Fruma Ya'el could never smell the spice without thinking of her. It was the reason Fruma Ya'el used cinnamon in her own soap making.

After their mother's death, Gittel had done her best to be both parent and sister to Fruma Ya'el. When Gittel and Hershel married six years before, he moved into their house, a devoted husband and older brother, he was affectionate and funny. It never seemed to bother him that his wife had borne him no children. He claimed she was all that he needed to make him happy.

While Gittel urged the horse on along the rocky path, she chattered like a robin heralding the first sign of spring. "Fruma, you'll have to make your best noodle kugel for dinner. I've invited your doctor friend. You know I'm going to miss you when you go to America."

"Silly goose. What makes you think I'm going? Besides, I'm only seventeen and Charles is almost twenty-six."

"I saw him talking to the matchmaker after shul Saturday." Gittel's eyes twinkled like black diamonds and she winked. "You think maybe he was asking for her chicken soup recipe?"

Half a block up the road Hershel and Charles sat on chairs in front of the house speaking with emphatic gestures. How they enjoyed a good argument. Hershel saw them, stopped talking, then grinned and waved.

Fruma Ya'el saw the snake in the road at the same time the horse whinnied and reared back. The otherwise gentle mare bolted and Gittel hauled on the reins to no avail.

The wagon lurched and careened wildly straight into a field where one of the wheels splintered on a large *stump. Fruma Ya'el's landing was cushioned by a freshly plowed furrow. Her sister was not so fortunate.*

*By the time the men reached the overturned wagon the damage was done. On its side, tangled in trace and girth, the horse tried frantically to escape. Its hooves beat a frenzied tattoo upon the earth and upon Gittel's broken body which lay beneath them.*

*Although Charles kept vigil at her bedside all night he was helpless to do anything but ply her with laudanum to ease her suffering. An hour before dawn her waning life escaped with a gasp through her swollen lips. Insane with grief, Hershel accused Charles of killing his wife and swore he would make him pay.*

"Ya'el, no one could've saved her." Charles' voice brought her back to the present. "Your father handed you over to Hershel as a peace offering, a consolation prize and Hershel married you to spite me."

"*Shah!* It's a sin to speak ill of the dead. It was all for the best." With her free hand, she held two fingers in front of her lips.

He grasped it with desperate force. "Look me in the eye and tell me again 'it was all for the best'." He pressed her captive hand against his breast. "Why Ya'el?"

"You're hurting me." She tried to free herself from his grasp.

"Hurt? Let me tell you a thing or two about hurt. I would have laid down my life for you, but you slammed the door in my face."

"Let go of me."

"I still hate your father and Hershel. I'm glad they're dead."

"Do you still hate me?"

For a brief moment it was as though thirty years had never passed. She relished the feel of his smooth hands caressing her face. His peppermint and cigar laden breath warmed her and his lips pressed against hers.

Reality snapped her back to the present.     She opened her eyes and shoved him looking around to see if anyone had witnessed her indiscretion.

Another doctor ran toward them, wringing his hands. "Dr. Rosenthal, we need you."

"Give me a minute, Doctor." Charles took a piece of paper from his pocket. He scribbled on it with a pencil stub. "Here's my address, Ya'el. Please write to me after you've settled."

With a kiss, this time a peck on her cheek, he turned and raced after his colleague. For a moment she lingered and stared at his rumpled note. Then she turned, and trudged toward the registry hall. Behind her, tattered bits of paper scattered on the wind.

Chapter Twenty-four

After spending a sleepless night on a hard bench, Havah's back, shoulders and neck ached. Brushing her hair out of her eyes, she reached for the hat that Ulrich had given her in Kishinev. Droopy and wilted, the once pink silk flowers had a gray tinge.

Grateful for her cane, she went to the ticket window, tucking her disheveled curls under her sagging hat. "What time to buy tickets on train to Kansas City?"

From under his black-billed cap, his eyes yellow walls of indifference, the concessionaire glared at her. His pipe, held between crooked teeth, exuded foul smelling smoke. "It's too early, Lady. Come back in an hour. Okay?"

"But you are here already."

"Look, sister, rules is rules."

"You are mean man."

"This job don't pay me enough to be nice."

To pass the time she hobbled the perimeter of the Registry Room, taking in the sights and sounds. Early morning sunlight poured through huge windows just below the vaulted ceiling between massive pillars. There were more people in the building than she had ever seen in one place at one time. Many came from Russia and other parts of Eastern Europe. Some came from Italy or France, places she had only read about. They sat on long rows of benches, waiting to register and be released to their new homes.

All over the great hall, children awoke, crying for their mothers. Their high pitched squeals made Havah's head throb. The odor of unwashed bodies mingled with pipe tobacco, coffee and other effluvium she did not recognize.

A wave of exhaustion coupled with nausea washed over her. She rejoined Arel on the bench where she curled up beside him and let her head sink into the folds of his woolen coat. "Your son is making me very sleepy, Reb Gitterman."

Instead of catching a short nap until the ticket concession opened, she fell sound asleep. To her horror, when she woke up, Arel smiled and said, "Good afternoon, Havaleh."

"How long have I been asleep?"

"Four hours."

"Why didn't you wake me?"

"A woman in your delicate condition needs rest."

She jumped to her feet and waved her cane in his face. "Do you know how long some people have waited to buy tickets? Days. Weeks. Even *months!*" She lifted her scraggly hat and, with one hand, jammed it down on her head.

Without a thought to her appearance, she hurried back to the ticket counter only to find two lines stretching from one end of the building to the other. Determined, she wedged in between the first person in line and the vender's counter.

"Please sir, I ask before about tickets."

"Listen, sis, it ain't my fault you lost your place in line. You're gonna have to wait like everybody else."

Angrily, she went to the end of the line. At least ten minutes passed before the person in front of her stepped forward. This would take hours. Her foot ached and hunger gnawed at her empty stomach.

Resigned to a long wait, she took a book from her bag but someone bumped into her from behind and knocked it from her hands. Her anger ignited against the clumsy stranger and she whirled about to confront him.

Instead of the impudent lout she expected, Shayndel dropped to her knees and picked up the fallen book. Then she stood, tears welling up in her eyes and streaming down her cheeks.

"Shayndel, what's the matter? Where were you going in such a hurry?" Havah's anger dissolved.

"It's David! He's run off. I put the boys down for a nap. Mendel went right to sleep but David was full of wiggles. I—I only looked away for a minute."

"Maybe he's with Itzak."

"No, Itzak and Arel are looking for him, too. I left Mendel with Mama and Papa and—oh, Havah, did I come all the way to this terrible land only to lose my baby?"

Havah stuffed her book back into her handbag and wrapped her arm around Shayndel. "Don't worry. We'll find him. He couldn't have gotten far."

"But this place is so big! How will I ever find such a small boy among so many people?"

"We will find him." She pointed to a row of benches. "You go down that row over there and I'll look down the next. With Itzak and Arel both looking, one of us is bound to have success."

With frustrated reluctance she relinquished her place in line and made a silent vow to spank David without mercy if she found him first.

After a frustrating hour of searching under benches, behind trunks and asking people, often resorting to sign language, if they had seen David, she caught a glimpse of the boy who ran headlong into a stout man in a tweed suit.

Instead of the irritation and the possible tongue lashing she might have expected from such a well-dressed gentleman, he laughed and swept David up into his brawny arms. With a nod to the concessionaire he had been speaking to, the man sat on a nearby bench and set the boy on his lap. Beneath a bushy moustache the man flashed a toothy smile. He pinched David's cheek, then took a silver coin from his pocket and pressed it into David's hand.

"Where's your mama, young man? Ah, you don't understand a word I'm saying, do you?"

"Oh, please to forgive my...my niece...no no...not niece...nephew." Havah stepped toward them. In Yiddish she reprimanded David.

"The lad's done no harm. He's a fine boy and I've one just like him at home." Eyeing her cane, he patted the bench beside him. "Won't you have a seat, madam?"

"Havah Cohen...Gitterman. David, he don't speak English. He like to talk so I think he learns quick."

"I dare say his auntie will teach him. Where are you from?"

"Kishinev."

"Kishinev?" His smile faded. "Then you are... Jewish?"

"What if I am? This is free country."

"It was a travesty—a dastardly travesty." He shook his head.

His blue eyes, moist and caring behind his spectacles, put her at ease. She showed him the scar on her hand. Trying to recount her history in her new language proved a challenge but he seemed to understand for his gaze never wavered except to wipe away a stray tear.

When she finished he pressed his handkerchief into her hand. "Where do you go from here?"

"A village called Kansas City." She dabbed her eyes with the handkerchief. "You know it?"

"I've heard of it."

"I have to buy tickets for train. But I have lose place in line. I am only one who speak the English and we will not be cheated."

His laughter echoed through the huge hall. "Bully! Bully for you, My Dear!"

He stood, hoisted David onto his shoulders and led her to the front of the line. "Make sure this lady's entire family is put on the right train immediately and sent on to their final destination."

"Yes, *Sir*! Anything you say, Sir. How many?"

With an almost frantic nod, the man who had been so gruff handed her eight tickets without hesitation. He even smiled at her.

The man with the bushy moustache planted a noisy kiss on David's round cheek and then set him on his feet. "I wish you a good life well lived, Little Man." He bowed and kissed her hand. "Godspeed and safe travel, Mrs. Gitterman."

"How do I ever thank you, Mr....?"

"Roosevelt, Theodore Roosevelt, at your service."

Chapter Twenty-five

Many of the synagogue members were emigrants from Russia who spoke Yiddish among themselves. Most had been in the country a long time and spoke English so rapidly Havah only understood every other word. Ulrich had cautioned her not to be impatient with herself. After two weeks in America what did she expect?

Across the large hall Itzak had already befriended a small group of musicians of the congregation. One of them, a lanky, dark haired man who played clarinet, reminded her of Evron. Another, a chubby gent with bulging whiskers and no hair on his head, pumped an accordion. Sweat beaded on his crimson forehead as he squeezed the instrument. Itzak winked at her over his violin.

Those who had finished eating formed circles and danced. Just like in the old country, one circle for women and one for men. It seemed some things changed while others did not.

Beside her Shayndel's hair shone golden under the electric lights. Her face reflected pure ecstasy. She licked her lips and patted her tummy. "Chocolate cake. The baby likes it."

"How can you eat?" What little food Havah had forced down threatened to come back up.

"Just wait until your fifth month, Little Sister. You'll eat everything."

"But you're no farther along than I am."

"I never get sick." Shayndel popped the last bite of cake into her mouth, took Havah's plate and proceeded to wipe it clean. She pointed to the dancers. "It is good to see my sister again."

Not much taller than Havah, Sarah bore a resemblance to Arel and Tova. Her thick black hair framed her delicate face. Although she lacked Shayndel's sparkle she was, nonetheless, handsome and poised. Between two women who towered over her, she giggled and danced with vigor; not at all the silent Sarah Yussel had described.

When the music came to an end, Sarah clapped her hands and grinned until her gray eyes met Havah's gaze. Sarah's smile faded for a moment. Then, with a curt nod she turned her head and struck up a conversation with another woman.

"Sarah doesn't like me." Havah looked down at the angry scar on her hand. She flexed and stretched her fingers in an exercise Dr. Nikolai instructed her to do three times a day.

"She's always been shy."

"No, it's more than that."

To avoid any further argument, Havah pointed to Yussel who sat at a table discussing Jewish law with other men of the congregation. "Papa's found—"

A shrill female voice a few feet away stopped her. She turned to see who was speaking. A well-dressed woman with wavy hair wagged her head and clucked her tongue. "Tch, tch, I just can't believe it, Nettie."

"You can't believe what, Zelda?" The plump woman with sorrel eyes and amiable features tapped Zelda's shoulder. "Lower your voice."

"Why should I? Those greenhorns don't understand English." With her pinkie finger at attention, Zelda sipped punch from a crystal cup. "As if it's not enough Sarah and Wolf took in her poor relations, now I hear two of those peasants are in a family way. Where are they going to put two babies, I ask you? They're going to run that nice house into the ground. Tch, tch. Why, it's practically a sin."

"What's it to you? Besides, they'll be moved into their own homes before the little ones arrive." Nettie, who had made a point of welcoming Sarah's family with food and gifts the second night after their arrival, winked at Havah.

Unaware of the exchange, Zelda continued. With each statement she raised her voice another octave. "I wouldn't trust them. Wolf's built such a good reputation. 'd hate to see things ruined by a bunch of *shtetl* peasants."

"Aren't you forgetting *you* were once, as you put it, a '*shtetl* peasant'?"

While it was hard for Havah to keep up with Zelda's rapid-fire accusations, she recognized the haughty woman's accent which betrayed her origins. Trembling with anger and thumping her cane along the way, Havah walked to where the two women sat.

She stopped in front of Zelda, glowered and searched for the right words in English. "I am not mean to intrude. I am one of '*shtetl* peasants' you speak of and I think already I don't like you."

Zelda's cheeks blanched and her mouth fell open. Nettie's eyes twinkled as she rose from her chair. "If you will excuse me, Mrs. Mayorovich, I mean Mrs. Mayer, I believe Mrs. Gitterman has more to say to you.

Havah's thoughts tumbled over each other with such reckless fury she reverted to Yiddish. "How is it you have forgotten where you came from? Why, you're no better than the rest of us! What makes you think you have the right to pass judgment?"

Past caring whether the other woman understood her or not, she pointed to Arel who had joined Yussel in his emphatic discussion. "You see my papa and my husband? They're not wealthy men but they are scholars!

Rabbis! Their knowledge is worth far more than all of your fine jewelry.

"My brother Itzak is a musician and a skilled cabinetmaker. He may not own a king's ransom, but he's a man of honor. His wife Shayndel, my sister, has a tender heart, which is worth ten times more than your precious reputation.

"Fruma Ya'el, my mama, is a midwife and one of the most beloved women in Svechka. Can you say as much for yourself? For all your affluence, *Froi* Mayorovich, *you* are nothing more than a '*shtetl* peasant' in a silk dress."

## Chapter Twenty-six

Not since her mother's death had Sarah felt so empty or alone. Sipping coffee, she chided herself. What did she have to be sad about? She had a decent roof over her head, ample food on the table and family around her.

Outside, two sets of twins tumbled and played tag. Already all four children spoke both Yiddish and English fluently. Every night Wolf praised Arel's talent as a tailor. And in just two months Itzak had a long list of customers. Shayndel and Fruma Ya'el were welcome companions who made her housekeeping burden lighter and more enjoyable.

Maybe today she would invite Havah to accompany her to the market. After all, she was her brother's wife. But try as she might to like her, something held Sarah back.

Since the night the plucky young woman put Zelda in her place the telephone rang at least three times a day. Everyone wanted to talk to Havah. No one sang Havah's praises more than Yussel, proclaiming her the most eloquent scholar since Ram Bam.

Licking her pencil point, Sarah hunched over her shopping list. Soft music from the living room broke her concentration. Who could be playing Chopin?

Last year on her birthday Wolf had surprised her with the upright piano. Embellished with floral carvings, the mahogany instrument glowed when afternoon sun poured through her picture window. After two months of lessons she realized that for her it would be never be anything more than a magnificent piece of furniture. Maybe someday Jeffrey or Evalyne would want to learn.

She picked up her cup and tiptoed to the living room. There sat Havah on the bench, eyes closed, an ethereal smile on her face. Her feet dangled above the floor like a child's.

Mesmerized by the music's poignancy and her sister-in-law's skill, Sarah set down her cup and propped her elbows on the piano top. At the end of the piece Havah opened her eyes, started and dropped her hands into her lap.

"I'm sorry. I should have asked permission."

"Wherever did you learn to play like that?"

With her left thumb Havah massaged the scar on her right palm. "Dr. Nikolai says I should play every day for exercise. I thought everyone else went out."

"Not everyone." Yussel's cane made tapping noises across the floor. Once he had navigated his way to the sofa he eased himself onto it. "My little scholar. She's a wonder isn't she?"

Sarah's tongue stuck to her teeth. "Yes...Papa."

Havah's dark eyes darted from Yussel to Sarah. She took her cane, stood, arched her back and patted her slightly rounded belly. "It's such a lovely day. I'm going to take my son for a walk."

When Havah donned her shawl and opened the door a frigid November wind blew through Sarah. She sat beside her father and watched Havah hobble along the sidewalk.

After a protracted and awkward silence Sarah cleared her throat. "Havah's really a lovely girl. I can see why—"

"Sarah, shhhh," Yussel held his finger to his lips. He curved his other hand around her wrist. "You're still very thin. Do you eat well? You're happy?"

"Yes, Papa. I'm very happy."

"You don't sound happy."

Father and daughter fell silent, hand in hand. She could not decide whether to excuse herself and go to the kitchen or think of something else to say.

"You were right, Sarah." A tear trickled down his cheek.

"I was right about what?"

"When you said I never saw you. Flesh of my flesh. You were different from the others…so…fragile. Maybe I was afraid to love you."

"You don't need to explain."

"Don't I? You were served a terrible injustice by, of all people, your own father."

Years of longing for his affection burst from her in choking sobs. He gathered her into his arms and, for the first time in twenty-nine years, neither of them pulled away.

Chapter Twenty-seven

The smell of fresh brewed coffee, oily latkes and buttery jelly doughnuts filled the room. Havah and Arel's new living room resounded with lively music and laughter. Candle flames cast quivering shadows on the floral wallpaper and filigree tile ceiling.

Beneath Havah's dancing fingers the ivory piano keys glistened. In time with her playing Itzak's bow darted and skipped across his violin strings. They hammered out the last few notes then yelled out, "Hey!" in unison.

Cuddled on Yussel's lap, Mendel pointed to the silver menorah on the coffee table. "Zaydeh, why do we light the candles?"

"To remind us."

"To 'mind us of what?"

"That the Almighty's light is never so bright as when it shines in the darkness."

"Huh?" For a lengthy moment, Mendel's eyebrows furrowed. "I don't understand."

"I hope you never do." Havah winked at him. From a glass dish atop the upright piano she grabbed a handful of raisins. Popping them into her mouth she savored their sweetness.

Beside her on the bench, Evalyne clapped her hands. "Auntie Havah, will you teach me to play the piano like you?"

"It will take six minutes to teach you everything I know."

"Don't listen to your aunt. Professor Dietrich said he'd never taught such a brilliant and talented student." Kneeling, Itzak gently laid his violin in its case. He reached up and tugged one of the girl's black braids and tapped her lump of clay nose with his fingertip.

With five-year-old impatience she bounced up and down on the bench. "I promise I'll practice every day. Please. Oh, pretty please."

"You'll have to make sure your mama and papa won't mind," said Havah.

"The question is, Havah, do *you* mind? It would mean Evie coming over here every day to practice since we no longer have a piano." Between Yussel and Fruma Ya'el on the sofa, Sarah waved her hand as if to shoo a fly.

Tears sprang to Havah's eyes. "You may have it back. It's much too grand a gift in any case."

"Perish the thought. I'm not moving it again." Wolf, who sat on the floor playing dreidel with the boys and Arel, pressed his hands against his lower back and let out an exaggerated groan.

"In my house it's a dust collector, Havaleh." Sarah leaned her head on Yussel's shoulder. "What you've given me is worth more than a hundred pianos."

## Chapter Twenty-eight

*How had they found her? How could all of them be here, so far from their graves in Moldavia? Yet tonight, in her front room, they lived.*

*"Auntie Havah, you won't forget me, will you?" Tuli cuddled close to her on the piano bench, his eyes like shining onyx.*

*"Forget you, Little Rooster? Never in a million years!" She kissed the top of his head.*

*Hand in hand, Ruth and Rukhel fluttered across the floor. Their moon glow dresses cast colorful patterns along the polished wood. Their words tumbled over each other until Havah could not tell which had spoken.*

*"What a pretty house!"*

*"Play us a tune, Auntie!"*

*"Oh yes, oh yes! Please!"*

*"Let's dance."*

*"It's too late for dancing. You'll wake everyone," whispered Havah as she grabbed for them. With dizzying speed, they spun out of reach.*

*"We're not asleep." Zelig, curled up on the sofa with a book, peered at her over his eyeglasses. Velvil snuggled beside him. The grandfather clock chimed three. She did not remember turning on any lamps, yet the room glowed with silver light. The flowers on the wallpaper swayed. By the blazing fireplace Katya sat in a rocking chair with a baby in her arms. Behind them Evron smiled as he reached over her shoulder tapped the baby's nose. "My daughter's a pretty one, isn't she? Please, Havah, play for us."*

*Gathered in a corner on ladder-back chairs, her brothers Mendel and David argued about passages of*

*Torah with Uncle Hershel. Their voices rose and fell. Then they stopped and David winked at her. "Play a song about a raisin, Bubbe Fuss Bucket."*

*"Play a waltz for your mother and me, daughter." Shimon Cohen curved his arms around her. The scent of bay rum filled her head.*

*Miriam shook her head. "Shimon, you push the girl too hard."*

*Tova's gray eyes flashed lightning bolts. "Play a victorious song!"*

*"Play something happy, Little Sister." Gittel's luminous green eyes shone like stars. In one arm she held a redheaded boy. Havah reached up but before their fingers could touch something cold slapped her face.*

Suddenly the room was cold, dark and empty. No longer did flames lick the hearth before the vacant rocking chair. The only light came from the streetlamp outside.

Wet washcloth in hand Arel scooped her up in his arms. Then he sank down on the sofa and gathered her onto his lap. His heartbeat soothed her. She relished his pajama's softness and his body's warmth.

To escape his anxious gaze she glanced out the window. Snowflakes, like tiny dove wings, glimmered in the streetlamp and floated to the sidewalk.

"Have you ever seen more beautiful snow, Arel?"

"Snow is snow. It's all the same."

Like a fish, their unborn child flipped inside of her. She grasped Arel's hand and held it to her belly. The baby kicked against his palm with such force Havah flinched. Brushing her lips across her husband's disfigured cheek she fought the stone forming in her throat.

"No, Arel, nothing will ever be the same."

Meet our Author

Rochelle Wisoff-Fields

Kansas City native Rochelle Wisoff-Fields is the author of *This, That and Sometimes the Other,* an anthology of her short stories, which she also illustrated. Her stories have also been featured in several other anthologies, including two editions of *Voices.*

A woman of Jewish descent and the granddaughter of Eastern European immigrants, Rochelle has a close personal connection to Jewish history, which has been a recurring theme throughout much of her writing. Growing up, she was heavily influenced by the Sholom Aleichem stories as well as Fiddler on the Roof. Her novels *Please Say Kaddish for Me* and *From Silt and Ashes* were born of her desire to share the darker side of these beloved tales—the history that can be difficult to view, much less embrace.

Before becoming an author, Rochelle attended the Kansas City Art Institute, where she studied painting and lithography. Her preferred media are pen and ink, pencil, and watercolor, but her artistic talent serves her well in her temporary career as a cake decorator. She and her husband, Jan, have raised three sons in the Kansas City metro area and now live in Belton, Missouri. When she takes a break from writing and illustrating, Rochelle enjoys swimming and dancing. She also maintains the blog *Addicted to Purple.*

Link to Rochelle Wisoff-Fields Art and Blog:
*http://www.loiaconoliteraryagency.com/authors/rochelle-wisoff-fields/rochelle-wisoff-fields-art-and-blogs/*

Link to Please Say Kaddish For Me Reviews:
*http://www.loiaconoliteraryagency.com/authors/rochelle-wisoff-fields/please-say-kaddish-for-me-reviews/*